LION LET LOOSE

So that was it! That was why he had been brought to France. Armour and tents bought for him. The possibility of knighthood and renown held out. To use him against the Scots forces.

James raised head high. "No, sir!" he said.

All were gazing at him now, tensely.

Henry's brows came down, at their blackest. "You say no! *You*, my pensioner! What have I ever asked of you, before? You refuse me this?"

James inclined his head slightly. "You command here, yes – you leave none in doubt! And you may possibly command James Stewart. But you cannot command the King of Scots. Not you, or any man! You cannot have it both ways, Henry. You cannot hold me a captive – and also have me to act as king over my subjects. It is one, or the other. If I must remain captive, I must. I will place myself under your command, here in France, as a private knight. To learn the arts of war under so famous a captain. This, yes. But if you would have *me* command my people – you must set me free to do it!"

"God's blood!" The other's fist smashed down on the table. "This is beyond all bearing! You . . . you are wholly in my power, and shall do as I command. *Command* – do you hear?"

Lion Let Loose

Nigel Tranter

CORONET BOOKS
Hodder and Stoughton

Copyright © 1967 by Nigel Tranter

First published in Great Britain in 1967 by Hodder and Stoughton Ltd.

Coronet edition 1993

British Library C.I.P.
A CIP catalogue record for this title is available from the British Library

ISBN 0 340 58698 2

Printed and bound in Great Britain for Hodder and Stoughton Paperbacks, a division of Hodder and Stoughton Ltd, Mill Road, Dunton Green, Sevenoaks, Kent TN13 2YA (Editorial Office: 47 Bedford Square, London WC1B 3DP) by Clays Ltd, St Ives plc. Typeset by Hewer Text Composition Services, Edinburgh.

Principal Characters
In order of appearance

JAMES STEWART: Boy Earl of Carrick, 2nd son of Robert the Third, King of Scots, later James the First.

KING ROBERT THE THIRD: Weak eldest son of Robert the Second.

KING RICHARD THE SECOND: Former King of England – or, perhaps, impostor.

DAVID STEWART, DUKE OF ROTHESAY: Prince of Scotland. Elder son of King Robert. Heir to throne.

WALTER STEWART, LORD OF BRECHIN: Half-brother of the King. Later Earl of Atholl.

ROBERT STEWART, DUKE OF ALBANY: Governor of Scotland. Next brother to the King.

ARCHIBALD DOUGLAS, 4TH EARL OF DOUGLAS: Scotland's most powerful noble, "The Tyneman".

HENRY PERCY: Son of Hotspur, grandson of Earl of Northumberland.

HENRY WARDLAW, BISHOP OF ST. ANDREWS: Primate and senior churchman of Scotland.

EARL OF NORTHUMBERLAND: English political exile in Scotland.

HENRY ST. CLAIR, EARL OF ORKNEY: One of the few friends of King Robert.

SIR DAVID FLEMING OF CUMBERNAULD: A loyal knight.

SIR ROBERT LAUDER OF EDRINGTON: Owner of the Bass Rock.

WILLIAM AND ROBERT LAUDER: Sons of above. Later to be important men in Scotland.

WILLIAM GIFFORD: An esquire, of the Yester family.

HUGH-ATTE-FEN: English merchant-skipper and adventurer.

SIR THOMAS KEMPTON: Constable of the Tower of London.

GRIFFITH GLENDOWER: Son of Owen Glendower, true Prince of Wales.

MURDOCH STEWART, EARL OF FIFE: Prisoner in England. Son of Albany. Later 2nd Duke.

KING HENRY THE FOURTH: English monarch. Formerly Bolingbroke. Successor, or usurper, of Richard.

LORD GREY DE CODNOR: James's keeper. High Chamberlain of England.

THOMAS, DUKE OF CLARENCE: 2nd son of Henry the Fourth.

HECTOR MACLEAN OF DUART: Highland chief and envoy.

MASTER JOHN LYON: Scots priest and secretary.

HENRY, PRINCE OF WALES: Eldest son of Henry the Fourth. Later King Henry the Fifth.

EARL OF WARWICK: Great English noble.

DAVID DOUGLAS OF WHITTINGHAME: Fictional character. Scots laird, prisoner in England.

CHARLES, DUKE OF ORLEANS: Brother of French King Charles.

LADY JOANNA BEAUFORT: Daughter of Earl of Somerset, grand-daughter of John of Gaunt.

SIR WILLIAM DOUGLAS OF DRUMLANRIG: Scots baron and envoy.

HENRY BEAUFORT, BISHOP OF WINCHESTER: Chancellor of England. Uncle of Joanna. Later Cardinal.

SIR RICHARD SPICE: English knight. Former Lieutenant of the Tower.

QUEEN ISABELLA OF FRANCE: Wife of mad King Charles.

KING CHARLES THE SIXTH: Mad French monarch.

CATHERINE DE VALOIS: Princess of France, daughter of Charles and Isabella. Later Queen of England.

ARCHIBALD DOUGLAS, EARL OF WIGTOWN: Son of "The Tyneman", later 5th Earl of Douglas.

WILLIAM DOUGLAS, 2ND EARL OF ANGUS: Nephew of King James.

LADY CATHERINE DOUGLAS: One of the Queen's ladies.

MASTER JOHN CAMERON: Priest and secretary. Later Bishop of Glasgow and Chancellor of Scotland.

ALEXANDER STEWART, EARL OF MAR: Illegitimate cousin of James. Son of Wolf of Badenoch.

ISABELLA STEWART, DUCHESS OF ALBANY: Wife of Duke Murdoch, daughter of Earl of Lennox.

WALTER STEWART: Eldest son of Duke Murdoch. Grandson of Albany.

ALEXANDER MACDONALD OF CLANRANALD: A Highland chief.

ALEXANDER, LORD OF THE ISLES: Earl of Ross, and greatest of the Highland chiefs.

SIR ROBERT GRAHAM: Tutor of Strathearn, uncle of the demoted Earl thereof.

SIR ROBERT STEWART: Chamberlain. Grandson of Atholl.

PART ONE

1

The boy slipped past the steel-clad guards at the side-door of the Great Hall of Stirling Castle, none paying the least heed. Down the stone-flagged, stone-vaulted corridor he turned, hurrying now. At the third door down, unguarded this, he halted. He thumped briefly on the oaken planks, flung open the creaking door, and entered without further ceremony.

"He's here. David's here," he announced. "He's drunk, I think. You had better come."

Two men occupied that small bare room. Both turned to look at the boy; one, crouched over the fire, vacantly, from strange, lack-lustre eyes; the other, standing near by, with a heavy and sorrowful stare. Neither spoke.

"Come, Sire," the boy repeated, urgently. "There may well be trouble."

For further moments neither man moved, the slovenly-clad croucher, wild-haired, prematurely grey, nor the tall older man, thin, sensitive-featured, white-bearded, stooping. Both, as it happened, could have acknowledged the boy's use of the royal honorific. The standing man sighed.

"Uncle Walter is . . . shouting," the boy added.

The crouching man abruptly whinnied a short high laugh, although his ravaged and saggingly-handsome features showed no trace of smile. He turned back to the fire, hunching closer. He was Richard Plantagenet, until three years before reigning King of England.

His companion moistened slack lips, motioned with his hand, and drew himself up a little, a complex gesture, part weary acceptance, part resignation.

3

"Aye, Jamie," he said. He had a gentle, melodious voice, tired but well matching the nobility of mien, the great pain-filled eyes – and the tell-tale weakness of mouth and jawline which even the most venerable white beard would not disguise. "I will come."

"Yes. Quickly, then." The boy James hurried forward, to grasp his father's arm, almost to pull him. "Come, Sire." He did not so much as glance at the other man.

The tall stooping man in the undistinguished, almost threadbare clothing, suffered himself to be led out – and it was he, not his son, who heedfully closed that door on the physical and mental wreck they left behind in the over-hot little room.

James Stewart sought to hasten along the corridor, and it is to be feared that the hand which he kept on his father's arm dragged rather than supported as it was meant to do – for the old man limped grievously. That damaged leg, kicked by a horse when its owner had been little more than a youth, had much to answer for in the troubled history of Scotland since. Significantly it had been a Douglas horse that had kicked him, that of William, Lord of Dalkeith – and loud had the Douglases laughed, then and ever since. As, from a Douglas viewpoint, they had reason. For a lamed and halting king, especially a sensitive, introspective and gentle one, was of no conceivable use to a Scotland which demanded for its rule activity and agility in body as in mind, a warrior's frame and a stout right arm ending in a mailed fist. Robert the Third, King of Scots, second of the Stewart line and great-grandson of the The Bruce, limped his reluctant, unhappy way along the corridor of his royal Castle of Stirling as he had limped all his pitiful, disastrous reign, a man all but broken by his fate.

They came to the Hall door, ten-year-old prince leading sixty-two-year-old king, and the royal guards stationed there made some half-hearted gesture at drawing themselves up. No-one however thereafter made any public announcement as to the monarch's arrival on the scene. King Robert was the last to expect anything of the sort.

4

He would, indeed, have taken a deal of announcing. A fanfare of trumpets would have been required to make any major impact on the Great Hall of Stirling Castle that autumn morning of the year of Our Lord fourteen-hundred-and-three. The vast stone-walled apartment, hazy with the blue of wood-smoke, was loud with the uproar of innumerable raised voices, ribald, excited, hilarious, angry or just plain drunken. A few women were skirling amongst it all, as well they might; but by and large it was a male company, vital, vigorous, vociferous, much of it steel-armoured, all of it aggressive. At sight and sound of it all, King Robert bit his lip, faltering. Young James tugged him forward.

Despite the noise, movement, and seeming confusion however, there were the elements of some order in that Hall – the order that acknowledged might as right. Crowded as it was, nine-tenths of the company present seethed and milled in one half of the floor-space, that part farthest from this private door – knights, pages, lesser courtiers, officers, priests, monks, serving-wenches and, outnumbering all, men-at-arms by the score, the hundred, colourful in the blazons of their various lords, most notably in the crimson-and-gold of the royal livery, the blue-and-yellow of Stewart, and the unmistakable Red Heart of Douglas. Of the remaining half, part was occupied less densely by sundry lords, bishops, abbots, envoys and chamberlains, with a breathless lady or two maintaining approximate decency with squealing but practised protest. What was left of the Hall, nearest to this doorway, with a vast fireplace of its own and raised a foot above the rest on a dais, was comparatively empty. Around a massive table set transversely across the head of the chamber, three men stood and one sprawled on a bench. One woman shared the space with them, acting indeed as a buxom and giggling prop to the youngest of the men.

As King Robert came hesitantly forward, some few there made acknowledgement of his presence by sketched bows, especially amongst the clergy – but most did not. The young woman at the dais-table flushed and sought to curtsy – but this was difficult without upsetting him who leaned upon

5

her, for his arm was around her gleaming shoulders and his hand indeed down the opened front of her gown where it stroked and probed at will.

"St-stand still, m'dear! A pox on it – stand still, woman, I s-say!" the young man requested genially if thickly. "Would . . . would you have me on my back, here? Again? Before all!"

"Where we'd see the best o' you, by the Mass!" the sprawling man hiccuped. To add, "My lord Governor – God save us!" Walter Stewart, Lord of Brechin, had some difficulty enunciating that last.

"There speaks j-jealousy, Uncle! Y'are past it, man, I swear! Too fat! Is he not, Jeannie, m'lass? Even you'd make naught of old Uncle Wattie, hot as you are . . .!"

"Peace!" a cold crisp voice cut in, like a whip-lash. "Peace, I say! Young man – your father."

That brought a momentary silence to all within hearing distance, as all eyes turned towards the owner of that harsh and chilly authoritative voice, darted over in the direction of the shrinking and at the same time noble figure of the King, and then back again to the speaker.

He was a tall, spare, dark-visaged man in his mid-fifties, greying only a little, with a rat-trap mouth and small pointed beard, richly dressed in black velvet trimmed with gold. He had something of the stoop of his brother – but where the King's was an infirmity, a physical shrivelling, Robert, Duke of Albany's was a menace, the hunching, head-thrusting stoop of a bird of prey, an eagle no less; a resemblance to which the notable hooding of the man's great Stewart eyes by extra large lids, gave additional point. Seldom could two brothers have been less alike – or three, indeed, for Walter of Brechin, fleshy, coarse and dissolute, was as dissimilar again.

"Ah yes, my lord Duke – peace!" the young man cried, with a laughing mockery that was a deal less unsteady than his stance – and still without abstracting his hand from its blatant fondling of the bulging breasts of his supporting young woman. "Who indeed more apt to cry peace th-than my Uncle Robert – who hasna the meaning o' the word in

6

him! And would have this bedevilled realm o' Scotland no' to know it, either! God save us – peace from *you*, man!"

"Silence, sir!" the Duke said, with a level chill. "You'll speak me respectfully, boy. Or suffer for it!" Albany never raged nor shouted, any more than he ever smiled. He was as tightly contained in sober, frigid arrogance as was his unhappy brother loose and lost in self-doubt and kindly uncertainty.

"Ha – respect! For you? This is rich, i' faith! And you would threaten, my lord! Me? Rothesay? Beware how you do that, by Christ's Rude! Have you forgot, Uncle – *I* am Governor, now? Master of this realm. Not you, any more! Heed it, I say!"

That was more than any empty boast. The fair and laughing, handsomely-dashing youngster of twenty-three, richly-dressed although travel-stained beneath his gold-engraved half-armour, was indeed Governor of the Realm; had been for almost two years. David, Duke of Rothesay, elder son of the King, and heir to the throne. Whether this made him master of Scotland was another matter – for that rugged and unruly northern kingdom took a deal of mastering. None knew this better than his uncle, Albany, who had held the Governorship before him for no less than ten years – and had yielded it only reluctantly after his nephew's majority. Grimly, the older man picked on the point.

"Master, say you? I think not. Have *you* forgot His Grace the King?"

Rothesay's laughter rose almost to a hoot. "God's eyes – this from you, Uncle! Have *I* forgot His Grace? Spare us, for very shame! I swear it was largely to spare my royal sire from your slights and afflictions that I assumed the Governorship!" Belatedly David Stewart turned to his waiting father, and with his free hand flourished the preamble to a bow – all but unbalancing himself in the process. "Your Grace – my lord King and noble p-progenitor!" he exclaimed.

King Robert cleared his throat. "Aye, Davie," he said, low-voiced, troubled.

7

There was a pause at that dais end of the Hall – not so much on account of the King having spoken as out of awareness of the drama here enacted and now, clearly, to be brought to a head. All knew that Rothesay, his first-born, was the darling of the old King's heart, that despite all his follies, extravagancies and mistakes, the love was still there. Nor was it all one-sided, for Rothesay was credited with having some fondness for his feckless parent, even though he showed him little respect. But then, who did? Respect was a commodity which John Stewart had had to do without, all his life – for John was the King's true name; he had only had the name of Robert thrust upon him at his succession and coronation – for John was considered to be an unlucky name for kings, a point which his almost equally feckless father might have thought of when naming *his* first-born. Not that the change of name had done any good. Love there was between these two, then – and mutual hostility to brother and uncle, the Duke of Albany. Though perhaps hostility is too strong a word, as far as the King was concerned – for he hated none; fear and complete incompatibility had always been the one brother's reaction towards the other, and undisguised contempt for Albany's reaction. Yet today, as even the scullions of Stirling knew, young Rothesay had been summoned in the King's name to be berated, humbled, and Albany to triumph. That the younger man knew it, with the rest, may have in some measure coloured his behaviour that morning.

It was Albany who spoke, sternly but levelly, with no hint of emotion in his rasping voice. "You are here, sir, on matters concerning the well-being of this realm. That being so, I suggest that you put that young woman from you, and behave as more befits your place and station."

"I am here, Uncle, because as Governor of Scotland, I chose to come. For no other reason." Rothesay was choosing his words carefully now evidently not only for the aid of his wine-thickened tongue. "I came at my father's request, but of my own decision. And as for this lady, she at least is honest in her behaviour and function –

8

which is more than can be said for all in this company! I brought her – and she stays!"

Young James Stewart felt the frail arm which he was still clutching stiffen a little. Surprised, he glanced up at his father.

"You'd have done better to have brought your wife, Davie, I think," the King said, mildly enough but, for him, significantly, however sadly. "Aye, you would, lad."

The boy was not the only one to be surprised at that. All there glanced sharply at the speaker, who did thus occasionally surprise. King Robert might be a fool, in one sense, but only the ignorant would deny him perfectly sound wits in another, however little he seemed to make use of them. Rothesay himself looked at his father quickly, and perceiving the direction of the King's uneasy glance, followed it to where a big, still-faced, indeed utterly expressionless youngish man stood, at the other end of the long table – Archibald Douglas, The Tyneman, new and fourth Earl of Douglas and head of the greatest family, next to Stewart, in the kingdom. Rothesay had been married to Mary Douglas for a year. She was The Tyneman's sister.

He cleared his throat. "My wife is . . . otherwhere, Sire," he said, a little uncertainly. He withdrew his hand, at last from the lady's bosom. She sniggered, with apt embarrassment, and would have stepped back and away, had not Rothesay held her firm by the arm even yet.

Albany took up his flat and toneless recital. "You are charged, Nephew, with the shameful misgovernance of this realm. With the wastage of the kingdom's substance. With the alienation of Crown lands. With the subversion of justice . . ."

"Charged, is it!" the younger man interrupted hotly. "How charged, sirrah? I was appointed Governor by the King in Council. If I, the Governor, am to be charged, it can only be by the said King in Council. Is this the Privy Council of Scotland?" He gestured around him. He had sobered, quickly.

"A warning, Davie," his father mumbled unhappily. "A warning just. No more, lad."

"You would prefer to answer these charges, in detail, before the assembled Council, Nephew?" Albany asked, thinly.

Rothesay frowned. "These are not charges. They are but vague accusations, unfounded. Representing but the spleen of an old man, jealous!"

"You would have chapter and verse for them, then? Such can be produced, readily enough . . ."

"You lie! These are but wild denunciations. Stone-throwing. I cast them back in your teeth – you, who trampled on the country for ten years! Besides, you would never dare to have the Council face me. I have too many friends there – and you too few, my lord Duke! Aye, and nowhere else indeed, than in this my royal father's Castle of Stirling, would you dare so to speak me – for you know full well that the folk of Scotland much prefer me to yourself!"

His young brother James all but exclaimed aloud his satisfaction with that – for he was nothing if not a partisan in the matter, careful, wary, thoughtful boy as he had grown to be. He greatly admired his good-looking, accomplished, exciting brother – although with certain reservations, for he hated to see him drunken and less than his brilliant best, or in the hands of these women. David was the finest swordsman in the land, the champion jouster, the best horseman and huntsman. He played lute and fiddle to break almost as many hearts as he did with his bold but haunting Stewart eyes and nimble poetic tongue; he sang tunefully, was generous beyond all telling, and scarcely knew the meaning of fear. His ready laughter alone would have earned him worship in the eyes of his brother – for there was little enough of laughter in James Stewart's life.

But, despite hero-worship, it was all true that Rothesay had asserted to Albany. Rash, pleasure-loving, indiscreet, he might be, and lacking in the sober qualities of rule and government; but the people loved him, and forgave him anything. Whereas, like young James, they loathed the cold, efficient and ruthless Albany.

The older man was not deflected for a moment from his purpose. "You are here that the King's will and decision shall be made known to you," he went on, as though the other had never spoken. "The Governorship is not taken from you – but you are to be restrained in certain respects. You will accept the guidance, in pursuance of your duties, of myself, along with my lords of Brechin, Douglas, Moray and Crawford, acting in the King's express name. And should you fail to do so, and not mend your ways, Nephew, I shall, with His Grace's and the Council's authority, resume the Governorship. You understand?"

"My . . . God!" Rothesay whispered into the hush which now gripped all that great room, staring. He turned from his uncle, to look at his father. "This . . . this is beyond all belief! All bearing! You, Sire – you heard? Spoken in your royal presence! To your son! To the heir to your Crown! You heard?"

Swallowing painfully, audibly, the King shook his white head. "Aye, Davie – I heard," he got out slowly, sighing. "It must be. You have brought it on yourself, I fear – the sorrow of it. See you, the rule o' this realm is no' a game to be played, a sport for braw laddies! God forgive me who say it – for my failure is the greater than is yours, lad. Aye, the greater. The fault is largely mine, I do confess before all." The King's head sank on his breast, "But . . . God's will be done," he ended, wearily.

"*God's* will, by the Rude!" Rothesay burst out. "Is that what you name your brother's intrigues and schemings, now? The Devil's will, rather! But . . . I'll not have it! There are more wills than Albany's in this realm, even if *you* have none! Aye – and more than words to count! There are such things as swords in Scotland!"

In the complete silence which followed that statement, the young Duke turned, to stare. First he looked at the Earl of Douglas.

"My lord. Good brother," he jerked. "How says Douglas?"

11

The Tyneman did not move a muscle. Not so much as an eyelid flickered. Silent, impassive, as though carved out of stone, the big man stood, while everywhere in that Hall breaths were held and men awaited decision, the fall of the scales.

As well they might. This one still-faced ponderous man represented so much in the land. Not only was he the head of the fierce Douglases, the most powerful and warlike family in Scotland, possibly, things being as they were, in all Europe – they were also the most united; which was where they differed from the Stewarts. At the drop of a glove he could field three thousand armed and mounted men, a week later double that number. Give him a month, it was said, and because of bonds of manrent and support, marriage links, and the threat of reprisals, he could raise half of Lowland Scotland. He was indeed brother to Rothesay's wife; but he was much more than that. His own wife was Rothesay's sister, the Princess Margaret, eldest daughter of the King; his cousin, George Douglas, first Earl of Angus, was married to the next daughter, the Princess Mary; and the third princess, Elizabeth, was wife to Sir James Douglas, Lord of Dalkeith. So Douglas's least word spoke loud indeed, anywhere – and Rothesay had reason to await it anxiously. A year before, he need not have worried; then The Tyneman's warrior father was still alive, and Archibald the Grim had been Albany's greatest enemy, and the strongest support of Queen Annabella Drummond – and therefore of her son Rothesay. He it was, indeed, who had forced his daughter's marriage to the heir to the throne – when the young man was in fact affianced to another, thereby laying up great trouble for Scotland. But now both able Queen and fiery old Earl were dead, and the Duke of Rothesay awaited his brother-in-law's verdict.

As the moments passed, painfully tense, it began to dawn upon all, not least the young Duke, that the dispassionate Douglas was not merely being more than usually slow of speech. He was not going to answer at all. Straight ahead of him he gazed, granite-eyed, wordless.

12

A long sigh escaped from the assembled company. A sob rose into the boy James's throat, and all but choked him.

Walter Stewart of Brechin, the other uncle, barked an abrupt laugh, harsh and savage.

Shaken, Rothesay blinked, biting his lip. Then he drew himself up, head high. He turned, to scan the ranks of lords and prelates who stood in the space below the dais.

Not a single glance met his own. He had friends of a sort there, drinking companions, adherents, collaborators, beneficiaries; none, this morning, after Albany's words, the King's falterings, and Douglas's silence, raised voice or eye.

Gripping the table-edge tightly, David of Rothesay looked farther still down the Hall, to where the press of folk was thickest, all listeners now. There, admittedly he could see not a few stout fellows dressed in his own colours – or, at least, in the royal livery, which up till now had been more or less the same thing – most of whom had come with him as the Governor's bodyguard. But they were far outnumbered by the minions of Albany and Brechin, not to mention Douglas. Moreover, in the presence of the King, how much reliance could be placed upon the adherence of the royal guard?

Drawing a long quivering breath, Rothesay swung back to face his accusers. Without taking his eyes thereafter from Albany's aquiline face, he groped out until his hand contacted the goblet half-filled still with wine, on the table before him. Raising it to his lips, he gulped down the contents in a single draught before them all. Then, holding it there, he spoke.

"My father's words I have heard," he declared strongly. "He says that the rule of this realm is no game. That I accept. As its Governor I shall see that none play it – I promise you all! Warning has been given – and taken. I add mine. Let none seek to govern save the Governor! When King, Council and the Estates of Parliament assembled command me to lay down that office, then I shall do so. Not before. His Grace says 'God's will be done!' To that I say Amen – but let us not confuse Almighty God with my Uncle Albany! I charge you all to say, rather – God

13

save the King! And, by the Holy Rude – to remember who will be King hereafter!"

With a sudden explosion of force, violent as it was unexpected, he hurled the heavy silver goblet, empty, down the littered length of the dais-table. Scattering and upsetting viands, flagons and the like in its course, it crashed at the very feet of the Duke of Albany.

In the resounding clatter, David Stewart, Prince of Scotland, flung around and, jumping from the dais, went striding down the hall without a backward glance, making for the outer door, to the main courtyard and his horses. Right and left men parted to give him room. After a little hesitation, the unfortunate young woman went hurrying after him, biting her lips.

In the uproar that succeeded, King Robert, empty open hand raised trembling after his son, dropped it, moaning useless and incoherent words. He took an uncertain step forward, to pluck at Albany's velvet sleeve.

That man turned stooping shoulder on his brother, ignoring him entirely. "Walter – come with me," he snapped. "My lord of Douglas – your attendance, if you please. Where is my son Murdoch? The young fool should have been here. Fetch him, I say . . ."

The boy James took his father's arm again. "Come, Sire," he said. "Better away. Aye, come you . . ."

Together, none hindering or indeed considering, the boy and the old man went unheeded through the side-door and back down the stone passage, the noise fading away behind them.

At the third door down, where Richard Plantagenet was kept, when James paused, the King shook his head. "No' in there, Jamie," he said. "I couldna bear His Grace o' England in this pass. I'll . . . I'll away up to my own chalmer. Aye, I want my bed, lad – my bed."

Saying nothing, the boy moved on, his open young face set. He was a well-built, sturdy lad, though not tall, with good regular features firm enough to balance the softness of the great Stewart eyes, his sensitive mouth offset by an already pronounced jawline. But there was an imposed stillness about his habitual expression which was hardly natural. For one so young, he was perhaps over-quiet, reserved, thoughtful. Though his mother had once said that he would out-sing his brother David.

Slowly they climbed the winding turnpike stair at the end of the long corridor, towards the royal bedchamber in the square flanking-tower, the lame King having to take one step at a time, the boy patient, silent, heedful yet withdrawn.

Half-way up, the man who looked so much older than his years, paused, panting. "Yon was ill done," he muttered. "Ill done. Wae-sucks, that it should have come to this!"

"It was ill done," James agreed flatly.

"It wasna how it should have been. I know it well. But . . . Davie was ower hasty. Stubborn. Prideful. And he shouldna have brought the woman. Yon was unseemly. But I grieve for him."

"You grieve for him, Sire – but you spurned him! You threw Davie aside. For Uncle Albany."

"No, no! Not that. I but warned him. What could I do, Jamie? They were at me. They are aye at me. Davie can be foolish. Head-strong. I had to warn him. You hear me? I had to."

"Yes, Sire."

They moved on.

Soon the King had stopped again. "What could I do, Jamie? Your mother . . . dear God, your mother would have known what to do!" His voice trembled. "But she is gone. My Anna is gone. Left me. Archie Douglas, too. He aye knew what to do."

"You could have spoken him alone, Father. Not before all. Not before Albany."

"Aye. But your Uncle said it must be so. Robert was fell fierce on that. He'd have it no other way – no' have believed that I'd spoken. He's a hard, unbelieving man, Robert! What could I do . . .?"

15

Tight-lipped the boy opened the bedroom-door for his father.

"I'll to my bed," the King of Scots said. "I didna sleep well, last night. I'm no' well, Jamie. I . . . I wish I was with my Anna."

"Yes, Sire."

The monarch sat down heavily on the great canopied bed, its gold tarnished, its heraldic hangings sagging and dusty. He hunched himself, gazing down at his open hands. "My robe, Jamie," he requested. "I'm cold."

The boy brought the bed-robe from a chair, and put it about his father's bent shoulders. "Shall I summon one of Your Grace's pages?" he asked, with oddly stiff formality.

"No. Leave them be. I would be alone."

"Then I have your royal permission to retire?"

"Aye. Gang your ways, laddie – gang your ways and leave an auld done man." But, as the boy bowed and turned to the door, his father raised his head. "Jamie – I'm thinking this is no right place for you, these days. No place for a lad. I'm no' well, you see – and if I should be blest enough to follow your mother quickly – och, then I'd no' like you to be left here alone. With . . . him. It wouldna be for the best, maybe. Mind, I like to have you by me. But you'd be better some other place, belike. Some strong place. In good hands. Aye, good, strong hands." He was staring down at his own hands again, with all the sorrowful knowledge that they were not strong enough to protect this child of his. "See you – send the good Bishop Trail to me, Jamie. Send my lord Bishop o' St. Andrews."

"Your Grace – the Bishop is dead. Have you forgot? Two months dead, and more."

"Eh? You say so? Aye – God's pity, so he is! Dead. All my friends are dead, I say! All gone. Then . . . then it must be Henry Wardlaw. Aye, send me Bishop Wardlaw. He is honest, a leal and godly prelate. And learned. I'll see that he gets St. Andrews. Raise him to the Primacy. I can still do that. And St. Andrews has a fine strong castle. You will go there, Jamie – with Bishop Wardlaw. He'll see to you.

16

Keep you safe. Better than can I, your father. Aye, and teach you what I canna do." The King almost straightened up, on the bed, with this unaccustomed decision. He actually pointed towards the door. "Send me Henry Wardlaw, the new Bishop o' St. Andrews. D'you hear, boy?"

"Yes, Father." Blinking, the boy bowed again, and backed for the door. Once outside, however, James, Earl of Carrick, turned and ran. He took the steep stairs two at a time, sure-footed as any deer. St. Andrews – where they said the sands were golden and the seas were blue! Not to be cooped up on top of a rock . . .!

2

Young Henry Percy came bursting into Prince James's little room high in the topmost garret storey of the Sea Tower of St. Andrews Castle. In a rush, he almost ran over to the window, where the other boy sat, book in hand, gazing out through the thick glass that even thus high was blurred with salt spray, looking over the grey, white-capped and rock-torn sea. Unceremoniously the newcomer snatched the book out of the other's hands, and flung it into a corner. Harry Percy was like that, a spirited youth – as became the son of the late and renowned Hotspur. Moreover he was a year older than James Stewart, and did not allow the younger to forget it.

"Stop reading that stupid book!" he cried. "What's wrong with you? Forever reading books! Listen, James – here is word to rouse you out of any book! Your brother Rothesay – he is dead! Killed! And you are to go away. To France!"

Uncomprehendingly, the younger boy stared, jaw dropping a little.

"It is true, I tell you! I heard it all. Every word. A messenger has come. From your father. From the King. The King of Scots, that is – not *our* King Richard. I was in the little chamber off the Bishop's library. Writing those devilish proverbs he punishes me with – the old owl! He forgot that I was there. I heard all, through the door!"

James gripped his fellow-pupil's wrist tightly. "What did you say?" he got out, from stiff lips. "My brother, you said . . .?

"Yes. The Duke of Rothesay. He is dead. Killed by the Duke of Albany. And my lord of Douglas. At Falkland.

18

Starved to death, the man said. You hear – *starved*! He even ate his own fingers! I heard the man say it. Chewed them all away, right to the bone! God be good – think of it, James! Just at Falkland. In Fife. Not a score of miles from here. All that time. Weeks in a deep bottle-dungeon, in Albany's castle. Just like the one we have here. And no food. In the darkness. Nothing to drink, either. At least, not exactly that . . ."

Henry Percy gasped, choking to silence, as without warning James Stewart leapt up and hurled himself upon his companion. Furiously he rained blows, from clenched fists, on the older boy, hammering wildly, unmercifully, on head and face and body, anywhere that his blows could reach, all without a word spoken. Only his sobbing breath answered the other's shouted protests.

Young Percy defended himself, of course, and once the surprise was past, gave back almost as good as he got. He was a head taller than James, and with longer reach – but more willowy, less broad and muscular. In the two years or so at St. Andrews, benefiting by the good sea air, and the untramelled life for a growing boy on coast and cliff and moor – as well as by the good Bishop's tutoring, discipline and regular hours – James had developed notably, in body as in intellect. Although he could have done with an inch or two more of height to carry his stocky breadth, he was now a compact, well-developed youngster, promising to become a man of powerful physique and solid presence. There was nothing wrong with his thews and sinews, that was certain.

The heir to Northumberland managed to free himself, and threw himself backwards, out of reach of those pounding fists, to grab up a wooden stool from the floor and use it as a shield and possible club.

"Ha' done! Stop it! Hold, I say!" he exclaimed. "What's come to you, James? Mary-Mother – ha' you run mad!"

The other, panting, stood still in mid-floor now, glaring. Gradually the black frown cleared from his wide brow, his arms sank to his sides, the white-knuckled fists relaxed, and his whole taut body seemed to sag. Turning about, he stumbled back to the window, to lean there, head on arm.

"I am sorry, Harry," he mumbled.

"I should say so! To turn on me like, like a wild boar! You've hurt my nose. I believe it's going to bleed!"

"Yes. I am sorry. When was it? When . . . did Davie die?"

"How should I know that?" the offended youth exclaimed, feeling his nose.

"You said that you heard all."

"Well – not that. But it would not be long since, I would think." Hotspur's son, in the exciting recollection, forgot his injuries. "This courier came from your father, he said. All the way from Dundonald Castle. Where is that?"

"Near to Ayr. On the other side of Scotland. The house my father likes best. In . . . in . . ." James shrugged. "In my earldom of Carrick!"

"I do not know where that is. But this man came hot-foot, by the sound of him. He fears for *you*, now – the King, your father. This uncle of yours, Albany, must be a great rogue, I swear! To kill him so. No clean steel! Or even swift poison! So, you are to be sent to France. Out of danger. I wish *I* could go to France. You are lucky, James. They say that they allow knighthood there as young as my age. I could be dubbed knight, even now. I am good with lance and sword – better than you. I would be a champion, and famous. Like my father . . ."

"How did it happen?" The other boy's voice was notably level, flat. "How did they take him? Why did none rescue him? Was he not still Governor of the Realm?"

"I do not know. They did not talk about all that. I but heard how he died. However Albany caught him, he put him in this dark hole. In the thickness of the walling of Falkland Castle. There he was to rot. But he took a long time to die, the man said. And d'you know why? Because of the women! Women, yes. I have heard that Rothesay was a great man with the women. Sandy, my groom, says he was always after them. Getting them to

20

have babies – dear God knows why! I think women are silly, soft . . ."

"Yes. What did the women do?"

"There were two of them. One was the keeper of the castle's own daughter. She must have been crazed. About your brother. For she found a crack through the mortar of the wall. He said Rothesay must have dug it out with his finger-nails! But could not move the big stones, you see. From the outside, after dark, she fed him through this crack with grains of oats. One by one. They kept him alive. Think of it, living on little hard grains of oats! But they caught this woman at it, at last. And she paid for it, by the Mass! Albany had her put to death, James!"

The other shook his head, wordless.

"That is not all. There was another woman. I do not quite understand this. She was . . . well, older, I think. She had milk." Young Percy produced an embarrassed half-laugh. "A wet-nurse, the courier called her. You know what women are like. They have these things – paps. With milk in them. Like cows. Disgusting, I say! Somehow she fed Rothesay with this milk. Through the crack in the mortar. By a straw, the man said. Do you think it can be true? I do not understand how that could be. Do you? He could not suck it, could he? Anyway, it is a filthy thing, don't you think? I would have died before swallowing such foulness! Wouldn't you, James?"

His companion still made no reply.

"They caught her, anyway. As well. And killed her, like the other. That would be when your brother started eating his fingers, I expect. It must have been terrible, there in black darkness all the time . . ."

"Be quiet! For sweet mercy's sake – be quiet!" James exclaimed.

"Well – if you do not want to hear about it, of course! I thought, Rothesay being your brother, you would have been interested. I know that I would."

"I just, just do not want to talk about it."

"Well, you will have to, you know. Everybody will be

21

talking about it soon – you'll see," his friend pointed out reasonably. "Especially if you are to be sent to France. James – see you! Could you not have me to come with you? That would be good! If we both went. I would like to go to France."

"I . . . I do not know."

"It would be better if we could go together, James. Do you not think so? Why should I not go? I am not a prisoner here. Or a hostage. And my grandfather is very rich. Richer than *your* father, I swear – even though he is not a king!"

There was truth in all that, certainly. The old Earl of Northumberland was one of the wealthiest and most powerful lords in England. He and his grandson were in no sense captives at St. Andrews Castle – guests of Scotland rather, although somewhat embarrassing ones. The Earl had, the previous year, led a rebellion against the usurping Henry the Fourth, in favour of Richard, the rightful King of England, the pathetic wreck then existing in Stirling Castle – whom Henry declared to be dead and ceremoniously buried. The rebellion had failed, and Northumberland, with his grandson and heir, had fled to Scotland. The old King Robert had kindly received them, and lodged them here at St. Andrews, Albany agreeing – that the responsibility and the cost might fall on the open-handed and kindly Bishop Wardlaw rather than on the realm's treasury.

Young Percy was pursuing his theme with vigour, when the door opened to reveal the Bishop of St. Andrews and Primate of Scotland himself. Henry Wardlaw, nephew of the late Cardinal-Bishop of Glasgow, was still in his early middle-age, a big, burly genial man of hearty appetite and brilliant scholarship – unusual concomitants. Renowned as much for his courage as his learning and boundless hospitality, he was one of the few men in high places bold enough to oppose the Duke of Albany and his friends – and with the See of St. Andrews, had the wealth and the all but impregnable castle with which to do it.

Now, the twinkling grey eyes in the ruddy countenance were clouded, and he dismissed Henry Percy with less than his normal amiability. The heir to Northumberland did not linger.

"Jamie, my son – I fear that I have ill news for you," the Bishop said gravely. "I am sorry, but you must hear it. My lord Duke, your brother, is dead."

"Yes."

"You know it?"

"Yes. He told me. Harry."

"Young Percy? He did? How did *he* know? He must . . . yes, he must have overheard! M'mmm. But – no matter. I do not know what he has told you. But your brother Rothesay has been cruelly done to death. It is no kindness to hide this from you, my son. Not only you, and your royal father, mourn him. He had been foolish, as young men are foolish. But this – this villainy, is beyond all condemnation!"

"Yes," James said.

Sorrowfully and with great sympathy, the man looked at the tense, strained-faced boy. "You will be brave, I know – you, who are of the line of the Bruce! Whose own brothers were slain as savagely; but who was not overwhelmed by the sorrow, and stood firm, to triumph over the butchers in the end!" The Bishop paused, frowning. "I do not know how much you have heard, how much that young scapegrace may have told you. And there is no profit in dwelling on the hurt of it. But you must know that it happened in the Duke of Albany, your uncle's, castle of Falkland. And His Grace, your father, believes that it was at Albany's behest. Although, no doubt, he will deny it."

James waited, still-featured, silent.

The other put out a hand to touch the boy's shoulder, and then thought better of it. "His Grace is concerned for you," he went on, with a shake of the head. "Concerned for your sorrow. But also for your safety. He believes you now to be in some danger. Not immediately perhaps, but hereafter. You understand?"

James nodded briefly.

"You perceive the consequence of this wickedness, my son? You are now the heir to the throne. The next King

23

of Scots. *You* are now Duke of Rothesay. And after you, your Uncle Robert of Albany is next heir."

"Yes, my lord," the boy said quietly. "If he might kill me also, then he would be King. When my father dies."

"Aye," Wardlaw agreed heavily. "That is the size of it, lad. So fears His Grace. So must fear any honest man. You are safe, to be sure, in this my Castle of St. Andrews. Neither Albany nor the Douglas can touch you within these walls. But I cannot hold you cooped here, like some trussed fowl, for years. Here would be no life for a lad of spirit. We must not make a prisoner of you in shielding you from your enemies. And the King your father is a sick man. He cannot protect you as he would. So – he would have you go to France. There you will be safe. He is in alliance with King Charles of France. There you will learn to be a prince and a king, secure from evil men. Until it is time for you to return to this your kingdom. To rule it then truly, firmly, strongly, as a king should. You will go to France, my son."

"Yes. Will you come with me, my lord?"

"Me? Alas, no, Jamie – no. I fear not. I can serve your father here best. In Scotland. I must keep the Church loyal to him, and to you. I am Primate of this land – chief bishop. With my responsibilities. But . . . my heart will go with you, lad."

"I am sorry."

This time the man's hand did go out to grip the sturdy, square shoulders. "I thank you, my lord Duke!" he said. "That is a word I shall not forget."

"When do I go?" the boy asked, with no lift to his voice.

"That we do not know. His Grace's trusted messenger, who brought me the tidings, says that you must wait. In readiness. It may take time to arrange. The King of France must be approached. Probably a French ship brought for you – lest one of our own should prove untrustworthy, betray you. It will not be done in a day or two. For all must be done in great secrecy. None of this must come to the ears of your enemies. His Grace is most strong on that. He did not even write me a letter – lest it fall into wrong hands. For

Albany has his spies everywhere. The courier came straight from Dundonald, a hundred miles away and more. With His Grace's orders. You are to be kept in readiness. To go secretly at a moment's notice. None to know of it. Meantime, you are not to venture outside the walls of this castle. It will be galling, lad – but your father's royal orders. And wise. Lest they snatch at you, anywhere. No more hawking or fishing, I fear, Jamie. No more riding the moors or sailing the coast. Happily, it is almost winter, and will try you the less. But . . . you are Scotland's hope now, my lord Duke. Else she enters a night of deep darkness! You understand? You will do it?"

"Yes, my lord. I understand. Will my father come to me?"

"That I do not know. But I fear not, Jamie. His Grace is sick. And it is a long journey. Moreover, to come here might but prejudice your safety. Make Albany suspicious. Act the more savagely."

"Then . . . then I may never see my father again? If I go to France . . .?" the boy said, voice cracking at last.

The Bishop drew a long breath. "You must not say that, my son. All is in God's hands. These are dark days – but the sun will yet shine from behind the clouds . . ."

"Yes, my lord Bishop," said the Prince of Scotland. "Perhaps."

The long months of waiting, frustrating for the boy James in that they represented cramping confinement, yet welcome enough since they allowed him to remain with his friends, came to an abrupt end on a stormy night of February, 1406. James indeed was haled from his bed in the high tower room by one of the Bishop's chaplains, told to dress and come down quickly to the library. Yawning, he donned his clothing in bemused fashion, while gusts of wind shook the casement shutters and draughts set the candle guttering.

Downstairs in the warm room that was littered with books, parchments, scrolls and missives, where he had done so much studying – he willingly, young Percy unwillingly – James found three men with Bishop Wardlaw. Though seated, two of these rose at his unannounced and modest entrance, and bowed to the boy with some formality, causing the third belatedly to rise also. This last he knew – the Lord Bardolph, an Englishman and colleague of the Earl of Northumberland, sharing his exile here.

"Ha, my lord Duke James," the Bishop said, holding out his hand. "The call has come. Here are two noble gentlemen whom His Grace your father has sent to take you from my keeping. My lord Earl of Orkney, and Sir David Fleming of Cumbernauld."

The newcomers bowed again. Orkney was youngish, handsome, elegant even in his travel-stained riding-clothes, a tall, pale man with a thin dark moustache and just the suggestion of a beard; Fleming, older, bulky, rugged, an unvarnished soldier – indeed a namely warrior and survivor of the recent Battle of Homildon Hill. James was impressed.

"It is the start of your long journey, my son," the Bishop went on. "It may seem a strange time to take the road. But secrecy is vital — more urgent than ever. Speed likewise. You will be leaving forthwith."

"For . . . for France?" James got out.

"On the road for France, yes. A long road, lad . . ."

The door opened again to admit the chaplain with two more charges — the Earl of Northumberland and his grandson Henry, the latter still lacing his doublet.

Northumberland, a grey-haired but vigorous man, hurried across to greet and shake the hand of Sir David Fleming. Apparently they were old companions in arms, and though they had fought against each other on many a bloody field, they were good friends. Henry Percy came to James's side.

"Is it France? At last?" he whispered. "Do I come with you?"

"France, yes. I do not know whether you are to go, or not."

"My lord of Northumberland," the Bishop announced. "I regret — we all regret — the disturbance of this late hour. But it is no time for niceties. I fear that you and Lord Bardolph must be gone from St. Andrews within the hour. The Lord James here, also. Ill night as it is, you must be far from here by daybreak."

The Percy straightened up. "So soon, my friend? You would not say that were there no need, no danger. I smell . . . treachery!"

"Aye," the Bishop nodded unhappily. "You may well. My sorrow that here in my house, in this my country, our guests should be the victims of such discourtesy. But . . . the Duke of Albany is Governor of the Realm again, and anything may happen in Scotland now!"

"Albany is no unfriend of mine, my lord . . ."

"No? Which makes the blow the more bitter. Sir David Fleming here has unearthed an evil plot. Against you, who are not captives or hostages, but guests, honoured guests. But Sir David can speak for himself."

27

"I can, my lords – though it sticks in my gullet to say it!" the knight growled hoarsely. "Two days back I learned of a foul ploy. Albany plans to seize you, and Bardolph here, and hand you over to the usurper King Henry, in exchange for his own son Murdoch, and the Earl of Douglas, taken at Homildon!"

"Satan seize him!" Northumberland cried. "He would do that? To me, Percy! I, who have eaten his salt, dined at his table! Knowing that it will cost me my head!"

An invasion of the North of England by the Scots, as reprisal for King Henry's constant attacks, ending in their defeat at Homildon Hill, had been a great disaster. Archie Tyneman, Earl of Douglas, in command, had proved that though a fierce fighter he was no general like his father. The numbers of slain had been enormous – fifteen hundred fugitives had drowned in Tweed alone, attempting to escape – and no less than eighty nobles and knights were taken prisoner, the Earl himself and Albany's heir, Murdoch Stewart, Earl of Fife, amongst them.

"Aye – that is Albany!" Fleming looked as though he would spit, but recollected his whereabouts in time. "Whenever I heard of it, I rode hot-foot to the King, at Dundonald. I havena bedded since!"

"And your King said . . .?"

Fleming shrugged, glancing uncomfortably towards young James. He turned to the Earl of Orkney.

That nobleman, something of a diplomat and one of the few who maintained an active loyalty to the unhappy monarch, took up the tale.

"His Grace was indignant. Wrath. But he is sick, and Albany is the Governor and holds the power. He sent us to warn you, to escort you from this place. For we have it that the Duke intends to come here in person tomorrow, to demand your persons from the Bishop." Orkney grimaced. "In the name of the King!"

Northumberland nodded. "Where do we go, then? If His Grace of Scotland cannot protect us in St. Andrews Castle, where are we safe?"

Orkney inclined his head, acknowledging the thrust. "His Grace believes that you would, indeed, be safer in your own Northumberland. If that does not commend itself to you, my lord, he suggests that you sail with my lord James, here, for France."

"France!" the older man cried. "God's wounds – I do not wish to go to France! How would I fare there? No – I shall return to my own country. I shall find refuge meantime in some remote place. In some Cheviot valley, belike. But . . . it must be done in all secrecy. None must know that I cross the Border."

"That is understood. In this, my lord, your situation exactly matches that of the young Earl of Carrick, here." Carrick was still officially James's title, for though now heir to the throne and entitled to the dukedom of Rothesay, no move had been made to instal him therein, and only Bishop Wardlaw named him Duke. "Indeed your cases are linked, for the King believes that Albany's coming here tomorrow to demand your persons, is also excuse to lay hands on the boy. That if the Governor demands entry to this castle in the name of King and Council, to take possession of the persons of English sojourners, my lord Bishop will not be able to refuse him access. And once herein he will seize the young prince also."

"I fear His Grace has the rights of it," Wardlaw agreed, unhappily. "Hence this midnight departure. James's whereabouts must be kept as secret as your own, my lord. A ship is engaged to come from France to fetch him – but it is thought still to be at Dieppe awaiting more favourable weather. So James must be taken privily to some secure hiding-place, near to which the ship can be directed. It was to come to Leith. So the Lothian coast is best. That is on *your* road to the Border, my lord. All can ride together."

"I have sent a messenger to my kinsman, Sir William Sinclair of Herdmanston, in Lothian," Orkney put in. "He is sound. He will meet us. Will know best where we can lie secure, in that country."

"So be it. We ride," the old Earl said. "For the Border. You agree, Bardolph?" he asked, belatedly.

That silent, swarthy, Italian-looking man nodded. "We shall do well enough in the Cheviots. Or the Cumberland fells, I vow," he said grimly. "And perchance strike shrewder blows at Lancastrian Henry from there, than here!"

"Truth in that. Come, then – we must gather such small gear as we may carry . . ."

James's parting from Bishop Wardlaw at the portcullis-gate to the castle drawbridge was the most sore that he had known. In a life wherein, since his mother had died, affection had been sadly lacking he had grown to love this kindly, able man. Now, he might never see him again, for to his young mind France was at the other end of the earth, and the years to be spent there a lifetime. So a great lump closed his throat and scarcely a word could he speak, as the Bishop held him close, wishing him well, bidding him to be of stout heart, and assuring him that the love and hopes of many in Scotland went with him – not least that of his prosy priest and book-bound tutor at St. Andrews. Wet-eyed and ashamed, for all his twelve years and more, James clung to him until Orkney's hand on his shoulder became urgent enough to draw him away.

Mounting, he did not look back.

They clattered off over the wet cobblestones of the narrow, night-bound streets of the ecclesiastical metropolis of Scotland. At least it was good, after all the months of incarceration, to feel a horse between his thighs again. Harry Percy had shed no tears over his farewells and was much excited – although disappointed that it seemed that he was not going to France with his friend, after all.

One of the Bishop's chamberlains accompanied them. He saw that the night-porter opened the gates of the West Port for them without trouble. Thereafter they were quickly into open country, a party of about a dozen. They settled down to simple hard riding.

It was a cold and blustery night, with successive chill rain squalls sweeping in on the east wind from the North Sea, the presence of which, though unseen, was ever with them. They were soon climbing, up from the coastal plain, for the intention was to ride by the most direct route, straight across country; no-one would be about, or looking for them, at this hour and in this weather. Moreover the high empty moorlands which formed the spine of the East Neuk of Fife, probably represented the safest route, however difficult going they made in the wet darkness – and however near it took them to the domains of Albany around his favourite seat of Falkland, messuage-place of his earldom of Fife.

James Stewart was young enough actually to enjoy the novelty of that headlong ride through the night, once he had mastered his sense of loss at leaving the only real security he had known in all his world – whatever his elders thought of it. Since they were heading south by west, the wind and rain was mainly at their backs. He was already an excellent horseman, and the Bishop was wealthy enough to afford some of the best horseflesh in the land. Neither of the boys held up the company in the least.

They went by Cameron and Lathones and Lathallan, the Bishop's man guiding them unerringly over the bleak uplands. After almost a dozen miles of it, they were being buffeted by the wind unmercifully, high on the bare east shoulder of Largo Law. Had it been daylight, here they would have seen all the great expanse of the Firth of Forth spread before them. Now there was only the vast void of the streaming murk.

Down on the less exposed south face of the hill, they were spared the worst of the storm. In snatches James heard Orkney and Fleming passing anxious exchanges about the sea crossing ahead. Two hours out from St. Andrews they came down to the little harbour of Lower Largo, an inn and a huddle of low-browed fishermen's houses, around a dog-legged stone pier and a projecting reef of rock which together enclosed the haven. Skirting the darkened cottages they rode straight down to the jetty, the noise of the sea already the ominous background to all things.

Amongst the scattering of small boats moored here, was one larger, a herring-buss of the Dutch type, for deep-sea fishing. No sign of life showed about the wind-blown, spray-drenched harbour, and noise of their hooves on the rough masonry of the pier produced no reaction. Cursing, Sir David Fleming dismounted and clambered down on to the larger vessel's decked-in fo'c'sle, to thump on its timbers with a spurred heel.

This produced voices and then shadowy figures emerging from the kennel, all, it seemed, protesting vigorously if yawningly. Fleming's great and authoritative roar silenced them, but even so it was quickly apparent that the fishermen considered the night much too rough to make the crossing to Lothian.

Fleming flayed them with his tongue for poltroons and knaves. But to no effect. They must await an abatement of wind and seas, they insisted. In an easterly gale the Forth could be the death of them.

The Earl of Orkney, with an oath, leapt down from his horse, and shriller even than the wind in the buss's shrouds, was the screech of steel as his sword was unsheathed. Lightly he jumped down into the boat.

"Death, my friends, is here! Now! On land. Death for you forthwith, if you do not put to sea – because death for us all, if we are found on this shore in the morning! You sail – in the King's name. Or you die! Choose!"

Fleming's sword was out now, also. Above, Northumberland, Bardolph and the men-at-arms followed suit. Sullenly, the fishermen bowed to the inevitable.

"James," young Percy said in his friend's ear. "Are you afraid? I am not."

James shook his head. "I am only a little afraid," he answered honestly. "I would rather go in the boat than stay here."

Leaving the horses with the chamberlain and the three Bishop's men, the boat party embarked, with the light baggage that they had brought along. It made a strange leave-taking.

With surly deliberation the fishermen cast off, long sweeps out to pull them clear of the harbour. Once outside its mouth, with the heavy lumbering craft already heaving ominously, a mere rag of sail was hoisted on the forward of the two stumpy masts. The loom of the land was lost almost at once.

"You have your orders," Fleming told the squat and shaggy skipper. "Put us across to Fidra Isle, off Dirleton, and you will earn the King's gratitude. And good payment."

"What profit frae either?" the other snorted. "If we're at the bottom o' the sea? Forbye, I canna say that I'll can put you at ae place on the south shore, in this blaw. We'll just hae to run before the wind, the maist o' the way. I'm thinking we'll end up nearer Seton than Dirleton. If we dinna founder first!"

"With your sweeps you can pull up the coast, can you not? Men and horses await us at the Dirleton shore. Seton is little use to us, man."

"Pull! In the cross-seas the likes o' what we'll get out there! Guidsakes, lord – you dinna ken what you're saying!"

The truth behind the skipper's fears was not very evident at first. Though the seas were short and steep and white-capped, the boat was able to maintain a rolling crabwise course through the jangle, the sweeps still out. Largo Bay is four miles wide and two deep, with the high cliffs of thrusting Kincraig Point shielding it on the east. Once past that shelter, however, the mountains of Norway are the nearest barrier to an east wind.

Despite the darkness none aboard needed to be told when their vessel crossed the unseen line of protection. The moan of the wind rose dramatically to a roar, and the waves grew quite alarmingly greater, their hissing crests whipped off in spray that blew like stinging hail in the driving rain. Squat and beamy as the buss was, she heeled over violently, the port rowers collapsing on their benches as their sweeps

33

flailed the air. Hastily the long oars were pulled in, and the helm thrown over, turning the bows points into the west. To have sought to maintain a true southerly course would have been suicidal.

Plunging fore and aft now like some great ungainly war-charger in the see-saw motion enforced by the long following seas, they pitched and wallowed ponderously, seeming to progress in a series of lurches. The buss, though clumsy and an uncomfortable sailer, was built for heavy North Sea conditions, and was probably the best craft of its size that could have been chosen for such a crossing. But her low freeboard seemed very close to the surging waters, which every now and again came snarling inboard. The surface of the sea had suddenly become more frighteningly visible, white instead of black, veined and creamed with foam.

The travellers had long been superficially wet; now they were all soaked through. Some had sought the shelter of the fo'c'sle – but quickly decided that the howling night was preferable to the stinks and suffocating gloom of that black hole. They huddled under the lee of the net-platform aft, little shield as that fish-smelling pile afforded.

Not so the boys. From one side to the other they stumbled, seldom still, their favourite position well forward, where they clung to the shrouds of the foremast, peering into the turmoil of the elements, exclaiming excitedly at everything, shouting delighted warning of giant combers, and helping the crew to bail out the water which splashed about their ankles. They were accustomed to boats and unquiet seas, at St. Andrews – but never had they been abroad in such weather as this.

It was as well that there was a deal of north in the easterly wind, otherwise their course would inevitably have been more up-firth than across it. Directly south-south-east of Largo, Fidra and Dirleton lay about a dozen miles off. Even giving more south to his course than his judgement permitted, the skipper reckoned that they had a twenty-mile voyage ahead of them, with probably Salt-Preston as their likeliest landfall, miles west even of Seton. His passengers could only fume and shiver; out here swords, like high rank, resolved nothing.

"You are not feeling sick, James?" Harry Percy shouted, presently, almost hopefully. "Lord Bardoph is sick. Trying to spew all the time. Availing nothing. And one of the men-at-arms. They should play the man better than this, I say!"

"I'll wager you are sick before I am!" James returned, with some spirit. "I have never been sick on the sea in my life."

"*I* shall not be sick, I promise you! You should see the storms we get at Alnmouth and the Farnes, off our Northumberland coast. That is the *real* sea – not a sort of river, like this!"

"The Firth of Forth is no river," the other protested strongly. "Any mariner will tell you so. Many stout ships have sailed here all the way from far lands, only to wreck in the Forth. There . . . there are probably sunken ships underneath us at this very moment!"

At this sobering thought even James himself eyed the chasing lip-curling combers towering behind them and around them with less appreciation, and the boys fell silent for a while.

It was two full and trying hours after leaving Largo before a slight and very gradual lessing of the sea's fury enabled the skipper to announce his belief that they had crossed far enough over to be in outer Aberlady Bay, within the modest shelter afforded by the series of low promontories of the Gullane coast.

He turned the buss's blunt bows a few more points into the south, but had to ease his helm again almost at once, as they began to ship water abeam. Clearly there would be no rowing down the coast that night.

"Where think you is the nearest you can put us in?" Fleming demanded, not for the first time. "If we are in Aberlady Bay, we are devilish close to Kilspindie, a Douglas house. We would keep our distance from all such!"

"Och, it's just the outer bay we're in, mind – no' the inner. There's a gey lot o' it. I'll do what I can, lord . . ."

"We do not want to land at Seton harbour, either. My Lord Seton is doubtful of loyalty."

"Man, man – what way's this to seek a landfall in a storm!" the sorely-tried seaman cried. "No' here, no' there! Hech, hech – I'll do my best for you, lord, but it's no' possible to put you east o' Gullane Point. Waesucks – even such as you should be able to see that!" The skipper, the worst over, was beginning to recover something of his spirit.

The knight forbore meet reproof.

Presently, despite the seas lessening steadily, a new thunderous roaring sound began to assail their ears above the din of the storm. The skipper, peering to the left, landwards, tugged at his shaggy beard.

"Yon's the bar o' Aberlady Bay – the inner bay," he informed. "Three miles long, and a killer! Dries out at low-water. But it's more'n half-tide now, and making. It's an ill place. But . . ." He scratched his chin. "Och, it might serve . . ."

"What are you talking about, fellow?" Orkney demanded. "Where *are* you going to land us?"

"Och, it's no' so easy, sir. This is a right wicked coast. On sic a night. No' like the Fife side, wi' wee havens and ports a' the way. It's just shoaling sand, banks and shallows, by the league. In a nor'-easter the likes o' this, it's a mariner's grave, just. And east o' Seton, no' a harbour in a score accursed miles."

"Well, man – well?"

"Yon bar, across Aberlady Bay. Nae craft could cross it. But, at its west end, see you, there's a bit gap. Where the river comes out, at low water. Cuts a passage through the sand-banks. If we could win through that, there'll be quiet water behind, in the deep inner bay. It runs far into the land. There's nae harbour – but I could put you ashore in the shallows, just."

"Do that, then . . ."

"How close would that be to Douglas of Kilspindie's house?" Fleming put in.

"Yon's on the west side o' the bay. The east side's empty

bog and links. That side I'll put you in. If the blessed saints will take us in through the gap . . ."

Although the thunder of breaking water, landwards, was ominous, the fearsomeness of the great sand-bar in a storm only began to be apprehended by the passengers when they perceived an eerie lightening of the gloom to their left, vague but continuous. This grew, as did the noise, with their slantwise approach to the coast, until all could recognise it for what it was – a vast area of tortured, boiling, spouting water about three miles long by a quarter-mile broad, where the great seas smashed themselves in white fury upon the serried ranks and ridges of shoaling sand which, only a foot or two beneath the surface, barred the inner bay, the waves blasting themselves into disintegration high in the air in an unending curtain of seething fountains, the stark white and phosphorescence of which lit up the black night. Awed, even veteran warriors like Fleming and Northumberland stared at this battlefield of the elements, and wondered whether the skipper was keeping sufficient distance. As for the boys, for once they failed for words.

Almost parallel with the awesome barrier the buss ran, for what seemed miles, the skipper watching it steadily from under dripping brows. At length, when it began to give the impression of lessening something of its fury, he suddenly shouted a command to get out the sweeps, and gradually put over his helm.

The heavy craft swung round, rolling and wallowing, and bore in at a steeper angle for the chaos. Immediately water, the tips of breakers, came hurling in over the dipping port freeboard. Save for the oarsmen, all aboard, even the earls, urgently began to bail, glad enough to be doing something other than staring at the horror ahead.

The gap in the rampart of exploding seas was not evident until they were almost upon it. Near the extreme west end of the bar, where it ended at the rocks and reefs of Kilspindie Point, the Peffer Burn, whose estuary this inner bay was, had cut for itself a channel, perhaps seventy yards wide, through the sand shoals. Here was deeper water which, though still tortured and seething, did not spout. Into it the clumsy, barge-like vessel lurched and plunged, the rowers labouring in panting desperation, the sail hauled down.

Through this strange corridor, high white menace towering on either side, the streaming spume of that to the east all but smothering them on the driving wind, they crawled and sidled. None spoke.

Then abruptly, almost unbelievably, it was all over. With little or no warning, they were through, into the great sheltered lagoon of the inner bay. The noise of the bar was almost worse, for now it was mainly to windward of them; but the water was comparatively calm, all the sea's force expended on that submarine plateau of sand. On into black darkness again they pulled, and though the wind still tore over them it seemed by contrast that they had miraculously come into a place of still peace.

In the flood of relieved and thankful exclamation, even the proud nobles found themselves wringing the skipper's horny hand in gratitude.

"I couldna hae done it, mind, in a nor'-*wester*," that man declared. "Then it a' just piles right into the bay, and there's nae way in or oot!"

"But if it had been a north-west wind we would not have been blown here!" Harry Percy pointed out loudly. He had not stopped talking from the moment they penetrated to safety. James Stewart, on the other hand, remained entirely silent.

The buss was now rowed south-eastwards across the great wedge-shaped bay, the skipper himself taking soundings with a lead continuously – for it was very shallow in here, indeed mere mud-flats at low tide. The craft was fairly shallow-draughted, but even so most of the time there was only a foot or two of clearance, and sometimes where mussel-beds rose above the muddy floor, their bottom scraped alarmingly.

At length, with a shuddering jolt, the buss ran her broad prow hard aground, and no amount of oarsmanship would refloat her meantime. It was not yet high-water, however, and the flowing tide would float her again in due course.

"We're no' far frae the tideline, here," the skipper announced, pointing due eastwards. "You'll can just see it, yonder. It's gey low, mind."

None other could in fact see any sign of the shore, but one of the fishermen jumped over the side, to prove how shallow was the water, which came up barely to his middle. Other members of the crew, suddenly affable now, offered to carry their passengers ashore on their backs. But all were now so comprehensively soaked that any such proceeding would have been as pointless as it was undignified. They would do their own wading.

Orkney paid the skipper handsomely, Fleming and Northumberland adding extra tokens of their own relief. The impact of that sand-bar had not yet worn off.

The shore party lowered themselves gingerly over the side. Wet and chilled as they were, they found that actually standing in the cold water was a grievous thing. There was no delay now. Clutching their belongings, they splashed their way unsteadily towards the unseen shore, with little leave-taking.

There was no beach here, merely saltings, an area of seagrass covered at high-water, and filled with holes and runnels – highly unpleasant for benighted walkers. Only the boys were able to find the situation less than intolerable.

After the saltings, they found themselves in a belt of level marshland and bog, through which they had to plouter – almost more unpleasant. The Earl of Northumberland, old enough to know better, wasted precious breath in a steady stream of cursing.

At least this waterlogged wilderness was a sufficiently secret place for their landing, Orkney pointed out.

At length these grim tidelands gave place to firm rising grasslands that lifted up and up. Evidently they were climbing a sizeable hill. None of them knew this country, but the skipper had told them that due eastwards would lie the village of Gullane, and that Gullane would be perhaps three difficult miles west of their desired landing-place at Fidra Isle, where their friends awaited them.

On the top of the ridge, where the gale met them full blast again, they held a huddled council. They calculated that there were yet perhaps two hours till daybreak – ample time to cover three miles in normal circumstances. But in soaking darkness, unknown territory and in the face of a storm, it was different, especially for men unused to walking. The great castle of Luffness must be somewhere near at hand – but its lord, Sir Walter Bickerton, was another of the prisoners of Homildon Hill, in English hands, and neighbouring Douglases might well be in possession. Young James remembered that there was a collegiate religious house at Gullane, under the see of St. Andrews, where they might get horses; but to go there would draw notable attention to themselves. It was eventually agreed that there was nothing for it but to trudge on north-eastwards avoiding the village if possible, until they struck the coast again, and then work their way along it until they reached the Dirleton shore – uninviting as was the prospect.

That grievous thing they did, stumbling their slow way across an infinity of sand-dunes, round wave-torn strands, over rocky promontories, negotiating little cliffs. Before long, old Northumberland was in marked distress – hotly as he rebuffed any who sought to aid him. Their pace slowed and slowed.

The day dawned late that cold February morning – but even so the last dire mile of their ordeal was traversed in a lessening darkness which progressively revealed the grim grey prospect of angry sea and ravaged coast. Indeed they were able to glimpse occasionally the rocky islet of Fidra half-a-mile offshore, lost as it was most of the time behind a screen of erupting spray.

The island formed something of a breakwater, and land-ward of it was a comparatively sheltered area, at the head of which two out-stretching arms of reef formed a natural haven which had been improved with stones and boulders. Here was a rude shelter of timber and turf – for the isle supported a small monkish colony whose hermit-like members devotedly kept a beacon for the warning of mariners, supplied with fuel from the woods of Dirleton. This was their ferry terminus.

Thankfully the weary wayfarers perceived saddled horses huddled in the lee of this shelter, and presently shouts announced that they had been spotted. Men came hurrying to meet them, anxiously exclaiming and questioning. James, for the first time in his life, found himself the recipient of the greatest attention and most concern. Sir William Sinclair and Sir Walter Haliburton, in their long vigil, had come to fear that the Heir of Scotland had been taken by the sea. Sinclair of Herdmanston was a kinsman of Orkney's, while Haliburton was his own mother's brother's son.

Cheered and sustained with strong spirits and cold meats, the entire party rode the mile or so inland, though by secret wooded ways, to Haliburton's fine castle of Dirleton.

4

It was two nights later that the fugitives again faced the sea
– or some of them. They had waited, at hospitable Dirleton
Castle, until the storm abated. Then, on the second day,
Haliburton had word that the Douglases and other friends of
the Governor, were scouring the country. The Prince James
had been stolen from St. Andrews, the rumour said, by
traitors in the pay of the English renegade Northumberland.
Great rewards were offered for captors and captive. East
Lothian was full of Douglases and their supporters – for
Tantallon, one of their greatest strongholds, lay only a few
miles away. Surer security than Dirleton was urgently called
for.

So again, in darkness, with the salt tang of the sea in
their faces, the secret party halted just behind the little
town of North Berwick, at the foot of its conical law, a
couple of miles east of Dirleton. It was the parting of the
ways. Northumberland and his grandson, with Bardolph,
here must strike inland, to avoid the area of Tantallon,
cross the Tyne at Linton, and ride into the empty hills of
Lammermuir on their way to the Border. James's party had
a less lengthy but more spectacular itinerary.

The goodbyes were not prolonged. James was sorry to
lose his friend, but he was growing used to that – and Harry
was not always the most easy of companions. They promised
each other that they would meet again, some day, in different
circumstances, renowned knights, noble champions – perhaps lead a new Crusade together, to free the Holy Land;
at any rate, to demonstrate how life ought to be lived.

The Englishmen, with only two men-at-arms as escort,

rode off southwards into the night, to murmured God-speeds.

Reining their beasts' heads round, due northwards, the rest of the company trotted down, across links of rustling marram-grass, to the sea.

Again they sought a boat, a smaller one this time – and dared not go to the harbour of North Berwick for it. This craft, waiting hidden in a sandy cove, was oddly enough a women's boat, the property of the Cistercian nunnery nearby, whose Prioress was a sister of Haliburton's. But the four fishermen who manned it were brawnily masculine enough, providers of fish for the nuns.

Only a much reduced party clambered aboard with James – Orkney, Fleming and Sinclair of Herdmanston, with three servitors. Where they were going, extra mouths to feed were not wanted. Sir Walter actually knelt there on the sand, to kiss the embarrassed James's hand, to wish him well, and to promise to send secret word to the French ship whenever she should arrive at Leith.

The wind remained easterly and cold, but greatly reduced in strength. The seas were still high however, though very different in quality from two nights before, and the entire coast shook to the slow thunder of long rollers. Once out of the sheltered cove, the boat seemed very small, like a tiny eggshell dancing on the great smooth-sided swell that rose and fell a score of feet in rounded ridge and valley to all infinity.

James was not sick – but very much aware of the supper he had eaten at Dirleton before setting out.

There were gaps in the cloud tonight, occasional winking stars, and somewhere a horn of moon had risen to lighten the overcast, so that there was visibility of a sort. The endless glass mountains of black sea were the more dauntingly evident in consequence – but the voyagers were also able to observe their progress, intermittently from the wavetops, as they were pulled almost due eastwards across North Berwick's two bays, roughly parallel to the coast and perhaps half-a-mile out.

43

This was no lengthy voyage. Quite soon they could discern ahead of them the monstrous and improbable stack of the Bass Rock, rising in dizzy precipices like a sheer pillar from the waves. High, remote, savage, it towered in their path, girdled with the white of shattered seas.

All but appalled, the travellers peered at it. That this could be their destination seemed beyond all belief.

They had not been so close to the Bass as they had thought, as became apparent by their delay in coming up with it – and the more enormous, in consequence, grew this majestic tower of rock. The boatmen said that it lay three miles out from North Berwick, but only half that from the nearest point of the mainland shore – on which point, as it happened, stood the mighty Douglas castle of Tantallon.

The rowers took their slight craft to the south of the huge pile, and as they drew close certain attributes of the place became inescapable to the newcomers. First, that as well as soaring physically, it stank to high heaven; then, that the surge of the seas, elsewhere impressive enough in all conscience here developed proportions that challenged all acceptance, rising and falling against the beetling cliffs in heights and depths that made the prevailing swell look puny, insignificant; and thirdly, in consequence, that the Bass was quite impossible of access.

Their steadily-pulling escort answered their concerned questions with a sort of soothing scorn. The musty smell was from the droppings of birds – for the Bass harboured more sea-fowl than all the rest of Scotland, they claimed. The great lift of the tide here was caused by the rock standing at the very edge of the land's shelf, where the sea-bottom dropped away into unplumbed depths. And there were means of winning on to the place, as they would discover.

As though to confirm this reassurance, a small yellow gleam of light now became apparent, skied perhaps one-third of the way up the south face of the stack – which, their informants declared, reared four-hundred feet into the air.

Almost directly below this lofty glimmer, they drew in close-soaring and sinking on the surge in quite sickening fashion. It became evident that there was a small re-entrant here, a sort of recess in the face of the cliff, which by its situation and the vast buttresses which flanked it, would be comparatively sheltered from all but due southerly winds. Herein, though the rise and fall of the swell was little abated, the seas did not break and spout. But the streaming black rock walls were as sheer as ever, with no possible landing-stage evident.

As the travellers were voicing disbelief, one of the boatmen produced a horn, on which he blew a succession of short blasts. The echoes of these, amongst the high precipices, had scarcely died away before an answering series sounded thinly from somewhere above. They waited, then, dizzily swooping and plunging, only a few feet from the rock-face. There was a great distant booming going on, from an unidentified source, ominous, to set the hair lifting at the nape of the neck.

At length, above this and other unchancy sounds, they heard the clanking of a chain, and down towards them came a great wicker basket, lowered jerkily from on high. Its descent was halted skilfully at approximately the highest point to which the seas reached. Ropes dangled from its rim.

The transference to this basket was an undertaking which none who experienced it were ever likely to forget. One of the boatmen, with enviable expertise, caught the thing on one of the upsurges, as his colleagues manoeuvred the boat close and launched himself up as the craft sank away, to hang there for a moment before nimbly vaulting over the rim and inside. Thereafter, he held out his hands to aid the first volunteer.

Young James, rising to the challenge, offered to go first, but Orkney would not hear of it. Sir William Sinclair elected to make the attempt – and with the fisherman's help, effected the alarming evolution successfully enough, although he seemed to hang for unconscionable time half-in, half-out, of the container.

With four hands to aid him above, Orkney allowed James

to go next, two surges of the tide later. The boy undoubtedly found the business less of an ordeal than did his elders — although there were moments when, clinging and scrabbling there, he was very much aware of the boat sinking away below him and the yawning emptiness all around. Then he was over, into the frail but so real security of the basket, and exhilaration welled up in him like a flood.

Orkney himself came next — and his sword catching in the wickerwork gave them all a few dire seconds before he was hauled inside, just as a new sea came boiling through about their legs. Then the boatman below blew his horn again, four being as many as the basket would safely hold at a time. The chain began to clank.

Being drawn, swaying and birling round, up and up into the emptiness, was another sensation which would stay in the memory. The sense of vacancy and isolation was very real. They seemed to rise a long way before the creak of pulley-wheels intimated the end of the ascent, and hands reached out to steady the basket and assist them over the side.

They were on a grassy ledge, not so broad as to feel very safe, where four men worked a capstan which raised and lowered the basket. Behind this the cliff-face slanted up steeply, but no longer sheer. Up this a flight of steps was cut in the natural rock. One of the men led them up, leaving the fisherman to help with the capstan.

Climbing those stairs, on slightly unsteady legs, James was even more aware, in the pit of his stomach, of the quality of the drop below. A stout rope hung beside the steps, as hand-rail — and none failed to avail themselves of it.

Presently the steps ended at a high stone wall, battle-mented and gapped with shot-holes. In this was a postern-gate, with a little porter's lodge and an iron yett. Here an elderly stooping but broadbuilt man awaited them. He bowed low to the boy.

"Welcome to the Craig of Bass, my lord James," he said. "I am Robert Lauder of Edrington, laird of this hold. Ye'll be safe here, laddie. My lords — come ye in."

Turning, he led them across a tiny courtyard to the open door of a squat, square keep that rose in a declivity of the cliff-face, as though itself growing from the living rock. It was from a window of this improbable fortress that the light shone.

So commenced an interlude in the life of James Stewart, extraordinary by any standards, a period so distinct, different and divorced from all that had gone before or was to follow on, as to seem always thereafter as though in another world, almost another dimension of living. For a full month James and his little party were destined to roost in that strange wind-blown eyrie above the wrinkled sea – while the land was ransacked for the missing Heir of Scotland, and men died horribly for failure to produce him. While they awaited the ship from France, it would indeed have been difficult to find, or conceive of, a more secure hiding-place than this.

The wonder of it commenced from the very moment of wakening, next morning – after dropping at once into a deep and dreamless sleep in the small garret chamber allotted to him within the parapet-walk. The noise was penetrating, shrill and incessant, a high-pitched screeching cacophony of such vehemence, volume and stridor as to beat on the brain and almost numb the senses. Leaping out of bed, the boy ran to the window.

Without actually considering the matter, he had assumed that it was as yet barely daylight. Peering out, he perceived that this was not so. The lack of light was caused by the air being so dense with whirling, circling, screaming birds as to darken the sky around the rock. In their hundreds of thousands the creatures wheeled and beat, sailed and swooped – all apparently yelling at the pitch of their lungs. There were birds and gulls of all shapes, colours and sizes in bewildering profusion and confusion, but the boy could not help but be particularly attracted by the largest and seemingly most numerous – huge white birds with black at their wing-tips, and with fully six feet of powerful wing in between. These James knew to be gannets, solan geese, the Bass's especial denizens. He had seen them often, fishing in the sea off St. Andrews; but never close like this – for they flashed past his window in unending succession near enough for him to gaze into their cold, bright, unwinking eyes behind the long spearlike beaks.

Pulling on some clothing, James hurried to the door which opened on to the parapet-walk, and out. There he gasped, faltering, unprepared for the impact on his senses. The noise here was deafening; the rush of the great birds almost terrifying as they swept close; the smell was choking, stirred up presumably by the turbulence of a million wings. Moreover, the parapet at this side of the keep overhung sheerly above the restless waves a couple of hundred feet below, and the sudden perception of the fact, with the stench, was almost too much for James's stomach. He realised that he was standing, there on the narrow walk at the wall-head, on perhaps six inches of white and dried droppings. Everything in sight was so coated.

Glancing to the right, he was the more astonished. There, only a few yards away, the cliff rose, soaring high above this level. And it was as white as all else – not only with the droppings but with roosting sea-fowl. Every crevice and cranny, every ledge and hollow, was occupied and crowded with sitting birds – gannets, kittiwakes, fulmars, puffins and every variety of gull. There they sat in their unnumbered thousands, most of them vociferously squawking – so close packed that the marvel was to imagine where room might be found amongst them for all the myriads already wheeling in the air.

If this was the first wonder to assail James Stewart, it was by no means the last. Another was to discover a little church, clinging like a limpet to the steep slope some way above the castle. This had developed from the hermit's cell of an ancient but presumably clearheaded saint called Baldred, whose reasons for selecting this spot for his devotions demanded no little explanation. It was now, actually, a parish church, the Bass representing a parish of

48

its own. It had a very odd and tiny congregation consisting only of Sir Robert Lauder's few men from the castle – and not a woman amongst them. In the weeks James spent on the Bass, no parish priest materialised. Just what Sir Robert kept a garrison here for, in itself, was never explained.

Higher still, when that forenoon James went exploring, and clambered up a zig-zag but well-made path to the dizzy summit of the rock, he found, of all things, a flock of sheep grazing, wind-blown but fat, on the few acres of lush grass that capped the gently-sloping top – grass richly manured by bird-droppings, to produce the famous Bass mutton that was known as a delicacy throughout Scotland.

James learned, also, that the booming noise emanated from a great cavern hollowed out in the heart of the rock, said to be nearly two-hundred yards long, where the seas ran in and smashed themselves in thunderous clamour. In a storm, he was told, the noise was like cannon-fire, the entire rock seeming to shake to the impact. Let him wait; this being February he probably would not leave the place without a demonstration.

For the next few days however storms withheld, and calm sunny weather, with frosty nights, smiled on land and sea. Although Orkney, Sinclair and Fleming soon began to fret and grow restive in these cramped quarters, whiling away the time in gaming and drinking too much – for though the diet was restricted there was certainly no lack of liquor in this airy stronghold – James himself was happy. Left entirely to himself, he clambered all over that exciting place – indeed, had his elders seen some of his exploits, they would have kept him as house-bound as themselves thereafter. He spent a lot of time, scarcely noticing the cold, up on the very highest north-eastern tip of the rock, where the most stupendous of the cliffs dropped four hundred feet sheer to the surging tide, lying on the grass and sea-pink plants and gazing down to watch the seals swimming or heaving themselves about on the tidal ledges far below, or admiring the magnificent diving of the gannets as they plunged arrow-straight down into the sea from hundreds of feet, to disappear far under the surface after their quarry – but usually to burst up again presently, with shining silver in their beaks. How they saw them, and seeing, were able so to descend upon the swiftly-moving fish and strike them, despite the refraction of the water, nobody could explain to him.

When James tired of looking down, he had only to raise his eyes to contemplate a prospect the magnificence of which would be hard to better – all green Lothian glowing in the sun to the south and west; the islanded firth spread far and wide around; to the north the distant shore of fair Fife with its hills – even on the clear northerly air, the smoke of St. Andrews blue above the East Neuk; and eastwards, the limitless plain of the azure sea, with only the Isle of May, dwarfed from here, to break its shining surface ten miles away. James looked for ships, of course, especially one that might have come from France – but did not greatly pine because none came near. More often he looked over at the frowning towers of Tantallon Castle, little more than a mile away to the south, and even on occasion shook his fist at the great Red Heart banner of Douglas which he could just discern flying from its topmost turret. If the Douglases only knew . . .

Not that even Douglas and the Governor could have achieved anything against the Bass had they known its present secret. Most obviously the place was quite impregnable. Even to starve out its garrison was scarcely possible, for once all the mutton that grazed here was eaten there was an unending supply of fish and sea-fowl – the gannets apparently were edible, though not to everyone's taste. Haliburton and Sinclair had carried out their monarch's anxious behests in no feeble fashion.

They were not entirely cut off from the rest of the world, however. At times, usually of a night, a horn would sound thinly, capstan and chain would go into action, and a messenger or select visitor would materialise with tidings or provisions. On one occasion, two sons of Sir Robert arrived from Edrington in Berwickshire – for Lauder only intermittently lived on the rock – cheerful and muscular young men, to one of whom James took a particular fancy. It was only when they were gone, after three energetic and companionable days, that he learned with surprise that his especial friend, Willie Lauder, was a priest.

Another night, just over two weeks after their arrival, it was Sir Walter Haliburton himself who came, to express his concern that there was no word of the French ship, and to tell of Albany's drastic methods of search for his nephew. His information was that the Governor believed that James had been in fact brought to Lothian, and was concentrating his search in that area – but not particularly in this easternmost corner. So far none had come chapping at his door at Dirleton Castle – though Herdmanston House, a dozen miles nearer Edinburgh had been visited and searched. The King's friends, unfortunately, were known and suspect.

It was a couple of nights later that James was awakened by the great concussions. At first he thought that his uncle had found him, and sent ships with cannon to blast him off this rock, so powerful were the crashes. Then he realised that though the tower shook to these explosions with monotonous regularity, they were not continuous, while the casement and shutters of his window shook all the time. A gale was blowing, evidently once more from the north-east. It was long before the boy slept again.

Next morning, he rose to find the Bass a different place indeed, and a fair representation of the Inferno. The halo of wheeling birds, which from daybreak to nightfall encircled its lofty brow, was gone. Now another whiteness than droppings and plumage coated everything – white foam and froth. Like a snowstorm this filled the air, darkening the day, covering keep and rock and crouching fowl alike. It was with something of a shock that the visitors came to realise that this thick foam, since the storm was from the north-east, must be coming right over the top of the Bass. The thought was a daunting one. What was going on in the great cavern below did not bear contemplation. Sir Robert had to reassure his guests more than once that having survived untold centuries, it was unlikely that his peculiar lairdship would split right open and disintegrate in this particular storm.

For four grim days men, like the sea-fowl – and presumably sheep – could do nothing but crouch and wait. There was no prospect, the spume blotting out all beyond a yard or two, no let up from the nerve-jangling crashes, and the howl and whine of the wind. The fourth night, however, the wind dropped quite suddenly – and in the morning the screaming chorus of the birds was back at its tireless circling.

Concerned for his sheep, Sir Robert led his guests up to the topmost plateau that forenoon, for an inspection. They had to go carefully, linked together by a rope – for the froth and spray and rain had made a slippery paste of the comprehensive coating of bird-droppings, and falls might have been as disastrous as they were easy.

They found the sheep huddled scarcely credibly in niches and corners immediately below the rim of the top, at this lee side. Counting them, Lauder could assess only five missing – and these might well be hiding in other nooks and crevices.

The grass cap of the Bass was a sight to see. Yellow-white with foam, it was littered with seaweed, shells, starfish, even squids and dead birds. That all this could have come up from so far below taxed acceptance – until they neared the outer edge and saw the fearsome seas reaching out for them half-way up that mighty cliff, and even yet throwing up a curtain of spume to soak them. It was not a sight over which even James wished to linger.

It was a week later before word came again from Dirleton. On this occasion Sir Walter could not come himself, for he was sure that he was being watched. A relative of his wife, married to a Douglas, had arrived unannounced to visit them, and other Douglases were much in evidence. The hunt was moving in. But he sent his steward to report that the merchant bark *Maryenknyght*, of Danzig, had limped into Leith at last, with a cargo of wines, after being blown off course by the gale and stormbound in Dundee. Conditions permitting she would sail again two afternoons hence, March

19th, and be lying off the Bass by ten at night. She would show a blue light, to guide her intending passengers.

And so the strange interlude came to an end. On a dark night of moist and warm westerly wind and drizzle, the visitors took leave of the Bass and their host, and were lowered to the same waiting boat which had brought them there. At first there was no sign of the ship, for with a westerly wind she was lying at the far lee side, where also no blue light might be visible from Tantallon Castle.

Rowing round, they soon perceived the *Maryenknyght*, rolling heavily, her tall masts describing strange patterns on account of the complicated swell and undertow occasioned by the abrupt change in the sea-floor level which made this area so wicked. The French shipmaster, already impatient and anxious, alarmed by stories heard at Leith, the state his ship was in, and the fear of worsening weather, shouted urgently for them to hasten. In the circumstances there was a hurried parting – for only Orkney and a couple of others were going on with James to France. Taking faltering farewell of Sir David Fleming and Sir William Sinclair, James climbed the swaying rope-ladder to the deck, the Earl at his back.

The Bass was already lost in the gloom, though he could still hear the hollow booming of the cavern. Quickly the little boat dropped away, without further ceremony, the boy perceiving no answers to his waving. He stared back into the night for as long as he could hear that strange sound, which was all that was left to him of Scotland, before swallowing and turning to follow Orkney and the French-speaking captain below.

The shipmen's fears about the weather, at least, were justified. By morning half-a-gale was blowing from the south-west, forcing the vessel farther east than was the intention. The craft's timbers had been strained by the previous storm, and gear damaged, and repairs at Dundee had been hurried and inadequate. They had not dared to linger at Leith. The intention therefore was to keep fairly close inshore during the run down the English coast – happily there was a truce in force meantime between England, Scotland and France – in case it became necessary to put into some haven or anchorage for further repairs and caulking. These strengthening south-westerly winds however made such a course almost impossible. Under minimum sail the *Maryenknyght* was pushed ever farther from the shelter of the land into a grey, hostile and tossing immensity.

The travellers were surprised to find that they had a fellow-passenger. Seasick below was a lanky ginger-headed young man, who turned out to be William Gifford, cousin to Sir Hugh Gifford of Yester, one of the late Queen's household, whom King Robert had sent to act as esquire for his son on his travels. If James was not a little impressed at thus having acquired, for the first time, an attendant of his own, he was meantime but little advantaged, for the unfortunate Gifford was wholly prostrate on his bunk.

Admittedly it made unpleasant voyaging, even for a boy undemanding of comfort and eager for new experience. The ship was sluggish and heavy, the crew ill-tempered and uneasy, the master preoccupied. Moreover a cargo of untanned hides and fleeces had been shipped at Leith, and the stink from these made the Bass bird-droppings aromatic by contrast. Below decks was all but unbearable – though Master Gifford stayed there.

All day they rolled and wallowed south by east in an empty desolation of angry waters, and the long and weary night brought little solace or betterment of conditions. But by morning the wind had dropped considerably and was backing into the north-west. The captain was able to star-board his helm and run south-westwards. The passengers received their first civilities.

They sighted land in the early afternoon, the North Yorkshire coast. Satisfied meantime, Monsieur Bereholt turned to run due south, perhaps ten miles offshore.

They passed one or two sail, at a distance, and were off

Flamborough when a small squadron emerged suddenly from behind that great headland. No port for large vessels lay yonder – and one of these newcomers was a taller ship than the *Maryenknyght*. M. Bereholt was a little perturbed, muttering about English pirates. He turned a few points into the east again.

The squadron also adjusted course forthwith, the large ship overhauling them fast. Alarmed now, the *Maryenknyght* put on all possible sail, amidst a gale of Gallic eloquence.

But neither sail nor eloquence was sufficient. The other ship most obviously sought their company, and having almost twice their canvas was in a position to attain it. And she had more than canvas. Presently the deep double boom of cannon startled them, and two white fountains rose in their wake, well astern but true as to line.

Confusion reigned aboard the *Maryenknyght*, loud and comprehensive. But there was no question as to procedure. Despite Orkney's pleas and curses, the captain would not hear of trying to make a run for it, much less a fight, and trusting to the early darkness to come to their aid. He ordered sail to be lowered.

The Englishman came up in businesslike fashion, gun-ports wide and cannon-snouts projecting threateningly. Nevertheless she appeared to be no king's ship but rather an armed merchantman – which made any such assault sheer piracy.

Warily the newcomer circled the Danziger and, satisfied evidently that no foreign guile was contemplated, moved in close, revealing herself to be the *Kingfisher*, of Great Yarmouth. Skilfully she manoeuvred alongside, under the threat of gunners with spluttering fuses in their hands and pointing bowmen and hagbutters stationed on fore- and after-castles. Grapnels and hooked cables were thrown over, to bind the two vessels together. Then, sword in hand and amply escorted, a burley blond giant of a man leapt with surprising agility aboard the *Maryenknyght*, summoning all to surrender in King Harry's name.

He was met by a spate, a torrent of words, of a profundity, vigour and expressiveness quite phenomenal. These he listened to with a grin of patience laced with mockery. But presently he had had enough, and with a chopping motion of his sword-hand, cut off the flow with surprising success.

"Enough, Master Frog!" he barked. "Save your breath. It's wasted on Hugh-atte-Fen, by the Powers! Peace, man! You are my prize – so make the best of it. Your cargo stinks – but maybe that's the least of it? The names of your passengers, sirrah?"

The Frenchman spread fluttering, outraged hands.

"I am the Earl of Orkney," that nobleman declared, haughtily angry. "Of the Privy Council of the King of Scots. With whom *your* king, fellow, is in signed truce! What is the meaning of this, this affront?"

"That you will discover, my lord! Meantime – greetings. At last. We have looked for you for many days, to welcome you!" The Englishman gestured towards James. "This lad, now? I'll wager he's not *your* son? At a guess, I'd hazard his name to be James! Am I right, my lord?"

Frowning, Orkney fingered his small pointed beard, and said nothing.

The English captain laughed, and flourished a scornful bow at them both. "Your servant, my good lords. Humble Hugh-atte-Fen, of Great Yarmouth in Norfolk, welcomes you to the fair realm of England! Will your honours step this way?" And he gestured to his own ship.

"What insolence is this?" the Earl demanded, but with only a hollow show of confidence. "We journey to France, on the business and under the protection of Their Graces of Scotland and France."

"Then now add to that the protection of His Grace of England also!" the other interrupted, with grim humour. "You will continue your journey, I vow, in more comfort and speed in *my* ship than in this stinking tub! Come, sirs – quarters await you."

"Where . . . where do you take us?" Orkney asked, from tight lips.

"A deal nearer to your destination, I promise you! At least as far as the Thames, my lords – most of the way to France! And have you there twice so fast as had you remained in this! You will thank me. Now – your chattels . . ."

5

From the high after-castle of the *Kingfisher*, James stared
unbelievingly at the crowded and jumbled skyline of
London. Throughout their interminable progress up the
Thames estuary, he had scarcely been able to credit that
people could actually live in such consistently flat, dreary
and marsh-like surroundings, with not so much as a tiny
hill in sight. He had waited for better things. Now, he saw
a great city built on the same dismal and level terrain, a
huddled infinity of walls and gables, roofs and spires and
belfries, crouching under a canopy of smoke that reached as
far as eye could see. And out of it, stark, uncompromising,
forbidding, rose only one notable landmark – a great square
ugly keep, huge, plain and featureless as a box of grey-white
stone – which could only be the dreaded Tower of London
itself, charnel-house of liberty. In vain the boy looked for
palaces and castles, the symbols of kingship and nobility.
In Scotland, such were usually set high on soaring rocks
and pinnacles, suitably crowning proud hills. But here there
were no hills nor rocks, no eminencies of any sort worthy
of the name – and no challenging turrets, citadels and
fortalices either, it seemed; only the vast ominous square
prison to reign over all.

The *Kingfisher* was warped in, to tie up at a wharf
projecting, amongst many, into the murky waters of the
river. Here was more shipping moored than James had
been aware existed in all the world. The bustle, activity
and noise from all around was as extraordinary – and, after
a while, James would have had to admit, heartening. Surprisingly, the people thronging the quays and rabbit-warren

of alleyways flanking them, seemed to be as cheerful as they were voluble and shrill.

There was to be no closer contact with all this novelty meantime however, it seemed. Shipmaster atte-Fen insisted that his guests return to their cabins for an unspecified interval – he had made a point of calling them guests throughout their four-day association, whilst nevertheless treating them as captives. He was going ashore – presumably for instructions. Orkney was indignant, recovering something of the suitable hauteur so difficult to maintain hitherto, now that they could see an end to the insufferable dominance of a mere merchant-adventurer. He demanded to be brought into the presence of men of authority and rank forthwith – Privy Councillors, the Chancellor, King Henry himself. Hugh-atte-Fen waggishly assured that this was indeed the entire object of his present mission – but locked his guests into their cabin nevertheless with something of a flourish. Since it was not high enough for the Earl to stand upright in, he forbore any demonstration of noble pride meantime.

It was a matter of hours before atte-Fen returned. He had with him an officer in royal livery and a party of men-at-arms. The officer, however, was obviously of no very high rank nor breeding, his manners rougher and less respectful even than those of the shipmaster. Curtly he ordered Orkney, James and Gifford to accompany him, all representations and protests ignored.

Down a gangway they were urged, to the wharfside, atte-Fen bowling ironic farewell. No horses were provided for their transport, as would have been seemly. Surrounded by the men-at-arms, the trio were marched off into the city.

The impact of London hit them like a wall – a wall of noise and smells and crowds, of sheer enclosure. James was used to the narrow streets of Stirling and St. Andrews; but here mere noisome tunnels winding into the tall cliffs of building, so close together were piled the houses and so projecting were the upper storeys that they all but met on either side, practically blotting out sky and light. Since the streets themselves had to serve as open sewers and garbage heaps, with poultry and even pigs rooting about amongst it all, the stench was such as to choke and overwhelm – for here were no fresh breezes from sea and hills to sweep and cleanse. Not that these conditions seemed to have any overwhelming effect on the city's teeming inhabitants. Never had James seen so many people, or known them so loquacious, so clamant of voice. Far from holding their breaths, as he was trying to do, they each and all seemed never to stop talking, shouting, scolding, laughing. And at all levels, for not only did they tightly throng the streets themselves, filling every booth, shop, doorway and closemouth, but they hung out of every window right to the topmost attics, yelling to their neighbours across the way – who might be only a yard or so off, in fact – down into the mêlée below.

Through this prolonged bedlam the men-at-arms pushed and jostled their captives – who very quickly had to give up any attempt to walk any dainty course through the mire. Their passage was a notable source of interest and amusement – and at such close range that there was no escaping the highly personal comments, remarks and even handling – to the Earl of Orkney's almost apoplectic offence. Young James's attraction seemed to be mainly to the women – and though he did not understand one quarter of what was said to and about him, he was aware of enough to make him blush more than in all the rest of his life hitherto. He likewise encountered more open thrusting female bosoms and bold glances than had been his privilege to date.

The English, he decided, were a very different folk to the Scots. William Gifford evidently seemed to think so too, blinking, coughing and looking guilty by turns. Orkney was much too outraged by the entire proceedings to show other than frigid disapproval.

Breathless, buffeted and bemused, they were presently brought out into a comparatively open space – open in that it was not built up with high, crooked, proliferating houses, that is, though full of booths, stalls, animals, and a different variety of smells. This seemed to be a sort of elongated market for fish, meats, cheeses, live poultry, even cattle – though how the latter were got here was a mystery. The space was comparatively narrow, but extended away on either side out of sight. Beyond it lay a deep and wide ditch, filled with foul and filthy water, in which all manner of refuse floated, and behind rose a high battlemented wall built of some soft chalky white stone – notable in that all the houses were made of wood – with squat round towers at intervals along it. Across a drawbridge and up to a massive door in this wall, the Scots were taken, and the officer pulled on a dangling chain which hung there, attached to a great bell.

As this clanged out its summons, just for a moment or two almost a hush descended upon all that noisy, boisterous throng, as everywhere folk turned to gaze at the party waiting at the gateway. In that brief significant interval, something more than unaccustomed quiet prevailed, some emotion was stirred in the brash and careless crowd. No single witticism or sally was tossed at the little company now – and here and there an old woman crossed herself.

The heavy door creaked open, armed guards appearing, to flank it. As the party passed within, and before the door clanged shut again behind them, the noise of the crowd resumed.

Before the escorted trio was another and wider moat, backed by high grassy earthworks that were topped by a second lofty stone wall, parapeted, where steel-clad guards paced between more squat round towers. Another drawbridge, upraised this time, was clankingly descending for them, from a gatehouse with portcullis and gunloops. And high beyond soared the blank, sheer frowning face of the Tower of London, up and up, stern, implacably hostile.

Orkney, biting his lip, turned to look at his charge, and shook a helpless head.

"I insist, sir, on being conducted into the presence of King Henry, without further delay!" the Earl declared strongly, his fists tensely clenched. "It is intolerable. For three days we have been held here. Like . . . like felons! Do none

61

in this realm of England know how men of lineage and breeding should behave?"

Sir Thomas Rempton, Constable of the Tower, pursed thin lips. "If your quarters lack comfort, my lord, I will see what improvement may be possible . . ."

"A tush for your quarters, man! They are well enough. If that was all, who would care! It is to be imprisoned thus, unvisited, ignored, like outlaws, like common rogues! Do you not perceive what you do, sirrah? My lord James here, is the Prince of Scotland, heir to the most ancient throne in Christendom! Our two realms are not at war. Yet he has been taken, and of set purpose, at sea savagely by your English pirates. On peaceful travel to France. Brought here, and held in this notour place, this Tower of London — instead of being greeted and comforted by your king, made amends to, and assisted on his way. Aye — and the insolent pirate hanged on this Tower-hill . . .!"

"My lord, these things are not for my decision . . ."

"No, sir? I swear by God they are not! They are for your liege lord's decision, as between princes. So we should have been taken before King Henry at our very landing. Not brought here, captives. But, being here, sir — how dare that you should pay no heed to our presence? How dare, indeed, to ignore *my* demands? A score of times I have sent for you — I, an earl of the Scots realm, of His Grace's Privy Council, chief of the name and line of proud St. Clair, a house more high and ancient than his who sits on your English throne . . .!"

"My lord — ha' done! Enough, of a pity! I but obey my orders, do my duty. His Majesty knows that you are here . . ."

"You say he knows it? Then, you make of your king an oaf! A clod-hopping churl! Do you that, Sir Knight? Do you make it that Henry of Lancaster is still so new sat on his usurped throne that he knows not how to behave towards fellow-princes? Towards the son of the King of Scots? Is that it? If so it is, I cannot think that he will thank you . . ."

"Christ God – I say no such thing! The like I never for a moment suggested . . .!"

"Then go you to King Henry, man, and tell him that I, St. Clair of Orkney, deem it so. Tell him that I cannot conceive him so ignorant and uncourtly as *you*, Sir Thomas, do make him! But that I shall come to believe it if he does not grant us audience forthwith. Go you!"

Frowning uncertainly, in some discomfiture, the Constable of the Tower bowed briefly to young James, stared balefully at the Earl, and hurried from the chamber.

"That was well said, my lord," James declared, shining-eyed.

"The Constable has not so been spoke since he came to this Tower, I vow!" That was said in a strange lilting, singsong voice, as though by one to whom English did not come naturally. The speaker was a boy not much older than James, and no taller, but dark, intense, wiry – Griffith, son to Owen Glendower the Welsh patriot and true Prince of Wales. He had been captured a year before, during his father's uprising against the English domination, and confined in the Tower since. A lively eager lad, he undoubtedly looked upon the Scots' arrival with satisfaction.

Whether as a result of Orkney's tactics, or not, next day a summons did arrive for earl and prince to appear before King Henry, at Westminster Palace. He even sent horses to transport them thither, Sir Thomas Rempton escorting them in person, if without enthusiasm.

James got little better impression of Westminster as a palace than he had gained of the rest of London. He considered it a poor unprepossessing place, compared with the towering royal strongholds of his own land, despite its undoubted size. It was in fact merely the converted monastic buildings of the old abbey, asprawl beneath the shadow of the great minster, and no king's castle at all. But internally it was very rich, with a superfluity of plenishings, hangings, tapestries, statuary, furnishings, floor-coverings and the like, in a strange mixture of secular and clerical, such as to make the Scots stone halls seem bare indeed.

63

The approach to the throne was very different also. It was a slow and delayed process, attained by stages. Through chamber after chamber the pair were conducted, with long waits between, passed from functionary to functionary, by way of assembly-rooms, ante-rooms, outer and inner halls of audience. The Crown of England, apparently, had no concern with approachability.

Even when they at last penetrated to the presence-chamber, the humiliating procedure was not finished. At the far end of the vast apartment, which had obviously been the abbey refectory, a figure lounged on a gilded throne – but neither he nor anybody else, near or far, paid any attention to the newcomers. There was no heralds' fanfare, no suitable announcement of the arrival and identity of important visitors, no ceremony of any sort – not even a pause in the general stir and chatter. After their initial bows towards the throne, which nobody acknowledged, Orkney and James were left standing alone near the door by which they had entered. Sir Thomas Rempton disappeared.

"God's eyes! Never have I been treated so in all my days!" the Earl muttered into his beard. "They are barbarians, nothing more! For all their wealth and pretence."

After perhaps ten minutes of waiting, with not a word spoken to them by any of the courtiers who thronged the lower part of the hall, Orkney was reduced to nibbling his nails and shuffling his feet.

"It may be that we just go forward, my lord?" James suggested. "I am sure that the King Henry has seen us, knows us here. He has looked this way more than once."

Orkney's lips formed words which it was as well were soundless, and side by side man and boy began to move towards the top end of the chamber.

Almost immediately two richly-dressed men materialised from amongst the chattering throng, one carrying a black rod of office, and this he held up in front of the pair, to bar their progress – as though they had been cattle straying at a fair. Back, he and his colleague gestured, with a shooing motion but without a word spoken.

Blazing-eyed, the Earl drew himself up. First he held down a hand to James, to halt any turning away. Then he deliberately folded his arms across his chest and so stood, there in the middle of the great room, face set, unmoving.

The ushers, or lords-in-waiting, or whatever was their function, frowned, glanced at each other, made more pushing gestures – but wisely forbore to lay hands on the Scots. After a moment or two of indecision, they turned their velvet-clad backs on the visitors, but continued to stand there in front of them, barring their way forward – with uneasy surreptitious backwards glances out of the corners of their eyes.

Although undoubtedly this pantomime had been observed by practically everyone in the hall, no direct notice was taken of it – nor of the protagonists. Men continued to talk, laugh and circulate – there were no women to be seen – and up on the throne the monarch still lounged, chatting to obsequiously-bending companions.

So, feeling as ridiculous as they were determined, the man and boy stood there in mid-floor, ignored save by the hostile backs of the two men in front. The minutes continued to drag by.

Then there was a diversion. A much over-dressed and affected young man came strolling up, to toss a word to the ushers, and then move round behind them, inspecting the visitors with a sort of surprised interest. He sketched the merest hint of a bow and smirked a condescending smile.

"Ha, Cousin," he said, "Welcome! A pox – you've grown but little these four years, I do vow! Orkney – y'servant. I heard it was yourself."

They both stared. The man before them was tall and well-favoured in a stiff and wooden way, almost handsome but with the fatal weakness of the mouth and jaw that beset so many of his house. James was hard put to it to recognise him nevertheless, so fanciful and foppish was his garb, so studied and unnatural his airs – and so mincing the attempts to anglify a broad Scots voice. That this was indeed his full cousin, Murdoch Stewart, Earl of Fife, Albany's eldest son

65

and heir, captured with the Douglas at Homildon Hill four years before, seemed scarcely credible.

The boy blinked and mumbled in embarrassment.

Orkney looked the other up and down with no joy. "My lord," he said stiffly.

"They tell me that you were bolting for France?" Murdoch observed. "A foolish exploit, was it no'? Being taken in war is one matter – but whilst bolting . . .!" He left the rest unsaid.

"Precisely!" Orkney snapped. "I am glad you note the difference! My lord of Fife – we are here for audience with King Henry. He does not appear to be acquainted of our arrival."

Murdoch began to guffaw – then altered it to a modish simper. "Ah! Umm," he said. "Think you so? Aye, well – I'll see if I may win you a minute or two of His Grace's time, Jamie. Presently – aye, presently." He strolled off.

"Popinjay! Ninny! Prancing coxcomb!" Orkney snorted – nor attempted to lower his voice.

James was watching where the other sauntered. He touched the Earl's sleeve. "See whither he goes. To whom he speaks, now? It is my lord of Douglas."

"Aye – you're right. Archie Tyneman himself! I fear we are in a nest of your enemies here, lad. They seem to enjoy a comfortable captivity, i' faith!"

Earl Murdoch made no attempt to approach the vicinity of the King. Indeed, after a few moments, he and the Earl of Douglas turned away to laugh and talk with another group. James could hear Orkney's teeth actually grinding.

Then, after a little, a supercilious young page came up, to exchange a word with the man with the black rod. The latter nodded to his companion, and turning a baleful glance on the pair behind, pointed ahead with his staff. They moved forward, slowly.

Orkney's hand came out to restrain James from following.

If it was not exactly a hush that fell now on that great apartment, at least there was a change of atmosphere.

Everywhere men turned and watched and nudged their neighbours, as the ushers paced solemnly onwards towards the throne – and nobody paced after them. There were sudden exclamations, stares, outraged looks, titters. The visitors were no longer ignored.

The ushers were not far short of the royal chair, in their dignified progress, before the agitated glances of some of the people around the King made them glance back, to perceive that they were in fact alone. Appalled, they faltered to a halt, looking from each other, to the monarch, and back behind them, uncertain what to do. One of them made urgent beckoning movements with a hand behind his back.

Ignoring them, Orkney and the boy stood their ground. There was silence in the chamber now, at last – until someone at the back laughed nervously.

The only seemingly unconcerned person in the entire assembly was the man who sat on the throne. After a single swift glance at the situation, he continued to chat and smile to the men standing at right and left behind his gilded chair, with no hint of unease or awareness of tension. The prelate in the gorgeous, jewel-encrusted robes at his right stooped in eagerly-nodding anxiety.

Allowing a few further significant moments to pass, Orkney touched James's shoulder, and together they moved forward, the boy seeking to match his stride to the man's measured pace.

The ushers, in evident quandary, hesitated, seemed as though they might interfere – and were all but brushed aside as the Earl came up, turned a lordly shoulder to them, and strode past.

Only a yard or two from the throne the Scots halted – by which time various armed guards and officers had taken tentative steps out from alcoves and corners. But the King still did not pause in his talk or make any sign of acknowledging the presence of his visitors – and Orkney, with a brief headshake, forestalled James's bow. They waited.

At length Henry turned, and allowed his glance to alight on the pair in front of him. They both bowed low.

For further long seconds not a word was spoken. Henry Plantagenet, once known as Bolingbroke, Earl of Derby, son of John of Gaunt and grandson of both Edward the Third and Henry the Second, gave little impression of regality. A big man of forty years, he looked like a yeoman farmer, heavy, fleshy, red-faced, blunt-featured. But he looked also like a fighter, and the small quick blue eyes were shrewd as the thrusting square jaw was determined. He was carelessly dressed, but a furred purple cloak was tossed back from his shoulders, and a slender plain ring of gold encircled his thick straw-coloured hair.

Staring, suddenly he bellowed a hoot of laughter, and slapped his thick thigh. "God's wounds!" he cried. "More Scots come visiting! On my soul, this realm of mine does hotch with the breed!" He glanced right and left, grinning – and everywhere men breathed again, and those nearby chuckled appreciatively at the monarch's clemency and wit. The Chancellor, Henry Beaufort, Bishop of Winchester, at his right, bent to murmur felicitation – but was interrupted abruptly.

"How old are you, boy?" Henry jerked, pointing at James.

"Thirteen years, Sire," James said. He drew himself up, raising his head and chin noticeably, as though to make up for his lack of height. "I am James, of Carrick, Prince of Scotland. And this is my lord Henry St. Clair, Earl of Orkney, my royal father's esteemed councillor and ambassador!" It was well and meetly said, with dignity as well as courage – even though the boy's voice cracked a little in the saying.

"Ha!" Henry considered him for a little, and then sat back, nodding acknowledgement. "So roars the whelp of a sorry lion! Greetings, lad. And to you, my lord of . . . of Orkney, was it? Some such . . ."

Stiffly the Earl inclined his head, as courtiers tittered. "Orkney," he agreed. "An ancient princedom of a thousand islands, Your Grace – where pirates are hanged, not nurtured and rewarded!"

There was an audible gasp from all around at this unheard of boldness – but Henry only grinned, much as Hugh-atte-Fen might have done. Indeed there was a marked similarity of manner between the two men.

"Aye – we hang pirates here likewise, at times, my friend. Also cut-purses, cattle-thieves . . . and Scots! You are much troubled with the like, I take it?"

"Only, Sire, since we sailed into English waters!"

"You say so? We must look to this. My lord Chancellor – note it. The Scots complain of pirates." Ruefully Henry shook his tow head. "The *Scots*, mind you!"

A gust of laughter shook the chamber.

Steadily, almost expressionlessly, the Earl of Orkney spoke through it. "On behalf of my liege lord King Robert and his heir the Prince James, I request Your Grace forthwith to take and hang the pirate Hugh-atte-Fen, of Great Yarmouth, Norfolk. Also to compensate His Grace of Scotland for injury done. And to assist our onward journey to France."

"God save us! Injury? Compensation? In what are you injured, my lords? As I heard it, the good Norfolkman but lifted you out of a leaking, sinking tub full of stinking hides, and brought you forward on your journey in his fair fast ship, in comfort. Where is your injury?"

"We did not voyage for London, Sire."

"No? You mean that the Prince of Scotland would have sailed secretly past my dominions and never thought to pay his respects to me? Here is unneighbourly conduct between princes, to be sure?"

Orkney controlled his voice with difficulty. "We were assailed by cannon-fire. Threatened with arms. And by a squadron which lay in wait for us. Behind Flamborough Head. Had waited for us long, they let fall. Waited for the Prince James – for the man atte-Fen named him before ever I did. Took him prisoner, and then brought him straight to Your Grace's Tower of London! Since when, for four days, we have been held unvisited . . ."

"In all comfort, I am assured, my lord? Lacking nothing?"

"Save our freedom, Sire. And your royal explanation!"

"God's eyes – you are bold, sir Scot! With your tongue! Less so on board ship, I am told! Explanations are not to be demanded of princes, by subjects, I'd remind you!"

"I crave your pardon. I ask then, what I am to inform *my* prince, King Robert?"

"Inform him, by the Mass, that I, Henry, am taking better care of his son than did he! Than, as I understand it, *can* he! Scotland is but an ill sanctuary for kings' sons, I am told! Assure him that the person of the Earl of Carrick is safer in my keeping than in his realm. By far. Or in France, where wars rage. Aye, and tell him that if it was for the prince's improvement and education that he was being sent to France, *I* speak not indifferent French myself, having dwelt there much! I am the rightful King of France, remind His Grace. As well as Lord Superior of Scotland! He could not have sent his son to a better master!"

Again there was a throbbing silence in the hall. None could fail to recognise the significance of all that.

Orkney chewed his lip, at a loss for comment. It was young James who spoke.

"You will . . . Your Grace will hold us?" he got out. "Not permit that we go to France?"

"You heard me, boy. I conceive you safer here."

"We are then . . . prisoners?"

"Guests, rather. We are hospitable, here in England!"

"Guests! In the Tower of London!" That was Orkney.

"To be sure, my lord. Your charge will be as free there as he was in St. Andrews Castle, I vow! As well as safer!"

The Earl drew a long quivering breath. "Have we Your Grace's permission to retire?" he jerked abruptly.

Grinning again, Henry flicked a derisive and dismissive hand. "You have, my lord of the thousand rocks of Orkney – and welcome!"

With the stiffest and briefest of bows, man and boy turned and went striding down the great room, James having to step hugely at the Earl's side. The ushers, who had waited to conduct a backing-out progress, now themselves had to back away before the Scots, in undignified haste. Even so they were brusquely elbowed aside, and completed the passage to the door behind their charges almost at a trot. Sir Thomas Rempton waited there, lips tight. Though he jerked head towards the throne, no final bows were offered, as the visitors left the presence-chamber.

No single word was spoken on the way back to the Tower.

It was on a sunny April afternoon three weeks later that Boyd of Ardneil, the Rothesay Herald, newly arrived from Scotland on a safe-conduct, was admitted to the Tower. Having spoken with Orkney, the latter led him down to that part of the outer premises of the establishment where, in a pit, the menagerie of ten lions and leopards were kept, captives whose still closer confinement was calculated to emphasise rather than ameliorate the restrictions on the human variety. James and Griffith Glendower spent much time, nevertheless, admiring these unfortunate creatures, all but mesmerised by their endless padding, pacing of their den, and the cold, glassy, yellow-eyed glare that spoke shiveringly not of patience but of disciplined savage waiting. Few adult prisoners found such contemplation bearable. Will Gifford, James's esquire, although he kept his charge in sight, preferred to sit some distance off.

The boys were there, watching, as the two men came up. Boyd stepped forward, and sank on one travel-stained knee before James

"Your Grace!" he said.

The boy looked at him strangely. "Why do you that, sir?" he asked. "You are . . . from Scotland?"

"Robert Boyd of Ardneil, Coroner of Ayr and Rothesay Herald," Orkney announced. "New come from . . . from Your Grace's castle of Rothesay, in the Isle of Bute." He paused. "Give the Herald Your Grace's hand," he directed, thickly.

James looked from the Earl to the still-kneeling emissary, and back again, uncomprehendingly.

71

"Your hand," Orkney repeated.

Wondering, James extended a hesitant and not over-clean hand. The kneeling man raised it to his lips.

"Sire!" he said, and rose to his feet.

The boy's eyes widened as something of understanding came to him, there by the beasts' den. He tried to speak, but the words caught in his throat.

"Ardneil has ridden day and night, Sire, to . . . to acquaint you. From your father's castle on Bute. At much danger to himself." Orkney stepped forward, and in his turn sank down on one knee before James, and took his hand to his lips. "God save the King's Grace!" he said.

"My . . . my father!" the boy got out, in strangled fashion.

"His Grace King Robert, my master, is dead," the herald said, in his singsong West Country Scots voice. "He died on hearing the word of Your Highness's capture by the English. It was too much for him. The final blow. His heart was broke, I think. He spoke never another word after the tidings . . ." The man's voice tailed away, as James, gulping, gazed down at his tightly clenched hands.

There was a long pause, with only the soft interminable scuffling pad-pad of the great cats' feet to underline the interval.

Orkney, standing again, spoke. "His Grace your father, and my friend, had no joy of his life, Sire. Since the Queen your lady-mother died, he has known no comfort in living. He is, I say, well quit of life. Grieve not too deep for him. He has his peace, at last."

Dry-eyed but stark of face, James looked at him, seeking to control his trembling lips. "Yes," he said. "Yes. He had no comfort. And now, nor have I! I have nobody. Nobody. All gone. Dead. I have nobody."

At the hopeless hurt and despair in that young voice, Orkney shook his head. He forbore to point out that not only had the boy three uncles and numerous cousins, but that he had three sisters also; these had all been married, as little more than children, at Albany's

72

instigation, to his Douglas friends, and James knew them not.

"You have many, Sire – a whole nation," the Earl said, at length, moistening his lips. "You are the King of Scots. King James, by God's grace – the first of that name. And I your devoted and leal subject."

"And I, Sire," Boyd declared.

"And I, my lord King," Will Gifford put in, coming forward to kiss the boy's hand, in turn. "You have us all. And all leal Scots everywhere."

James looked from one to the other, but there was no lightening of his set features. Slowly he nodded. "Can I go home, now? To Scotland? Now that I am King?" he asked, but flatly.

Orkney blinked, and took a deep breath. "I fear not, Your Grace," he said. "Not yet. If King Henry found you a notable prize, as heir to the throne, how much more valuable to hold in his hands the King of Scots himself! I fear much that he will not let you go. Not yet."

"When, then?"

"Who knows? He is a hard man, and ruthless. He will achieve all that he may by holding you. A treaty in his favour, perhaps. Some bargain. Possibly some of your Scots territory . . ."

"A ransom, it may be, Highness," Gifford suggested. "Some great sum of money, to be paid for your release."

"His Grace is not some mere hostage, taken in battle, to be valued and bought back, sir!" Orkney said shortly, frowning.

"No. But if it would gain our release . . .?" James said, clutching at a straw. "I have friends in Scotland. You have just said it. Who would find the money. I am the King. The good Bishop Wardlaw, for one. He is rich . . ."

The Earl shook his head. "I am sorry, my lord James – but I advise that you should not so cozen yourself. For it is not only King Henry whom you have to fear, you must remember."

"You mean . . . my Uncle Albany?"

73

"Aye – Albany! The man who undoubtedly betrayed you to Henry. Sent word that you would be sailing for France. The man who rules in Scotland. Think you he will be eager for Your Grace's return?"

"But – now that I am King?"

"Now less than ever, I swear. 'Fore God, I believe that Henry is right! That you are safer here than in Scotland! Even as King."

"Then . . . my friends that you spoke of? What of them? The leal Scots everywhere who love me? They mean nothing, my lord?"

"Never say it, Sire. You have true friends, a-many. But . . . by the Rude, it costs dear to be your friend in Scotland today! As Ardneil here can vouch. He has just told me. Your friends who aided you out of Scotland – they paid the price. After the Bass, Albany was waiting. Returning to their own places, after they saw us aboard the ship, they were caught. The Douglases were waiting, round my kinsman's house of Herdmanston. Sir David Fleming is dead. And Sir William Sinclair and the others now lie deep in Douglas dungeons."

"Sir David – slain!" Appalled, James stared. "Dead? Sir David – dead also! Killed. For . . . for aiding me!"

"Aye. To counter the ambition of my lord Duke of Albany is a dangerous business!" Orkney said grimly.

"Then what hope is there for me?" the boy cried. "There is only sorrow for myself, and death for my friends! I can never win back to Scotland. Nor wish to, I think! No – nor wish to! It is a land of blood. And treachery. And hate. My house is accursed – all the house of Stewart!"

At the normally quiet and contained boy's outburst, the others exchanged glances.

"Do not say that, Your Grace . . ." Boyd exclaimed.

"It is none so ill as that, Sire," Orkney declared, hurriedly. "We must just work for betterment. We shall change all, in time."

"Now it is *you* who cozen! How can there be betterment? What hope is there? We can do nothing."

"Not so. We can do much, I think. But it must be featly and skilfully done. We must fight evil and bad faith with cunning and subterfuge . . ."

"In the Tower of London, my lord!"

"Your Grace – I have been thinking much, these last sorry weeks," the Earl said slowly. "Ardneil's ill tidings but make the issue the more urgent. See you – Henry is for France again. To war. He requires money. He would not ransom you, Sire, I fear – but myself he might. I should be loth to leave your side – but back in Scotland I might serve Your Grace the better. Do much to prepare your return. Prepare a party to seek and demand your return. A party to oppose Albany."

"Leave me, my lord? Here!"

"I fear that King Henry will not suffer me to remain with you in any case, Sire. Already there is word of it. He conceives me to influence you but ill! If we are to be parted, better that I should be working for you in Scotland, for your return."

"But what could you do? Alone? Would not my uncle slay you also?"

"I think not. I am warned, and would be careful." Orkney drew himself up a little, perhaps subconsciously. "I am no simple knight or laird for him to crush. I am St. Clair, with a great earldom at my call. I can field a thousand men, from Orkney and Caithness. More. And I have potent friends. Aye – and better! I think to *make* another. The *most* potent!"

At the Earl's tone, the others eyed him sharply. Even James found a spark of interest.

"Douglas!" Orkney went on. "Archie Tyneman himself. I love him not – but believe he could be weaned away from Albany. He is a strange secret man, and not to be trusted – but that should be made to work against the Governor – or the Regent, as now he is styling himself – as against others. And he is chief of the most powerful line in the land."

"You will not win over the Earl of Douglas to any cause but his own, my lord!" Gifford asserted.

75

"Perhaps not. But we might make the King's cause his. Rather than that of Albany. Already he is something out-of-love with the Regent. Twice I have had privy word with him, and am beginning to see inside his mind, I think. He is fretting for his release. Unlike Earl Murdoch, captivity irks him sorely. And he sees his friend Albany doing nothing to gain him his freedom. Four years he has been a prisoner now, since Homildon – and it was at Albany's behest that he rode to Homildon! The Regent is more concerned with getting his son Murdoch freed, than Douglas!"

"And how shall that serve King James?" Boyd asked.

"Thus. Henry's need for moneys for his French war. And his need that the Scots should not assail his rear while he fights in France. Archie Tyneman could aid him with both, if he would – for he is passing rich, and the Douglases control half the Borders. If I can work together with Douglas for our release, make him beholden to me, and further turn him against Albany and Murdoch – then who knows how the King's cause in Scotland may suddenly prosper!"

"You think it so, my lord?" There was hope in the boy's voice again.

"I do, i' faith! I think that I have sounded the Douglas's depth. And, mark you, whoso counts Douglas amongst his allies lacks not for supporters! Even if slippery ones!"

"Even if they helped to murder his brother?" James asked, huskily. He seemed to have taken on added years in the last few minutes.

Orkney nodded, sighing. "A king may not always choose the allies he would wish," he said. "A king must needs use the tools which come to his hands."

James looked down at his hands, and then suddenly held them out towards the others, in a strangely eloquent and pathetic gesture – small hands, open, empty and less than clean. Then, without a word, he turned his back upon them all, to stare down at the lions and leopards.

76

Presently, from behind, Orkney asked if they had His Grace's permission to retire. The King of Scots nodded, still wordless, and kept his eyes on the pacing cats until he was alone.

PART TWO

6

The two youths drove their sweating, steaming horses through the crackling undergrowth and over the fading golden bracken and ferns, crouching low in their saddles beneath the spreading branches of tall trees, twisting their mounts skilfully at speed to avoid trunks, fallen timber and snaking roots. Apart from the crash and beat of their own going, only the distant baying of hounds, at a loss, sounded through the forest glades.

"Hear them? As I said," James, slightly in the lead, threw back over his shoulder. "He's made for the mere – the water. Trotter's Mere. Hounds are held. We'll save half-a-mile."

"To be sure. Never doubted it," Griffith panted. "But is it worth . . . broke necks?"

He could have spared precious breath. When James Stewart got his leg across a saddle, and opportunity to escape the cramping restrictions imposed by others, he seldom failed excuse to break out in some such headlong chase. It was as though bouts of such furious activity, such violent and demonstrative freedom of action, were recurrently necessary to him, safety valves in the long and weary captivity normally borne with such contained calm and apparent patience. That was why Nottingham Castle was James's least irksome prison of the many fortresses and abbeys which, with the Tower of London as base, for nearly five dire years had constrained him – for the proximity of the great Forest of Sherwood offered the most frequent release; and the Lord Grey de Codnor, their keeper, was notably fond of the chase.

James drove on through the thickets of alder, hazel and even holly, apparently by sheer instinct – for there were no prospects of any distance in the greenwood, and unlike the main hunt which they had so cavalierly left, they followed no tracks or grassy rides. James seemed to have some inborn feeling for direction, country, and the ways of wild things, so that even Grey grudgingly admitted, on occasion, that he was more to be relied upon than were the professional huntsmen, verderers and rangers, disapprove as he might – for Lord Grey, High Chamberlain of England, disapproved of most things. Griffith Glendower, the leader in many of their activities, in social matters – and in the baiting of their jailers – was content to follow James when in the saddle.

The great trees, beeches and oaks, were thinning away now to little more than scrub, as the ground beneath the horses' hooves became softer, damper. The bracken was being succeeded by reeds, tussock-grass and mosses, and ducks and snipe were beginning to burst out from cover around them, rather than pheasants, woodcock and pigeons. This was territory the hunt tended to avoid, hating the treacherous, water-logged ground. But James plunged on unhesitant, despite the cloying, sucking sound of hooves in sodden mud, hooves which indeed were now throwing up black mire at every pace, spattering the riders. None of the rest of the hunt followed the two rash young men, not even Will Gifford.

Light, air, space before them, with the suddenly louder belling of hounds, heralded their goal, if not their quarry. Trotter's Mere opened in front, a long narrow winding stretch of water, rimmed with reeds, the largest and most obnoxious in this southern section of the vast Sherwood Forest. Normally the deer avoided it and its treacheries, and could be all but guaranteed to bolt for the higher, surer ground where their narrow pointed hooves would give them fleet advantage, or for the dense thickets of abounding cover. But just occasionally a wily old stag would turn this way, for the hollow low-lying bottom-land around the mere, knowing how the deer-hounds loathed it, and the horsemen likewise. This morning's beast, raised in the coverts of Bulwell, only a couple of miles from Nottingham Castle, had taken an unusual circling line, and James, ignoring the chief huntsman's prognostications and lead, had sensed that the brute was heading for Trotter's Mere – and taking French leave of the rest, had cut off hither in consequence.

Cantering heavily round the boggy rim of the mere, James made for where four tall and long-legged shaggy deer-hounds fumed and pranced and milled in slavering, loud-voiced frustration, savagely howling their hate, but daintily lifting their paws whenever they chanced into the slime of the mere's edge. For though a long narrow sheet of open water, the lake was bordered by no true shore but by a belt of soft and quaking mire and mud. The deer-hounds would swim in water if they must – but they would by no means soil their feet in such filth and slime.

Pulling up where a willow-clump's roots provided rather surer footing for the horses, James pointed.

"There he is! On the island," he cried. "See him? Sore spent. Head down."

The mere held a scattering of islets – although they were scarcely that, being little more than piers of tangled roots thrusting up through the shallow water, whereon grew dense brakes of willow scrub and hazel. On one of these in mid-mere, little longer than himself and perhaps one hundred yards away, a large stag could be seen wedged amongst the shoots and branches, standing still, antlered head lowered.

"The fool brute thinks that he is hidden! That we cannot see him!" Griffith shouted. "Have you ever seen the like!" He jumped down, and began to urge on the dogs with cries and gestures, to play their part and forget their finicking fear and dislike of the soft marshland.

James was staring towards the islet. "He is no such fool," he declared. "See the grey of his mane. He is an old beast – and any who survives so long so near to Nottingham is no fool! His head is caught – that is what it is, Griff! His antlers. See how his head is down, held down. As he climbed out of the water, his antlers must have tangled with the thicket. The beast is held, trapped."

The Welsh prince was now picking up sticks and turfs to hurl, firstly into the water in an effort to make the hounds plunge in, and then at the yelping, dancing creatures themselves, in his exasperation.

"Stupid, cowardly brutes!" he panted. "Frightened for a little mud! Too nice to wet their feet . . .!"

James was paying no heed. Dismounting, almost before he touched the ground he was commencing to throw off his clothing. Hurriedly he undressed, tossing his things to hang on branches of the willows, kicking off his long riding-boots.

"Mary-Mother – what's this?" Griffith cried, catching sight of his friend. "James – what do you do, a' God's name?"

The other was stripping off his trunks. "I do what these hounds will not," he said. "You will not make them take to that mud, Griff – not deer-hounds."

He stood stark-naked now, reaching for the hunting-knife sheathed at his belt. At nearly eighteen, James Stewart presented a tough and muscular figure, its white already more than usually furred with body hair. He would never be tall, but his shoulders were broad, his chest massive, his hips slender and his legs sturdy as well as shapely. There was notable physical strength in that body, and no slackness nor hint of fat.

Griffith shook his dark head. "James, *bach* – you cannot do this! The mud! It is deep . . ."

His protest was cut short. Clutching the knife, James stepped back a few paces, and then, with an vigorous burst of energy, launched himself forward to race down over the soft ground and on to the yielding belt of bog.

There were perhaps a dozen yards of that mire, before the actual water, and though inevitably the young man's feet sank, his rush carried him over two-thirds of it before its clinging grip began to slow him down and each step sank deeper. With an evidently enhanced fury of effort he plunged on for five, six, paces, at each the black stockings of slime climbing higher up his legs till the very knees were reached. And then, as the dragging clutch of it all but held him, in a convulsive jack-knife explosion he hurled himself bodily, horizontally on in a dive that carried him forward sufficiently for him to hit the shallow water with a resounding splash, arms already flailing, dirk gleaming.

He gasped with the cold of it, for it was late November, and there had been even a touch of frost the previous night.

With a powerful over-arm stroke James struck out across the open mere, and quickly the black was washed from his kicking legs. On the islet for which he headed, the stag, although it was obviously struggling and plunging, still remained gripped by its antlers entangled in the thick willow scrub.

The youth swam close, and then trod water, wary on two counts. The coiling roots beneath the surface could trap him, as their upper growth had trapped the deer; and the animal's powerful legs armed with sharp hooves, could rend his unprotected flesh. Slowly he swam round, prospecting.

Just when the curious notion came to him, at complete odds with his so energetically prosecuted intention hitherto, he did not know; certainly it was when he gazed for a moment at close range into the great liquid brown eye of the noble brute struggling helplessly there, that he was conscious that a decision on it had been made. As he pulled himself up out of the water, dripping, keeping a screen of stout willow-wands between himself and those wicked hooves, he knew what he was going to do.

Reaching over, he grasped the beast's heavy mane with one hand – feeling the creature's almost electric start at this alien touch – and swept down with the sharp knife in the other hand. With a slash and a jerk, it was done. In his left hand he clutched a fistful of the coarse grey-brown hair of the mane.

Quick as thought he thrust this between his teeth, to hold it there and edging round and leaning over farther, went to work with hands and knife – but on the willow-saughs and tangled branches this time. He was in danger now from lashing hooves, and knew it – but that only gave added energy and urgency to his heaving and tugging and hacking, to clear the spreading white-tipped antlers. Panting, snoring almost, through the bunched hair in his mouth, he worked beside the heaving, twisting animal, indeed leaning against its warm flank.

Then, almost before he realised it, the obstruction was cleared, the springy entanglement was loosened, and with a fierce toss the stag raised his proud head high. For brief seconds the deer's large hazel-brown eye and the somewhat similarly liquid Stewart eye looked one into the other; then, with a single great standing bound the creature leapt right off the islet and into the water with a mighty splash, to swim strongly away north-westwards up the length of the mere.

There was a burst of shouting from the other shore. James turned, and saw that the main body of the hunt had arrived – and was at gaze with a rapt regard such as few chases were apt to engender.

He raised a hand to them all, half in salute, half in mockery, and dived cleanly back into the mere.

The young man was half-way back to his clothes when he remembered, with a start, that on this occasion, as was not usually the case, there were women riding with the hunt. King Henry was ill again, and his sons and brothers had been summoned to his bedside at Nottingham Castle, and had brought their royal ladies with them, Nottingham being a favourite with all. Some of these had insisted in hunting today, despite the Lord Grey's disapproval.

James's preoccupation with this distressing recollection, even though it perhaps slowed down his lusty stroke a little, did not last long. Or, at least, it was somewhat jockeyed aside for another. That belt of mud and slime. It was one thing, he now realised, to rush lightfoot over it from a running start, and altogether another to drag himself across it as he heaved himself up out of the water. Of a sudden James's vehement swimming died away, and he began to tread water, raising himself as high as he could, to consider the prospect. He must find a better place to emerge, if he could, than where he had plunged in, there in front of all that staring company.

There was plenty of alternative water's edge – but little evident improvement of accessibility. The only possible betterment that he could see was well over to the right, fully another hundred yards away, where a great forest tree, its roots rotted by the seeping waters, had crashed seasons earlier, its naked whitened trunk now lying part on land but mainly in the mere. It might make him some sort of a bridge.

So thither James swam, while the watchers chattered and laughed and advised.

The tree undoubtedly was a help – but unfortunately even its furthest tip was still very much in the shallows. Which meant that, standing up to climb on to its welcome firmness, the youth was still above the knees in mud. By the time that he had dragged himself on to it, he had black hose of slime half-way up his thighs again – and, glancing down, heartily wished them longer, to cover his naked loins. A ragged, chuckling cheer rose from certain of the hunters.

Working his way along that tree-trunk, although undignified, at least allowed him to retain a certain modesty of posture, bent down, monkey-fashion, aiding his slippery progress with his hands, knife in one and bunch of deer's hair in the other, and leaving a trail of mud and water behind him. But when he reached the end of it, to continue this would have been absurd. What should he do? There was an appalling area to cover to his clothes. Should he scurry along primly hiding his manhood with his hands? Could he walk half-turned away towards the mere, without looking a complete fool? Griff Glendower might at least have had the wits to hasten along with some of his clothing . . .

James jutted his chin and stood upright. Dignity was difficult in this situation – but such dignity as was possible he must maintain. He was, after all, King of Scots. He would not hurry nor bend nor hide himself.

So James Stewart paced along the rim of Trotter's Mere, head up, slow-strided, arms swinging at his sides determinedly – even if his fists were tightly clenched and his teeth bit his lip. No-one was more aware than he was of the indecent effect of those long black mud-stockings against his pallid remainder.

It seemed an endless journey – and seldom had a young man had more urgent desire to shorten it by running. But James was growing to be a man of no little determination; he actually slowed his pace. Oddly, that naked knife in his right hand was the only gleam of comfort that he knew.

Belatedly Griffith saw his duty, and came hastening to meet his friend, with his trunks and shirt.

Without haste, without a word, without even turning away, James handed the other the knife and mane, stopped to snatch up some tussock-grass to wipe down the worst mud off his legs, and then donned his trunks. He kept the shirt in his hand, and with the other, took back knife and hair from his friend. Then, swinging the shirt, he strolled on towards the rest of his clothing.

"My lord James!" a rasping voice barked behind him. "What a God's name's here? What folly is this? What . . . what shame? The saints grant me patience! What's to do?"

James turned. "Ah – my lord Grey! You have arrived?" he said pleasantly, though his voice quivered a little. "Too late for the sport, I fear. You were delayed?" None knew how much that easy pleasantry cost him.

Grey, a hard-bitten veteran of the French and Welsh campaigns, and one of Henry's most trusted captains, had little talent for diplomacy. "What do you mean by leaving the hunt, sir?" he demanded. "Without my leave? I'd remind you that you are in my charge. That you ride at all only out of His Majesty's notable clemency." Fairly clearly the Chamberlain considered King Henry's clemency overdone. He did not enjoy being jailer to high-spirited young men, and was not at pains to hide it. "Your bolting exercised me greatly. When I was told. I sent your squire, Gifford, seeking you. Where is he?"

"That, my lord, you should know better than I – since you saw him last! As to bolting, we but used our wits, to head off the quarry. Is not that the object of the hunt?"

Grey glared, snorting. "My lord James – you will not bandy words with me!" he exclaimed. The designation "Lord James" had been adopted by his captors on Henry's orders, since it would have made an embarrassing mockery of kingly titles to accord them to this youthful prisoner. "I'll not have it, d'you hear? And you have not answered me. What are you doing, thus? Mother-naked! Exposed, like some savage! In the water . . .?"

"I but did what your hounds refused to do. Pursued the hunt to a finish. They would not soil their feet, my lord. As you see, I was less nice! I conceived a good run to deserve a better end than baying and dancing round a pond!"

"But – to take to the water! The mud! Like some low-born varlet!"

James produced a smile. "I do not need to fear, my lord, that *I* shall be mistaken for a low-born varlet!" The faint emphasis on the personal pronoun, and the equally slight lifting of the chin, was very telling. It produced a murmur from the watching, listening throng on the steaming horses.

Frowning, Grey changed his line of assault, like the soldier he was. "It was folly. And you failed to kill, in the end. Nothing was served, boy. You did not use your steel! You ended nothing of the hunt."

"You think not?" James tossed the handful of wet hair at the Chamberlain's horse's feet. "I did not kill, no. But let that serve for trophy! I cut it from the brute's mane. I deemed that end enough."

Grey huffed and hawed, jerking his mount's head this way and that. "Folly!" he reiterated. "King Henry shall hear of this! Unworthy of his care of you! His tutoring and education! Unbecoming, I say . . ."

Hot words were springing to James's lips – for no youth of spirit could relish this hectoring in front of all the company. But he was forestalled. A tall thin youngish man, too richly dressed for hunting, on a magnificent white stallion, reined forward.

"I' faith – I think you are too hard on the lad, Grey," he said. "It was but a thoughtless prank. I vow we should be grateful for the entertainment."

"My lord Duke – the boy is in my charge and keeping. His training is in my hands. When he behaves amiss, I bear the responsibility to His Majesty . . ."

"To be sure, to be sure. But – in that case, my friend, no doubt you also bear the responsibility for his continued good health? His Highness of Scotland is shivering! He is like to die of cold, with your scolding, I vow!" The tall man shrugged, and pointed at James, who indeed was beginning to tremble somewhat in the chill November air – though as much from suppressed anger as from cold perhaps. The speaker was the Duke of Clarence, second of the King's sons, whose new Duchess and her ladies were amongst the whispering company behind.

Grey blinked, in sudden alarm. The thought of his deplorable but valuable charge catching a chill which could be laid to *his* account, obviously shook him.

"Get your clothes on, sir," he ordered. "At once. Standing there, half-naked, before all! Dress – and then return to the castle. Forthwith. Young Glendower also. Sir George – see you that they do so, without further waste of time. See that my lord James is dosed. Put to bed, perhaps . . ."

"My lord!" Blazing-eyed, the youth took a step forward. "I'd have you remember that I am King of Scots! No child, to be put to bed . . .!" With a great effort he controlled himself – though not altogether his chattering teeth. "I shall do very well. The cold is nothing. With your permission my lord, I shall run."

"Run . . .? Save us – run?"

"Aye, run. I like to run. It will warm me, very well."

"Run? On your feet? By the Mass – here's madness!"

"Ha – run!" Duke Thomas smiled. "On my soul, the best thing he could do! Let him run, Grey, if he will." He cackled a laugh. "The Scots were ever good at running, as I mind it! Let their king give us demonstration, by all means!"

A shout of mirth greeted this sally.

Humour of this calibre appealed even to the unsmiling Lord Grey de Codnor. He nodded.

So all sat and watched while the set-faced James Stewart savagely donned shirt and hose and pulled on his long riding-boots — far from the best footgear for running. Doublet, short cloak and bonnet he thrust at the darting-eyed, uneasy Griffith. The commentary from all around was unfailingly witty.

When he was ready, James straightened up and looked round at them, a level, lowering look. "If any English think they could outrun me to Nottingham Castle — let them try!" he said, raising his voice. "It is but six miles, to be sure! No great distance. And some of you have longer legs than mine!"

There was a pause, then. None spoke, much less took up his challenge.

James nodded curtly, and turned to gesture Griffith to mount. Then, with the merest hint of a bow to Grey, the Duke and the ladies beyond, he set off at a loping stride, hands down at his thighs to hold up the flapping tops of his long soft-leather boots.

Leading his friend's horse, Griffith Glendower followed after, and behind him Sir George Sowerby, Lieutenant-Keeper of Nottingham, with two or three others, reined round in turn.

With a blare of horns, the hunt moved on to seek further sport elsewhere.

James had not lied when he said that he was fond of running. Next to the tourney and the hunt indeed, he preferred it above all other outdoor pursuits. His wide shoulders and barrel of chest indicated excellent lungs, and his tapering hips and muscular legs spoke of light-ness of foot allied to bounding energy. Many an abbot and castellan had looked wonderingly on their prisoner's strange and tireless running round and round the pur-lieus of their establishments — and only, possibly, Will Gifford, had related the phenomenon to the endless pacing

91

of those caged lions and leopards in the Tower menagerie.

He ran now, for pride rather than pleasure, mile after mile through the November woodlands, scorning even to hold Griffith's stirrup-leather as support. Behind, Sowerby and the others marvelled but soon ran out of quips and merriment.

Four miles, and two-thirds of the way back to Nottingham, Will Gifford came up with them, near Basford, in some distress. Being esquire, page, usher and factotum to his unpredictable prisoner-monarch was a taxing task for a sober, conscientious young man, old for his years.

Though breathing deeply – and cursing his boots, albeit wordlessly – James was still running strongly and refusing to remount his horse forty minutes or so later when they entered the streets of the town, to face the stares of the good folk and the climb towards the twin eminences crowned by the royal Castle and the towering church of St. Mary. This was the obvious point for James to resume the saddle – but he would do no such thing. He had said that he would run to Nottingham Castle, and he would do just that. Such was the sort of man that fate, experience and temperament were making of James Stewart.

Although he asked for no respite, he was granted one. At the wide market-place below the hill, one of the finest in all England, there was a blocking, milling crowd of people, who shouted and laughed. And not at the running youth and his escort, on this occasion. They were all looking the other way, indeed, towards the far end of the market-place, where the road from the north-east came in, pointing and gesticulating. Sir George and his men had to draw swords to beat an indignant way through the crush with the flats of their blades. Even from the saddle Griffith could not tell James what the to-do was about.

At length, exclamations of surprise and wonder from the Welsh youth overcame James's stubborn determination to remain on the ground. "Mercy on us – did you ever see the like?" Griffith was saying infuriatingly. "Here's a sight, indeed to glory! What mummers can these be?"

James swung himself up on to his horse's back at last, to stare over the heads of the crowd. And he caught his breath.

It was indeed a strange sight, such as Nottingham certainly had never seen before. A cavalcade, quite a large one, part mounted, part on foot, had entered the place from the north-east and was making its way diagonally across, on a converging course with their own, for the street which led up towards the castle. Outlandish, splendid, colourful this travel-stained but formidable company of about fifty moved through the goggle-eyed townsfolk like a plough through sand. Nottingham, though it stared and hooted, gave it wide berth.

James was moved and intrigued at once, for a variety of reasons. For one thing, here were more runners. Those not mounted loped along beside the shaggy, short-legged, long-tailed horses with a steady, tireless striding that clearly was their accustomed and natural mode of progress, with no hint of breathlessness or wilting. These were clad in short roughly plaited skirts or kilts of tartan or saffron, hide brogans, and in the main nothing else save wide leather shoulder-belts supporting basket-hilted broadswords which they bore tucked under one arm. Some wore loose sleeveless jerkins of calfskin, flapping open to reveal hairy chests, but most were bare to the waist, a hirsute, brawny, bearded company.

The mounted men whom they escorted, about a dozen in number, were still more spectacular. They were led by an enormous individual under a great white banner on which was devised an oared galley in black, its sails furled. Red-haired, red-bearded, red-faced, this colossus was dressed almost wholly in red tartans under a long open coat of brown-and-white calfskin, hair side out. This man did not wear a kilt, but tartan doublet above long tartan trews, cut on the cross, which clung lovingly to tremendous legs right down to his silver-mounted brogues. The gleam of silver and great jewels came also from elsewhere about his person, from sword-belt, dirks, the clasps of his coat, and the sporran at his loins, a glittering and archaic array. But most striking and archaic-seeming of all was his headgear, a pointed black steel casque inlaid with gold and flanked on either side by the great pinions of sea-hawks – a helm which harked back to the days of Vikings and sea-rovers, fierce and arrogant. To complete all, a huge two-handed sword five feet long was slung upright at his back, its enormous cross-hilt rising up behind his head – whence it could be reached up for and brought slashing down in one mighty overarm sweep which no armour on earth might withstand.

His companions were somewhat similarly, though less dramatically clad, some wearing long belted saffron shirts instead of the calfskin surcoats. The entire entourage fairly bristled with arms.

"God be good – Highlandmen!" James cried. "Not mummers, Griff – Scots! Highland Erse – from the Isles, I think."

"Scots, eh?" Sir George Sowerby repeated, looking sidelong at James. "Aye, to be sure – I can well believe it!" He sniffed eloquently.

"Hieland *stots*!" the Lowland Gifford muttered, frowning.

"I said Scots, Will! My people. My subjects," the young King cried. "Let us to them."

"They're little better than savages, Sire. And rebels, mind," Gifford maintained. "Your subjects such may be – but how many of them will acknowledge it? I say they're the kind of subjects best dangling on a rope!"

For the reserved and cautious Gifford this was a notable outburst – but it was a fairly typical reaction of Lowland Scots towards their Highland compatriots.

James frowned. "How dare you speak so?" he demanded. "They are as much my subjects as are you, sir! Do not forget it. Sir George – let us hasten. I would speak with these people of mine."

Sowerby looked doubtful. He had no instructions as to how to deal with such an eventuality.

The crowd, however, prevented them from catching up with the fast-moving cavalcade until the latter was held up in front of the castle drawbridge itself by the somewhat alarmed watch. James and his party arrived just in time to hear the gigantic individual under the banner announce that he was Eachann Ruadh nan Cath mac Gillean, Red Hector of the Battles, Maclean of Duart and Morvern, come to treat with the King of England on behalf of his potent prince, Donald, Lord of the Isles.

If James was just slightly put out at the lack of any mention of the King of Scots in this recital, he was too excited by the entire situation to elect to stand on any dignity. Couriers, visitors and missions from Scotland had come to James sundry times during his five years of captivity – but this was the first occasion that Highlanders had been seen or so large and colourful a company had arrived. Ignoring Sowerby's gesture of restraint, he rode forward to the newcomers.

"I bid you welcome, Maclean!" he cried. "I am happy to see you. To greet you – to greet you all. It is good to see Scots again. The tartans. Good. I am James. The King. James, King of Scots."

The big man, who at close quarters seemed even more intimidating, with startlingly fierce blue eyes amongst all the redness, looked him up and down slowly. Then, fractionally, he inclined his winged head.

"James Stewart, is it?" he said, again in the lilting, strangely mild and musical voice of the North-West. "I have heard of you. Well met, Cousin."

James paused, blinking. Life had not been such as to make of him a stickler for form and a stander on ceremony; but this huge Isleman's greeting was hardly what a king might have looked for, however gentle the tones. It sounded like one prince to another.

"Ah . . . yes, no doubt, sir," he answered thickly. "You have come far. To see me. It is a far cry from the Hebrides to this Nottingham."

"Far," the other nodded. "And I came to see King Henry, Cousin."

95

The youth bit his lip. "I think, sir, nevertheless, that it would be seemly first for you to pay your homage to your liege lord!" he jerked, flushing. "Even though he *is* a captive."

The Maclean chief raised bristling brows. "My liege is Donald of the Isles, my mother's brother. I call no man lord. And Maclean pays homage to God only," he said softly. Then he smiled faintly. "But I wish you very well, Cousin James."

As though he had been struck, James flinched back in his saddle. Abruptly he reined his horse around.

He came face to face with Sowerby, who was grinning a little. The smile faded however as he looked past, to the Highlander.

"I am Sir George Sowerby, Lieutenant-Keeper of this royal castle of Nottingham," he said. "His Majesty of England lies sick within. I will enquire whether His Majesty will grant you audience Master, h'm, Maclean, is it? Meanwhile, you may enter, with one or two of your, your people. But these . . ." He gestured towards the foot gillies.". . . these must remain outside. It is not permitted that armed bands enter one of His Majesty's castles, Master Maclean."

"Then I shall wait with my friends here, also," the big man returned. "We shall do very well outside your king's walls, I promise you! Your town shall feed us – well, I hope! It had better! And, hear me, Englishman – do not name me *Master* Maclean, by the Lord God! I am Maclean – that and nothing else. Mind you it!" That was said in little more than a sibilant whisper, but it made Sowerby catch his breath nevertheless. The chief turned away, heeling his shaggy garron through the press. As one man his party turned to follow him.

Both somewhat put out and at a loss, but without a word to each other, James and Sir George rode in over the drawbridge, set-faced.

James paced his chamber, back and forth, and the two men watching, waited silent. Gifford had already had his head all but snapped off, and was risking no more advice meantime.

The visitor in the long black travelling-robe of a priest, ragged and travel-worn, never took his dark glowing eyes from the young monarch's troubled features.

"You say that he means me no slight? No affront? Yet he showed me disrespect before all! He denied me, his King. Why should I now receive him, Master Lyon? Show him the courtesy he has not shown to me? And his duty."

"For more reasons than one, Sire, I do assure you," the priest declared earnestly. His voice was not Highland, although he was one of Maclean's company. John Lyon, though one of Donald of the Isles' chaplains, was no Gael, but an Angus man, a cadet of the house of Glamis. "Firstly, it could be to Your Grace's most real advantage. Secondly, he has been charged to speak with you, by Donald. And moreover has a message for you from my lord of Orkney. And thirdly, Sire, Hector Maclean is a courteous man, however puissant, and intended no disrespect, I swear . . ."

"On my soul – did you not hear him? What he said to me?"

"Maclean was in a difficult position, Sire. He is here as representing his uncle, Donald, Lord of the Isles. And Donald, howsoever Your Grace sees it, howsoever the rest of Scotland sees it, considers himself to be an independent prince. As have his forefathers. Maclean holds Mull and Tiree and Coll, and the rest, of Donald, not of Your Grace. The Isles have ever deemed themselves as independent of the Crown of Scotland."

"I told you they were rebels, Sire!" Gifford growled.

"Not rebels, as they see themselves, my friend. They see their lordship as springing from the ancient Norse kingdom. Therefore had Maclean acknowledged Your Grace there, before all, as his liege lord, he would have been denying the authority of his present mission to King Henry."

"How dare any subject send his own missions to such as the King of England?" James demanded. "Is that not treason?"

"The Lords of the Isles have been doing it for many a day, Sire. And none has yet paid the penalty of treason!"

"Because they sit secure amongst their outlandish islands – only so!" Gifford said.

The priest spread his hands, French fashion, and said nothing.

"You say that Maclean has a message for me from the Earl of Orkney? Has my lord, then, been keeping company with Donald of the Isles? Why this?"

"I think because he could win no-one else to Your Grace's cause, in Scotland! No-one powerful enough to gainsay the Duke of Albany – since Douglas went back on his word. So he came to the Isles. To Islay, two months back. After all, Donald is Your Grace's full cousin. His mother, the Princess Margaret, was one of your royal father's sisters."

James had forgotten that – though he supposed he had been told it once. His father had had five sisters, after all – and he had never met one of them. That the old King, his grandfather should have been prepared to let one of them marry a Lord of the Isles was strange – but probably he had hoped thereby to pacify those wild and troublesome parts.

"And Donald . . . Orkney thinks to aid me through Donald, now?" he demanded. "What do they plan, Master Priest?"

"That is not for me to tell you, Highness. Maclean is Donald's envoy – not I. I am but a humble secretary."

"But . . . how can I receive privily one who does not acknowledge me publicly?"

"Receive him as your cousin, Sire. As he is, to be sure, since he is sister's son to Donald."

"M'mmm." The youth stared out of the window. "Very well. Tell him that I will see him. When will he come?"

"He is with King Henry now. In the evening, perhaps . . ."

When the priest was gone, Gifford shook a foreboding head. "It is ill done, Sire," he said. "To receive an open rebel. It but compounds the treason . . ."

"I care not. Half of Scotland is in treason to me, it seems, Will – or will do naught to help me. If here is a man who will, then must I refuse him? Unheard?"

"*I* could have heard him, Sire . . ."

James was not listening. "It is near four years since Orkney and Douglas rode for home – four long, sore years! I was to be ransomed, released, within the first of them. But Douglas, false as ever, turned coat so soon as he was back over the Border. He has not even paid his own agreed ransom to Henry, letting his hostages, men of his own name, rot here – like his King! He is Albany's man again. And Orkney, who misjudged him, has now to skulk and go secret – for though he won Douglas out of Henry's grasp, Douglas would now silence him." The youth was pacing again. "None other of my people dare raise voice or hand against Albany or Douglas. Save, it seems, Donald of the Isles, whom you name rebel! Must I refuse to hear what he proposes? Whose is the greater treason? His – or the others?"

Gifford had no answer to that.

Later, Master Lyon brought Maclean of Duart to James's apartment. Red Hector of the Battles was redder than ever – for he had shed his calfskin coat and extraordinary helmet for a vivid red tartan shoulder-plaid, in lieu of cloak, and a bonnet from which three eagles' feathers soared proudly. Seeming to fill the small room with his presence, he addressed the young man more affably. He did not remove the bonnet, however.

"Greetings, Sir King!" he said. "At least this king is on his feet, and hale! To Donald's salutations I add my own. He wishes you a speedy deliverance from your bondage."

"In that we are wholly agreed, at least, sir! You have seen King Henry? What did he say?"

The big man raised bushy brows. "So fast?" he said. And then smiled. "You weary of waiting, I see."

"Would not you?"

"Aye. No doubt. Even so, I cannot be telling you what King Henry said. That is for me to be telling to Donald, who sent me."

"But . . . you spoke of my freedom?"

The other shook his red head. "That was not the purpose of my embassage," he declared.

James swallowed, and looked at the priest. "I thought . . . I thought . . .?"

John Lyon spread his eloquent, delicate hands. "Your Grace perhaps mistook? What Maclean came to discuss with King Henry is other than what he has to say to you."

"I see," James said, set-faced.

Not unkindly the chief eyed the youth. "You are sore, lad – and have reason to be, whatever. None will deny that your case is hard. What so ill as a king lacking a kingdom! And disappointment is sorry meat. But, see you – I bring word of better things. Of hope. From Donald, my cousin and yours. And from Orkney, your friend . . ."

"Hope! Aye – hope is all that I have, sir! What hope have you for me? After five years!"

"This," the other told him. "The man Albany, your uncle, has taken many an evil step. Now he has taken a foolish one. The Earl of Ross died five years back, leaving only a daughter, Euphemia. Now Albany has had her to resign the earldom and take the veil. Her mother was the Princess Isabella, Albany's sister and your father's. Now Albany has taken the earldom, one of the richest in the land, that covers half the Highland North, and given it to his younger son, Buchan. Whereas it should have gone to Donald who is wed to the Earl's sister. Who should now be Countess of Ross. You have heard of this?"

James shook his head.

"It is a notable matter," Maclean went on, in that gentle singsong voice. "Is Albany mad, whatever, that he thinks to rob the Lord of the Isles of what is rightfully his? Donald ever fights for his rights, by the Lord God!"

"What has this to do with me?"

"Much. *You* are King of Scots, not Albany. Donald asks that you, as King, confirm the earldom of Ross to him, over-ruling the Regent. The priest, here, has a charter for you to sign."

"Sign? *My* signature on a paper? What will that serve, sir – when my uncle holds Scotland?" That was bitterly said.

100

"It will serve very well, boy. With it, Donald can land on your territories. From the Isles. On Scotland. To enforce your writ. To *take* the earldom of Ross. And to teach Albany a lesson, see you. He can land twenty thousand men of the Isles on the mainland. And call on all leal subjects of the King of Scots to join him. The mainland clans. Lowlanders, also. And having taken Ross and the North, march south!"

James stared, his breath catching in his throat. "You mean . . . war!"

"Aye, lad – war! War on *your* behalf. With your aid, to take Ross. Donald promises to make Scotland yours. He is your cousin, and royal. All who hate Albany and Douglas will join him. Orkney has sounded out many, in Highlands and Lowlands both . . ."

"Orkney would have this?"

"Orkney devised it, whatever!" Maclean opened his sporran, and drew out from it a ring. "Here is his token to you. He said that you would know it. He sends it – and says that this thing he would have you do. He says to tell you that this is your opportunity. For Donald of the Isles is the only power who may challenge Albany and Douglas together."

"Aye – this is Orkney's ring. But . . . war!" James took a turn away, and back, suddenly a boy again, with a man's decision to make. "And what . . . what if I do not do this? Sign this charter?" he asked, uncertainly.

The giant shrugged vast shoulders beneath his plaid. "Donald will fight, whether or no," he said. "He will land his galleys in Wester Ross, and take what is his own. He will take the North from Albany. But you will remain here, boy – a prisoner. He would liefer, I say, land in Scotland in its King's name, and have your leal men to join him."

"Aye – a prisoner still!" James took him up. "Why should my case be changed, even if your Donald defeats my uncle? How will that cause King Henry to release me?"

"Henry requires something of us. He plans to go on a crusade, of all things! You will have heard of this? To the Holy Land. Och, the man is not what he was, at all. He is oftentimes sick – and so thinks the more on his latter end. He has sins to wash away – and so would lead this crusade before he dies. For this he requires much money. But more – he would have his rear secure. The Scots not to invade his borders while he is gone. He does not trust Albany – with reason. Nor Douglas. He trusts Donald."

James saw it all now. "You mean – the invasion of the North, by your Donald, is to take place as Henry departs on his crusade? To distract Albany! He will not venture across the Border while the Islesmen advance in the North. That is the real meaning of your visit here!"

The other shrugged. "Have it as you will, boy. But . . . Henry requires Donald's aid. And will pay Donald's price. He will demand a ransom for you – but you will go free."

The young man took a deep breath. "It is a dire choice you offer me, sir! War – for my freedom! Men's lives, for mine . . .?"

"Do not rate your choice too high, Sir King!" the Maclean told him grimly. "The war is decided, whether you are or no. Already the galleys muster, by their scores, their hundreds. When the brackens next show green in the Isles, the clans will sail. Men will die, yes – but not for you! Whether you come back to your kingdom, thereafter, to rule it – or leave that to others – that is your choice today!"

"And my lord of Orkney says to sign?"

Maclean held out the ring again.

John Lyon also held out something, a small roll of parchment, briefly inscribed. James scanned its few and simple phrases.

"This charter makes Donald of the Isles my vassal. For the earldom of Ross!" he pointed out. "For Ross he must do me, the King, homage!"

"I'ph'mmm," Red Hector said, enigmatically.

"A pen, Will," James demanded abruptly. "Ink. And my seal. Wax. Quickly."

And so the charter was signed and sealed, the decision made, James's first act of kingship performed. And hope was rekindled, precious, vital hope – at the hands of a proud

102

rebel, who bowed to him now with a strange admixture of mockery and sympathy.

"The priest, here, shall return to you with tidings, in due course," he said. "If stout hearts and true steel mean aught, they shall be good tidings, lad. I bid His Grace of Scotland a goodnight!"

"Yes," James said. "Yes."

It was August, nine months later, nine months of high hopes of anxious waiting, before John Lyon made his promised return – and not to Nottingham but much farther south, to the Abbey of Stratford in Essex, near to London, where King Henry had moved his Court. James now was considered old enough to be taken with the Court, wherever it went, like Cousin Murdoch of Fife, to enhance the English monarch's prestige and fame at having a captive king and princes in his train.

The priest's tidings, though he made the best of them, were such as to all but quench the precious flame of hope in the young man's heart. Donald of the Isles had indeed landed on the mainland of Scotland, in May, as planned. He had conquered his great earldom of Ross. Having subdued all the North, he moved southwards, captured Inverness and advanced on Aberdeen with a mighty and augmented Highland army. Albany himself had not gone to meet him, nor Douglas, but sent another nephew, the vigorous Alexander, Earl of Mar, illegitimate son of King Robert's third brother, the notorious Wolf of Badenoch. Mar was as urgent as his father – but a skilled leader of mounted knights. The two armies had met at Harlaw, outside Aberdeen, on July the 24th, and for a whole summer's day had fought the bloodiest internal battle of Scotland's long history, steel-clad mounted chivalry against Highland broadswords. Men died by the thousand – and neither side would yield. Who could say who won or who lost that grim day – although, despite their armour, on Mar's side more men of note fell at Harlaw than in any other battle that the bloodstained land had seen. But when night fell at last on the scene of carnage, Mar himself and a small remnant still stood fast – and by morning, Donald's mauled host was retiring on Inverness. For what it was worth, Harlaw's reeking field was Albany's.

Red Hector of the Battles fought his last battle there. At the height of the fray he had sought out and challenged Sir Alexander Irvine of Drum, the champion of Scotland's knights. They had slain each the other.

Mar had retired south as Donald had north. The latter had his earldom of Ross – but Albany still ruled Lowland Scotland. King Henry's rear would not be secure for him to go crusading yet awhile.

With a tight hold on his emotions, James listened to the dire news. Men would die, Maclean had said. Stout hearts and true steel were not sufficient, then. The sword had failed. Through the haze of red, blood-red, the young king looked at his future – and saw only grey upon grey.

Donald of the Isles, Earl of Ross, had sent one word however, not of hope perhaps but at least of encourgement. He was the King's man for this his earldom, and would not forget it. What he might do in James's cause, he would. In token of which, on Orkney's advice, he had ordered his trusted secretary, the priest John Lyon, to remain with King James as his envoy and go-between, to seek to advance their mutual causes. God willing, they would yet turn the tide.

James Stewart forbore to say that he doubted it.

7

In the fine hall of Archbishop and Chancellor Arundel's great manor of Croydon, the young man who plucked at the lute strings held all eyes, not only by the pure liquid notes of the instrument but by the sweet haunting loveliness of his singing. Everywhere men and women stood or sat entranced, gay, noisy and drink-taken as had been the company hitherto. Even Earl Murdoch Stewart of Fife looked soulful, his vapidly handsome features rapt – though he was drunk, of course.

One man, however, did not watch the singer – though he it was who had taught him the lilting, repetitious melody of the Isles, though not the words, which were James's own – John Lyon, priest and secretary. His darkly burning eyes were apt to stray elsewhere, over to the other side of the huge fireplace where a youngish man sat with a flushed girl on his knee, her clothing not a little disarrayed. This man was good-looking in a hatchet-faced and arrogant way, his features strong though dissipated. Henry of Monmouth, the King's son and Prince of Wales, now in his twenty-sixth year, was not the man to sit long patient whilst another held the stage.

Lyon's thoughtful and alert glance slid further over still, to a far corner where Griffith Glendower stood alone, slight, dark, intense. These two in the same room ever made for tension, for the title which the King's heir bore was claimed as rightfully his by Griffith's father, in revolt amongst the Welsh mountains – a situation which Prince Henry was the last to seek temper by tact or moderation.

As James commenced the fourth and final verse of his new song:

> "To see the world and folk that went forby
> as for the time, though I of mirth's dear food
> might have no more, to look it did me good . . ."

Henry rose abruptly to his feet, unceremoniously unseating the young woman.

"Come, Cousin James," he interrupted loudly. "Enough of moping and brooding! I vow you'll have us all in tears! If you cannot pipe more joyfully than this, a God's name give way to one who can! Dickon! Where's Dick Pryor, the ranter?"

Into the sudden hush that followed, some murmured, some tittered or laughed outright, some rose to their feet – for though Henry was not the King, in the absence of the monarch he did represent the Crown. Only embarrassment was general.

"For shame!" Clear and distinct, though low-spoken, the two words came from the corner of the room.

Henry turned slowly to look in that direction, and white teeth showed in a wolfish grin. "Did I hear a mouse squeak?" he asked. "A Welsh mouse? Or a rat, maybe? A Welsh rat that thinks to squeak, while yet stuffing its belly at our good English tables!"

"I said, for shame," Griffith repeated tightly. "Shame that King James's fine singing should suffer such unmannerly intrusion!"

"Ha! You say so, Welshman!" Henry snarled with cold menace, and took a step or two towards the younger man. "Shame, you say? I vow, here we have a very judge of shame – a dastard rebel from the bogs and hills who for eight years has enjoyed my father's ill-judged hosp . . . hospitality . . ."

"My lords! My lords . . .!" The Countess of Warwick, their hostess, whose birthday celebration this was, came forward anxiously protesting. "Here is no way to take our pleasure. You are my friends, all my friends. Do not spoil my pleasure in your presence here . . ."

"Friends, Kate?" the Prince barked. "Save us – you n-name as friend the lowborn son of a Welsh outlaw, who should be shortened by a head – not cherished at my father's Court! If you do, then by God's favour count me no fr-friend of yours, in con-consequence!" If Henry made but a botch of that last, the guilt lay with the wine that he had taken, and the circumstances which found him in that chamber at all. For Henry Plantagenet had no faltering tongue, any more than a faltering spirit. Undoubtedly he was not at his best this Candlemas of 1413.

As Griffith Glendower, blazing-eyed, had his lips parted to make hot rejoinder, four clear, slow rising chords, plucked from the lute-strings, turned all heads. James Stewart rose to his feet, and bowed to the Countess – who it was, indeed, had asked him to sing.

"My lady," he said, "have I your permission to offer my poor services, then, like my lute, to the Prince Henry? Understandably he finds my halting verses something dull – as indeed they may be. He would have more lusty fare. Pray His Highness to provide it, himself, for our entertainment. Whatever his choice of song, these fingers will seek to support him on the strings."

"Why, my lord James – I thank you!" their hostess cried. "Yes, yes – that is well said!" Her relief obvious, she turned back to the Prince. "Sing for us, Harry," she pleaded.

"My songs are of the camp and the field, Kate," the Prince of Wales declared, a little put out. "Not apt, I fear, for women's ears." Though he addressed the Countess, he was narrowly eyeing James. "When I am in the boudoir – why, my mind is on other matters than lutes and singing!"

The laughter which greeted that was not confined to the sycophants. Even John Lyon found himself joining in, thankful for tension lowered. James himself, having drawn the fire from his friend Griffith, smiled, nodding easily.

"Your prowess, Cousin, in such case, is well known," he acceded. "The pity you will not sing of it?"

"Unlike yourself – who *only* sing!" Henry jerked.

James's nostrils flared. But he inclined his head. "My opportunity is something less than yours," he said quietly.

"With women, perhaps. With others . . ." and he flashed a glance over at Griffith Glendower, ". . . who knows!"

Indrawn breaths all around registered the return of tension with a vengeance. Relief had been short-lived.

James flushed slowly, and the hand which gripped the lute grew white-knuckled. Sensing Griffith's hot fury, he raised his other hand in that direction, nevertheless, though he did not turn.

"I must await my time for prowess in the bedchamber, perhaps," he said, even-voiced. "As Your Highness of Monmouth must for the Council-chamber!"

"Christ God!" Henry panted.

None there failed to recognise the lash behind the younger man's seemingly civil words – the double lash indeed. To name the other of Monmouth, his mere birthplace, instead as of Wales, his proud title, was publicly to deny the authenticity of the latter, by implication to substantiate Griffith's father's claim. But more cutting still, because more immediately personal, was the reference to waiting for the Council-chamber. At that very moment a Parliament was meeting at Westminster, not a dozen miles away, in solemn conclave over the forthcoming crusade – the King presiding – and Henry, Prince of Wales was not present. And not through disinclination. He had been deliberately excluded, by his father's express command. Not only from this Parliament, but from all meetings of the Privy Council. In consequence of his riotous living and dissolute ways. Not only weak and ineffective kings could have unmanageable sons.

There was a strange and involuntary movement discernible in that hall, amongst those near the two protagonists – arising out of the universal awareness of Prince Henry's violence of temper. Many, probably subconsciously, edged back, away; but one or two, including John Lyon, Griffith Glendower and Will Gifford, moved forward. No clearer evidence of the accepted character of the heir to the throne could have been demonstrated.

But Henry's behaviour was not always predictable, and his character more complicated than was generally realised. Though he stood now actually trembling with rage, and the livid scar at his temple, which had been left by a Welsh arrow at Shrewsbury field when he was only sixteen – for he was a fighter even then – could be seen to pulse and throb painfully, yet he controlled himself with evidently tremendous effort. His quivering hand rose, to point at James – but it was long moments before words came.

At last he got them out. "K-kennelled dogs should beware how they b-bark!" he stammered – and it was no longer the wine which affected his speech; there was no trace of tipsiness about the man now. "Remember it, Sir Scot!" He swung on the Countess. "My lady of Warwick," he jerked. "You will permit that I take my leave?"

"But, Harry . . .!"

"It would be more suitable that *I* should go," James put in. "With the Lord Griffith, here. Back to our kennels!"

"Oh, my lords . . .!" The Countess began, when she was interrupted. The hall door was thrown open, and two urgent cloaked figures burst in. One of them was the Earl of Warwick himself.

"My lord Prince!" he cried. "Highness! The King! Your father! He is stricken down. Seized of an apoplexy. Sore stricken. At the White Friars. He calls for you. It is . . . it is . . . the end, I fear. Quickly, Highness . . ."

Pandemonium broke loose in Croydon Manor.

King Henry the Fourth was dead, and a new and forceful hand reigned over England. The land was not slow to be aware of it; indeed, even before the ink on the first swift edicts was dry, the story had swept London and prepared the folk – how, as he had lain dying on a bed in the White Friars monastery in London, after the Parliament, the old King had sent for his crown to be brought and laid on the pillow beside him; and coming in booted and spurred, his son Henry had waited there a while, and presently conceiving his father dead had picked up the crown and put it on his own head, and hurried off; but the old man was still alive, and rallying a little had opened his eyes to find the crown gone, summoning enough strength to demand its whereabouts – so that the Prince had to return, and receive sundry reproaches and charges at the dying man's lips before finally all was over. It was said that one of the charges was to relieve the old King's conscience by releasing the captive King of Scots.

The said King of Scots was, in fact, one of the first to be made pointedly aware of the change of hand on the helm of state, for almost the first act of Henry the Fifth, the very next day after his accession, when he had dismissed Chancellor Arundel and appointed his own illegitimate uncle Henry Beaufort in his place, was to order James Stewart and Griffith Glendower back to strait confinement in the Tower of London, on the pretext that they were a focus for disaffection in the land. It was exactly seven years since the Tower gates had first clanged ominously behind the boy James; now he was a man, with his twenty-first birthday only a few months off. The sensation was none the happier for that.

8

The two men strained hugely yet almost motionlessly on the grass, grunting, muscles standing out, rippling, on their bare arms and torsos in the mellow October sunlight, whilst the onlookers watched enthralled but silent. At first glance, it might have seemed strange that the two wrestlers should be thus almost immobile, in apparent equipoise of effort, for they were far from a well-matched pair. One man was heavy, gross, obviously enormously strong, in early middle years; the other was young, finely-made, of little more than half the weight, but with great breadth of shoulder and depth of chest. That the latter should be able even to hold back the mighty, sweating bulk of his opponent was a wonder. Yet few there had any great doubts as to the outcome of the struggle. This was the third bout of the forenoon, and James Stewart had easily won the other two.

The big man, who was in fact Sir John Pelham's chief cook at Pevensey Castle, suddenly bent his knees, so that his whole great body sagged backwards. Since his arms were wrapped tightly around the other's rib-cage, James inevitably canted forward over him. Then, as the younger man's wide-legged stance was momentarily shaken, the cook convulsed with a violent explosion of force. Up and up he raised his opponent, and with sheer, irresistible muscle-power tossed him right over his own head and shoulders in a magnificently spectacular throw. As James came down on the warm grass beyond, on his back, with a jarring crash, a quivering sigh rose from the watchers. But none cheered or shouted either encouragement or advice. When one of the contestants was a king, even a captive one, it scarcely seemed suitable for scullions and castle-servants to applaud their own champion; and John Lyon was not a shouter at wrestling matches.

James, despite the force of his fall, had not allowed his grip of his opponent to be jerked loose. One arm he still held encircling the other's thick middle. Scarcely had he hit the grass before, with a complicated movement almost too swift for the eye to follow, he had doubled himself up at the back of the other's knees, and jerked with all his might, in his turn. The big man toppled backwards over the bent body.

None, including the cook himself no doubt, could have said how it came about that by the time they were both stretched recumbent, James was on top. Uncanny swiftness of action, notable agility, and sheer knowledge of the art he practised, had tipped the balance against weight and superior strength.

But in the tense moments that followed, strength itself was on trial – that and nothing else. For though the cook was on his back, the bout was not finished. His bullet head and brawny shoulders were raised – and those shoulders must be flat on the ground before victory could be claimed. James, one knee in the other's groin, had a hand against each heaving shoulder, and despite the spasmodic efforts of the older man to throttle him with one crooked arm and to break his back with the other, he was steadily, consistently, inexorably bearing down on the man beneath, drawing on some seemingly inexhaustible and improbable reserves of vigour and main force. Slowly, inch by inch, both men groaning with the effort, perspiration running from the cook's rolls of fat in streams, those shoulders were forced lower and lower. Stalemate appeared to have been reached in the last centimetres, and for endless straining seconds there was no discernible movement. Then abruptly the cook went slack, his head hit the grass, and all was over.

It was a moment or two before James rose to his feet, breathing deeply and swaying a little. He reached down a hand, to assist the other to rise.

112

"A good fight . . . my friend," he panted. "You near had me, there. You have a . . . mighty grip. My ribs . . . will be sore . . . for a week!"

The cook hung his head, shuffling his feet and saying nothing.

John Lyon came forward. "Do not take it amiss, sir cook!" he said, smiling. "It is no disgrace, I swear, to be beat by the finest wrestler in all England!"

"A man of God should speak only truth!" James declared. But he could not hide something of pleasure in the saying, exaggerated as it might be. In the two years since the new King Henry had ordained his closer confinement, the captive had determinedly set his face to prevent the degeneration and flabbiness, both of body and spirit, which prolonged imprisonment could so grievously engender. Now that there was no more hunting, jousting and similar untramelled sports permitted, resolved to keep his body hard and fit, and finding the endless running round and round the restricted purlieus of London Tower insufficiently effective, James had taken up this wrestling, unsuitable as it was deemed to be for the loftily-born. And when James Stewart took up an activity, nothing would do but that he must excel at it. Everyone of the Tower's inmates and garrison, who would, had been wrestled with, and as the months turned to years, defeated. Now, these past weeks transferred to this Pevensey Castle on the Sussex coast, with plague once more in London and Henry away fighting wars in France, he was but keeping his hand in. One day, he promised himself, he was going to require all his bodily and mental powers.

On the narrow ribbon of greensward between the inner and outer baileys of Pevensey's ancient and crumbling Norman castle – which represented as much freedom as the royal captive was permitted these days – James was rubbing himself down with a cloth and asking the assembled servitors and men-at-arms whether they knew of anyone locally who might be persuaded to come and wrestle with him, when shouting turned all heads. On one of the

113

round flanking towers of the inner bailey, the Deputy-Keeper stood waving them in.

"Back to your places, knaves!" he shouted to the servants. "Quickly! Enough, I say. The Keeper returns." And as these departed without argument or delay, he turned to James. "My lord," he cried, "Sir John Pelham is crossing the marsh causeway. Dress yourself quickly, of a mercy! Let him not find you so. He mislikes it. Considers it unworthy . . ."

"Yes, yes, friend," James called back. "Never fear – he will not learn that you permitted it. We have swords down here. Master Lyon will engage me in play with them. Even Sir John cannot frown on swordery as unsuitable, surely?"

The priest groaned. The Deputy-Keeper shook his head. "Better if you came in, my lord James. To meet Sir John and these new captives . . ."

"Never!" the younger man returned strongly. "Think you that I am going, hands out, to meet my insufferable Cousin Murdoch! Or this wretched Douglas! I am a king, I'd remind you, sir – and these are subjects of mine. Kings do not go to meet subjects . . ." He paused, listening. The distant clamour of church-bells, pealing from Pevensey village across the marshland, sounded clear. "What is that?" he asked. "Why ring church-bells at this hour?"

"I know not, my lord. Sir John will know belike. I must go meet him . . ."

John Lyon preferred to wield words rather than swords – with which anyway he was less than expert. "Sire – I'd counsel you to keep open mind as to this Douglas who is being brought here. I have heard well of the Laird of Whittinghame."

"He is a Douglas!" James commented briefly.

"Aye – but they say that he is something different from the others. He loves neither the Duke of Albany nor his son the Earl Murdoch, for a start."

"A sign of grace, admittedly!"

"Also, he is said to hold a notable grudge against his chief, the Earl of Douglas. As is little to be wondered at. He was amongst those sent from Scotland seven years

114

ago as hostages for the Earl's great ransom of one hundred-thousand crowns – and he is still here! The Earl has stopped paying – indeed he has now gone to France, has Archie Tyneman, to aid the French against King Henry. Nothing has been paid for two years. This David Douglas of Whittinghame is the last of the hostages – and like to remain one. And one less than beloved by his captors! That, no doubt, is why he is being brought here, for closer confinement."

"It may be that we both have reason to mislike the Earl of Douglas, then. But so, no doubt, have many . . ."

"Yes – but is this not an opportunity for you to drive a wedge between the Douglases? Next to your uncle of Albany, Sire, they are your most potent enemies. This Whittinghame is of the Dalkeith family, one of the greatest branches of the house. Linked with those of Drumlanrig and Cavers and Morton. There must be much resentment over his sorry state. Use his resentment at his chief to make him your friend – and who knows how one day he may serve you! And others with him."

"M'mmm. You have the mind of a serpent, I think – despite the eyes of a saint!"

Nevertheless, when presently Sir John Pelham, the King's grizzled Keeper of Pevensey, brought the new captives to greet King James, that young man was more affable than he might have been – the more so perhaps because there was no sign of the Earl Murdoch, who had been expected likewise. There were a dozen or so extra and assorted prisoners, French, Welsh and the one Scot, being concentrated here – for though Pevensey was not important as a royal castle, it was one of the most secure as a prison, being sited in the midst of salt-marsh and fen, approachable across a maze of moats only by a narrow causeway.

Pelham was another veteran captain of the earlier French and Welsh campaigns, like the Lord Grey, and an even greater martinet, resenting his isolation here in the Sussex marshes when he should have been teaching King Harry's pups how to fight. His prisoners, like his staff, had to pay for this oversight of the King's. But today, as he curtly introduced the new captives and hostages, he was in better temper than his usual.

"Hear you yonder bells?" he said to James. "Heed them well, my lord. Those are victory bells. Young Harry has proved himself. Won a great victory over the French. Greater than Harfleur. At a place named Agincourt, they say, near to Calais. I know it. I campaigned thereabouts once. It has been a mighty slaughter. They say one-hundred-and-twenty great lords of the French are slain, seven dukes amongst them. And eight thousand gentles, knights and squires. All North France is Harry's! God save King Harry, I say!"

Perhaps not unaccountably none of the captives joined in the hurrahs of their bodyguard.

"I take it that King Henry survived the battle, Sir John?" James said – and managed to convey a mild regret, without the words being such as could be seized upon.

Pelham's square face grew turkey-red. "He did, my lord James, God be praised – he did! He will soon be king in France, see you, as he is here in England. Aye, and in Scotland too, belike! As in Wales and Ireland!" The Keeper glared round upon them all. "God and King Harry will see to it!"

"Ill-assorted allies as they may be!" James acceded. He turned his shoulder on the seething knight. "So this is the Laird of Whittinghame! Welcome, my friend, to King Henry's hospitality!" And he held out his hand.

The fair-haired, open-faced, powerfully-built young man with the Red Heart of Douglas embroidered on his doublet, three or four years older than James, stepped forward and sank on one knee to kiss that hand.

"Your Grace's true and leal servant," he said.

"And yet a Douglas!"

"Aye, Sire. There are more sorts of Douglas than one!"

"You say so?" James shrugged, and smiled. "Ah, well – there are more sorts of Stewart than one, also, I think! You

116

have not brought my cousin Murdoch of Fife with you, I see?"

"He is gone . . . elsewhere," Pelham broke in, shortly. "On orders from my lord Chancellor Beaufort. Now – to your quarters, gentlemen. I expect all at table sharp, at Pevensey. None enters my hall later than five minutes after the horn is sounded. Is it understood?"

"King Henry's hospitality, that I spoke of," James added. He eyed David Douglas's sturdy and well-thewed frame. "Tell me, Whittinghame – do you wrestle?" he asked.

Snorting, Pelham waved them all indoors like a flock of poultry.

Later, in James's own chamber which looked out over the flat saltings to the gleaming Channel, David Douglas of Whittinghame unburdened himself.

"I was to be married," he declared. "All was arranged. Then the Regent Albany summoned me to Edinburgh. The Earl was there – Archie Tyneman. They said that I must go to England. Only for a short time, they said. Only while the Earl gathered the remainder of his ransom money. No great sum was still owing, they said – but King Henry was demanding notable hostages for it. Or else he would not consider releasing the Earl Murdoch . . ."

"Releasing the Earl Murdoch? Not King James!"

"Murdoch, yes. That is what they said. When I asked, why me – they answered that it had to be some of the foremost of the name of Douglas. For the honour of the house. Honour, by the Rude! That was seven years ago. I did as they asked. I came south. And others with me. Now the Earl, and his sons with him, ruffle it in France. And I rot here . . .!"

"You have our sympathy, friend!" James said gravely.

At something of the King's tone, the Douglas recollected. "I crave Your Grace's pardon. Your state, of course, is more evil than mine. Yet you, Sire, at least, can look for early release . . ."

The younger man barked a mirthless laugh. "Have your trials addled your wits, sir?" he demanded harshly for him.

117

The other raised fair brows. "But . . . this matter of the Pope? The papal moneys. That must win Your Grace's freedom soon, to be sure?"

"What is this? What do you mean – the Pope?"

"Have you not heard?" The Douglas looked from James to the priest, and back. "The great Church moneys. That the Regent has negotiated. For your ransom. And that of his son, Earl Murdoch. The word of it has been abroad for months . . ."

"The walls of the Tower of London are thick, sir! As are these of Pevensey, you will find," James said. "We hear little that our gaolers do not wish us to hear. I know naught of this. I wrote letters to Pope Benedict, yes. More than once. Seeking his aid to gain my release. As I have written others amany, God knows! But I get back only fair words . . ."

"This is more than words, Sire. As I heard it, the matter is well forward. Pope Benedict at Avignon requires money. Because of this schism, this split, with two popes, the Churches of Christendom have been holding back their dues which should go to the Vatican, waiting some sure settlement of the dispute. Scotland, like France, supports Pope Benedict, yes – but still the papal dues from the Scots benefices have not been sent these last years. Now, Albany and the Pope Benedict have reached an agreement. The Regent, with Bishop Wardlaw's help, will collect the moneys from the Scots Church, and send half of it to Avignon. The other half will remain with Albany – on condition that he uses it to pay the ransoms of yourself and Earl Murdoch. It is a great sum, which has been a-growing for years . . ."

"God be praised! The Church!" James turned on John Lyon, shining-eyed. "You hear? The Church – coming to my aid, at last! This will be the good Bishop Wardlaw's doing. How could we have heard naught of this, man? Had I known, when I sent Will Gifford home . . .!"

The priest shook his head. "I knew only that the Earl of Orkney had gone to France, with Douglas. But not to fight. To see Pope Benedict. I told you that, Sire. But, I feared, ~s fruitlessly as the rest. This of the money is new indeed.

118

If it is truly half of all the yearly dues, the annates as they are called, on all Scottish bishoprics, abbeys and foundations, to the Holy See – then it is a great matter, a vast sum. For near half the best land in the realm is the Church's."

"Aye." James's breath came out on a long sigh. "Here is news indeed. Mark you, we must not count on it too greatly. For if these long years have taught me anything, it is that – not to count wholly on any thing or on any man!" For a young man of barely twenty-two, that was caustically bitter. "But at least, my Douglas friend, you have brought me hope again. And if hope for myself, then hope for you also. For I will not forget my friends. Pray God, this time, that it may not fail – since it is His Church that takes a hand."

"Aye, Sire . . ."

"Murdoch!" Lyon interposed. "Could this be why Earl Murdoch was not brought here today, as intended. Sir John Pelham said that he had gone elsewhere. On the Chancellor's orders. Could that mean that the matter is in train? That negotiations are sufficiently forward . . ."

The three men eyed each other, doubts and fears writ large on each face – yet hope, blessed, vital hope, there also, clearest of all.

London Town seemed to have gone clean mad. The late plague appeared to have damped the spirits of the ebullient citizens no whit – though more had died there than Frenchmen at Agincourt. Despite the cold, damp weather of late January, every Londoner was in the streets, every church-bell clanged incessantly, every drum in the city was beat, every trumpet and horn blown, every voice was upraised. Flags, arras, tapestries, hung from every window or were draped across the narrow streets, evergreens had been plundered from great men's gardens to deck the town, towers and stages erected all around still further constricted passage, and the city conduits actually ran with wine. Highest holiday reigned, to welcome the victorious King Harry back in triumph to his capital.

119

James had been brought back to the Tower for the event
– and, he hoped, for better things than this. For now, as the
mile-long procession wound its tortuous way from Aldgate
through the narrow, crowded, stinking streets, he walked,
set-faced, alone. He was spared the symbolical rope which
the others had to carry, wrapped once around each middle
and linking one another – for he could scarcely be claimed as
a prisoner-of-war; but in front of him, to make it clear who
he was, two mounted knights dragged in the mire at their
horses' heels a captured royal standard of Scotland. King
Henry, on in front, was punishing him for the fact that
Scots had fought on the side of their ancient ally France.

Behind James paced, limped and stumbled much of the
flower of that France. First came Charles, Duke of Orleans,
brother of the mad French king. Pale, delicately fastidious,
he glanced neither left nor right at the crowds who hooted,
laughed, mimicked, even spat, concerned apparently only
where he trod in the filth of the gutters. Linked to him
by rope was his uncle, the elderly Duke of Bourbon,
wounded and in pain but grey head held high. Next
came the royal counts of Vendôme, Richemont and Eu,
followed by the Marshal Boucicault, so bandaged as to be
scarcely recognisable, tied to the chief herald of France,
the King-of-Arms Mountjoye. After these leaders came
so many lords, nobles and knights, three by three, that
even the London crowds began to weary of the sport and
flag in their witticisms. Good King Harry might almost be
said to be overdoing things.

The procession was to end at the Guildhall, off Cheapside,
where the Lord Mayor, aldermen and craft-guilds were
giving a great banquet for the hero-king. Needless to say,
the prisoners were not to be participators; so, at the Poultry,
east of Cheapside the long straggling column of illustrious
captives was headed off, under strong guard, down the
Walbroke, making for East Cheap and Tower Street, to
their grim destination by the river-side.

That night the Tower was full, as possibly it had never
been before. Every cellar, dungeon, storeroom and corridor

overflowed with much of the cream of Continental chivalry – a woeful company, glad to huddle together against the draughts and chill and rats.

James's own small room in the White Tower contained two new occupants – the Dukes of Orleans and Bourbon. Charles of Orleans was good company, even if his uncle was doleful and complaining. There was nothing deranged about the mad King of France's brother. Approximately James's own age, he was talented, intelligent and lively – and if notorious for his association with the Queen Isabella, his brother's German wife, famous also for his poetry, painting, and virtuosity in music. James perceived a kindred spirit.

But it was not the arts and graces of living which they discussed over their frugal meal that evening. Orleans, although philosophical about his own state, was not unaffected by the concern which prevailed amongst the crowds of his compatriots that thronged the Tower.

"Henry is no brute, no ogre," James sought to reassure him. "He is a strange man – but with his virtues. I do not love him – but he has his own notions of honour. This day's play-acting was but mummery for the crowd – a Roman triumph staged for the multitude. He will, I believe, treat you more honestly than this."

"Myself, perhaps," the Duke conceded. "It is for the others that I fear. As do they. Henry is a great warrior, and bold, I admit – *parbleu*, who in France could deny it this day! But as to his good faith, his humanity – that is less certain, Your Majesty."

James stirred a little uncomfortably at the unaccustomed honorific. Majesty was not a phrase the Scots used, preferring Grace; and the English, on policy, granted him neither, on the convenient fiction that since he had not had any coronation he was not yet truly a king.

"Henry is fierce and ruthless, yes," he acceded. But since assuming the crown he cares much for his reputation as the right hand of God Almighty! And, mark you, he is very English! The English, you will find, are a strange people – with much good to them. They have many faults –

121

but they are, on the whole, trustworthy. And cheerful. But they are merchants, all of them — a race of pedlars and hucksters. Even their nobles. Henry himself. This undignified concern with ransom. I do believe that this is why they go to war! To gain prisoners, whom they can sell back! No more than traders in flesh and blood! Your Highness, and your friends, like myself, are no more than so much merchandise to be bought and sold for the highest price possible. And merchants, see you, do usually take fair care of their goods!"

"It may be so. Yet this Henry slaughtered thousands of prisoners after Agincourt! Men who had surrendered honourably. Is that Your Majesty's man of honour? Or even your careful merchant?"

James nodded grimly. "I heard of that, yes. A shameful deed which I think Henry will never forget. But . . . it is said to have been something of a mistake, done in misapprehension. After the strife, when still on the field of battle, marshalling the prisoners, gathering the booty, stripping the dead, and the like, a large company of French was seen reforming and coming in on the English flank. A cry went up that the enemy was renewing the assault, after surrender. Whether it was so or no, I do not know. But Henry, in the confusion, this once appears to have given way to panic. He commanded all prisoners to be slain, lest they encumber him, or turn on him again. It will stain his name for ever — but I believe it done in hasty error."

The other shrugged, Gallic fashion. "You may be right, Sire — but even so, having made such error, might he not make more? My friends out there fear for their lives. There is scarce gold enough in all fair France to ransom all of them! And this Henry is not the man to entertain useless captives. Nor to send them home unredeemed — perchance to fight against him later. *Mon Dieu* — he will be so glutted with French gold, after this, that he will be the richest man in Christendom! Can you wonder then that many out there doubt if they will ever see France again?"

Orlean's words were like a sudden stoun at James's heart. And shamefully, it was not the thought of possible death for many unwanted prisoners that smote him; it was purely selfish, his own less desperate case. If Henry was indeed now to be glutted with French money, what of his own prospects? Might Pope Benedict's dues from Scotland no longer seem of vital import? And what difference could that make? Might Henry be prepared to send him home with the less fuss and delay? Or . . . might he rather decide to hold him fast, spurning the money, preferring to hold Scotland's king to bolster up his recent presumptuous claim to Scotland's overlordship?

It is to be feared that James Stewart scarcely heard the rest of the Duke's anxieties, so suddenly agitated had he become. He had scarcely realised how much he had come to build on the tidings which Douglas of Whittinghame had brought him.

He was still making vague and distracted replies to the other when the door opened to reveal David Douglas himself. In the three months which had elapsed since their meeting, Whittinghame had unofficially, almost involuntarily, moved into the position formerly held by Will Gifford, of esquire to the King.

"Your Grace," he announced. "A visitor craves audience." Glancing a little uncomfortably at the two Frenchmen, he cleared his throat. "Not, h'm, a captive!"

A tall and elegant young man, richly dressed in the height of fashion, pushed past the Douglas, with just the hint of a swagger. Slender to the point of thinness, his hair curled, and jewellery glittering about his person, he at first appeared a complete stranger to James – and no very welcome one.

"Ha – James!" the apparition exclaimed, in loftily affected voice. "James Stewart, i' faith – my good Jamie! *King* Jamie, no less! Greetings, my friend!"

It was something about the voice that James recognised. He started to his feet. "Henry Percy!" he exclaimed. "Save us – it is you! I scarce knew you. After all these years.

Nine long years!" He strode forward, hand out. "Greetings, indeed!"

The newcomer made no move to kneel, even bow, or take the hand, much less kiss it. He glanced around him, slim nostrils wrinkling a little, "My God – Harry does not deem you worthy of great regard, I swear!" he commented.

"Undoubtedly," James agreed briefly, withdrawing his hand. "Here are their Highnesses the Dukes of Orleans and Bourbon, brother and uncle to the King of France. Henry Percy – now, I understand, Earl of Northumberland."

"I have heard of the famous Hotspur, Monsieur," Orleans said, bowing. "A renowned warrior. Your father, that would be?"

The other inclined his head only slightly. "Yes. My father, however, had not a monopoly of military prowess, my lords!" He turned a slender shoulder upon the Frenchmen. "May we not speak alone, James?" he demanded.

James frowned. "You saw the state of this place, as you came, surely? This chamber, I believe, will be one of the least crowded in the Tower, tonight."

"Your Majesty – with your gracious permission my uncle and myself would retire, for a space," Orleans said. "We have matters to discuss with our comrades . . ."

"There is no need, Your Highnesses – "

With great dignity the two dukes bowed themselves out.

"That was ill done, Henry," James said. "They are king's sons."

"They are Frenchmen!" the other amended. "This is better. I vow I find foreigners . . . unappetising!"

"Perhaps. But it comes to me that you were something of a foreigner in a strange land yourself, once! Captive of a sort, also. It might have bred in you some fellow-feeling? Indeed, even now I believed you to be in Scotland. Held there in ward, since Bramham Moor, in . . . 1408, was it?"

"I was released," the Percy said briefly. "King Harry required my services."

"Ah. So simple as that?"

124

"Harry *is* King of England, James. What he desires, he is wont to get."

"I recollect that his father was also King of England, Henry. Yet you and yours esteemed him so little as to rebel. Thrice. Indeed, was not your grandfather slain battling against him at Bramham? Two years after we parted that night at North Berwick. And you fled again into Scotland?"

"Those days are by with," Northumberland said stiffly. "Harry is a different man from his father. A man Percy can work with. Moreover a man who needs Percy!" He drew himself up a little further. "I am Warden, now. Warden of the East March. In room of the Duke of York, who fell at this Agincourt."

"Warden – you! Warden of the East March!" The words aroused in James Stewart a great wave of nostalgia; he saw a warm picture of the Borders of his own land, near four hundred miles away, so that his voice quivered. "The Marches! The Borderland . . .! Dear God, Henry – I do envy you!"

The other shrugged. "It is but my birthright, after a fashion. Only Percy may truly control the North. Always it has been so. But, James – I will do what I may for you. I will speak with King Harry . . ."

"That was scarce my meaning!"

"Think naught of it. Harry will heed me – nothing more certain. I am but new come from his side – his table at this Guildhall. I am as good as his gossip. Summoned south in person to attend on him, at this his triumph. I thought of you there, Jamie – in the Guildhall. And swore that I must come visit my old playfellow."

"You are vastly kind!"

"It is nothing. I bring you news of Scotland. The good wishes of your friends there . . ."

"Good wishes!" James swallowed, apparently with some difficulty. "I think that I require more than their good wishes!"

"At least they have not entirely forgot you – as they might have done. For it has been a long time, see you. Murdoch of Fife, in especial, sent his greetings . . ."

125

"Murdoch? You have met with him? I have not seen Murdoch for months. Where do they hold him now? He was not at this banquet? What was his message?" James's quickened interest was evident.

"Why, just to keep in good heart, he said. As he had done. Your turn will come – as had his, at last. Fourteen years he had been held in England – a great time, you will agree. But he had never lost heart . . ."

What . . . what are you saying?" the other broke in hoarsely. "Where is Murdoch? Where did you see him?"

"At Berwick, to be sure. Where we were exchanged, and the ransom money paid. Only a few short weeks ago. It was a notable occasion . . ."

"God in Heaven!" James had actually to grip the table to hold himself steady, so grievous was the shock. "Murdoch is . . . free? Released? Ransomed? Exchanged . . . for you!"

"To be sure. I told you, King Harry required me. And no doubt your Albany wanted his son. Though why is less clear, I grant you! For, on my soul, your Cousin Murdoch is but a wind-bag, a strutting clothes-horse . . .!"

James had turned, and gone pacing blindly, as though drunkenly, to the small barred window, to stare out into the darkness. No words would come.

Surprised, Northumberland eyed his back. "Is aught amiss, James?" he wondered.

It was moments before he found his voice, flat, level, thick. "There was no word . . . of me? Of *my* release?"

"Why, no. Did you expect it? Albany had enough to do to raise the £10,000 Harry demanded for Murdoch, I swear – though, mark you, *I* had to find some of it! Where he got so much, God knows – for Albany spends money like water. They say that most of the royal lands have been alienated, sold . . ."

"The money came from the Church. A great sum. The Annates. Papal dues from the Scots Church." The words came out individually, separately, like beads on a rosary, heavy with hurt. "Greatly more than any £10,000!"

126

"You say so? I know naught of that. I would scarce have thought it – for Albany and the Church scarce agree! Bishop Wardlaw, our old tutor, does not love him. Nor do most of the other prelates. Indeed I do not know who does love Albany! Myself, I found him less than agreeable. Mark you, he is not a fool like his son Murdoch . . ."

It is to be doubted if James Stewart heard any more. Certainly he took in nothing of his visitor's subsequent gossip of Scotland, prolonged as it seemed. He continued to stand over at the window and contributed never a word.

At length, even Henry Percy perceived that, despite old times and boyhood memories, his company was being insufficiently appreciated. With not a little stiff reproach eventually he took his leave.

The King of Scots moved over to the rough bench beside the table, and sitting, dropped his head between his hands.

9

The morning was fresh, sweet-scented and very fair, and somewhere a nightingale poured out its heart in glad fervour to the new day. At the narrow iron-barred window, James twisted his head this way and that, even pressing his cheek against the cold stone, to try to perceive from whence came the joyous cascade of melody.

He could not place it. Darting, skimming swallows he could see everywhere; from near at hand the murmurous cooing of doves sounded, and two, their fantails spread, were strutting on the terrace below his window; from over by the Thames, where white mist-wraiths coiled into the still night-washed May air, cuckoos were calling with haunting gentle persistence. But where the nightingale sang, he could not discover.

The young man gripped the iron bars in a sudden rush of blind rage, all out of tune with the fair morning. For a moment blood sang in his ears, drowning the songs of the birds, hot tears of sheerest frustration stung his eyes, and a surge of bitter gall filled his throat. He began to beat a clenched fist against the stonework. Then, with a vehement effort, he controlled himself – as he had done so many times, as indeed he spent much of his life doing. It was not for this that he had left his bed so early, to add extra hours to another interminable day.

This early rising had become something of a habit with James these last years. To be up and about, even in the limited confines of his own room, before others were astir, somehow was apt to give him some illusion of freedom. This, too, was when he best could write his poetry – though not always, for his muse was erratic and wayward, as with most poets; but it was when he could write most freely. Also, despite the bitter-sweet hurt of it, he liked to watch the world of men awake — or such tiny segment of it as he might view from a slender arrow-slit window. And if this had been his frequent habit in London's Tower, looking out over the stinking kennels and befouled reaches of that river, how much more did it apply here.

For the Thames where the white mist rose before him now was not the filthy and swollen London river; the doves that cooed were not the cocky, brash city pigeons; and the levels over which he gazed were not the roofs of teeming human warrens but the rich and lush, cattle-dotted pastures of Windsor's royal park. James, in fact, leaned at a second-floor window of a tower of Windsor Castle that May morning of 1419, King Henry having brought his Court here a week previously, and a selection of his most illustrious prisoners with it, for reasons undisclosed — but not out of undiluted love, indubitably.

Forcing himself to it, James opened the ink-horn and picked up the pen, testing its quill-point against his thumb-nail. In frowning determination he smoothed out the paper, and point spluttering with the undue pressure, wrote:

"Where Spring-tide sets the seal of youth
   on brow and heart;
And I stand here, in very sooth,
   a man apart . . ."

It was the nightingale again that stopped him, chiding him with its notes of true clear loveliness. Here was no way to write poetry, to write anything, this sweet morning, with such sounds in his ears and the scent of clover from the park in his nostrils. Better not to write at all, if this was the style of him . . .

Another sound came to him, on the still air — the silvery tinkle of a tiny bell. High, distinct, yet inconsequential it

129

sounded – and in the peculiarly aware mood in which that young man found himself, told him that he was a fool, that all men's activities were folly, that life itself was vanity – that only beauty, the liquid, unthinking, prodigal beauty of the nightingale, was of any true worth or virtue.

The sudden certainty of this truth set his pen-point hovering above the paper. Could he capture it in words . . .?

But something in the very mockery of that small but so potent tinkling drew him back to the window, to discover what caused it. Looking directly downwards, he saw a small white dog, trotting over the short, dew-silvered grass of the terrace. From its collar a tiny bell gleamed in the stripling sunshine, and tinkled.

A little dog! A lap-dog! What deathless verse, what verities of the unstained morning, could spring from such a source? Not even a true hound or honest mastiff . . .

Then James Stewart caught his breath – and was not aware when he was permitted to release it again.

A young woman had come into view from his narrow vantage-point, pacing slowly behind the dog. And seeing her, James was abruptly and totally overwhelmed, a man smitten as with a blinding light.

In those first few breathless moments before she passed out of sight from his infuriatingly restricted view, he did not seek to analyse what he saw. Undoubtedly she was fair, young, serene – but of details he was scarcely aware. All he knew was that here was the true, essential and crowning beauty which not only the nightingale but all the fair morning had been awaiting, natural and prodigal, yes – but not unthinking, heedless. Here was warmth and life and understanding, in the guise of beauty. With searing certainty the man knew it.

James discovered that he was trembling, as well as breathless. Nothing like this had ever happened to him before. Men, poets in especial, talked lightly of falling headlong in love; indeed he himself had glibly written and sung such nonsense. But this was nothing like that. Love came not into it. How could it, when he knew nothing

130

of the creature? Save that in this unlooked-for moment of blazing clarity, he knew her to represent for him all beauty, delight, truth and purity.

Heart beating wildly, he waited. She would return, she *must* return. It was inconceivable that she would not show herself again. Somehow, those small regular footmarks dark on the dew of the grass, promised it. He stared down at them, in a fever of anticipation.

She did return, presently; and, joy of joys, at an angle of approach which allowed him to watch her for precious moments longer than formerly. Though slightly light-headed, James this time did manage to drink in something of detail.

That she was very lovely went without saying, in person as in features. Sufficiently slender to seem fairly tall, she was yet shapely of figure and carried herself gracefully with a proud upright carriage which was as natural as it was unconscious, and made a poem indeed of her very move-ment. She wore her long rich chestnut-brown hair simply looped back with a fillet instead of being elaborately built up under either high-crowned steeple or fanciful horns, as was the fashion. Her features were winsome, regular, finely cut and moulded without being over-delicate, with a noble sweep of brow, chiselled nose, and sweetly-curved mouth over a firmly-rounded chin. She was too far away for him to discern the colour of her eyes, but her complexion seemed to be of a warm honey-hue to match the gentle warmth of her expression. She wore a simple but cunningly-cut gown of a cornflower blue, wide enough of neck to reveal something of white shoulders and the hollow between full breasts, high-waisted to mould lovingly her figure above, the full flowing skirt not so long as to trail upon the dew-drenched grass.

The man gazed, enthralled – and then drew back sud-denly, almost guiltily, as she seemed to glance up towards his window. Why he should have felt thus an intruder he could not have explained. Nevertheless, as soon as she was past his narrow line of sight, he was back to the window

131

again, peering after her for the few yards more in which vision was granted him.

Thereafter, James was a man transformed. For long he stood at the window, unaware that he did so, full of the lightsome glow which the girl had kindled so astonishingly within him – not looking for her again, but content to be filled with the knowledge that she walked the same earth as did he. Though content was scarcely the word which applied to his state; uplifted, charged with strangest emotion, irradiated, better described him.

Presently he reached for his pen again, and began to write. Now the words flowed in a vivid, joyful stream:

"Beauty, fair enough to make the world to dote
   Are ye a wordly creature?
Or heavenly thing in likeness of nature?
   Or are ye Cupid's own princess, come here
   To loose me out of bonds . . ."

He was still writing when John Lyon came to him, to say his morning office – of which today James heard never a word – and when later David Douglas informed that breakfast awaited His Grace in the ante-room which he shared with the Duke of Orleans. The Duke had to make all the conversation that morning – at which of course he was proficient – though it did not take him long to disabuse himself of the flattering impression that James's rapt expression was the result of his own untimely eloquence. None of the trio had, in fact, ever seen James Stewart like this before – faintly smiling, courteously if silently attentive yet with his glance far, far away.

At Windsor, the prisoners were permitted more of freedom than was possible in the Tower of London, though they were still not allowed to hunt or hawk, or indeed ride a horse, or venture beyond the extensive terraces and gardens and the inner rim of the great park. It had been indicated that they might attend, in a discreet way, at sundry activities of the Court, and Orleans, a sociable character if ever there was one, had availed himself of this from the first. Not so James, who though no recluse or hater of his fellows was concerned to avoid King Henry as much as he might. Indeed they had spoken only distantly and formally in all the three years that had passed since Henry's triumphant return from Agincourt, each manifestly uncomfortable with the other. James went so far in the matter as to post David Douglas at some distance from the tennis-yard when he played there – which he did each day, in his determination to keep fit – to warn him should King Henry appear to be coming thither. It was fear that motivated the younger man in this – fear that he might not be able to restrain his deep hurt and resentment before the Plantagenet, and so fail in his dignity and in the façade he forced himself to present to his restricted world.

This sunny May forenoon, however, James rejected all suggestions of playing tennis, wrestling with Douglas, fencing with Charles of Orleans, or running round the long perimeter of the castle gardens – though his refusals were gentle, if abstracted. There was in fact a mild and congenial preoccupation about him which was entirely new to them all. He was content to stroll or sit on the warm grass of the terrace-garden, directly below his tower window, doing nothing else at all – a thing quite unheard of. In the afternoon, he was back in the same place, this time with his lute, and striking occasional pellucid chords. He was composing a new song, John Lyon decided – but evidently not with any urgency.

The prisoners' wing, needless to say, was not in the best part of the huge castle, being near to the kitchens and the servants' quarters. There was little or no passage of courtiers or quality in its precincts, or its part of the gardens, save for the captives themselves. Certainly no fair ladies strolled that way, by day, with dogs or in better company – though bold-eyed kitchen wenches on occasion did find their way thither, not infrequently to disappear giggling behind bushes and shrubberies with love-starved hostages.

James showed no signs of impatience or disappointment.

In the evening there was dancing and song in the Great Hall, as usual, but James still would not go to watch. Orleans was not the man to miss such, even as a spectator, and James was glad to push off Douglas with him, and even a not entirely reluctant John Lyon, to get back to his pen and paper until the light failed him. He was in bed long before the others returned.

In the morning he was up betimes, foolishly early indeed, to take up his stance beside the window. His heart sank when he saw that it was nothing like so fine a day, with grey skies and a fitful wind. Nevertheless the nightingale sang again, and the cuckoos still called, and he had hope – all of which he needed before at last, after it seemed endless waiting, he heard the tinkling bell again, and saw the little dog come bounding.

The same heart missed a beat thereafter, however, and for an instant its owner knew utter despair, as another young woman, plump and comely enough, appeared in view. Then he perceived that she was smiling and talking – talking to his own fair creature of the day before. All was well with James Stewart's world again.

She was as before, save that today she had a light mantle cast over her shoulders against the slight chill of the morning. Listening to the other though not herself talking at this moment, her face was the more animated and alive. She was all loveliness, entirely to be worshipped and adored.

Grievously brief was the arc of his vision, and she was gone. But in a few tense minutes he was uplifted, for not only were the pair coming back but this time they had taken a turn round farther across the terrace; now, returning, they were fully fifty yards away across the grass but coming directly towards his window at an angle which kept them in his view for greatly longer. He blessed his beauty for this act of charity, unconscious as it must be. And for the slowness of her pacing.

The other girl's glance was never still, just as her lips seemed never to cease their chatter. Time and again she seemed to look up towards his window – as no doubt towards others in that tower. But her companion kept her gaze downbent; that is, until they were almost below the walling, and hateful stone and lime were about to interpose. Then she lifted her eyes to look full at his window for wonderful, glorious seconds – and James this time did not draw back. For a timeless moment their eyes indeed met and held, before masonry came between.

It was some considerable while thereafter before the poet was in a condition to take up his pen again.

For the time being, the prisoner's life was altogether changed. Indeed, for the first time in thirteen years, he felt scarcely a prisoner. It may have been that the incident happened at an exceptionally impressionable moment in his career. Undoubtedly the unnatural conditions in which he lived, allied to a romantic temperament kept rigorously under control, rendered him particularly vulnerable to the effects of some such experience. Probably, too, his intense and wholehearted reaction was something in the nature of a release-valve, or a subconscious grasping at a life-line, much needed, when his desperately stretched self-discipline had come near to breaking-point. Be that as it may, James Stewart's horizons were suddenly and joyfully vastly enlarged, and the bonds of his captivity in consequence lay infinitely more lightly upon him.

Strangely perhaps, for the moment he was content with this shining revelation, happy to clutch his new awareness and felicity to himself, to worship thus from afar. He made no attempt even to discover the identity of the young woman. When, next morning she came walking again, with friend and dog, even though there was rain in the air and she must wear cloak and hood – so that he could not be sure whether or no from its shadow she looked up at his window – he knew only jubilation and a great gratitude.

That day, however, the real reason for his being at Windsor at all was revealed. In the late afternoon a chamberlain brought a summons for the Lord James to attend on

King Henry forthwith. Envoys from Scotland had arrived, it seemed, at the castle.

In his previous frame of mind, James would have resented and probably rejected this peremptory summons on grounds that if the King of England desired to speak with the King of Scots then let him come to do so. But because of the new warmth within him, he forbore to criticise openly, and delayed the chamberlain only for sufficient time to indicate that he was not to be ordered into the presence like some lackey. Moreover, he insisted on taking his secretary, John Lyon, and his esquire David Douglas, along with him.

They were escorted to a handsome high-roofed chamber, hung with armorial shields and banners, in the principal part of the castle. Henry sat on a raised chair-of-state at the far end of the apartment, with a table before him and perhaps a dozen men standing below it.

Although the chamberlain led the way forward, James, with vivid memories of another such occasion, at Westminster Palace thirteen years before, stood his ground at the door, waiting. When, presently, something of a silence fell upon the room, he nodded to John Lyon.

The priest lifted up his voice in richest intonation. "James, King of Scots, Duke of Rothesay, Earl of Carrick and Baron of Renfrew!" he cried.

In the hush that followed there was some small confusion at the other end of the room. All heads turned. Approximately half of those present, the six Scots envoys, bowed deeply. Some of the Englishmen inclined uncomfortable heads and others looked back at their own monarch. That man sat still, watching.

Henry had changed not a little during his six years' occupancy of the throne. Now a man in his thirty-second year, he was lean almost to the point of emaciation, and looked older. Always he had been hatchet-faced; now his features were fined down, as though by steel, his eyes dark, swift and searching, his chin jutting sternly below a tight mouth. Gone were the marks of dissipation which once had marred him; now his was the ravaged face of a king and warrior who ruled all – all save some gnawing doubt within himself, a man assured of all save his own conscience. He was at present home in England only for a brief interlude from his now almost permanent French warfare.

At length he raised his hand, in a gesture that might have been salutation, or equally well an autocratic beckoning. James chose to interpret it as the former, and moved forward unhurriedly.

As he came close, one man detached himself from the bowing group at the left of the table and came to meet him, to drop on both knees before him, arms unashamedly outstretched. Thicker, heavier, grey-haired now, it was Henry St. Clair, Earl of Orkney.

"Sire!" he exclaimed. "My lord James! At last! God bless and save Your Grace!"

Much moved to see his old friend, James raised him up and embraced him, before them all.

The other five Scots came forward, each to kneel and kiss the royal hand, Orkney naming them – Sir William Douglas of Drumlanrig, Sir James Douglas of Balvenie, the Abbot Hailes of Balmerino, Sir John Forrester of Corstorphine, and Sir Walter Ogilvy of Lintrathen.

Before the last had risen, Henry broke in, tightly. "A touching scene, i' faith! And I ever believed the Scots lacking something in display! Now – may we to business, gentlemen?" He leaned forward over the table. "My lord James – I have brought you here that you might be acquainted with what progress we have made in these negotiations. I do not say that all is yet agreed, but . . ."

"Did I hear you say negotiations, sir?" James interrupted, and deliberately – for to interrupt the king's speech was something that no-one else in all England might presume to do. "Or did I mistake you?"

Henry frowned. "I said negotiations, yes. With these emissaries of Scotland."

"On what subject, sir?"

"On subjects not a few. On the shameful Scottish aid to France. On the question of a Border truce. On my

137

suzerainty. Aye – and even on the matter of your own, h'm, enlargement, my lord."

James drew a deep breath. "I fear Your Majesty is in some error here," he said. "These are not matters on which you *may* negotiate. Talk, yes. Discuss, maybe. But for negotiation, sir, you require the King of Scots, do you not?"

There was a quivering and appalled silence. Henry half-rose from his chair.

"You dare . . . you dare to chaffer words with me, sirrah!" he demanded, eyes blazing. "With me, the King!"

"I do, sir – since I also am King! And in affairs of my kingdom, you must negotiate with *me*!"

"God's death! Are you clean mad, man? I, Henry, negotiate with whom I will! In this case with the rulers of Scotland – the Regent Duke Albany and his Council. Note it, sir – note it well!"

"Which Regent and Council only act in my name. When I can be present in person, their authority lapses. Do you, sir, allow your subjects to negotiate affairs of your realm, when you are at hand?"

"*I* am not a warded captive, by the Mass! A wretched prisoner and pensioner! Without a rag to his back or a crust to eat, that is not of my providing!"

James inclined his head. "King Henry's hospitality is famous!" he said stiffly. "On a balance with his courtesy!"

As they eyed each other, Orkney spoke up, urgently. "Your Graces! Most noble princes! Let us not dispute over a form of words, I pray you. We have but talked, yes. Discussed. Hitherto. Reached nothing of conclusion. Sire – my lord James! *We* sought your presence from the first . . ."

"That I believe, my good lord. I reproach not you."

The Lord Chancellor, Henry Beaufort, Bishop of Winchester, raised his voice. "Your Majesty – this is not to be borne!" he declared. "Here, in your own palace, to be outfaced by these, these . . .!"

Henry raised his hand. "To be sure, Uncle," he said, suddenly soft-voiced. "But we must recollect that our Scots friends have not our . . . advantages!" He sat back in his

138

chair, and actually smiled, if thinly, as all men stared at him, surprised. Henry the Fifth had always had this peculiar and upsetting faculty for doing the totally unexpected, on occasion; of, without warning, reversing his entire position – an unpredictable quality which no doubt contributed not a little to his successes in war. "Let us not waste further time. The Lord James is now present, and we may proceed. Refresh our memories, I pray you my lord Chancellor, as to the matters under discussion."

His uncle, illegitimate son of John of Gaunt, Duke of Lancaster, a proud but able prelate, cleared his throat, frowning. "As Your Majesty wishes," he said shortly. "Proposed by Your Majesty and Council. That a three-year truce be signed forthwith, to halt all further Scots raiding and invading across your Borders. That Scots forces at present aiding the enemies of England be withdrawn from France. That the undoubted suzerainty and paramountcy of the King of England over the realm of Scotland be duly acknowledged and subscribed, once and for all, in a solemn treaty. And that in return, the realm of Scotland be received into the love and peace of Your Majesty, and the Lord James of Scotland to be released from bonds, and after doing due homage, be permitted to return to his own country. These, Your Majesty, are the main heads."

"I thank you, my lord Bishop."

James's bark of mirthless laughter rang out abruptly. "You brought me here to listen to . . . this!" he jerked. "Think you that I would agree to my freedom on such terms?"

"Are they so harsh?"

"They are impossible! You would have me to sell my country's independence for my own release? Would *you*, sir, do such a thing?"

"H'mm. I cannot conceive of the King of England being ever in a position to needs make the choice, my friend!"

There were smiles from the Englishmen present.

James turned on Orkney and the other Scots. "*You* would not consider negotiation on such terms?" he demanded.

139

"No, Sire – no!" Orkney assured him. "This of suzerainty was not so much as mentioned before we left Scotland. Any word of homage. The truce we were to consider. The matter of aid to France, also. But this of paramountcy – no!"

"Yet I did not fail to raise the issue in my letter to your Regent, inviting this embassy," Henry mentioned.

There was silence in that room.

James broke it. "Gentlemen – no purpose is to be served by this meeting, I fear. To my regret. I bid you all good-day!"

As he was turning away, Henry stayed him. "Do you not desire your release, my lord James?" he asked. "Do your bonds so become you? Your warding – has it grown so comfortable?"

"How think you?" James's voice both grated and quivered. "I desire my freedom from this fell bondage more than any words of mine can express. God knows, I have had thirteen years of it! Most of my life. But . . . I will not purchase it at the price of my honour."

Henry treated him to a long, hard look. Then he nodded briefly, apparently in acceptance.

Orkney intervened again. "In default of this of suzerainty, Sire, there is still the wherewithal to bargain. It was on such indeed that we came. His Majesty of England desires an immediate truce, above all. This, with the question of withdrawing the Scots arms and aid from France, is no small abatement. His Majesty has intimated that, lacking what he first asked, he would still treat on these."

"So!" James stroked his chin. Henry, as all knew, had left his armies besieging Rouen, the capital of Normandy. He was about to go back there. When Rouen fell, he would be master of all North France. He could turn his attention to the heart of that unhappy and divided country – Paris. But to do so, he needed to know that his rear was safe, as his lines of communication lengthened seriously. He had made some sort of peace with the Welsh; Owen Glendower was dead, but his son Griffith had at last been sent home. The Irish princes were being placated.

140

Scotland, it seemed, had still something with which to bargain.

"What do you, sir, offer for such concession?" he asked of Henry, slowly.

The other was as careful about his answer – but definite. "I would consider your temporary liberation, my lord," he said. "*Temporary*, I repeat. Your return to ward warranted by the provision of suitable hostages. And the payment of one hundred thousand marks guaranty."

James drew a quick breath, and looked at Orkney – and almost imperceptibly that man nodded. "You . . . you ever deal in money, sir!" he said huskily. "One hundred thousand marks is a vast sum."

"Those are my terms. I shall not change them. Do you accept?" Henry shrugged. "Although, by the Mass, it is not *your* acceptance that signifies in this, so much as your Uncle Albany's!"

The younger man bit his lip, glancing again at the Scots envoys. Their faces betrayed a variety of emotions – though clearly Orkney at least was for acceptance. "I . . . I must consider this well," he said, at last. "I must have time for thought. For reflection. With my friends . . ."

"Very well. You have until tomorrow. Tonight, I give a banquet in honour of the Scots embassage. You, my lord James, will be welcome. You may there discuss with your friends." Crisply he spoke, and rose to his feet. "My lords – this audience is ended." Turning about, he strode to a side door – before his fellow-monarch might make a move.

Coldly, the Chancellor took over. "This way, my lord James, if you please . . ."

Later that evening, James sat in Windsor's Great Hall like an honoured guest and no prisoner. But not a guest too greatly honoured. Henry had been clever about this. The positioning of the awkward royal visitor posed a delicate problem. His rank, of course, entitled him to sit at the host's right hand at the dais-table – but such placing was not to be considered in the circumstances. On the other

141

hand, since this great repast was ostensibly in honour of the Scots envoys, it was out of the question to place their monarch less honourably than themselves. Henry had got over the difficulty by providing a small special table for the Scots party, placed sideways on the dais, at the head of which he set King James.

The Earl of Orkney was talking earnestly, his voice lowered. ". . . not to accept, Sire, would be folly, I say. Temporary liberation is better than no liberation. Once Your Grace is free, you may well be able to prolong that freedom!"

James did not answer. He was gazing abstractedly towards the main dais-table.

Orkney went on. "All these so many years, Sire, you have waited – and I have sought fruitlessly to gain your release. At last, after all the failures and heartbreaks, it becomes possible. Do not let it fail again – this time by your own too nice scruple!"

"You think scruple would be but folly, my lord?"

The older man looked quickly at his young liege lord, so greatly changed by the intervening years. James's question had sounded hypothetical, almost absent-minded.

"In this case yes, Sire. Your capture, in the first place, was against all law and justice. Piracy. Your prolonged captivity has been infamous, without scruple. Henry, who is no fool, knows that well. Why must *you* show all the scruple? Accept, I say." He lowered his voice still further. "Mark you, Albany will foil all, if he can. He will prevent your return to Scotland by any means to his evil hand. He did not want to send this embassage – but Bishop Wardlaw prevailed upon the other bishops and prelates in the Council to force him." His glance slid round the Scots table. "Do not trust all these, Sire! The two Douglases, Drumlanrig and Balvenie. They are Albany's men. Forrester, Ogilvy and the Abbot are all sound."

"Ah, yes. Indeed. Good!" James nodded – but his eyes, and the nod itself, seemed to be directed elsewhere. "See you that loveliness which sits at Henry's table?" he asked.

"Between the young Earl of Somerset and the Archbishop. Who is she, do you know?"

"What is that?" Frowning, the Earl turned. "No – I do not know, Your Grace. As I was saying, Albany will try to ensure that this matter comes to naught, as he has done all others – whilst seeming to seek your release. He will fail to find the moneys . . ."

"Ah!" James said.

"Yes. But the Church may find it. The Primate, Wardlaw, remains your true friend. And even those bishops and abbots who are less leal to Your Grace hate Albany – who has enriched the nobles at the Church's expense. Nor have they forgot how he kept Benedict's Papal Annates to ransom only Murdoch, and to line his own purse! The Church, I believe, will find your hundred thousand marks, great sum as it is. Despite Albany."

"That is well. I shall be much beholden to Holy Church." James was only toying with the rich food, different as it was from his normal plain fare. "She must be high-born indeed, to be sitting there amongst the great ones. She is of the most perfect beauty, is she not?"

"Eh . . .? Orkney drummed finger-nails on the table. "No doubt, Sire. I am no judge in such matters. Now – on the question of the hostages. Here, I say, is your great opportunity! Guile must be fought with guile." He was whispering now. "Once you are back in Scotland, there is no lack of enemies of Your Grace whom you may choose to send as hostages for King Henry! Many bearing the name of Douglas, no doubt! Such as would serve you a deal better out of Scotland! And . . . there need be as little haste to redeem them as there has been' you!"

The other sighed. "My lord – you would make a rogue of me?"

"A king, Sire – a king!" the Earl amended. "Kings must needs use the tools which come to their hands."

"Aye. Perhaps." James leaned forward, to speak down the table to where John Lyon sat at the foot with David Douglas. "Master John – you know much that goes on about this

143

court, I believe? Who is the lady who sits yonder between Somerset and the Archbishop?"

The priest turned on his bench. And even as he did so, the young woman in question raised her eyes towards the Scots' table, as though she was well aware that she was being spoken of – to James's somewhat evident confusion.

"Why, Your Grace – that is my lord of Somerset's sister," Lyon informed. "The Lady Joanna Beaufort. Daughter to the former Earl of Somerset, who was eldest natural son to John of Gaunt, Duke of Lancaster and brother to the Chancellor Beaufort – and half-brother to the late King Henry. Therefore she is cousin to the present king."

"Ummm." James's face fell. "So . . . so near to the throne! A Beaufort!"

"Nearer yet, Sire. For her mother, I have heard, was daughter to the Earl of Kent, and therefore niece to Richard the Second, of the other line! Moreover, who married again after Somerset's death, and is now Duchess of Clarence, and so sister-in-law to King Henry!"

"You say so!" James muttered. "Is it so, indeed!" He relapsed into silence.

It is to be feared that he heard little more of Orkney's important, indeed vital, talk thereafter.

The meal over and some entertainment offered by singers, players and tumblers, the ladies retired, and King Henry shortly afterwards. James immediately rose to leave, whilst men were still on their feet. He told Orkney and the other envoys that he would give them his decision on the morrow.

Whatever it was that preoccupied his mind on the way back to his quarters, he plucked a red rose from a bush as he went.

The morning dawned wet and blustery. No nightingale sang, no cuckoos called. James, too early risen, paced his small chamber more fretfully than he had done for days, unsettled. Because of the gusty wind, he did not hear the tinkling of the little dog's bell, so that only out of the corner of his eye did he glimpse, in his striding, a slight figure,

144

heavily cloaked against the weather, hastening by below. In a surge of joy returned, he pressed himself against the window-jamb, looking for her return. He saw the dog come first. At sight of it, he snatched up the rose which he had pulled the previous night, and threw it out of the open casement.

Unfortunately the wind caught the flower and whisked it away, so that where it fell James could not see. Indeed, he caught only a brief sight of a miniver-edged cloak that passed too close below the walling for him to see more. He was reasonably content, nevertheless.

In the forenoon, when the Scots party came to enquire of his decision, he told them that he would agree to the idea of the temporary release, and to Henry's terms therefore.

That evening there was music and dancing as usual in the Great Hall, and with the Scots envoys due to leave for home the following morning, James was again specifically invited to attend – and could scarcely refuse to go.

On this occasion there were no formalities. Henry was already present when James arrived – indeed dancing. The younger man's heart missed a beat when he perceived that it was with the Lady Joanna Beaufort that the King danced. It missed several more when, as the slow and stately measure brought in turn each couple close to where James stood, with Charles of Orleans and Orkney, he saw that on the swelling bosom of Lady Joanna's white-and-gold gown was pinned a single distinctly limp and faded red rose.

Henry was not a man who could ever be really genial or relaxed. But tonight he was in a good mood, jerky and less than gracious, but affable after his own fashion. After dancing, he moved round amongst the thronging courtiers and guests. Presently he came to James's side. Orleans and Orkney moved discreetly back.

"So, Cousin – we are in agreement, for once!" he said. "Here is cause for celebration indeed!"

"If it give *you* cause for satisfaction, then perhaps it behoves *me* to think again!" James returned grimly.

"You see it so? Might it not be, conceivably, to our mutual benefit?"

"Has anything, in the last thirteen years, worked to your advantage – and mine?"

The other shrugged. "No great deal, perhaps, as yet. But who knows – we may do better hereafter." He paused. "Your Uncle Albany grows old," he added.

Sharply James glanced at him. "Yes?"

"He may not live much longer. Then . . . there may be occasion for some co-operation between our realms, Cousin."

"I think that there has been some co-operation already, sir! For . . . for those same thirteen years, in fact!"

Henry frowned. Then forced a smile again. "We may find it possible to do better," he repeated. "For our two realms' sake."

"Pray God so, indeed! But – not while you presume to claim paramountcy, overlordship, over mine!"

Henry looked almost as though he would move on. But he unclamped his rat-trap jaws again. "That we shall see," he said. "But, see you, there may be areas of co-operation open to us, otherwhere. In France, for instance. I shall be King of France one day. Soon."

James said nothing.

"When that happens, it would be well that we were friends, would it not? Well – for Scotland!"

The younger man could not deny it. The entire balance of power had for centuries demanded that Scotland and France be always in mutual alliance, in order to contain the dynamic and aggressive England, north and south. Albany's support for the Auld Alliance had been markedly feeble, however – and Henry now controlled a third of France. If he gained it all, it would indeed be politic for Scotland, isolated, to be England's friend rather than her enemy.

"Friendship I would welcome," James said slowly. "Scotland's thralldom, under English suzerainty – never! I have had my bellyful of that!"

"It is friendship that I think of, Cousin." Henry actually touched the other's arm. "How think you to come campaigning with me in France, James? Ha – cousins-in-arms, eh?"

James stared, swallowing. "What . . . what mean you?" he got out, thickly.

"Just what I say, my friend. I return to France within the month. Come you with me. This temporary release need not take you forthwith to Scotland. Where, if my spies speak true, the Regent, your uncle, and his powerful friends, scarce pine for your return! Whatever my lord of Orkney there says. The two Douglases, I swear, sing a different tune! What is to be gained by an immediate return to Scotland? Let us have this truce – and then come with me and earn your spurs in France! It would be my pleasure to knight you, in person, on the field of battle. As a king should be knighted! Albany is now seventy-nine, no less. And, I am told, failing. When he is gone – then the way will be open for your return to your realm, as a monarch, not as a suppliant!"

That was potent talking. Henry was no fool, and no doubt knew well how tempting was his proposition. James came of a proud and warlike race – however feeble his father. He was aged twenty-five years, and had never acted the warrior, drawn sword in battle or known the glory and chivalry of knighthood that was his birthright. To a young man of spirit, heir of Bruce, Canmore and MacAlpine, refusal to exchange his four prison walls for a place at the side of the most illustrious warrior in Christendom scarcely bore contemplation. And what Henry said of Albany was nothing less than the truth.

"I . . . I . . ." James began, and stopped, biting his lip.

It was the Lady Joanna who came to his rescue – if that is what it was. She was dancing now with the Earl of Warwick, and as they came sailing gracefully past in a slow Provençal waltz, her eyes met and smiled into those of James. He perceived that they were hazel, flecked with green. She swept on, to leave him as though invigorated.

147

He drew himself up, following her with his glance, and it was moments before he spoke. "I thank you," he said carefully. "I will consider what you have said."

Henry's brows came down in a dark bar across his narrow face – but he followed the direction of his companion's gaze thoughtfully. "Aye – do so, my lord James," he said, his voice changed. He moved on.

As soon as the waltz ended, James threaded his way through the colourful company to where Warwick chatted with his partner. There he was content to stand a little way off, drinking in her beauty. She had a sort of latent vivacity about her of which he had not been aware.

She quickly perceived him, and a faint flush mounted from her throat. With a word to Warwick, she sank down in a deep curtsy.

James shook his head, and hurried forward to raise her up. Her hand in his sent shivers through him. He raised it to his lips, eyes searching her lovely face. He, to whom words were important, could not think of a word to say.

Warwick, brows raised, bowed himself off.

"Your Majesty greatly honours me," she murmured.

"No!" That was almost a hot denial. "*You* do the honour. You only." He paused. "The rose . . .!"

"Yes," she said, and her fingers went up lightly to touch the faded petals.

They both smiled, nodding.

So they stood, side by side now, in that crowded place, while the courtiers eddied around and eyed them with undisguised interest. Strangely, at the moment, there seemed to be no need for words.

"You are very beautiful," James declared, at last. It was a statement of fact as he said it. "The most beautiful I have ever looked upon. And kind."

"It pleases me that Your Majesty should think me so," she answered simply. "Even though it be less than truth. And though I feel kind now, it is not always so."

'You have been kind to me," he said.

She shook her head. "Not kind. I think that Your Majesty is so little used to kindness that you mistake. Beauty also, perhaps."

He shook his head. "I do not mistake. I think much of these things. Having perhaps little else to do! And do not call me Majesty. Others do not."

"Shall I not then be different, Sire?"

"Nor Sire, either. Yonder strange man only is Sire to you." He nodded across the floor to where King Henry could be seen talking with the Earl of Orkney. "I would have you different, yes. Call me only James."

"Would that not be presumption?"

"It would be my command — were a captive king's commands of any worth. As it is, I make it my plea."

"I accept it as a royal command," she said. "But before others, I must still call you Majesty. The more so in that others do not!" There was a spurt of spirit here.

He sighed. "Majesty I have none of — in person or in state. But a little grace I do ever seek. Grace is our Scots custom. If you must, call me that. Before others."

"I shall . . . James."

"I' faith — I had never thought it a sweet name! Until now!"

They were silent again, and for long, but without unease or embarrassment. It seemed that they could converse together very well without words.

Presently, up in the minstrels' gallery amongst the musicians a pair of Spanish singers sang a duet, a strange song apparently of love and war and conflicting passions, now stirring, now languorous, now jarring in sudden savage discord. The words were unintelligible, but more than once James and the girl found each other's eyes involuntarily at certain passages. Here also they found no need for words.

"It was well sung," the Lady Joanna said, when it was over. "You also sing, they say? And divinely."

"Who so says?"

"The Lady Warwick, who is my friend. She says also that you play on the lute, like a very angel. Other instruments

149

likewise. Aye, and that you make up your own songs. That you are a poet, indeed!"

"I scribble poor verses, and string a chord or two, yes – lacking more manly employment. The Lady Warwick, I think, must lack judgement – save in that she chooses good friends!"

"Do all the others lack judgement also? Who say that the Lord James of Scotland is one of the best swordsmen in England. Likewise one of the best horsemen, hunters, wrestlers, tennis-players." She smiled. "Even, I have heard it whispered on the best authority, notable at swimming and running."

He looked at her quickly. "Swimming . . .?"

"To be sure. Like any . . . stag!"

"Ha! The Forest of Sherwood! Trotter's Mere." Suddenly he faltered. "Save my soul! You . . . *you* were not there?"

"No. I would be then but ten or eleven years. But my mother was . . ."

"Of course – the Duchess of Clarence!"

"Often she had told me. How the King of Scots went swimming. After a hunted deer. To save it, not to kill it. When the hounds would not enter the water. And came out of the lake, to walk with all the dignity in the world, mother-naked before all! And then challenged the Lord Grey, or any man, to outrun him back ten miles to Nottingham Castle . . ."

"Six," James corrected. "Six miles, only."

"Since when I have never failed in my interest in James of Scotland!"

He cleared his throat. "I was . . . very young," he said.

A minuet they danced, the first measure James had trod for many a day. Then the young Earl of Somerset, brusque and awkward, came to claim his sister, saying that King Henry was holding private entertainment in another chamber – and making it clear that he did not consider James to be invited. Joanna, flushing, seemed as though she would not only rebuke her brother but refuse to accompany him,

150

when James took her hand, to raise it to his lips again. She sank then in another deep curtsy, her eyes holding his, and so stayed until he turned away – to the annoyed mutterings of John Beaufort.

James, heart singing, was anxious only to escape from the throng now, to win out into the May night where he might be alone with his thoughts. But Orkney waylaid him.

"Your Grace," he said, "a word in your ear. I believe that we are in a stronger position than we knew. I have been speaking with King Henry and his Chancellor Beaufort, both. It seems that they are more concerned for the French situation than we understood. Henry is wholly set on gaining the French throne. All else is to be subservient to that. Consequently he needs Scotland's good will the more. We must take advantage of this, Sire."

"To be sure," James nodded, moving on.

"We might have won better terms for your release, had we realised it," the Earl went on urgently. "Even now something may be possible. But . . . it augurs well for the future, I swear. I think that we need no longer fear that your freedom will be only temporary."

"I rejoice to hear it, my friend. Now . . ."

"Sire – King Henry would have you accompany him to France. Has he spoken of the matter to you? Here is a most happy proposal. You will serve your own cause better in France, meantime, than in Scotland, I vow. At this moment, Albany and Douglas are assembling a great army to go to France, to aid in their struggle. Many thousands. Douglas himself to command. Some have already sailed. No doubt Henry's spies have informed him – and this is part reason for his new policy towards you. Use it, Sire, to your own advantage – as he would use you. These are *your* subjects. If you were in France also – see you how the situation would be changed. A great army of Scots, and you their liege lord! They will not all love Douglas, that is certain – for he is a man whom few love. You could displace him – the King! And then, Sire – when you return to Scotland, you would have an army at your back! To face your foes in Scotland. What think you of that?"

James had paused, tapping toe on the floor, and frowning. He did not answer.

Orkney went on. "Moreover, this of your marriage. This also should aid your course . . ."

"Marriage?" the younger man interrupted swiftly. "What are you saying, man?"

"Chancellor Beaufort let fall this project, Sire. That Henry would have you to wed one close to his own royal house. Would seal and confirm your friendship and co-operation thus. Admittedly it would serve his cause – but yours also. To be allied to the mightiest prince in Christendom today, in marriage, would be no disadvantage. Especially when you return to Scotland. I cannot think that Albany would rejoice! And an heir to the throne ever strengthens a prince." The older man smiled. "And if my eyes do not deceive me – you would find the prospect none so ill!"

Orkney's smile was wiped off his face by the other's reaction. James gripped the Earl's arm fiercely. "God's mercy – you say that this is Henry's doing?" he cried. "*He* planned this? Planned it all . . .?"

"Why yes, Sire. But . . . is it not well? To your great gain . . .?"

Violently the older man was flung aside as, without another word, his companion strode for the door.

James thereafter had indeed an hour alone with his thoughts in the May night, before guards came to conduct him back to his own chamber, a man near stricken.

Next morning when the Lady Joanna Beaufort walked her dog on the terrace below the castle walls, though the sun shone and the nightingale sang, no eager eyes watched for her at the arrow-slit window. James Stewart, though awake, lay still abed with his face to the wall.

10

Still another castle's walls to enclose the captive; another terrace on which to stalk back and forth like a caged lion; and most strangely, another Joan Beaufort to rub salt into an open wound. This was Raby Castle in the County of Durham; the lady was the Countess of Westmorland, aunt to the younger woman; and Scotland's border lay little more than fifty miles to the north. In consequence of which, the guard on the royal prisoner was increased and strengthened as never before.

Here at Raby, indeed, there were few signs of King Henry's new policy of friendship and leniency towards his captive, apart altogether from the precautions necessitated by the geographical situation. James, it could be said, had only himself to blame. Since that night at Windsor, he had been scarcely co-operative.

This fine warm afternoon of June was more apt for sitting at ease in the castle pleasance, idling the waiting hours away, smelling the scents of the flowers and new-mown hay, and listening to the drowsy hum of the bees and the distant lowing of cattle across the water-meadows. Some did that, indeed, in three distinct groups, watching and waiting. But not James Stewart. He paced alone, back and forward, back and forward, over the same stretch of turf, a stocky, tense, lonely figure – but one that most evidently cherished its aloneness.

This was his sixth day at Raby – and unless the Scots came today, it would be his last. One week was all that Henry, wary, suspicious, and affronted, was permitting. Already the English patience was strained. The Scots ambassadors, with the money and the hostages, should have been at Pontefract, in Yorkshire seventy miles farther south, ten days ago at least. James had awaited them there for two impatient weeks. When they did not come, he had urged and pleaded that they be given a little longer, that a move further north, to meet them, be made. Reluctantly the Bishop of Durham and the Earl of Westmorland, in charge of the exchange arrangements, had acquiesced – but sent couriers hot-foot south for royal confirmation. Henry, in the act of setting out for France, had acceded; but no farther north than Raby, he said – and for a further seven days only. If the matter was not settled by then, the prisoner was to be returned to the Tower of London forthwith. And let every precaution be taken against anything like a rescue raid across the Border.

In all the young man's years of bondage he had never known bitterness such as this. To have tasted the sweet fruits of love, and anticipated freedom, both, and to have them turn to gall and wormwood in his mouth – this was too much. Perfidy in his captors he could accept; but perfidy in that fairest of all creatures was beyond all bearing. And now, it seemed, perfidy in his own countrymen and subjects, humiliation, shame.

Worsening his hurt and mortification, of course, was the knowledge that he had in some measure brought it upon himself. He had brusquely rejected Henry's invitation to go with him to France, insisting on the fulfilment of the agreement for his temporary release and return to Scotland, commanding Orkney to see that the business was expedited. And here he was, only fifty short miles from his own land, after three weeks of waiting – and neither envoys nor hostages and money had appeared, as arranged.

Yet, as he paced there, truth to tell, it was not so much his humiliating and unwanted state that exercised the young man's mind as the other, more personal, matter. The questions never left his mind in peace. How could she have done it? How could anyone so lovely, so pure-seeming, so proudly honest, have allowed herself to be used to ensnare him in a base plot? How could she so act bait to trap him into Henry's scheme of marriage?

A thousand times he had asked himself if he could anyways have misjudged her. Could she be innocent in it all? But the facts would offer him no gleam of comfort. Henry had decided to try to make him subservient to him for life by marrying him to one of his own near kindred. Joanna was the only woman who might fit the case, the only close cousin Henry possessed, unmarried and of suitable age. She did not normally attend his Court – but he had brought her to Windsor, and within a day or two she was making her cunning, sweet but false assault upon the prisoner. The timing was exact – just when he was to be uplifted and aroused by hopes of freedom and possible knightly renown in France. It was inconceivable that she did not know – for assuredly she lacked nothing in wits and intelligence.

James could find no comfort anywhere – and certainly none in the hopes which had buoyed up David Douglas, that at any moment a hard-riding, mosstrooping force of Scots Borderers might appear on the scene in a gallant dash to rescue their monarch. The Laird of Whittinghame and John Lyon sat nearby watching their unhappy liege lord, reluctantly admitting to themselves that it would demand a very large and desperate force to effect such rescue now, for all the country between Raby and the Border was standing mobilised and alert. The three men who formed the second of the lounging groups in that pleasant terrace garden in fact controlled between them almost the entire North of England – the Prince-Bishop of Durham; Raby's own lord, Ralph Neville, Earl of Westmorland, Warden of the English West March; and James's old fellow-pupil Henry Percy, Earl of Northumberland, Warden of the East March. These, however anxious they might have been earlier, when no envoys appeared, were now at ease and relaxed. Their people roused and on the watch along every mile of the Border, and standing to arms in depth at innumerable points between, meant that no raiding column could make any move into England without being at least spotted and delayed while word was sent to Raby. The expected envoys had been sent strict instructions to come only by the coast road, via Berwick and Alnwick; no other approach was to be permitted. But from that direction also no message came. Unless they travelled furiously and by night – which scarcely was to be expected of a diplomatic party – the matter was finished, the period of grace over.

The third group of watchers was rather differently concerned. This comprised the Countess of Westmorland and her ladies, sitting in an arbour of the pleasance near to one end of the prisoner's promenade space. James undoubtedly had come to have a certain attraction for the other sex – partly of course because of the romantic character of a king in chains, but more particularly on account of his known poetic temperament and the sombre, smouldering good looks which he had developed. These ladies were much intrigued, pleasantly titillated and mildly distressed by the plight of their royal visitor, the Countess Joan in especial.

Presently that lady rose, and laying aside her tambour-frame came over to intercept the man at his striding. She was a tall angular woman, thin as a rake but handsome in a haggard fashion, with great dark eyes – youngest of John of Gaunt's illegitimate Beaufort brood, and therefore half-sister to the late Henry the Fourth. She was reputed to be something of a dragon – but perhaps not where personable young men were concerned. At anyrate, her attitude to James, as she came up, was solicitude itself.

"My lord James," she said, "it is too hot a day for all this grievous marching! I vow you have us in a sweat but watching you! Come and sit with us, I pray you. It is known that you sing fit to charm a bird from a tree . . ."

"I thank you, lady," James returned, "but I feel like walking – and by no means like singing!"

"No? I am sorry. Then, will you not pleasure us with the lute, perhaps? Since in this also you excel, I have heard." She smiled. "If your playing must needs be sorrowful – then that we shall accept."

"My regrets. I would not wish to offend – but I am scarcely in a mood for dalliance. The reasons should be evident . . ."

"Why yes, my lord. Fate uses you ill in certain matters, to be sure. But . . ." She smiled again. ". . . there are compensations, are there not? In other matters, are you not rather to be congratulated?"

"It may be so, lady – but if it is, it has escaped my perception!"

"La, sir – do not cozen an old woman!" Playfully the Countess tapped his arm. "We are not so remote up here in the North that we do not hear whispers of what is toward at Court. I think Your Highness may not be altogether heart-broken if you have to return to the South tomorrow! Is there not a certain young woman whose charms may serve to console you in this pass?"

James drew himself up stiffly. "Your ladyship has been . . . misinformed," he said.

"Sakes! Are you ungallant? Or bashful? Or but wary, my lord! Come – you need not dissemble before me – for am I not one of the family, to be sure."

"One of a family, since you say it, ma'am, of whom I have discovered good reason to be wary!" he returned. "You must forgive me if I watch all such more heedfully in the future!" With a curt bow, he turned on his heel, to stalk in the other direction.

James had only gone a few paces from the affronted lady, however, when he was brought to a halt again by shouting from the far end of the terrace, where men were pointing. He turned, to see, riding swiftly across the level parkland towards the castle, a tight body of men, armour glinting in the sun. For a moment, his heart rose.

But only for a moment. The banner that fluttered at a lancehead behind the foremost rider, he perceived, bore three golden leopards on red – the royal arms of England. It was no large banner, however, and must signify only one of Henry's couriers. But one in a hurry, it seemed. And well escorted.

157

James resumed his walking.

It was not long until a weary and travel-stained knight was brought before the Prince-Bishop and the two earls – and but a little later all four came together to confront the pacing captive.

"My lord James," the stout Bishop Langley announced, puffing. "Here is Sir Richard Spice. He brings new orders from King Henry."

"I am acquainted with Sir Richard," James commented grimly. "He was long my jailer in the Tower – lieutenant to the Constable. Has he come to take me back there?"

"Not so, my lord. Sir Richard's instructions are otherwise. If the Scottish envoys, with the moneys and hostages, are not here at Raby by sundown tonight, it is His Majesty's wish that you be carried south tomorrow. To join him in France, forthwith."

"France . . .? Tomorrow?" James swallowed. "What is this? France? I told Henry that I would not go to France."

"His Majesty's command," Sir Richard said briefly.

"I would remind you that no man *commands* me to do anything, sir!"

"Tut, my lord – the commands are for Sir Richard," the Bishop put in hurriedly. "He requests, as instructed, that you accompany him. Tomorrow. For it is impossible now that your ambassadors should come in time. Word would have been brought us had they crossed the Border."

James inclined his head, lips tight.

"On my soul, James – here's good fortune for you!" Henry Percy cried. "Better fortune, I swear, than a cold welcome in Scotland! Would that it was myself! That I could accompany you. I besought King Harry to take me – but he would have it that I must needs hold the East March secure for him. In France, I say, you will find what you will not in Scotland – battle, glory, honour!"

"His Majesty acts you fair in this," the Earl of Westmorland said, not unkindly.

"If so, it is for his own purposes," James answered levelly.

"I shall withhold my thanks until I discover what they are! Meantime, consider me at your service, gentlemen."

Nevertheless, next morning, when James, with his two companions, turned his back on Scotland and took the long road south, strongly escorted, he did so with a certain relief. Since he could do nothing about his two great problems, it was perhaps as well that those facing him now were likely to be new ones. And France . . .!

PART THREE

11

Two days out of Southampton, James paced the poop-deck of his ship, and eyed the white chalk cliffs of Dieppe with mixed feelings. It was fourteen years since he had set sail from Scotland for fair France – and now, at long last, he was about to reach it. He was to have been kept safe and educated in France, until Scotland called him back; but Scotland had not called him back, and he had been held all too safe in England instead, and educated as an Englishman – well educated too, as he had to concede. And now the France which he belatedly approached was as different a place as was James Stewart a person. It was a war-torn, shattered, betrayed and almost hopeless land – and he was an emotion-torn, betrayed and not notably hopeful man, brought here at the caprice of others. So much for fourteen years.

And yet, James could not but know an upsurge of spirit and vigour and some sort of hope. From the moment of feeling the heaving timbers of a ship beneath his feet again, he had become almost a new man, his head held no higher but less stiffly, his eyes brighter, his tread more lightsome. Until then he had scarcely been able to accept the change which had come over his circumstances; the feel of the vessel and the sea had made it real to him. He was still not a free man, of course – but the walls of his prison had drawn back mightily. No doubt he would have trials and distresses to face in France also, and almost inevitably a clash of wills and loyalties – but surely there would be space about him, new experiences, adventure, sheer action, for a vigourous young man who had mouldered within walls for too long. James Stewart was not fundamentally stern, sober, or proudly awkward; only circumstances had imposed these characteristics upon him. Now his two faithful companions, John Lyon and David Douglas, saw another James emerging – and rejoiced.

They landed at the wharves of Dieppe, within the Arques-mouth, busy with the transport of war rather than the trade for which they had grown, still under the escort of Sir Richard Spice and his men-at-arms. They wasted no time in Dieppe, however much James would have liked to look about his first French town; Spice most evidently took entirely literally his instructions to deliver the Scots king to his own monarch as quickly as possible. Within half-an-hour of landing, the tight and well-armed company was trotting southwards along the straight road to Rouen. Behind the men-at-arms came a small baggage-train of pack-horses bearing the armour, tents, banners and weapons, to the value of £150, which Henry had apparently authorised Spice to purchase for the due equipping of the new royal campaigner. James had not been consulted in the matter, and was under no illusions as to the disinterested nature of this sudden generosity.

That first ride through France opened the captive's eyes to another aspect of war than that imbued in him by his upbringing, knightly training, the talk of Court and the songs of minstrels. He saw a countryside which should have been rich – however flat and monotonous – fertile and prosperous, as now a man-made desert that stank of death and corruption. Everywhere were ruined empty villages, burned farmsteads, desecrated churches, broken bridges and untended fields now rioting with weeds. Gib-bets, well-laden, decorated every cross-roads and deserted market-place – symbolic of King Henry's stern determina-tion to put down brigandage and restore law and order to this occupied area, Sir Richard explained. Apparently quite small children were amongst the most active brigands.

They smelt Rouen, capital of Normandy, on the warm southerly wind, long before they reached it. Though the city had fallen, after its prolonged siege, fully a year before, it still was one vast shambles, witnessing to the ferocity of victors and vanquished alike; its proud cathedral rising amongst the ruins, superficially undamaged, seeming both a mockery and an indictment of men. It was evening when they approached the city, but they did not enter within its grim and broken ramparts, preferring to spend the night at the English army encampment outside, to the east. Great armies of French prisoners and peasants were being forced to clear the place, it seemed – but disease stalked apace. Twelve thousand useless townsfolk had been thrust out, between walls and besiegers, to die of starvation under the eyes of both sides.

Spice would by no means allow James to inspect any closer than the shattered main gates.

Next day they changed direction to head almost due eastwards, making for Beauvais – a long day's ride of sixty miles through ever more newly devastated country. The Dauphin's forces and the Orleanists or Armagnacs had held this area until quite recently – and many of the sad scars were old enough to be of their making, equally with those of the English. France's civil wars between the Orleans faction and that of Burgundy – respectively brother and uncle of King Charles – to gain control over that mad king's domains, were fully as destructive as the activities of the invaders.

Still farther east, the day following, to Soissons – this to avoid the Paris area, still held by the Dauphin, King Charles' heir. English garrisons held these Picardy towns – but thereafter the occupying troops were largely Burgundian. Sir Richard did not trust them, and chose to requisition any suitable shelter for the night that he could find, away from towns. The fall of Rouen to the English had to some extent helped to heal the breach between Burgundy and Orleans, and the Duke had at last agreed to aid his nephew the Dauphin in resisting the invaders. But in September last Burgundy himself was treacherously assassinated, the Dauphin looking on, and the fragile French harmony was shattered. His successor, Duke Philip, furiously turned to

Henry, and now the Burgundians and the English were allies, facing the Dauphin and Orleans faction plus the Castilians and the Scots. Nevertheless Spice's attitude was typical of the English; you never trusted a foreigner.

From Soissons the travellers turned south again, and in two hard-riding days through the rolling Champagne country, reached the upper Seine, and journey's end at the splendid city of Troyes.

Troyes, Henry's headquarters, and capital of Champagne, was so far untouched save by the more picturesque and colourful aspects of war. A handsome and exciting city in its own right, it was now ringed with the many-hued pavilioned encampments of much of Europe's chivalry, and its narrow streets, tall palaces and quaint timbered houses seethed with half of Christendom's nobility. Scarcely a building but flew the heraldic banner of some duke, count, lord or baron; knights roosted in garrets and cellars; and their trains jostled each other in proud and frequently violent rivalry in every lane and alley and all the thousand wine-shops of this the wine metropolis of France.

James's reception at Troyes was almost laughably other than he had anticipated. After all Sir Richard's to-do and haste, his charge was two whole days and nights in Troyes before King Henry so much as recognised his presence there – two days which, however, James and his two companions made use of to good effect in savouring the excitements of the busy town, little less than free men for once.

Henry, always a man for sudden and unexpected decision, was in process of getting married. Dissolute to a degree before his accession, he had surprised all by remaining unmarried thus far. Now, abruptly, he decided to consolidate and regularise his French conquests and ambitions by taking to wife the Princess Catherine, eldest daughter of the King of France – and sister of his chief enemy, the Dauphin.

In order that there should be no mistake in any minds – particularly French minds – of his intentions in the matter, Henry turned his marriage contract into a treaty, signed well

166

before the nuptial ceremony took place. In it he stipulated that, on his union with the princess, he, Henry, should immediately become Regent of France. And on the death of King Charles, King of France. In the event of his own previous death, his heir on the throne of England should also succeed to that of France. It was a notable treaty. Owing to the unfortunate state of the said King Charles, this undertaking was signed by his wife, Queen Isabella, and by Duke Philip of Burgundy – her current principal lover, as his father had been before him – as royal commissioners.

Perhaps understandably, then, Henry had little time to spare for receiving such as James Stewart.

The younger man's presence was not altogether overlooked, however. On the third evening of his stay in Troyes, a royal page arrived at the modest lodging where Sir Richard Spice and his charge were housed, bearing a bundle of handsome-looking clothing and King Henry's compliments. He requested the presence of the King of Scots at his marriage ceremony in Troyes Cathedral next day at noon. The clothing turned out to include a cloth-of-gold tunic embellished not unworthily, back and front, with the tressured red Lion Rampant of Scotland.

James, of course, perceived very clearly the motives behind this gift and summons. He was to be shown-off again, to the greater glory of Henry Plantagenet, before all the glittering assembly, like a tame lion indeed. But was there any point in seeking to make protest? Henry could enforce his wishes – and everybody knew that he was his captive, anyway. At least, he was apparently to be treated, on this occasion, something like a king – which was always a step in the right direction.

Next forenoon an esquire came to conduct James – looking in fact exceptionally well, his powerful and manly figure more resplendent than ever before in his life – to the cathedral. Although he entered humbly and unannounced at a small side door, he was led to a very lofty position indeed, to the right of the sanctuary steps, where he was left in lonely magnificence for the best part of half-an-hour, before all

167

the vast, crowded and noisy nave. He strolled about in his limited space, in a gallant attempt to appear nonchalant.

Presently he was joined by Thomas, Duke of Clarence, Henry's brother – the curtness of whose nod may have been inspired personally, over James's rejection of the marriage scheme with his step-daughter, Joanna Beaufort; or generally, in that as heir-presumptive to his brother, he was scarcely likely to rejoice at Henry's wedding.

Two gilded throne-like chairs were then carried in and set down beside them, and, following a fanfare of trumpets Queen Isabella entered the cathedral in a flurry of pages and ladies-in-waiting, to take one of the chairs. James eyed this notorious woman with interest. Middle-aged, heavy, almost gross, far from being attractive she was all but repulsive – save for her eyes, which were dark, vivid and shrewd. She was a Bavarian and reputed the most evil woman alive. Weighed down with jewellery, she sat, and gazed about her. Presently James found her lively black eyes fixed upon himself, and stirred uncomfortably.

He was quickly distracted. After the Queen, four liveried servants came half-carrying a bent, shambling and jerking figure between them, whom they set down on the second chair, and proceeded to strap therein. Twitching and gibbering, this astonishingly overdressed apparition pointed to the diamond-studded and ostrich-plumed bonnet which had fallen to the floor from his over-large and lolling head – but was ignored by all. His Most Christian Majesty, the King of France, was gracing this special occasion.

James stooped to pick up the hat and give it to its owner. Charles clapped it awry on his head – and then reached out a claw-like hand to grasp and cling to that of the younger man. Embarrassed, James stood. Queen Isabella uttered a throaty laugh.

More trumpets announced the arrival of the bride. Preceded by a choir of singing eunuchs she came pacing up from the main doorway, on the arm of a weedy-looking young man who was Philip, Duke of Burgundy, her cousin. James forgot for a moment the twitching hand which so tightly

168

clutched his own, in considering the young woman whom Henry had chosen to marry.

Catherine, though not beautiful or particularly attractive, was nevertheless a notably normal-looking daughter to have been produced by such parents. Fair-haired, plump and still with something of the bloom of youth – she was now nineteen – she had a somewhat foxy look, emphasised perhaps by her very pale eyelashes. She seemed to have some difficulty in walking, so stiff was her gown with sewn pearls. Her head also drooped a little – but that could be explained by the weight of the tall, jewel-encrusted steeple-head-dress with its train.

"Keep your head up, girl, for good Christ's sake!" Queen Isabella growled, in guttural French, as her daughter passed.

The Cardinal-Archbishop, the Bishop of Troyes, and other clergy, now moved into place in the sanctuary. Then the trumpets rang out again, this time in a fanfare many times louder and longer than previously, reinforced by the clash of cymbals.

Up through the crowded nave strode a single figure, and everywhere men and women drew breath in surprise. Henry marched purposefully, only just short of hurriedly. He had no train, used no ceremony. He was not actually in armour, but otherwise he was clad as though for the field, not only without magnificence but in entirely plain, functional, indeed well-worn clothing. Save for the slim gold circlet round his dark hair, he was almost certainly the most poorly dressed individual in all that huge and glittering concourse. As, head up, hatchet-face grim, he stalked up towards the altar, he could not have made it more evident to all that this marriage was no more than part of a campaign, a victor's campaign, with but one purpose, one end in view.

James, while he knew pity for the bride, sympathy for the French, and something like hatred for Henry, knew an unwilling admiration also. This man was at least a king, in face of the travesty of kingship which watched him.

169

The nuptial ceremony was of the briefest, cut to a bare minimum, with the wordless protests of the prelates almost evident. James Stewart listened and watched in no very pious or worshipful frame of mind. He saw it all as a mockery, the merest caricature of holy matrimony. Incurably romantic in mind, despite the blows he had received – especially in the matter of Joanna Beaufort – he could not accept this union as anything other than an insult not only to the young woman but to the Creator who was being confidently assumed to be a party to it. The thought of marriage as it affected himself, also, was not to be banished from his mind – and the hurt of it welled up within him. Moreover, though he had at last managed to disengage King Charles's grip, he was still very much aware of Queen Isabella's calculating scrutiny of himself.

The Cardinal's benediction was barely over when Henry turned, with his wife, to face the congregation, and gave a flick of the head. Immediately, from one side, the Garter King-of-Arms stepped forward, with his flamboyantly tab-arded heralds. His trumpeter sounded, and into the echoes he intoned sonorously the titles and dignities of the most puissant, noble, high and mighty Prince Henry, by the grace of God, King of England, of Ireland, Heir of France, Prince of Wales, Duke of Normandy, Lord of Aquitaine, Brittany, Maine, Anjou, Touraine and Guyenne, Regent of the French realm; and of his wife the Princess Catherine, Daughter of France, Queen-Consort. A brief pause, and in the same tone the herald announced the solemn deposition and disinheritance of Charles de Valois, former Dauphin of France.

Another fanfare, and Henry took Catherine's arm and started to stride, in businesslike fashion, for the nearest door, while overhead the clamour of the cathedral bells broke out – and forthwith, great and small, all the other churches, abbeys and religious establishments of Troyes joined in, with almost military precision and timing. Henry Plantagenet could order well more than battles.

James found himself unclenching tight fists. In the Garter

King's resounding recital of Henry's assumptions he had not included that of suzerain or paramount of Scotland. Had the man done so, James would have to have acted, done something. That Henry had not ordained this, whilst so comprehensively rubbing the French noses in the dust, meant presumably that he required something of the King of Scots. It behoved a wise man to walk warily still.

That evening, in the Bishop's palace which Henry had taken over, James, once again specifically invited, indeed escorted thither, discovered what was required of him. But he had some time to wait for it – for, though the evening's entertainment was in the nature of a bridal feast and celebration, over much of the time there was no sign of the bridegroom.

James, on his arrival, paid his respects to Queen Catherine, a somewhat lonely figure – for it did not take long to perceive that the centre of attraction in the great crowded salon was her unlovely but vital mother, whom the newcomer was glad to avoid.

"We are in something of the same case, you and I, are we not?" Catherine said, as they stood side by side, looking down the room, after James's brief and formal greetings. "Your Majesty, I note, does not congratulate me, as do all others!"

He considered her carefully. He was sorry for her – but apart altogether from her parentage, there was a slyness about her which behoved a man to take heed. "Your Highness is the wife of the most powerful monarch in Christendom," he said. "And I – I am but a captive on a chain. Would you so liken our cases?"

"We both must do what King Henry says, must we not?"

"Say rather that Henry would *have* us do as he says!"

"There is a difference, Majesty?"

"For myself, there is." He paused, and shook his head. "Or . . . shall we say that *I* would have it so!"

"And do you ever succeed?"

"Only, I think, when Henry requires something of me."

"Ah. But with me has he not already gained what he required?"

James was silent.

She eyed him from under those pale lashes. "Is . . . is Henry not interested in women?" she asked, low-voiced. "I have scarce seen him since we left the church. Is it myself? Or is he ever thus? You have known him long. What do I look for?"

James cleared his throat. It was no easy question to answer, to a bride. And it did not fail to occur to him that few brides would have asked it. On the other hand, most brides would not have required to. "Henry is not cold, I think – if that is your meaning, Highness," he said slowly. "Once, he was notably otherwise, indeed. But he is a man consumed with a purpose. All things must be bent to that purpose."

"And the purpose is the conquering of France?"

"More than that. Or less. The purpose is but *conquering*, I think. Power. France it is today. Scotland it may be tomorrow. Thereafter, who knows?" James bit his lip. He had not intended to go thus far, to talk so freely. This young woman could be a danger to him if she made him talk so. He was, unfortunately, too little used to conversation with young women.

"Power . . .!" she echoed. "There are more kinds of power than one, I think." Her voice was strained. "Let Henry watch to his!"

Surprised, James studied her. Did this frail nineteen-year-old think to pit her immature woman's powers against Henry's ruthless drive and experience? "He knows how to use women also, when need be," he said – and Joanna's fair, false face rose before his inner eye, so that the words choked off unevenly.

Catherine was too concerned with her own mental imagery just then, to notice. "Let him watch!" she repeated, tautly. "One kind of power may feed on another! Let him look to his – in his bed this night! Lest . . . lest he discover himself with the wrong partner! To his cost!"

172

James was taking this extraordinary statement to be but the folly of a young woman slighted on her wedding-day, when he perceived the fierce direction of the other's gaze – and more than that, the blaze of hatred in eyes which no veiling under pale lashes could hide. She was staring directly at a nearby group – four laughing, eager men clustered round one uncouth, leering woman, who was Isabella of Bavaria, Queen of France. There could be no doubt as to her meaning.

Appalled, he almost drew back a step – and as though sensing it, Catherine turned her young-old eyes full upon him, frank for the moment.

"What is my wifely duty, think you?" she asked levelly.

James could find no words adequate to the occasion. In his confusion, strangely enough, it was the older woman who came to his aid. Turning at that moment, she looked at him there with her daughter, and laughingly dismissing her quartet, she came simpering towards the couple at what could only be described as a waddle.

"God's eyes – my daughter would seem to have taken possession of the wrong king!" she exclaimed, in her deep, hoarse but undoubtedly attractive voice, as she held out a podgy hand so glittering with rings that fingers were scarcely visible. "Do you seek to oust Henry already, young man? Or are you perhaps his proxy in this matter? His, shall we say, viceroy!"

James was thankful that it was the rings which he must kiss, rather than the woman's flesh. "I congratulate Henry on his wife, Madam," he said stiffly. "That, at least."

"That is what I feared! Do you also congratulate this minx of mine on her husband?"

He discovered that he had been previous in his satisfaction about the fingers, for Queen Isabella was retaining her grip of his hand, and however podgy, her grasp was strong. It appeared to be a habit with the King and Queen of France.

"Henry . . . is Henry!" James answered. "His renown in all matters, depends not on the commendation of such as I!"

"Ha! You do not love the Plantagenet, then! A dangerous man to be consoling his new wife! Begone, child – and leave this menace to me! Who can better deal with him. Off with you!"

Without a word, Catherine swung round and moved away.

James found himself envying her in that – but the other had him held tight. She had transferred her grasp to his arm now.

"You have strong arms, boy," she said, probing with her fingers. "Good muscles. I hear that you are a wrestler, amongst other accomplishments. That is . . . admirable! I find strong men to my taste!" She laughed. "I have some little strength myself! We might even try a fall together, you and I!"

He could think of nothing to say to that.

Standing back a little, the better to look him up and down, she considered him, frankly assessing. Almost, those gleaming eyes seemed to devour him. "You are a well-made man, Name of a Name! For a king! God help us – for a king!"

James, scarcely appreciating being summed up, like a bull before a baiting, sought to free his arm – but unsuccessfully. "I am as God made me, Madam," he grunted.

"Aye – and there's the splendour of it, boy! As God made you!" The Queen moistened thick lips. "A captive. Since childhood. I swear that you will certainly lack something in experience! In some matters! Eh?"

He cleared his throat.

Her finger-nails were digging almost viciously into his arm, one at a time, in a rhythmic succession. "I should not wonder but that Henry, and his father before him, have neglected your education? In some respects? How say you, my young friend?"

By main force James wrenched his arm free at last. "I say, Your Majesty, that in some matters, even a captive may remain his own man! In that respect at least, I am well content!"

"Your own man? God be good – here is delight! Can it

174

mean . . .? Can it be true? The Virgin King!" She was advancing upon him again, her massive, heavy body notably light on strangely small feet. "My dear – how fortunate are we both! Are we not?"

He discovered that he was actually retreating before her. This would not do, with half the eyes in that great salon undoubtedly upon them. Allowing the woman to grasp him again, he forced a smile. "I fear I must disappoint, Madam," he said. "My experience is perhaps more catholic than you credit!"

"With women?"

"Henry's Court is not devoid of women, Majesty."

The other's deep chuckle was purely amused. "Not Frenchwomen, I think! Nor German, for that matter! I shall be surprised if you have not much learning – much pleasurable learning – ahead of you, young man!"

James, near to desperation, looked about him – and proof of his urgency was forthcoming in that he positively welcomed the sight of Sir Richard Spice most obviously making his determined way in his direction.

"No doubt, Madam," he said. "But . . . here is one of King Henry's messengers, if I mistake not."

Isabella frowned – and jerked something rude enough to make James start, blinking.

"My lord James – His Majesty requests your presence," Spice declared – and recollecting, bowed belatedly to the Queen.

"Where is King Henry, sir?" that lady demanded, gratingly.

"In, h'm, another apartment, Your Majesty," the knight said. "Dealing with business of state."

"Which state, man?"

Spice looked quickly at James, but got no help from the younger man. "The King did not confide in me, Madam. He but commanded me to fetch my lord James."

The Queen snorted. "Then you will go and tell King Henry that His Majesty of Scotland is meantime engaged with *me*, sir!"

175

James hesitated. Glad as he was of the opportunity to escape from this alarming woman, he was not prepared humbly to obey such peremptory summons forthwith. "I shall see your master presently," he told Sir Richard.

That man tugged at his beard, eyeing the two royal speakers with undisguised disapproval. Evidently he was not disposed to go back to Henry with such answers.

It was Isabella who resolved the situation. Suddenly she changed her attitude. "Come, my friend," she said to James. "We shall *both* go to see the Plantagenet! Discover where he hides away. And why!" And still holding his arm, she moved off, signing imperiously to the very doubtful Spice to precede them.

What the watching company, Queen Catherine included, might think of King James's withdrawal, arm-in-arm with Queen Isabella, the man at least did not care to speculate.

They were led by sundry corridors to the Bishop's library, where a group of men stood around a large table littered with maps and papers. As well as Henry, there were his brothers, Thomas, Duke of Clarence and Humphrey, Duke of Gloucester; also the Earls of Warwick, Salisbury and Suffolk, and one or two other top commanders of the English army. At sight of the newcomers, all stared, scarcely welcoming, before they thought to bow.

"What secret conclave is this, Henry?" the Queen asked, though she smiled. "Strange company for a bridegroom, is it not? Is my daughter's company so distasteful?"

Henry straightened up from the table. "Convey to the Lady Catherine, my wife, my regrets, Your Majesty," he said crisply. "I shall join her so soon as urgent matters allow."

"On a wedding-day, my friend, urgency is usually, and decently, otherwise!"

"Perhaps, Madam. But the circumstances are not usual. I have much to see to."

Isabella sighed gustily. "Ah, me! Were I the bride, I might think to prove the mistress of circumstances! And

176

master them!" She relinquished James's arm at last, and moved determinedly over to Henry's side. "Lacking, of course, such manly concern in the bridegroom!"

Henry frowned. "No doubt. But I am fighting a war, Madam. First things must come first."

"I could change your mind, I think, as to which are the first things!" she said, holding him with her glittering eyes. "Try me!"

Even Henry faltered, coughing. But he recovered himself swiftly. "Your Majesty would do better to devote your attention to your son, in this matter," he said harshly. "To Charles de Valois. He it is who comes between me and my bride. He has moved out from Paris, and taken the towns of Sens and Montereau. With much slaughter."

"Charles was ever headstrong," the Queen murmured. "But, I swear, I should require better excuse than this, sir, of *my* bridegroom! Sens and Montereau are near twenty leagues away!"

"It may be, Madam, that we see marriage differently!" Abruptly, as though breaking off an unsatisfactory engagement, he turned. "My lord James – I required your presence here for a purpose. With Her Majesty's permission, my lords, we resume our business."

James, who had been too much interested in this exchange to consider his own position, nodded. "We all know, sir, that you never do anything *lacking* a purpose! This is my third day in Troyes. After travelling in haste all the way from Durham . . ."

"Would you have preferred to return to the Tower?" Henry barked.

"I should have preferred that our agreement on my release and return to Scotland should have been proceeded with."

"Tush, man – Albany does not want you! And there's an end to it. Remember it! Your uncle desires only to injure *me*, not to aid you. He has sent seven thousand of your Scots subjects to withstand me, here in France. Under his younger son, Buchan – your cousin. They are the spearhead of the Dauphin's . . ." He corrected himself. ". . . of the former

177

Dauphin's forces." Henry stabbed a finger at a map on the table. "They led, I am told, in the attacks on these towns. It is intolerable."

"Perhaps, if I had been allowed to return to Scotland this would never have happened."

Queen Isabella, who had not taken the very broad hint to retire from the company, hooted a short laugh.

"The former Dauphin no longer represents France," Henry went on, heavily. "I am Regent, and the King of France is in treaty with me. There can be no possible cause for the Scots to take up arms against me – save spleen. Albany's spleen. The spleen of an aged doting man!"

Again the Queen laughed. She undoubtedly had a strange sense of humour.

James waited.

"These people are your subjects, Cousin. A proclamation by yourself, commanding that they lay down their arms, on pain of rebellion to your royal self – that is what is required. A proclamation. Signed by you."

So that was it! That was why he had been brought to France. Armour and tents bought for him. The possibility of knighthood and renown held out. To use him against the Scots forces.

James raised head high. "No, sir!" he said.

All were gazing at him now, tensely.

Henry's brows came down, at their blackest. "You say no! *You*, my pensioner! What have I ever asked of you, before? You refuse me this?"

"I do."

"Why? Why, in God's name? When the cause is just?"

With difficulty James kept his voice even, level. "Because, so long as I remain a prisoner, it becomes neither myself to issue such a command, or my subjects to obey it. Irrespective of the cause, sir."

"Becomes you! *Becomes* you, you say! Who are you to say what becomes you and what does not? I, Henry, say that you shall do it! I command here, I tell you. And decide what is becoming, by the Mass! And for whom!"

James inclined his head slightly. "You command here, yes – you leave none in doubt! And you may possibly command James Stewart. But you cannot command the King of Scots. Not you, or any man! You cannot have it both ways, Henry. You cannot hold me a captive – and also have me to act as king over my subjects. It is one, or the other. If I must remain captive, I must. I will place myself under your command, here in France, as a private knight. To learn the arts of war under so famous a captain. This, yes. But if you would have *me* command my people – you must set me free to do it!"

"God's blood!" The other's fist smashed down on the table. "This is beyond all bearing! You . . . you are wholly in my power, and shall do as I command. *Command* – do you hear?"

Henry Plantagenet in a fury was a terrifying sight. All in the room were clearly in a state of alarm, even his brothers – save only Isabella of Bavaria, who actually looked as though she was enjoying herself. James himself knew fear – but forced himself on. He even mustered the travesty of a smile.

"You claim, sir, with no least cause, to be suzerain of my realm," he said, holding his voice steady. "In such case, issue you your own proclamation! And see whether my subjects obey it!"

Only Isabella saw any humour in that.

Henry appeared to be speechless, for the moment

In the throbbing silence, it occurred to James that he might at least now take advantage of one of the few privileges of his royal position; he did not have to obtain another monarch's permission to retire. It seemed to him that all that was to be said on this subject had been said; it was not necessary that he await the explosion. He nodded, therefore, to Henry, and bowed to the Queen of France.

"I bid you all a very good night," he said, and swung on his heel.

Isabella's deep laughter and Henry's tight words sounded

together, as James reached the door – and the expected explosion did not materialise.

"We ride at first light, Cousin. Armoured and full harnessed. An esquire will await you." That was rasping, but level.

Surprised, the younger man turned in the doorway, to look back. "Very well," he said, and closed the door quietly behind him.

In the turmoil of his thoughts, as he made his way through the noisy city towards his humble lodging, he recollected that at least he had to thank Henry for delivering him meantime from Queen Isabella's unwelcome attentions.

12

The bright fresh morning brought a notable change not only in prospect, programme and mood, but in King Henry himself. The entire army, of course, had suddenly changed its mood, almost its character, with the smell of action in the air, and Troyes and its surrounding encampments hummed like a wild bees' nest. Henry had nearly twenty thousand men thereabouts, who had come to France to fight.

When, a few miles out of Troyes on the road to the west, riding at the head of a splendid knightly cavalcade of perhaps one thousand of his most illustrious chivalry, Henry summoned James to his side, it was as to a different man. Almost gone was the tense, self-conscious autocrat; in its place a confident and comparatively uncomplicated soldier, cheerful, good humoured, a man evidently himself and not playing a part. Here, it seemed, was Henry Plantagenet's true role in life – a captain in the field, at the head of his forces, perhaps the greatest warrior Christendom had produced in two centuries.

He greeted James easily, almost cordially, and gestured him to his left side. Philip of Burgundy rode on his right, and immediately behind came his brothers and then a galaxy of great English, French and Holy Roman Empire lords under a colourful forest of banners. James was very much aware of his own plain and not very well-fitting armour – in which, to tell the truth, he sat less than comfortably – his uncrested helm and modest mount, in so magnificent a company so superbly horsed and caparisoned; he held his head the higher. Nothing was said of proclamations, not indeed of the entire previous evening's encounter. And James forbore to comment on the nuptial position, mother-in-law, or this peculiar way of celebrating a marriage.

Henry was full of the military situation. He held all the north of France, down to Paris. Also a sizeable area in the west, based on the old English-held dukedom of Aquitaine. Burgundy, in the south-east, was now in alliance. Fully half the entire country was his. Moreover, the remainder was riddled with disaffection, suspicion and divided loyalties. The Dauphin Charles was no heroic figurehead to rally patriots, a sulky, ill-tempered and ungainly young man, stubborn rather than strong, and unpopular. The civil wars which for so long had rent the country had left a legacy of hatred, and the Dauphin's main supporters, the Orleans faction, or Armagnacs – led by the fierce Count of Armagnac, since their Duke was still a captive in England – were cordially loathed. Basically, then, the invaders' position was excellent, now that the nominal French throne and government had come to terms.

Unfortunately however, though the capital Paris itself might fall like an over-ripe apple, the strong Orleans country lay immediately to the south of it, keeping open a wide avenue of support for all the hostile south. Also, it kept open the links with Spain, and the King of Castile was supplying the Dauphin with an army and supplies. He had also sent no less than forty ships to transport the Earl of Buchan's army from Scotland to La Rochelle. Spain, of course, was concerned with the balance of power, and alarmed at the notion of an English-dominated France on her doorstep. And now the Scots held Touraine, to the west of Orleans, and all the land between to their base on the coast at La Rochelle.

The key to it all therefore was the hinge south of Paris, in the Duchy of Orleans, where a number of strong fortified towns held the country secure for the Dauphin and his allies. Now, from this base, Charles de Valois had moved out to the east, into this Champagne, to capture the fortresses of Sens, Montereau and Melun, held by the Burgundians. This must be changed forthwith, for the enemy move was clearly an attempt to link up with hostile Lorraine in the east, and so cut off Burgundy from the rest of the country – an insolent gesture. These towns must be retaken, and then a general attack launched westwards through the province of Orleans, to cut off Paris from south and west.

Sens was their present objective. It lay about forty-five miles due west of Troyes, through the wooded country of the Forêt d'Othe, on the bank of the Yonne.

James, whatever his feelings on the matter of policy, could not but find his spirits soaring this fine morning, riding at the head of so gallant a company through a handsome rolling land so far little disfigured by war. Scouting outriders kept Henry informed that there was no enemy force meantime seeking to bar their way. This was a vast improvement on imprisonment.

It was not until early evening that scouts came to report that a small enemy skirmishing force had materialised on a low ridge ahead, between them and Sens, which was now only about ten miles distant. Henry called forward Warwick to go with a company of cavalry to clear any obstruction, and then to look for a suitable site for the main host to encamp, before attacking Sens the next day. After giving this order, Henry glanced at James.

"How say you, Cousin?" he asked. "Would you care to ride on this little canter, with Warwick?"

James, perhaps foolishly, found himself so almost overcome with delight that he had difficulty in answering. Only the scion of a proud warrior race, bred on knightly tradition and held captive into his mid-twenties, might fully appreciate what this offer of action meant to him. He sent for David Douglas of Whittinghame, as esquire, and ranged himself behind the Earl of Warwick – with whom he had always got on well. He cared nothing for the smiles of many at his eagerness.

Warwick's company of about two hundred was perhaps somewhat heavily weighted with knights and lordlings, as distinct from rank and file men-at-arms – for James was not the only one anxious to whet his sword, in a campaign which had hitherto been little more than a political progress. Led by the scouts, they rode forward at a brave canter, armour clanking encouragingly, behind the black-and-gold banner of Warwick.

For two or three miles they went through fairly thick old woodland, with no prospects. Then the ground began to rise steadily, and the trees to thin, and presently they came to an open lip or edge, where a veteran knight, leader of the scouting advance-guard awaited them. They were in shadow here, with the forest and the westering sun behind them. In front the ground sloped down through scrub to a shallow boggy bottom, perhaps half-a-mile wide, beyond which it rose again, through scattered thorn trees to a higher bare limestone escarpment. Along the ridge of this, picked out in the flooding golden sunset light, was a long line of horsemen, banners and armour glinting.

"How many are there, sir knight?" Warwick demanded. "Are these we see backed by greater forces beyond the ridge?"

"Not unless they have come up new, my lord," the other said. "We have been in contact with this Armagnac skirmishing force for some hours. They number about eight score and have been retiring before us. They look like to make a stand on this strong position – and my men are weary. So I sent for help."

"Aye." Warwick was eyeing the low ground in front. "This is ill country to charge across. They will have no cannon, if they are skirmishers. But have they archers?"

"No long-bows. Only a few hagbutters, that we have seen. They are light cavalry, as are we."

"What of the flanks? Can we turn them?"

"Not easily. This swamp grows but worse on the left. To the right is the river. And the road, by which His Majesty comes. There is a bridge, yes – but strongly held by the enemy."

Warwick nodded. He seemed hardly to be listening. A skilled campaigner, he was gazing across the marshland

184

towards the opposite escarpment, lit up by the level beams of the sinking sun.

"They have a strong position, to be sure. But, see you, without cannon or archers they cannot use it to best advantage. We cross under their very noses, and deploy beyond, my friends. They watch us, but cannot touch us – without forfeiting the strength of that position. Your scouts out to pick the best way across yonder, sir knight. We follow in columns."

So down into the thicket-strewn unpleasantness of the bogland they rode, in full view of the enemy. The bottom was soft and waterlogged, hopeless for any fast cavalry advance, but passable so long as the horsemen picked their way carefully, willing to twist and turn to use what firm ground there was. Under cannon-fire it would have been a death-trap; a few English long-bowmen could have held the foot of the escarpment at will. But armoured cavalry up on the ridge could only sit and wait – or dash down the steep to contest the issue with the enemy as they emerged from the bog.

Undoubtedly not only James and other unfledged warriors felt singularly naked and vulnerable as they picked their slow and winding way in three or four single files, horses stumbling and slipping, mud splattering over gleaming armour – all under the regard of the Armagnacs half-a-mile ahead and above.

"A wager, my lord James," Warwick cried, smiling. "That yonder messieurs do not leave their high safety, to come down and throw us back into this sink!"

"They could do it, could they not?"

"They could try it. But . . . if they failed, they would have that steep face behind them, to cut off any escape. They cannot be sure that there are not many more of us, coming up through the forest. No – I say they will wait. Too strong a position has cost the day for many a side. It can stop freedom of action – aye, and the will to fight!"

Although it was a heart-in-mouth business for the last hundred yards or so, Warwick was proved right. His

185

mud-stained columns at last won their way out on to firm ground again – and no thundering charge came down from the ridge to sweep them back into the swamp. Indeed, because of the steepness of the escarpment, they now could not see the enemy above – and consequently were themselves out of sight in dead ground.

Warwick was crisp and businesslike now, splitting up his force. He sent large parties off left and right, to make flanking assaults on the ridge at quite distant points, which he had selected on the way across, ordering them to keep sending bugle-call signals – indeed to make as much noise as they could. His own trumpeter, with the main body, was to blow his instrument frequently, as they waited.

"We will keep those frog-eaters aloft in a sweat, my friends," the Earl chuckled.

James was in a fever of impatient excitement before Warwick at last gave the order to start the climb. Although the Earl said that the ascent should be made methodically, so that as far as possible all reached the crest together, James, with Douglas close at his heels, was quickly ahead. This was because, while others less active and eager allowed their mounts to pick their own way up the steep bro-ken incline, the two Scots at once dismounted and led their horses up by much more steep and direct routes than the beasts themselves would have chosen. James, of course, from long years of determined training, was probably the fittest man in the field – and one of the most muscular. He had to be, to do what he did – for climbing a steep slippery escarpment in full armour, leading a reluctant armour-clad horse, demanded major effort.

Warwick more than once had to call him to a halt, lest he face the enemy, at the top of the hill, alone.

Just under the crest, the Scots fretted while the others came up. The evening was loud with bugling and shouting, far and near. What effect this was having on the Frenchmen above they could not tell – though that their present nearness was known was evidenced by the heads which every now and again showed against the skyline – watchers to report progress.

Panting, for he was a middle-aged man and heavy, Warwick was in no hurry. "They will either seek to hold us, at the edge, on foot. Or retire back some way, to give their horses room for action," he declared. "Since they are cavalry, I think they will stay on their horses – though the first would be of greater danger for us. They will be anxious about their flanks. So spread out, my friends. Try to come up to that ridge as near the same time as you may. But once there, do not advance in line, but in wedges. When I signal. The crest may be bloody – but I think not. On then, gentlemen – for God and King Harry!"

James frowned at that last – but it did not prevent him from surging ahead again.

Warwick was right, once again. The French did not attempt to exploit their advantage by holding the lip of the rise – since they could only have done this effectively dismounted, broken up as was the limestone edge. A few hagbut shots were fired by the forward watchers, but with little effect. James, who was actually the first man to top the crest, found no opposition awaiting him – and, indeed, climbing back into his saddle, saw sundry watchers running back to rejoin the enemy line, which had now withdrawn perhaps three hundred yards down the slight grassy slope to the west, and waited in extended order, drawn up in disciplined array – and admittedly on good cavalry ground now. But, equally clearly, they had thrown away all the advantage of their strong defensive position. It was James's first lesson in military tactics.

Fuming at not being able to advance until Warwick's trumpeter sounded the charge, James waited. Men had come up behind him now, and without pausing to enquire who might be senior, he gestured them into a solid wedge formation at his back, Douglas acting as whipper-in. When at last the trumpet neighed its high challenge, the King of Scots' wedge was off at the first shrill note.

There was not much of military tactics or expertise about

187

what followed, as far as James Stewart was concerned. His lance couched and levelled at his right side, with his left hand he beat with the pommel of his drawn sword on the armouring of his mediocre horse, to urge it to its utmost speed. The shield on his left arm was hampering. His fear was only that the better-mounted knights behind him might get in front.

He had never a moment's doubt as to his due objective – the very centre of the Armagnac line, where a large red-and-white banner flew over, presumably, the enemy commander. This was what his code demanded and all his tourney jousting had prepared him for.

So they thundered across the three hundred yards of turf and tussock, in shouting, clanking clamour – and if James shouted for Saint Andrew and Scotland it did not matter for nobody could hear anybody else. They had not, in fact, three hundred yards to gain momentum – for no cavalry commander would sit tight and await a charge to hit him. The enemy must either take avoiding action, or advance to meet impact with impact. The Frenchman chose the latter.

The slight downward slope of the ground gave some advantage to the attackers. On the other hand the latter's mounts were weary, with the plouter across the bog and the scramble up the hill, while the Frenchmen had been resting. In numbers, too, the Armagnacs had a decided advantage at this point, since Warwick's force was reduced heavily to provide the flanking parties. But those flankers, of unknown numbers but loud trumpeting, obviously were worrying the enemy – and no man fights at his best with the thought that his foes are circling round behind him. Odds perhaps were fairly even.

Something of all this flashed through James's mind as he drove down on the red-and-white banner. He was aware, also, of two other matters – one, that he had forgotten to close the visor of his helm; and the other that the incesssant bellow close behind him was that of "A Douglas! A Douglas!" – an ominous slogan in Scottish ears for centuries, and one strangely disturbing to a Stewart.

188

With abrupt suddenness there was his target before him, a massive figure in battle-stained steel with a tattered heraldic surcoat above – most evidently the French leader. Whether he recognised the significance of the Rampant Lion of Scotland, painted not very flatteringly on the shield of the plainly armoured young man, he undoubtedly perceived well that it was against himself that the apex of this first wedge was driving. As James's lance came straight at him, at the very last moment the Frenchman skilfully reined back his mount on its haunches, front feet pawing, and thus presented the smallest possible target, his own lance high. Too late to alter anything, James's point, instead of crashing hard, went slithering along the other horse's neck-armour, and up the Frenchman's steel-clad arm and gorget, to glance off harmlessly. Then the other's own lance came down, not in any thrust, but in a wide sideways swipe.

It was not decent chivalric jousting behaviour, by a long way – but if James had swung his horse to the left to avoid a scraping collision, as was instinctive, he would in fact have been wiped right out of his saddle by the swinging force of the blow, to be skewered thereafter on the ground. But, with a lightning awareness of his danger, he wrenched his mount's head hard right, to crash directly into the other's flank, with a fearful clash of armour-plating and a jolting inside his own steel casing that all but numbed him. His lance was at this side, and useless now, point up, and his left and sword arm was weighted down with the heavy shield slung thereon. But, standing in his stirrups on his reeling, floundering mount, he brought round sword and shield both, in a furious body-twisting swing that almost unhorsed him. As the other's lance clattered comparatively harmlessly against James's back, to pitch him forward a little, his own sword struck the Frenchman on the back of the neck, sending him slewing half out of the saddle.

In the chaotic mêlée that ensued, it was not so much skill as impetus and equilibrium which dictated events. Because the French horse had not all four feet on the ground at moment of impact, it took the crash more grievously, indeed all but went over. On the other hand, James could by no means control his own beast's frantic onward plunging, to keep himself approximately upright demanding all his efforts. As a result the knight was left behind him, and before he could attempt to turn his horse round, he was immediately confronted with a new enemy – the banner-bearer.

It was in fact a fortunate chance for James, though normal that this man should be immediately behind his master. For this was no mere pennon at a lance-head, but a full heraldic banner – and its bearer could not carry a lance as well. So he was armed merely with a sword. James's own lance, at this abrupt new encounter, was still high in the air – so high indeed that in seeking to bring its point down to bear again, he entangled it forthwith in the silken folds of the flag. The force and weight of its descent brought the white raven on red down with it, in torn silken ruin on top of its unfortunate bearer, just as he had his sword raised to smite at his oncoming and almost involuntary assailant. Sword and wielder disappeared momentarily under the colourful coverlet.

James was almost under that banner himself. Swerving bodily in his saddle just in time to avoid its folds, he drove a wild back-handed blow with his sword at his muffled opponent, in passing, felt the jarring contact as the sword was wrenched right out of his steel-gauntleted grasp, and was carried onward in the rush. But making an instinctive grab after his flying blade, he caught instead only the silken folds – and rode on, dragging this trophy more or less involuntarily with him.

There were still French men-at-arms before him, but they were reining round, getting out of the way of the charge, rather than seeking to halt this swaying paladin, peculiarly draped in their own banner, swordless and lance askew. James, still under the impetus of his onset, found himself carried through the enemy's narrow line and plunging on.

By the time that he had pulled up his frightened, cavorting mount, and turned back, all was practically over. Most of the

Armagnacs were in full flight pursued by many of Warwick's men who obviously had not had a chance to cross swords. A few individual scuffles were still going on, but by and large the fight was finished. The field was theirs.

James Stewart was in a state of major embarrassment. It was his first real fight – and he had lost his sword. How many had noticed? Could he find it, retrieve it, unperceived?

That did not seem likely, for men were already pointing at him, shouting. Infuriatingly, David Douglas was foremost in this, coming riding to him.

It was some moments before James realised that he was being hailed as something of a hero, and that loss of his sword went quite unnoticed against the fact that he had captured the enemy standard. Moreover, Douglas's shoutings were that His Grace of Scotland had also so mauled the enemy commander that he, Douglas, had only had to push him out of his saddle thereafter. In consequence of which the French had the more swiftly lost heart and broken. Hurrah for King James!

The veteran Earl of Warwick had come up and was considering proceedings with a somewhat cynical eye. James decided that he at least was not deceived. He was not wasting time now, either, but already giving orders for his force to reform and ride northwards along the escarpment, in order to take in the rear the enemy reported to be holding the bridge over the river. His trumpeter was braying the recall to those who pursued the fleeing Armagnacs.

James was not the man to bask happily in unearned glory. He briefly discounted both heroism and expertise in his recent confused clash – but he also was sufficient of an opportunist not to fail to redeem his awkward swordlessness in a suitable fashion by requesting his esquire to hand over the forfeited blade of the fallen French knight – a handsome weapon much finer than his own. He was relieved to see that the Frenchman was able to stand on his feet, more bruised and dazed within his armour than seriously wounded – however unsuitable a sentiment this was. Likewise pleasurable was the discovery that he had

191

acquired a horse much better than that King Henry's bounty had found for him.

James avoided Warwick's close proximity as they rode for the bridge, suspecting that shrewd warrior to have a less high opinion of his activities than had some others. They found the bridge-holders discreetly retiring at their approach.

Encamped before the walls of Sens that night, Henry was gracious, and for him, relaxed. He summoned James to his great pavilion under the streaming Leopards and St. George's Cross of England, and poured him a goblet of wine with his own hands, before all his lords and commanders.

"I hear, Cousin, that you distinguished yourself today," he said. "A very rampant lion of valour!"

The younger man flushed quickly, glancing over at Warwick where he lounged with Clarence and Gloucester. "You jest, sir," he said shortly. "I shall do better, in time."

"I' faith, James – is this modesty? Or the opposite?"

"My lord of Warwick knows that my faults are those of inexperience. The jousting-yard is only doubtful preparation for war, I find."

"By the Mass, here's a strange candidate for knighthood! Wait, says he! Until you see what I shall do hereafter! We must look to our laurels, my lords!"

The laughter which greeted that set James biting his lip. He took less kindly than he should, perhaps, to being laughed at.

Warwick spoke up. "I ask no better comrade in the field, Sire, than my lord James. If at times he was over-keen for me – it may be because I am getting old! And so steals my worn renown." He raised his own goblet. "I pledge you, my lord."

James's breath caught in his throat. The Earl was not jesting, but speaking generously, kindly. He had not told Henry, then, of the hot-headed impatience, the presumption, the bungled charge and the almost accidental triumph. Henry was perhaps not mocking him – not deliberately, at anyrate.

"We all pledge you, Cousin," Henry was saying. "You have made a fair start to winning your spurs. And the Sieur de Dax may even fetch you a handsome ransom, so Burgundy here tells me!"

James was better at carrying off contumely – since he was the more used to it – than praise. He mumbled, and shuffled feet, as men drank to him.

"I thank you," he said, thereafter, jerkily. "But you are all mistaken. I botched my assault – taking a lead which was not mine to take. I would have been unhorsed at the first blow, but for a lucky chance. The standard I did not seek to capture – it but got caught on my lance-point. And I want no ransom for the French knight – who deserves, I think, rather my apologies! Save only his horse – which is a deal better than the one Your Highness gave me! And his sword – to replace mine own, which I lost somewhere in the business!"

The great shout of laughter which shook the royal tent was as wholehearted as it was general. Even Henry joined in. Men surged over to clap the speaker on the back – and if, so doing, they overlooked the fact that he was a king, equally they did his captive's status.

It was the beginning of James Stewart's acceptance as a man amongst other men.

If this colourful initiation into active warfare had its comic side, and its rewards out of all proportion to its importance, the siege of Sens which followed was the reverse – dull, uneventful and unrewarding. For a full month the pride of Henry's chivalry sat down around this small fortress-town, and its near neighbour Montereau, and achieved little more than frustration and boredom. The fact was that Henry Plantagenet was not so notable at siegecraft as at a war of movement; he had not the temperament, the patience, for it. Nor had he the artillery, on this occasion, the engines of assault. Whereas these fortresses were armed with good cannon, their walls lofty and stout, their positions strong. When Rouen had withstood siege, Henry had fairly quickly returned to England, leaving its slow reduction to others.

Now, after a few days of stirring summons to the defenders to come out and fight like men, he found other matters elsewhere pressingly demanding his attention, and left his brothers, Clarence to command at Sens, and Gloucester at Montereau. He would try to decoy the wretched Charles de Valois out of Paris, he declared, to fight a decent Christian battle. It was noticeable thereafter that his ridings about the country did not take him back to Troyes and his new Queen.

The Dauphin, for his part, apparently preferred to stay in Paris.

The sieges, of course, consisted of more than mere sitting down. Battering-rams, slings, balistas and the like were built, and as far as possible, put to use; Henry scoured France, and even sent to England, for heavy cannon; sapping and mining parties went to work. But so long as the artillery within outgunned in range and power that without, there was little that could be effected. And heavy cannon took an unconscionable time in coming.

James was not wholly idle during the waiting period — even though Henry did not take him on any of his various excursions. Once or twice he went out with foraging bands which had the task of requisitioning sufficient meat, meal and fuel — not to mention women — to maintain the army; but he very quickly had his bellyful of that side of warfare, sickening at the sights he saw and the tasks he was expected to share in. After the pillaging of a nunnery near Villeneuve, and the shameful sport made of its inmates, he requested Clarence to spare him any more such duties. Thereafter he used up his surplus energies in organising and taking part in sport — wrestling, races, jousts and contests of every description. As a consequence, his popularity grew greatly amongst the rank and file, but rather noticeably less so amongst the knightly class — since he was altogether too apt to excel in all, himself. Latterly he was deliberately holding himself back.

It was a mixture of disease and treachery which eventually brought the fortresses low, rather than any prowess of the besiegers. The Orleanist commander of Montereau, the Comte de Forquier, sent out a secret message that his people were dying in large numbers and he feared a major plague; he was short of all medicaments, and even space to dispose of the dead. On promise of a safe-conduct for himself and personal entourage, and honourable surrender terms for his soldiery, he would have the north gate opened at dusk the following evening, and the cannoneers there removed. Evidently he had to face opposition within.

King Henry was hurriedly sent for from Chablis, that he might make the victorious entry in person, and the next night Montereau duly fell – though there was some internal fighting before all was under control. If the unfortunate townsfolk had little reason to rejoice thereafter, almost certainly they were little worse off than they had been under the Orleanists.

James had his first encounter with his own subjects – a small detachment of Scots footmen from Buchan's army, whom he advised to make their way home to Scotland as best they could rather than try to rejoin their compatriots in the west. They were permitted to march away, disarmed.

Sens fell within the week, for no evident reason other than the contagion of defeat. There were no Scots here – and the garrison did not escape so lightly. A large number were declared rebels against the King of France, and summarily hanged – despite the surrender terms – as a disincentive to other would-be defenders of fortresses.

This unhappy development much upset James Stewart. His protests all brought the same answer – that it was by King Harry's personal command. Moreover, he was considered to be too lily-livered altogether. He was unable to make any representations to Henry until he, with the entire army, had moved on some twenty miles nearer to Paris, through the Forest of Fontainebleau, to the great fortress of Melun, now the greatest single obstacle between the invaders and the capital. Depressed at the thought of still another siege, James nevertheless sought out Henry, uninvited, at nearby Corbeil, where he had now brought King Charles, Isabella, and Catherine.

Despite their improved relationship, almost soldierly camaraderie, Henry kept the younger man waiting for two whole days at Corbeil before he would see him. Then he brushed aside James's expostulations, about the hangings, brusquely.

"Your soft heart would do credit to a priest, Cousin," he declared. "But not to a general. Or a king! You will learn that, one day – and the sooner the better. For your subjects. Often a hard-headed ruler serves them kinder than a soft-hearted one. Your father's son should perceive that! These men were rebels against their liege-lord, Charles, who is in treaty with me. All deserved to die – but I only hanged some few. As a lesson, a warning. Their deaths, I swear, will save the lives of many, by example. And therefore save many English lives also – that it is my duty to save."

"Yet these men surrendered on honourable terms. So you are forsworn, in the deed!"

"Honourable terms are not for rebels. *I* promised them nothing."

"Your brother Clarence did. Does he thank you for his fame reduced?" They were alone, for once, and James could speak freely. "Moreover, aside from your good name – was it good policy? Will it indeed save lives? In Melun now, will not the Orleanists resist the more fiercely? Knowing that they may well hang if they surrender! Your lesson will, I think, be learned backwards!"

"In Melun they will be the more ready to capitulate – those in command. Before they anger me more sorely! See you, James – I hanged no knights or gentles, only the common soldiery. At Sens and Montereau the leaders made their peace with me, and went free. One must divide, to win. In Melun, the men-at-arms may fear a hanging – but their leaders, who make the decisions, will be the more anxious to negotiate."

"I cannot say that I admire such policy . . ."

"Perhaps not. But then, you were not asked, were you!"

Henry shrugged, mustering a grim smile. "But . . . at least, I am glad that you are concerned for the speedy capitulation of Melun, my friend. For in this you may assist. There is, I am informed, a fair contingent of Scots in the town."

James frowned.

"A proclamation from yourself, declaring these to be in rebellion to their liege-lord if they persist, would no doubt help speed the surrender, Cousin."

"I told you. A captive king's proclamations are not to be regarded by free men."

"Nevertheless, such might have notable effect – since these Scots can scarcely hope to win out of Melun free men! And are you indeed so much a captive now, James? I had not thought it!"

"My conditions are greatly improved, yes. I acknowledge it. But as far as my kingship is concerned, I am still in bonds. I cannot act King of Scots to these subjects of mine."

"Then, at least, act their friend, Cousin. Urge that for their own good they should surrender now, rather than prolong the defiance. Melun must eventually fall to me – for I will never lift the siege. And Charles de Valois is not the man to risk his neck to succour it! Better for all that it be finished quickly. Certainly for your Scots therein. Tell them so, my friend – and theirs!"

James paced the floor of the abbot's room of the Abbey of Corbeil, at a loss. "I do not know. What is best. What is right. I shall have to think on this . . ."

"Go think then, Cousin. Think well. Remembering that every day that the siege is prolonged more men will die. And fewer Scots will return home to Scotland. That, whatever else, is certain."

James all but groaned.

Riding north again into the flat plain of Normandy, James did not know whether to be relieved or downcast. It was now September and after long weeks of the weary and depressing siege of Melun, it was good to be on the move again. Nevertheless, he felt that he had lost ground. Gone were the high hopes and chivalric excitements of July; siege warfare in a conquered country was like that. Moreover he was largely back to being a prisoner again, he felt – for riding beside him were not only John Lyon and David Douglas, but Sir Richard Spice, his old gaoler, and an escort of men-at-arms. He was not to go riding about France a free man. And James could not but feel that this detachment north to Rouen was little more than an excuse of Henry's to be rid of him; that having got his proclamation out of him, his usefulness with the English army was for the meantime past and his company dispensable.

His errand, in theory, was acceptable enough – if hardly such as demanded a monarch's attention. The Scots from Montereau had reached as far as Rouen on their way home, and there got into some trouble. Not altogether to be wondered at, for men left leaderless and with no means of support other than what they could find for themselves. The military governor of Rouen had held them there. Other small parties of Scots from lesser places had been sent to Rouen likewise, as a sort of clearing-house. King James was to establish himself in that city, and see that his countrymen behaved themselves. Also to aid their onward passage to various Channel ports, and embarkation thereafter, where possible, in returning English supply ships.

Providing that there were enough Scots to see to and repatriate, it was a useful and necessary task, however humdrum. But it was galling, if not insulting, that James must have Spice and his men always at his shoulder. Evidently Henry feared that he might desert to the enemy. That had been Orkney's idea once, of course – though James had never seriously considered it.

There were not, indeed, enough Scots to keep James occupied in Rouen – nothing like it, once he got the first batch off to a returning transport at Le Havre. Long autumn days and nights of boredom ensued, in the plague-cleared city which had now become no more than a great military supply base for the conquered North of France. As the weeks passed James slept more than he had ever done, even during his most rigorous confinement, drank more, even tried his hand at wenching for want of other occupation – although the female company available at Rouen was scarcely for the fastidious, however accessible. He could not decide whether such activities helped to take his mind off Joanna Beaufort, now that he had over-much time to think of her, or the reverse. In general, in the furtherance of his education in soldiering, his experience now was probably basic, almost essential, and well calculated to dispose of knightly fantasies. It was not so very long before he was wishing that he was back with Henry and the others, and wondering how he might effect his recall – for his instructions had been to stay at Rouen until further notice.

His opportunity came in unexpected fashion. On the last day of October a different kind of Scots soldier arrived at Rouen, under safe-conduct and an English escort – Sir William Douglas of Drumlanrig, seeking King James. A big, forceful red-headed bull of a man, of the Dalkeith branch – a kinsman of Whittinghame – James already knew him, for he had been one of the five Scots envoys who had accompanied Orkney to Windsor Castle to treat for his temporary release two years before. Orkney had warned then that he was Albany's man rather than James's. Now he came from Albany's son, the Constable, John Stewart, Earl of Buchan. He had journeyed from Buchan's headquarters at Tours, in Touraine, midway between Paris and La Rochelle, had seen King Henry at Corbeil, and so come to Rouen.

"Your Grace," he said bluntly and without preamble, almost before decent greetings were over. "This ordinance of yours – this proclamation. It is ill done. My lord the Constable is much displeased. As are all honest men. You ar'na to be congratulated, Sire, on this!"

James restrained himself. "You speak of my advice to the Scots in Melun, Sir William? To lay down their arms. I regret it if this displeases you. And my lord of Buchan. But – I gave this advice not lightly. After much thought. Believing it for the best. For these my countrymen." Deliberately he forbore to say subjects.

199

"The best? For the Scots? Or for the English!"

The younger man frowned. "I would remind you that it is Scots who are besieged in Melun – not English," he said, as patiently as he might.

"Melun is the least of it," Douglas asserted strongly. "It is the doubts, the mistrust, you sow in all the Scots host, that concerns us."

"Do no doubts afflict *you*, Sir William? About the rightness of shedding Scots blood in this cause? Now that the French king and government has gone over to Henry. With more than half of France. You are no longer fighting for France – only the Dauphin and the Orleanists."

"Think you we ever were fighting for France?" the other asked bluntly. "We fight for Scotland only. We'd liefer fight the English here, in France, than on our own Scots soil! That's the whole of it."

Slightly taken aback at such unvarnished frankness, James was silent.

"If King Henry wasna hammering France, he'd be hammering Scotland," the Douglas went on. "That one must be fighting somebody. We must hold him, if he's no' to be master in France *and* Scotland! And Your Grace's edict makes him the more ill to hold, i' faith!"

James rubbed his chin. "Surely you make too much of this, sir?" he protested. "Melun will fall. Henry is set on that. I but advise the Scots therein to urge surrender now, rather than later. For their own good. And that of all the garrison. And it is no edict. Since I am not ruling my country, in captivity, I do not, cannot, issue commands to my people. I but advise. And only these men in Melun."

The visitor searched his youthful monarch's face. "You say so, Sire? Yet all through France it is being announced otherwise. On Henry's authority. That the King of Scots commands all Scots in France to lay down their arms forthwith. On pain of treason."

"No!"

"But yes! That is the way of it."

"It is not true. I gave no such command. Refused to give it, indeed. This is damnable . . .!"

"It is Henry, lad! The English! It seems he has outwitted you."

"Outwitted! You mean cheated, forsworn me! Used my words . . ."

"I would have thought Your Grace would have known King Henry by this time! Known that he uses all. For his own ends. Always."

"I must see him," James muttered. "This is not to be borne."

"Think you Henry will unsay it? It is too late, Sire. The ill is done."

"At least, I shall speak him my mind. And you, sir – you will tell the Constable, my cousin, the truth of this. I do not know him, have never met him. But I have heard better of him, at least, than his father, Albany . . .!"

"Whose soul may God keep, Sire."

"Eh . . .? What do you say? Albany's soul? If he has one . . .!"

"God save us! Is it possible? That you do not know? King Henry has not told you? Albany – the old Duke – is dead. Has been, for months."

"Dead! Albany dead? For months . . .?" James swallowed. "And . . . and I was not told!"

"The King of England knew. He spoke of it to me but two days back, at Corbeil. I vow his spies had him the word within a week!"

"Aye." That came out on a long exhalation of breath. "And it was no man's duty to inform me? The King! That the Regent of my realm had died. Orkney? Has he also forgotten me?" That was bitter.

"Orkney? Sire – my lord of Orkney is dead, also. Of a fever. Before the Duke . . ."

"Dear God! Orkney – dead! My friend!" James sat down suddenly on a bench, overcome.

John Lyon and David Douglas, who had stood listening throughout, hurried forward to their master's side.

He waved them away, and presently looked up. "Your tidings are bitter, Sir William," he said thickly. "But I must needs swallow them. Complete them, sir. Tell me – what is done in Scotland now? Who rules? In Scotland today, with Albany gone?"

"Why, Sire – who but Duke Murdoch. Albany's heir. He was appointed Regent and Governor of the Realm, in his father's stead."

"Murdoch! That popinjay! That . . . that posturing weakling!" James was on his feet again, fists clenched. "Murdoch Stewart – Regent of Scotland!"

"Aye, Sire."

"Then, may God in His heaven have mercy on my poor unhappy country, I say!"

Two afternoons later a grim-faced James rode into Corbeil, the still protesting and uneasy Sir Richard Spice at his heels. Also Sir William Douglas. But King Henry was not there. Melun had surrendered the day before, and the king had gone to superintend the taking over of the town and fortress.

James was not to be diverted or delayed. Leaving Douglas of Drumlanrig to head back westwards to his own people, James rode on the few miles to Melun, despite Spice's opposition.

Threading the seething military encampment outside the walls, they learned that Henry was within the captured fort itself.

Outside the main gates of Melun they reined up, James at least aghast. Before the gates huge timber frameworks had been set up, enormous gibbets, from which dangled scores of hanged men, who birled and twirled in the gusty November evening breeze.

"They said . . . they said . . . honourable terms!" James got out from between tight lips. "What terms . . . are these?"

Spice did not reply. But one of a group of English soldiery standing there overheard, and spoke up, grinning.

202

"No terms for such cattle, lord! These are just the rascally Scots. King Harry does not treat with such!"

For long James sat his mount there, staring. At length he turned the beast round, to ride blindly away – away from gibbet and gates both. He could not trust himself to speak – least of all, to Henry Plantagenet – that night.

13

James Stewart's military education proceeded – at the hands
of a master. He had much to learn, and he learned it hardly.
But undoubtedly it was all profitable learning for a king,
and one who was monarch of a fighting people such as the
Scots – profitable if less than romantic or flattering to his
self-esteem.

He learned, first of all, that commanding generals are
not to be argued with – however loftily-born the protester.
Henry was busy, and could by no means make time to see
him – at least not alone or in conditions where the latter
could make representations. In the end James wrote down
his indictment, both on the matter of the false issue of the
alleged proclamation by the King of Scots, and on that of the
shameful hanging of the Scots from the garrison of Melun;
wrote in angry resentment – and received no reply, nor
any better satisfaction than the mere setting of it down.
The audience he demanded did not materialise. Instead he
found himself two days later peremptorily commanded to
return forthwith to his post at Rouen, left against orders –
a grim Sir Richard Spice and increased escort seeing that
he did so. Another soldier's lesson was learned, however
unwillingly. Spice made it very clear that he considered his
charge to have got off lightly.

So James was back in Rouen, kicking his heels, while
Henry celebrated his triumph. For with the fall of the
three fortresses, and a swift subsequent thrust westwards
into the main Orleans territory, the Dauphin's forces had
lost heart, and retired all along the line. The Castilians
retreated southwards and the Scots west, while Charles

de Valois himself abandoned Paris and fled, none knew for certain whither. Save for the south-west corner, all France was now Henry's. He entered Paris in triumph on the first of December, with his mad father-in-law carried at his side. The next day the two queens were brought there from Corbeil, and a programme of elaborate celebrations instituted, to continue right over Yuletide.

The King of Scots was not invited to any of it.

After the first bitterness, James summoned all his hardihood and philosophy both, in order to live with himself. One by one the veils had been stripped from his too romantic Stewart eyes. Clearly he was not to be allowed the luxury of illusions. In all things he was learning to face stark realities. He was a puppet, no more than that. To be used. And when his usefulness was past, to be discarded. Until the next time. And once there was no foreseeable next time, his discarding would be final and drastic. Henry Plantagenet was the supreme realist. Chivalry, James perceived, was outdated quite, a mere pretty screen to erect while harsh realities ruled behind – if it had ever been anything else.

Sometimes James almost wished for a return to his old captivity, where at least his illusions might have remained safe, sheltered, unshattered.

But Henry was not finished with him yet. One bleak January day Rouen was galvanised. King Harry was coming, on his way back to England. That night, James was summoned to the royal presence at last.

It was not a private interview, of course. There would be no more such. Rouen's military governor had been ordered to provide a banquet in the Archbishop's palace, and when James presented himself he was kept waiting in an ante-room until Henry and Queen Catherine arrived and were seated. Thereafter he was conducted to a place at the dais-table at Catherine's left hand, three down from Henry – with no further acknowledgement from that monarch than a raised eyebrow; and none from anybody else save the Queen herself.

Catherine admittedly seemed pleased enough to see him,

in her lack-lustre, slightly shifty way. She talked to him, rather than to Philip of Burgundy on her right. Indeed, as the evening progressed, it became apparent to James that this young woman was to be the go-between; that Henry was going to convey his wishes and decisions through her rather than at first hand, thus insulating himself from argument and wordy warfare. James learned, for instance, that he was to accompany the royal pair to England, and on a triumphant tour of the land thereafter.

"Why?" he demanded. "Henry despises, mocks and mis-uses me. What cause has he to drag me round England in his train? I can serve him nothing there. Nor pleasure him with my company!"

Her darting eyes considered him sidelong. "You under-value yourself, sir," she said. "Henry is an able merchant, who well knows the value of his wares! When to display them in his booth – and when to return them to his storerooms! That I was not long in discovering!"

A little shaken by this shrewd summary on the part of Henry's young wife, James inclined his head. "Perhaps, Madam. But I, you will recollect, am but old and shop-worn goods! I have been England's prisoner for nigh on fifteen years. And Henry's for seven of them. I have been of use to him here in France, yes. Or, not myself, but my name and style. A puppet to be seen to dance to his tune. But in England I am stale tidings . . ."

"I think you mistake, my friend," she returned. "In England your name and plight is known – but you have not been seen. You have been kept hidden, a prisoner, I believe? Now, you are to be seen. As am I. And others. Philip of Burgundy, here. And my uncle, Charles of Orleans, still captive in England. Henry requires a show. He is the bear-leader – and we are all his bears!"

"For what purpose? Why should Henry require this show?" James had dropped his voice, glancing along the table, past the Queen.

"That is no secret, at least," she said. "Henry, because of his very victories, needs men. Soldiers. English soldiers.

Since I think he scarce trusts us French! He has so many cities and fortresses to garrison, so much of France to hold. He must have more men, ever more men. That is the way of the conqueror, is it not? And his English nobles do not send him the men. A king who leaves his own country for long must pay the price. His brother, the Duke of Bedford, next heir, who governs in England, fails him in this. Perhaps of a purpose. So we go to England, my lord James – for men! To all its cities and towns – to show how great a warrior is King Harry. How glorious his triumphs. How noble a thing to be his soldiers! Thus and thus it is, my lord James – and we, his bears, must dance for our suppers!"

James was silent, perceiving that he had misjudged this young woman. She was a deal more clever than he had realised. And undoubtedly the more dangerous therefore. That she should speak so, only a few feet away from her puissant husband, to her husband's captive . . . Was this perhaps all part of Henry's greater cunning?

"We are in like state, you and I, are we not?" Catherine went on, softly. "We should be friends, my lord James." And so lightly as barely to be felt, her finger-tips brushed the back of his hand.

James drew in on himself, with an inner stillness, whatever words he used to hide it. This woman, he reminded himself, was the outrageous Isabella of Bavaria's daughter – and mad Charles's also. He had need to watch his steps – even if Henry had likewise.

Queen Catherine was accurate as to her information, at anyrate. Two days later the royal cavalcade set out northwards for the Channel, travelling by Amiens to Calais – and James went with it. There was quite distinctly a King's entourage and a Queen's; James's place was clearly with the latter.

It was a bad time of the year for journeying, but Henry seemed to be in a fret to get back to England. He was leaving behind his brothers Clarence and Gloucester, and most of his commanders, to keep France in order – the obvious inference being that he would be back shortly and that he by no means believed his warfare here to be over. The Dauphin was reported now here, now there, and there were rumours that Queen Isabella was secretly encouraging him. Moreover the Scots were said to be sending reinforcements, and the Spanish likewise. It was perhaps a little early for triumphal progresses.

After a stormy crossing, they landed at Dover at the beginning of February. All the way to London, despite the weather, there were set welcomes in each town they touched at, with deputations and loyal addresss. If there was a certain monotony about these occasions, and a certain mechanical quality about the hurrahs for King Harry – with no hurrahs for the new Queen Catherine – that was perhaps inevitable. The fact that these demonstrations of acclaim were scarcely spontaneous, indeed were ordered and arranged by Henry himself as he went, held the greater significance. England, it seemed, was growing tired of perpetual war, and its drain on her resources in treasure and men – the more so that, now that Henry was Regent of France, the lucrative business of French prisoners to ransom no longer was suitable. Henry had reigned for seven years – and five of them he had spent campaigning in France, inevitably neglecting his own realm. Now he had brought back a French wife, and a largely French train. And, it was said, he wanted more Englishmen to take back with him to France, many more. The enthusiasm was not there. Moreover, this time there had been no dramatic victories, like Agincourt; only a succession of dull sieges. There was a strain and urgency about Henry Plantagenet, the paladin of Western Christendom, which went but strangely with a victor's triumph.

James once or twice found himself almost sorry for his renowned fellow-monarch.

London, admittedly, greeted her king with rapture – for London was different from the rest of England, a world in itself, excitable, boisterous, ever seeking sensation and an excuse to abandon the daily round for carnival. Even Catherine was impressed by the Londoners and their evident pride in King Harry. She made one of her unexpectedly shrewd comments, to James, as they entered Westminster Palace.

"Henry, I see, is King of London – whether or no he is King of England! Or of France!"

James was seeing a deal more of Catherine de Valois than was his desire. He was sorry for her – but he could not find it in him to like her. They were inevitably thrown together – which seemed to be Henry's intention, a circumstance which in itself made James the more uneasy, since the Plantagenet always had reasons for his actions. The Queen was apt to show him favours, and to care not who perceived it. He could almost have welcomed the confines of the Tower, again.

But, no. James was now installed at Westminster, with the rest of the Court – admittedly in small and remote quarters but still within the palace precincts. John Lyon and David Douglas remained with him.

The new Queen's arrival was to be celebrated by a coronation ceremony, and great were the immediate preparations. This was to be a resplendent occasion. Henry's own coronation had been a somewhat scamped and hurried affair, overshadowed by his unfortunate and notorious assumption of the crown before his father was truly dead, and the doubts of most of his magnates that he was fit to rule. Now all this was to be put right in no uncertain fashion; and swiftly – for Henry was anxious to be off on his recruiting drive with the minimum of delay. So planning, precedencies, dressmaking and rehearsals were the order of the day, and activity was almost feverish. Without it being actually stated, and without any clear reason being evident, Henry gave the impression of a man working against time.

James was involved in all this in some measure. He was on his guard that it should not be in too great a measure, for Catherine was eager, apparently artlessly, that he should take a prominent part in the proceedings – whereas he perceived only too clearly the guiding hand behind her plans, that would have the King of Scots playing a humbly significant part in the worshipful coronation of England's

Queen-Consort, with all the homage and duty to an overlord king which such might be held to imply.

On one of his many summonses to the Queen's quarters, one February afternoon, however, James found himself much shaken in his careful role of limited involvement. Catherine desired him to make the ritual presentation to her, at the Abbey ceremony, on behalf of the non-English and non-French chivalry of Christendom, immediately after the Papal Legate's presentation. Surely he would not refuse to do her this service, which would in no way make him seem subservient to Henry? The Queen hung on his arm, prettily beseeching, in her plea – while James was in fact speechless, struck rigid. Amongst the French ladies whom Catherine had brought with her, stood two new ladies-in-waiting – the Countess of Warwick and Joanna Beaufort.

James recovered himself sufficiently to bow stiffly – but not sufficiently to prevent himself from thrusting off the Queen's person rather more abruptly than was fitting.

Catherine's quick eyes darted, and narrowed.

It was eight months since he had seen her, and Joanna had grown only the more lovely in the interval. She was looking at him now, after a deep curtsy, directly, calmly, but far from coldly, one would have said transparently honestly and with just a trace of sorrow, certainly with no hint of shame or discomfort.

Thickly, jerkily, he greeted first the Countess of Warwick and then the younger woman. His words were random, almost gruff, for him. Lady Warwick murmured gentle acknowledgements. Joanna inclined her chestnut-brown head, but said nothing.

"Your husband. My lord of Warwick. He is well," James went on. "I left him in Amiens. He was good to me. Most kind. I hope that I see your ladyship well, also?"

"I am well, yes. Though sorely missing my lord. But happy that you, at least, are come home again, my lord James."

"Home . . .?" he said, brows raised. But his eyes never left Joanna's face.

The Countess looked confused, but it was the Queen who spoke. "These ladies — they are your friends, James?" she asked, apparently prepared to overlook his curt withdrawal from her touch.

He hesitated for a moment. "They have offered a prisoner . . . of their various kind attentions . . . in the past," he said, in stilted, laboured fashion.

"And hope to again, Your Grace," the younger woman returned quietly.

Again Catherine's swift glance, at this Joanna's first remark. It was the first time that she had heard James referred to as Your Grace — when there was the well-known court edict that he was to be acknowledged only as the Lord James.

The Queen took his arm again. "Come, my friend — you must see the gown which I am to wear for the crowning. It is now finished. With a train four ells of length, embroidered with the Lilies of France and the Leopards of England, all ringed with pearls . . ."

Instead of exclaiming over the magnificent coronation robes, James questioned Catherine, low-voiced. "Your new ladies? How came you to choose . . . these? Was it Henry's choice?"

"Who else? I know no Englishwomen. Are they not suitable? The Lady of Warwick — she is wife to Henry's friend. And the Lady Joanna is Henry's near cousin, is she not? A convenient choice, no? If I must have Englishwomen!"

"Convenient, indeed!"

The convenience of Henry's choosing was less than apparent, at least as far as Joanna Beaufort was concerned, in the days that followed. Whatever Queen Catherine's reasons, she appeared to single out Joanna for her displeasure, berating her, setting her the most demeaning tasks for a lady-in-waiting, deliberately snubbing her — especially if James Stewart was nearby. James saw it all — for he was, to all intents, now part of the Queen's household —

211

and seethed with a strange conflict of emotions. There were times when he could barely hold himself in, his heart bleeding for the young woman – although at calmer moments he told himself that such treatment was little more than she deserved. For her part, Joanna accepted her humiliations with quiet dignity, patient without being meek. She was younger than Catherine by a few months, in her twentieth year – but she gave the impression of infinitely greater maturity.

Matters reached a climax two days before the coronation. At a rehearsal, in the abbey church, of the Queen's procession under the guidance of the Chancellor of the realm, Bishop Henry Beaufort, Joanna's uncle – King Henry being absent in the West, having more important things to attend to than such play-acting – Catherine, with seeming clumsiness, dropped on the floor the missal handed to her by the Abbot of Westminster upon entering her stall. As the cleric would have stooped to pick it up, a swift movement of the Queen's hand restrained him. Instead, she turned to her ladies behind her, and deliberately singling out Joanna, with an imperious gesture pointed forward and down.

There was an audible gasp in the great church – not least from Chancellor Beaufort of Winchester. With pages, esquires and junior clerics present, such a behest was nothing less than a studied insult to the highest-born of her ladies. Yet it was, at the same time, most clearly a royal command, even if unspoken, and men stood rigid.

Not so Joanna Beaufort. Inclining her head, she moved forward unhurriedly.

Then, even her serenity faltered. From the side, from one of the lesser stalls into which he had been shown, the King of Scots strode swiftly. Even as the Queen's hand went out again, forbidding it, he bent to pick up the missal, and with a bow handed it back to her. With a second bow he looked at Joanna – and saw her face flush hotly and her eyes widen. He turned, and went back to his place.

For a few moments there was a profound hush. It was Catherine who broke it. She slapped down the missal on her stall, and twisted around – much upsetting the pages with her train.

"It is enough!" she cried. "Enough for this day!" In the stress of the moment she spoke in French. Even as she spoke, she was hurrying back towards the main entrance, courtiers and clerics scattering to give her passage.

At the true ceremony two days later, Joanna Beaufort was not present, dismissed as lady-in-waiting. James however appeared to suffer no diminution of the Queen's favour, little as he sought it. Richly clad in a handsome tabard trimmed with fur, bearing the royal Lion Rampant of Scotland back and front – a last-moment gift from Catherine, which must of course have been in preparation for some time – he duly played his part in the magnificent spectacle by making the presentation of a great jewel to the Queen, as representing the knights of Christendom, catching King Henry's cynical eye in the process. Thereafter, at the banquet in the Guildhall, he sat at her left hand at the Queen's table, when she addressed herself considerably more to him than to the stiff Bedford, Henry's least favoured brother, at her other side. James noted, over at the King's table, Joanna, seated between her uncles, the Chancellor and the Duke of Exeter. He sought not to catch her eye – and failed consistently.

Henry allowed little time to elapse between the finish of the celebrations and the start of the projected great triumphal tour of England, which was to be his answer to the charge that his people did not know him, and his method of raising reinforcements sufficient to secure him France, once and for all. In a glittering cavalcade two miles long and unsurpassed in brilliance, Majesty took the road north out of London supported by sufficient lesser luminaries to dazzle the most phlegmatic of insular English. As ever, James found himself allotted to the Queen's train, and rode with her uncle, his late fellow-captive Charles, Duke of Orleans, and her cousin, Philip, Duke of Burgundy.

It was when riding up Hampstead Hill that James noticed something familiar about the single cloaked figure riding at the tail of the galaxy of ladies immediately behind the

Queen. It was the beautifully upright and proud carriage in the saddle which caught his attention – and almost before his eye had sought for the rich chestnut-brown hair, he was spurring forward leaving the Frenchmen without a word.

He reined up beside her, doffing his velvet and plumed cap – but finding words difficult to come by, though she smiled her welcome.

"You are back?" he jerked. "Amongst the Queen's ladies. I had not looked for it."

"Nor had I," she agreed. "But . . . I am back. By royal command!"

"Ah! Not . . . not Catherine's?"

"Not Queen Catherine's, Sire."

"So-o-o!" He frowned.

Into his silence, she spoke presently. "I have not had opportunity to thank Your Grace. For what you did in the church, that day. It was kind, noble."

"It was nothing. I could do no less," he said, almost gruffly, dismissing the matter with a wave of his hand. "Tell me – does Henry command that you return to be one of the Queen's ladies in order that you should be near her? Or near me! Tell me frankly."

She nodded her head, almost as though acknowledging a charge fairly made. "I believe to be near *you*, Sire – since I think I have ever been frank with you."

He opened his mouth to speak – and then thought better of it. But his frown was eloquent.

She sighed a little. "It is King Henry's desire that I should be wed to the King of Scots," she said.

"God – you are frank indeed!" he ejaculated.

"To my sorrow, Sire."

"Ha! You say so! Your *sorrow*, you say!"

"Yes."

He looked at her, sidelong. "You . . . you do not wish this?"

She answered slowly, as though picking her words. "I do not wish . . . to be wed . . . to the King of Scots."

"M'mmm," he said.

214

Wordless they rode for a distance. It was the young woman who spoke first. "Your Grace – my aunt, the Lady Westmorland, sent me a letter. She wrote that you had spoken with her. Said that you had declared yourself to have reason to be wary of the Beaufort family. That you would watch all such heedfully, in the future. She wrote that she did not believe that it was of my uncles that you spoke!"

He moistened his lips. "The Countess spoke truly – if unadvisedly," he admitted.

"It seems then that I have offended." She shook her head. "We spoke together but once – although other times we . . . we saw each other." Her voice came a little unsteadily now. "That last time, we parted as I believed . . . friends. I was aware of no offence. Your Grace said, indeed, that I had been kind. That was scarce true . . ."

"Aye, and there you have it! My sorrow – that it was scarce true!" His voice quivered. "As I discovered!"

"I was not kind – although I would have liked to be. But nor was I unkind. You . . . you never looked towards me again. In what, I pray you, did I offend?"

"God be good – you can ask that? When you have but finished telling me that it was all Henry's will, Henry's scheming! That you should ensnare me. As, by the Rude, you almost did! I learned, that night, that it *was* all Henry's doing. That Henry planned that I should marry you."

"And *my* offence, Your Grace?"

He stared at her, at a loss. "You do not see it . . .?"

"I see only that Henry, for his own ends, would have used my . . . my regard for you. As he uses all things, for his own ends. But the fault here lies surely with him, for conceiving the use. Not with me, for . . . discovering the regard?"

"But . . . but . . ." James shook his head. "It was a deep-laid design. Undoubtedly he brought you to Windsor for that purpose. And you carried out that design . . ."

"All unknowing. As did you not yourself, Sire? In some measure carry out his design. But also unknowing?"

He swallowed. "You knew nothing of this? Of the design?"

"Nothing. Perhaps I was foolish. A simple, foolish girl. Always I had heard of you – the prisoner-king. My mother told me of you, so often. You had much moved her, at Nottingham. Long I had thought of you – as a young girl may think, and dream. Injured by fate. A figure of . . . of high romance and chivalry! I desired to see you. And when I did contrive it . . . dear God, I was nowise bettered!"

"You say that you *contrived* to see me? Then . . . those mornings? In the garden? Henry did not send you there . . .?"

"Send me?" Almost her eyes flashed. "*Send* me! Mary-Mother – you can ask that! Your Grace suggests that I . . . I would so behave? At the behest of any man, king or none! Stoop so low! Act the mummer and the mountebank . . .!" Even beneath her travelling-cloak the heaving of her fine bosom was evident.

It was probably that heaving which overturned James's doubts. It went straight to his heart – a heart which, of course, unlike his head, had never truly defected from its allegiance, given that May morning, and thereby much added to his long turmoil of spirit. Though a romantic, James Stewart was entirely masculine.

He gripped her arm fiercely, now, through that cloak. "God ha' mercy!" he groaned. "Forgive me, Joanna – forgive my crazed and wicked folly! If you can."

"You believed . . . that I could do this!" That was little more than a whisper. "Almost play the whore, the wanton! At Henry's bidding?"

"No, no – never that! Never. Only that you knew his mind. Did as he commanded. I was mad to doubt you. I see it now."

"You went away. Went to France. To the wars. Believing me false. Without a word . . ."

"Aye – God forgive me. And to my own grievous hurt. Joanna – believe me. If I have hurt you, myself I have hurt a score of times as much!"

216

"You think so, my lord James?"

That use of the commanded style for him, completed the man's rout. "I am sorry," he said flatly. "I crave . . . only your pardon."

They rode wordless for a long way, lost in their own thoughts, uncaring how many eyed them and commented. It was indeed, not of their own volition that the silence was eventually broken. The Sieur de Maurville, one of the Queen's gentlemen, rode down the column to them, to flourish a salute.

"Her Majesty requests Your Highness's attendance at her side," he said.

James frowned. "Convey to Queen Catherine my duty, sir," he said. "I shall attend her presently."

The other raised expressive brows, spread protesting hands, and rode off.

"You should not have done that, I think," Joanna said, troubled in voice. "The Queen will not take it kindly . . ."

"I care not how she takes it!"

"Perhaps not, Your Grace. But *I* do. Since I it is, I fear, who will bear the weight of her spleen!"

"M'mmm. I see. Yes – there may be truth in that. I had not considered it."

"Go forward then, Sire. Before she takes it too much amiss. And . . . leave me to my thoughts."

"Thoughts that are bitter? To my hurt, my undoing?"

"Undoing? Of that I do not know. Bitter, yes – and no. Not altogether. Since I must be frank with you, even yet. Bitter-sweet, shall we say?"

"Frank! Aye – from now, may we be frank with each other! For I, at least, have learned my lesson."

"Have you, Sire?" She looked at him, searchingly.

"Yes, i' faith, I have!" He held out his hand. "Joanna – this Sire, and Your Grace. Between us, must you have it so? I mind, we had a compact once, did we not? That you should be different. From all others. That you should call me James. Only you."

"Much has happened since then, has it not?"

217

"Then – I am not forgiven?"

She smiled faintly. "Go forward to the Queen, Your Grace. And let this poor woman's head of mine look in at itself. Head . . . and other parts! Go!" But as she said it, she reached out lightly to touch his wrist.

Bitter-sweet, Joanna Beaufort had said, and it most aptly described the relationship between herself and James Stewart in the strange, busy weeks that followed, as they travelled the length and breadth of England. It could hardly have been otherwise. King Henry and his designs came ever between them, so that their very association was soiled. Catherine seldom lost opportunity to hurt Joanna – a situation for which James knew himself to be responsible. They were, of course, the objects of every unkind glance and whisper. And save when they managed to trot the roads side by side, they were never alone together. The strain on them both, inevitably, was great.

Nevertheless, if the bitter was all too evident, the sweet was not to be denied. James knew an enormous weight to have been lifted from him – especially after, that same evening, at St. Alban's Abbey, he perceived pinned to Joanna's gown a most ancient and faded rose, now brown rather than red; and next day, when she called him James. He was brisker, brighter, basically happier than he had been for long – and few there were who did not notice it. He even began to compose poetry again. As for the young woman, her beauty but bloomed and burgeoned like a tended plant, as that spring of 1421 burgeoned in England.

Week succeeded week of that fantastic progress, as they went by Dunstable, Bedford, Northampton, Lutterworth. Easter they spent at Leicester. Then on to Warwick, Kenilworth, Coventry. Frequently Henry left the Queen's entourage and took his own on sallies right and left, to lesser towns and the seats of great lords and proud prelates, in the pursuit of allegiance, men and money – though on these occasions he never took James. Indeed now it was established that the two kings were never together, save in a crowd; and that the King of Scots was part of the Queen's household.

The reasons behind this much exercised James – since, with Henry Plantagenet, reasons there must be. One day, he put it to Joanna, as they rode north towards Nottingham. She nodded gravely.

"I fear it, think of it often," she admitted. "There is purpose behind it. What I fear is that you may be made scapegoat, James. Should Henry think to get rid of his Queen!"

"Get rid of Catherine . . .!"

"It may not be so – but I dread it. He has never made pretence that he loves her. He married her only to gain the French throne. And an heir. If she does not produce him an heir, he will require a wife who does! Henry is ruthless. They have been married nine months – and she is not pregnant. It is my fear that if she is not with child soon, he may choose to put her away. He would need excuse. And you – you could be the excuse!"

"Me! God in heaven – why me? When he would have me wed *you*!"

"Because you are royal. A king. Henry is proud. If he must claim to have been cuckolded, he could only admit it by a fellow-monarch! With any subject it would be *lèse-majesté*, treason. Demanding a trial, and execution. With you it would be different, James. The accusation would be enough. No inconvenient trial. Catherine could be put away, in divorce. It may not be so – but I think it is in his strange mind. So you are to be seen as ever with the Queen. I . . . I pray God she conceives quickly!"

"But . . . this beyond all!" he said. "Is this the man who would teach me kingship!"

Nottingham, Pontefract, York, Beverley – and it was there that all changed, abruptly, entirely. Fate, history, caught up with Henry Plantagenet at Beverley – in the shape of a weary, travel-worn courier on a dying horse. He bore a letter from Humphrey, Duke of Gloucester, in Rouen. There had been a great battle, at Baugé, in Anjou, on Easter

Eve. Led by the Earl of Buchan, the Scots forces in France had defeated an English army under their brother Clarence. Clarence, indeed, left governor of France, was dead. As were no fewer than five English earls and a great host. Joanna's two brothers, the Earl of Somerset and Lord Edward Beaufort, were captured, with innumerable others. All Anjou, Brittany and even some of Normandy had gone over to the Dauphin. Paris was wavering. Henry must return to France, forthwith, if all was not to be lost.

Henry's strange urgency, his seemingly uncalled-for race against time, was seen to be justified.

The man showed now the other aspect of his quality. There was no panic, no confusion of alarm. Immediate action there was. The great cavalcade was turned face-about. Orders were despatched by swift courier all over the kingdom – not least north to the Border, to cancel the talks which Henry had arranged with Scotland's Regent Murdoch at, as it were, the apex of the royal progress. And a tight company of Henry's most useful and vigorous companions were commanded to prepare themselves to ride fast and far, at once. James, to his surprise, found himself included in this party. It was understood that they were for France direct. Before the Queen and her ladies though it was, James crushed Joanna to him almost wordlessly, and stumbled away after the others.

Thereafter all England heard of her puissant monarch was the pounding of his horse's hooves as they thundered southwards, ever southwards, for the distant Channel.

But the King of England was nothing if not a realist. The hard-riding band went by Windsor, where Henry had ordered others to assemble. And at Windsor, on 23rd April, St. George's Day, James found himself abruptly accorded the accolade of knighthood, along with some others, at Henry's own hands. He was not so simple, now, as to imagine that it was earned by past prowess rather than by the hope of future services. He remembered that it was the Scots who had won the Battle of Baugé.

14

James, in France again, was not long in discovering Henry's mind. A great council of commanders was held at Rouen, and while James was not included in this, he was summoned to appear before the rump of it before it dispersed. With the return to France, Henry's attitude towards his prisoner had subtly changed again. James was once more the junior officer, under military discipline; but there was a greater frankness, less of the distant constraint.

Now James found himself facing a group of the highest-placed leaders around King Henry – such as had survived the disaster of Baugé. They looked grimly determined, and not over-friendly – although James was comforted to see at least one kindly glance, that of Richard Beauchamp, Earl of Warwick. Henry, tired-looking, wasted few words and made no attempt to put a gloss on them.

He rapped out the current situation, *vis-à-vis* Scotland. He could no longer have dealings with Murdòch Stewart, who was not only a weakling and a fool but a deceiver and an ingrate. He had greatly reinforced his brother Buchan – and Baugé was the result. He, Henry, had intended to conclude a generous treaty with Scotland – but that was now out of the question. At least with Murdoch. His information was that even now the Earls of Douglas and Mar were gathering a further large Scots army to bring to France. Murdoch was bleeding Scotland white in this infamous adventure.

Murdoch, therefore, must be first countered and then brought down. This demanded both short term and long term policies. The first could be accomplished by com-motion in Scotland and division amongst the Scots here in

France. The second must see the displacement of Murdoch by King James's return to Scotland, in strength.

James listened to all this, set-faced. He did not comment; obviously no comment was expected or desired, at this stage.

To send James back to Scotland at once was not practicable. For one thing, it would look as though it was as a result of Baugé – which was not to be considered. Secondly, it would be useless unless James returned powerfully supported by armed men – otherwise he would find himself *Murdoch's* prisoner. And he, Henry, could not spare an army to go to Scotland with him, meantime. Therefore, this must wait.

But there was this Scots army here in France – James's own subjects. Led by Murdoch's brother, yes – but he might be disposed of; their allegiance transferred to their rightful lord . . .

James spoke up. "I shall not be a party, sir, to any attempts to subvert the Scots armies. I have learned my lesson! There will be no proclamations issued to them in my name, whilst I remain in your hands – true or false!"

"Tush, man – be not so prickly, so hasty! I have said naught of proclamations," Henry snapped. "The subverting, as you name it, will be done by another. One meantime more potent than you! Archibald Douglas! Your Tyneman!"

James showed his perplexity.

"My lord of Douglas is a slippery fish – as you, I think, know well! But he is the most powerful lord in Scotland – and does not love Murdoch Stewart! He worked well enough with your Uncle Albany – but he cannot work with Albany's son. Nor does he relish *Murdoch's* sons running wild in Scotland, as they are doing. He believes Murdoch seeks the throne for himself – *your* throne! Archibald Douglas is prepared to change sides!"

"How . . . how do you know this?" That was strained.

"On the best authority, my friend – Douglas's own! He has never failed to confide in me, since he returned to Scotland from our, h'm, hospitality. As well he might, since

222

I have paid him a generous pension, most regularly! Today, with Mar, Murdoch's cousin – and yours – he is preparing to bring Scots reinforcements to France. On Murdoch's orders. Let him bring those men to *me*, I say – or rather, to you! Not to Buchan. And much good is accomplished. Murdoch and Buchan are confounded. And you – you have struck a blow for your throne."

James found difficulty in speaking. "How . . . how do I know this to be true? Of Murdoch seeking to be king? Of the Douglas? How do I know that it is so much less false than much else?"

"You have my word, sir!" That was fierce. "Murdoch already uses a seal with his own head upon it! His son boasts that he will be Scotland's first King Walter! All my spies report it. But . . . ask Douglas!"

"What do you want me to do?" the younger man asked hoarsely.

"That is simple. Summon the Earl of Douglas to your side, here in France."

"To *my* side! To yours, you mean. I suggest that you summon him yourself, sir. Since he is your pensioner!"

Henry frowned. "Douglas has few scruples. But he perceives one here. He is willing to bring over a force of men – he even numbers them; 200 knights and squires, 200 mounted bowmen, and an unnumbered host of foot. But he cannot bring them, he says, at the behest of the King of England. Only of the King of Scots."

"I' faith – a nice distinction! Here is a nimble traitor!"

"Traitor? To you? The only man in Scotland who can save you your throne, I'd remind you!"

"My sorrow, then! Even so, I have said that I will not play the king while I remain in the hands of another. I will not command Douglas to come here, sir. Even to save my throne."

Henry glared at him, his features working, as the moments passed. At his side, Humphrey of Gloucester spoke in his brother's ear.

"Do not *command*, then. Consent. Consent to his coming," Henry jerked. "Give him something to cover his scruples. Write that you conceive him loyal to yourself. As against Murdoch's pretentions. And agree that he should bring this array of men, in token. Will you throw away all your heritage? For a word? Consent – and I will promise on my royal honour that you shall return to Scotland whenever this French campaign is over-past."

James drew a long breath, and nodded. "That I will agree to. I will not command the Douglas – but I will consent. Since it seems that only so may I save Scotland's unhappy throne from greater woe! And I shall hold you to your royal word, sir – before all these!"

Henry rose to his feet. "This audience is terminated!" he said bringing his hand down flat on the table.

Henry Plantagenet was not long in making his presence felt once more in France. Even before his massive reinforcements began to stream across the Channel from England, he had laid siege to the fortress of Dreux on the Loire, and effected its reduction. He then turned his attention to Beaugency, farther south, near Orleans. Smaller, highly mobile striking forces made swift and vigorous sallies in many directions, to remind the French who was master in their land – though meantime the dangerous Scots-occupied West was left alone, with the lost provinces of Anjou and Brittany. But Paris was secured again, and the Armagnacs driven off southwards. Warwick was one of the leaders of these busy flying columns, and James was glad to be attached to his company, and to see considerable if minor action under his banner, uncomplicated and militarily satisfying. He had a new watch-dog now – Sir William Meryng, a sardonic and hard-bitten veteran campaigner, but much better company than the sour and anxious Spice. The King of Scots' "train" consisted of six esquires, ten mounted archers, and two valets, under Meryng – but these, of course, were in reality his guards to ensure that he did not elect to slip away westwards to

224

the Scots armies. His own faithful friends Lyon and David Douglas were still with him.

It was on the return to Rouen from one of these sallies in the neighbourhood of Mortagne, that they discovered Henry to be in an unusually expansive mood. Two messages had just reached him. One, brought by Thomas Myrton, Vicar of Cupar, a Scots cleric with political interests, was that Earl Archibald Douglas had landed in France, and now awaited safe-conducts from King Henry, for himself and his force, to join the English army instead of the Scots. The other was from London, to inform him that Queen Catherine was pregnant.

James, while having his reservations about Archibald Tyneman, was unfeignedly relieved over the news of Catherine.

It was typical of Henry's methods that, having gained what he required from James, in the shape of what might be made to look like an invitation for the Douglas to defect to the English in France, he arranged that James should be out of the road thereafter – presumably lest he should be in a position to use Douglas's Scots force to his own advantage. Warwick, and James with him, was sent south to Beaugency, nearly a hundred miles south-west of Paris, to assist at the siege there, and to keep watch on the Dauphin, who was now known to have made his headquarters at Bourges, on the Cher, another sixty miles to the south. Douglas and his monarch, therefore, did not meet.

So the summer and autumn passed, campaigning in Orleans, Cher and Touraine. Beaugency town fell, but its strong castle defied the besiegers still. James was, on the whole, not unhappy. Warwick was good company and an excellent tutor in the art of soldiery – and the new keeper was a marked improvement on Spice. Their warfare was uncomplicated and honest, even comparatively chivalrous, with the scheming and the double-dealing left behind. And he had the thought of Joanna Beaufort to comfort and sustain him now, even though the future was uncertain and tangled indeed.

225

Henry's affairs in France prospered. Everywhere the Dauphin and his allies were forced back, out-manoeuvred and out-schemed. Baugé had been almost entirely a Scots victory, but now the Scots were doubtful and divided – even though their leader, Buchan, had been appointed Constable of France by the Dauphin. Undoubtedly Douglas's defection had shaken them grievously – especially as the Earl of Wigtown, Douglas's son and heir, was Buchan's second-in-command, and there were a great many Douglas supporters in the army. Mar, illegitimate Stewart cousin, had duly arrived to reinforce Buchan, and now the old Stewart-Douglas suspicion and rivalry was rampant. Archibald Tyneman himself, with his token force, was more or less inactive – except to line his purse at French expense – for Henry had well said that he was a slippery fish, and preferred to keep him in reserve, not to rely on him in any major action. The purpose of the exercise had been achieved, however; the Scots were at a loss and disunited – and the Dauphin's most valuable allies largely neutralised. No doubt, back in Scotland, the repercussions were making life difficult for Duke Murdoch.

By the onset of winter, all the North of France, right down to Berry and Touraine, was securely in English hands again, save for the extreme western provinces of Brittany, Anjou and Poitou held by the Scots, and the isolated and immensely strong fortress of Meaux, on the Marne, which still held out for the Dauphin.

In December, Henry, with his army encamped around Meaux, learned that Queen Catherine had given birth to a son at Windsor. England had an heir, at last – heir to France also. Christen him Henry, the King commanded, and ordered rejoicings on a vast scale throughout both realms. The Plantagenet cup was near to overflowing.

Nevertheless, when James Stewart saw Henry again, at Rouen in February, he was shocked. He had seemed to be tired, previously, for some time, though driving himself on by his nervous energy, and there had been rumours that he was not well. But here was a man only a shadow of his former self, his hatchet-face so gaunt as to be little more than a caricature, his spare frame stooping, though tense, his eyes burning. That he was only in his thirty-fourth year seemed scarcely believable. James was warned not to comment on his appearance nor ask after his health – for such only threw Henry into furious and uncontrollable rages. He was said to spend a deal of his time alone now, in private prayer and devotions. His veteran commanders were alarmed and unhappy men.

Yet they could not complain that there was any neglect in their business of warfare. However great the change which had come over the English king in these months, he did not allow his new preoccupation with worship to hold up his campaigning. With an urgency which was now almost feverish, he prosecuted the war along ever lengthening lines of communication – and with consistent success. That spring of 1422 saw the Leopards of England, quartered with the Lilies of France, triumphing everywhere – even though Meaux itself did not fall until early May, its leaguer, in fact, Henry's masterpiece in siege-warfare. Although there were some few Scots amongst the surrendered garrison, none was executed on this occasion.

Hardly had Meaux fallen than Queen Catherine arrived from England, in answer to her husband's summons. But, to his fury, she did not bring his son. The child was sickly, she said, unfit for the long journey. Henry, eaten up with his urgency, had thereafter little time to spare for his wife, indeed little use for her, without her child. And James Stewart was no longer desirable as her constant companion – and therefore not available. He was despatched south again, out of the way.

When Henry made his formal entry into Paris, in some pomp, on the last day of May, it was not now thought necessary that the King of Scots, any more than the unfortunate King of France, or even the Duke of Burgundy, should accompany him.

It was at the beginning of August that James was ordered to Cosne, in the Nivernais, one-hundred-and-thirty miles

227

south of Paris, where a Franco-Scots force had had the effrontery to encircle one of Henry's garrisons, and there were insufficient English troops available to deal with them summarily. But though it was Henry who had summoned James to confront his awkward subjects, it was not he whom James found at Cosne when he arrived, but the Duke of Bedford, his brother. The King had turned back at Corbeil.

So unlike Henry Plantagenet was this that the entire English array was in a ferment of misgiving. When, the very next day, one of Henry's privy couriers arrived, it was to spread further alarm – even though it was not from Henry himself that he came, and not to Bedford that he was directed. He brought an urgent message from Queen Catherine to the Lord James, to come to the Bois de Vincennes near Paris, at once. Unofficially, the courier admitted that King Henry was gravely ill.

Bedford handed over his command to Warwick and, with James, took the long road for Paris forthwith and with all speed.

With relays of horses, and snatching only an hour or so's sleep, they rode into Vincennes less than twenty hours later. An air of gloom hung over the French king's hunting palace. James, leaving Bedford, made straight to the Queen's quarters.

Catherine greeted him warmly. She showed no sign of distress, indeed tended to fuss over him. Tired and in no mood for by-play James cut her short curtly.

"You sent for me urgently, Madam," he said. "Not for pleasantries, I take it? Is it Henry? He is ill, they say."

"You are ungallant, sir! We have not seen each other for a twelve-month, and you scarce glance at me! I conceived us to be friends? Whereas you ask only for Henry – who is your enemy!"

"My regrets," he said. "My apologies. I need scarce ask for Your Highness. You are the picture of health. Whereas your husband . . .!"

"You say I look well? You do not think that I seem too fat?" She outlined her heavier breasts. "Child-bearing can make a woman so. Myself, I think not perhaps . . .?"

"Ah, yes." He drew a deep breath. "The child? Your son? He is better?"

"Better . . .?"

"I heard that he was sickly. Less than strong. I should have asked . . ."

"Indeed you should! He is well enough, I hear." She looked away. "But, I would not think that he will be . . . better!"

Her manner of speech drew his swift glance. "Yet you say that he is well?"

"There are more sorts of health than one, are there not?" she answered, her voice strained. "My son, I fear, takes after his grandsire rather than his puissant sire!"

"Grandsire!" James caught his breath. "You mean . . . King Charles? Your father!"

She nodded, head still turned.

"Dear God!"

"The dear God, indeed! Whose mercies, they tell me, are ever new!"

James could find nothing to say.

"I pray that the child is not . . . fatuous," the Queen said. If the word came out almost on a giggle, it was not a mirthful one. "I think not. Simple, perhaps. It is hard to tell, so young. But he lacks, he lacks!"

James cleared his throat. "Is this . . . part of Henry's trouble. What has stricken him?"

"Henry does not know it. At least, *I* have not told him. It would scarce help his present state, I think. That is why I did not bring the child from England, said that he was sickly . . ."

James looked at the young woman with new eyes.

She was plucking at her gown. "I am afraid, James," she went on, voice uneven. "Greatly afraid. Henry is going to die. I know it. What will become of me? And the child?"

229

The man shook his head. "Is it so black? So ill? Henry may but need rest. He has been campaigning for too long, sparing himself nothing. Give him rest and quiet . . ."

"Come," she interrupted him, beckoning. "See for yourself. Rest will not save Henry now. And he gains no rest." She opened a door, and led the way along a passage, where armed guards stood, at intervals. "He asks for you. *You,* James! Continually. You plague his mind. You, and St. Fiacre!"

"Fiacre? What is this?"

"It is *le mal de St. Fiacre*. The physicians say that he is smitten of this evil. He ordered the ravagement of some lands, it seems. During the siege of Meaux. Dedicated to St. Fiacre. And this Fiacre was a Scots prince. Long ago."

"I never heard of such . . ."

They came to a doorway round which a group of men clustered, speaking in low tones. These opened the door for the Queen, and stood aside.

The room within was darkened, and heavy with the odour of sickness. Two physicians and the Earl of Stafford bowed and withdrew at their entry, leaving them alone with the still figure on the great bed.

Henry lay on his side, with his face from them. He did not turn.

"My lord," Catherine said. "It is I. The Queen. Catherine. I have brought you James. King James, of Scotland. Are you . . . are you anything easier?"

There was no answer. After a few moments a hand was raised. It pointed to the door.

Catherine inclined her head and moved away. But she signed to James to remain. Quietly the door closed behind her. The two monarchs were alone together for the first time in nearly two years.

James cleared his throat. "I regret to see you in this case," he said, to the other's back, cursing his own stiffness.

"You are come to mock me! To exult!" That was hoarse accusation.

"I am come because I was sent for. Commanded to come. Your prisoner!"

"No!" Henry heaved himself over, the sorry, wasted wreck of a man. "No – my father's prisoner. Not mine!"

Looking into the tortured, pain-clouded eyes that yet burned with a fire from deep down, James forbore to make the obvious retort. He shook his head wordlessly.

"What could I have done, man?" Henry demanded wildly, his thick voice cracking. "If I had sent you back to Scotland, it would have been to your death! They would have slain you – Albany and his crew. Now Murdoch. They are barbarians, savages! I could not send you . . ."

"You *did* not, at least," James said briefly, grimly.

"I saved you! I preserved your life. I fed and housed and clothed you. Gave you moneys. All that a man could do for another, I did, I say! God is my witness! I gave you great freedom, a household, taught you statecraft," Henry was almost gabbling in the intensity of his agitation. "I received you into my Court. I knighted you – made a soldier of you. I would have given you a wife, of my own close kin . . ." He choked. "God's blood – is it not true?"

James nodded. "Am I denying it, sir? There is truth – of a sort – in all that you have said."

"I have cherished you. Used you like a brother. I have . . . I have . . ." Panting, Henry sank back, exhausted.

"I question the brother. But you have used me, yes!"

For long there was silence, save for the sick man's harsh and uneven breathing. James would have sought to comfort the stricken Plantagenet had he known how – for the wasted, trembling frame, the hollow skull-like features, the grey lifeless colouring, and above all those dull-glowing but almost opaque eyes, told their story all too clearly. Catherine was right. Henry was dying.

"A . . . a king is not as other men." The voice, when it went on, was weaker now, thinner. "A king cannot be judged with lesser men. He must act ever for the greater weal of his realm. You . . . you will discover it. One day. Always he must weigh . . . weigh the price of every act.

231

Not for one man or two. Not even for himself. But for many." Henry raised a quivering finger to point at James. "You hear me?" he croaked.

"I hear you. It may be true. But I would remind you that there are more kings than Henry Plantagenet! There is, for one, Charles de Valois, of France. Even James Stewart, of Scotland!"

"Scotland!" The very word seemed to act like a goad upon the sick man. "God's curse upon it! Scotland!" His voice was high and wild again. "Ever that plaguy land has been my undoing. A knife in my back! Wherever I go, whatever I do, the accursed Scots! This evil – this Fiacre! They say 'tis his vengeance. For some sacrilege. By the Mass – wherever I go I am bearded by Scots, dead or alive!"

"Superstition!" James declared, deliberately scornful now. "You, of all men, to believe such! Henry of England – accepting the tales of begging friars and old women!"

"It is true, I tell you! This of Fiacre. This new and vile sickness. I have been ailing for long. I have known it. Felt the evil thing feeding within me. Like a worm, a serpent. Cutting short my time. So I must needs make haste. So much to do. But this – this new foul distemper. That smites me unawares. Of Fiacre – of Scotland! The Scots again – ever them! Wherein have I wronged them? I could not send you back. I hanged some few, yes – but they were but rogues, in treason. What have I done . . .?"

He had tired himself out again, and lay gasping.

"Do not harry yourself, scourge yourself so," James found himself urging. "What good in it? All is done now. It is not to be undone. But these dark humours serve none any advantage. Rest, Henry – rest, man."

But the other's lips were still moving, as he stared upwards at the ceiling. "Say it," he whispered imploringly. "Say it. That I have not wronged you. Or your people. I cannot die in peace else. My father . . . my father . . . You hear me?"

James had to lean close – and the stench of the other's breath was foul.

"My father – he bade me send you home. When he was dying. I said that I would." The whisper was very faint now. "But how could I? How could I? Forging a brand. To smite myself. To smite England! He should not . . . have made me say it. James – say that . . . you are not . . . wronged!"

The younger man stared at the other, brows lowered, lips tight. His jaw was working, but no words came.

"Of God's mercy – say it!" A hand groped out, to feel for his. "I have . . . given orders. You are to go. When you will. Back. To Scotland. When I am gone. I have . . . told Humphrey. He will rule. In England. All else . . . is settled. Say me this . . . of . . . of your charity!"

"Aye," James mumbled, all but groaned. "You wronged me . . . nothing. It is done – all done."

He took the feeble, flaccid hand and pressed it. Faintly, so very faintly, he felt the grip returned. He thought of that other king's hand in his, in the cathedral of Notre Dame, and this time he did groan.

There were no more words from Henry.

Presently he would have gone, but the limp hand in his retained just sufficient strength to intimate that he was to stay.

For long he waited. Men opened the door, peered in, and closed it again. At length, the hand slipped away. He leaned over, to listen. Henry still breathed, but lightly, shallowly. James Stewart tip-toed to the door, and out.

Against all indications and probabilities, Henry Plantagenet did not die that night. His heart was strong, and he rallied. Next day, although scarcely conscious, his breathing was stronger. Day after day he lingered on, a mere living hulk that clung tenaciously to the last spark of existence. It was two weeks later, on the last day of August, St. Fiacre's Day, with Catherine summoned to her mother's palace of Senlis, twenty miles away, and James sent to Rouen by Bedford, when the word came for which all France and England now waited. King Henry the Fifth was dead. Long live King Henry the Sixth!

All was changed, now, for much of Christendom.

To Rouen, presently, came Henry again, in funereal state, with Queen Catherine and many of the high officers of both realms. James joined the solemn cavalcade there, so much slower than Henry's usual, to turn face for the Channel and England again. Duke John of Bedford remained behind, to govern France – if France would be governed.

Though it was a sombre procession, James Stewart could not mourn. Life would be different now.

15

James was part of Queen Catherine's household again. He had no wish to remain close to her, but she clung to him, suspicious indeed of all others save the Earl of Warwick. She was a frightened woman now – and James, though he sought to reassure her, would have been the last to believe that she had no cause to be. The foreign relict of a dead king, with an eight-month infant as new monarch, was in a position which few would envy. The struggle for power, inevitable hereafter, would scarcely be kind to her.

Moreover the alternative, for James, to the Queen's entourage, was apparently the Tower again – for whatever Henry's dying commands about his release and disposal, no man now seemed to have any instructions on the matter, much less any urgency. Negotiations, they said vaguely – negotiations must be instituted. Meanwhile, however, James Stewart was still England's prisoner. Sir William Meryng remained his close keeper.

Naturally, he hoped that the Queen would at least bring him to his love. But arrival at Westminster revealed no Joanna Beaufort amongst the Queen's ladies. She had been Henry's nominee, not Catherine's.

James learned that Joanna, with her twice-widowed mother, the Duchess of Clarence, now was living at the palace of her uncle, Bishop Henry Beaufort, at Southwark across the Thames. Another uncle, Thomas Beaufort, Duke of Exeter, had been in charge of the Queen's cavalcade from France, and was now appointed, with Warwick, one of the two guardians of the infant king. Learning that Catherine was to be sent to Windsor, with the baby, and that no doubt he himself would be taken there also, James prevailed upon Exeter to allow him to accompany him across the river, on a visit to the Bishop.

Bishop Beaufort was no more interested in James than he in him. After the briefest of stiff courtesies, he went in search of Joanna. He ran her to earth, unfortunately in the company of her mother, in a pleasant room of a minor wing of the palace, where a fire of aromatic logs held at bay the grey November chill.

At sight of him in the doorway, Joanna rose, eyes shining, lips parted. She took a couple of steps towards him before she recollected, and sank in a curtsy. This more or less constrained the Duchess to do likewise, though in perfunctory fashion. James was the recipient of few curtsies. He hurried forward to raise them up – and only just in time remembered to greet the Duchess first.

"I came . . . so soon as I could," he declared, without preamble. "Your brother, ma'am, my lord Duke of Exeter, brought me."

"Thomas? He is here? I must go see him," the lady said. But unfortunately she made no move to do so. "He is well? And you, of course, my lord James? You look it, I vow. The wars have dealt only lightly with you, I think." That was almost grudging. "Unlike . . . others! Have you seen my sons?"

"My lord of Somerset is well, ma'am. As is the Lord Edward. I saw them at Rouen. They remain with John of Bedford. They suffered no hurt, I believe, in their captivity. In Scots hands." Though he spoke to the older woman, his eyes devoured the younger.

"Their ransom cost me dear! Those Scots! Rapacious caitiffs! Barbarians!"

"Mother – you speak to the King of Scots!"

"Oh, yes. To be sure. Your pardon, my lord James. You have been reared otherwise, of course. Here in England. Your countrymen will be just as uncouth and graceless to you as to us! It was Henry's great heart that saw to this. You owe him much, my lord."

"Mother – of a mercy . . .!"

"Quiet, girl! Henry was a great and noble king. This young man has reason to know it. Poor Henry – so mighty, so goodly a man! Always it is such who are taken. As my Clarence, his brother . . .! And . . . others are left!" The Duchess looked accusingly at their visitor. "You . . . you were with him at the last, my lord? Tell us of it. And sit, I pray you."

The young man and woman exchanged glances.

"My Uncle Thomas . . ." Joanna reminded.

But the Duchess, scatter-brained as she might be, was not to be diverted. Nothing would do but that she must hear a step-by-step account of Henry's illness, symptoms, treatment and passing. Joanna came to stand at the side of James's chair, where at least he felt her close presence and sympathy.

At last the inquisition seemed to pall, and the older woman remembered her brother. She rose – and never was a lady more eagerly escorted to the door.

Thereafter the young people all but fell into each other's arms.

"James, James, my heart! My fond love! My joy!" Joanna sobbed – until the man effectually closed her lips.

They had so much leeway to catch up, so much to say to each other – and so much alternative communication to experiment with in this so rare experience of being alone together, that even their speech was of secondary importance. James, lost in enchantment and delight, yet retained sufficient of his wits to draw the girl back – so that he at least leaned against the door's panels, and none could open and take them unawares.

At length, with fear of imminent interruption goading him, but having to overcome an almost insuperable physical resistance, the man stood back, holding Joanna at arms' length, searching her flushed and lovely face. Then, sliding his hands from her shoulders down her arms until he held only her fingers he deliberately knelt down on the floor, looking up at her. When she protested, first seeking to draw

237

him up again, and then to come down beside him, he held her back, almost peremptorily, shaking his head.

"Wait," he commanded. "Wait – and hear me. Joanna Beaufort, my English rose – I, James Stewart of Scotland, do ask you, pray you, plead with you to be my wife. On my bended knee I ask it – and crave your forgiveness for having failed to ask it long ere this. Will you wed me, Joanna?"

"James! My dear! Heart of my heart – what are you saying? Can this be true . . .?"

"True, aye. Do you not see? It was only Henry's will that came between us. His decision that we must wed – for *his* own ends. He would have used our marriage as he used all else. That I could not accept – for our sake, for Scotland's sake. You know it well. But that was all – that and my wicked pride! Now, all is otherwise. Henry is gone. He will use us no more. I can wed you now – of my own will and choice. By the Rude – *will*, do I name it? Choice! Woman – if you refuse me now, I shall run mad! Deserve it though I do. Say it, Joanna, my love – will you take me to be your husband?"

He was not holding her away now. She slid down beside him on the skin-strewn floor. "Dear God be praised!" she murmured, as her arms enfolded him. "Take me – now and always. Yours to have and to hold – as you are mine. I will wed you, James – and joy in it."

"Joy! Aye – here's joy indeed. Joy that has been with me also, since . . . since, God forgive me, that day at Vincennes when I saw Henry dying, and knew only this! That the way was opening, clearing. If you would have me. Was that sin? To joy at another's dying? I saw it then . . ."

"Hush, my dear. Do not blame yourself. Here was no sin. *You* did not encompass Henry's death. But . . . is it not strange that greatly as he hurt you, over the years, his dying should have given us to each other? When he would indeed have had it so! Yet he alone kept us apart . . ."

"It *is* so, is it not? There could be nothing else? To keep you from me? Your mother? Your uncle, the Bishop? They do not greatly esteem me, I fear. They will not seek

238

to forbid it? Marriage to me, a captive? The Beauforts are rich, powerful. And I am poor. Have nothing – save a realm which cares nothing whether I come or stay, live or die!"

"No – do not say it, my heart! It is not true. Your people will care. When they see you, know you." She shook her head. "No – none shall prevent our wedding. I am of age now. Moreover, all must see it as to England's gain. As, pray God, it may be – without being to Scotland's hurt. *Henry* may have envisaged Scotland's hurt, as well as England's gain. But there is no Henry now, to exploit that hurt. Surely the gain will remain?"

"Aye – for I desire no war with England, God knows. And his brothers are different from Henry. Gloucester, who is Regent here in England, for the babe, is an easy man. Not driven. No fighter. He will take the facile way, if he may. Bedford, in France, is a fighter, yes – but not a schemer. A simple warrior. They will not hold me back from Scotland, I think. But, nor will they hasten me on my way, I fear! And others may seek to thwart me." He looked past her towards the door. "Catherine may. Who knows? But . . . the man I fear most between me and Scotland now, is in this house!"

"You mean – my uncle? Exeter?"

"Not Exeter. We are on good terms – or I would not be here today. No – it is the Bishop. He is another schemer – an able man, and powerful. Aye, and ambitious. He has been Chancellor – and will be again. For the present Chancellor, Bishop Langley, is only his lieutenant. Latterly he fell out with Henry – but he will dominate Gloucester. And he mislikes the Scots – of that I am sure."

"You think it?" Joanna said thoughtfully. "He is ambitious, yes. And clever. He was almost Pope, when Benedict was put down. Only the opposition of the French cardinals prevented it. And Henry, probably, who did not want him Pope!" She smiled faintly. "Uncle Henry may mislike the Scots – but he does not mislike *me*! I flatter myself that if anyone may win him round, I can! Is that vanity? Whether it is or no, I shall work on

239

him! With Uncle Henry, you have a friend at Court, my love!"

"Praise heaven for that!"

"There perhaps is something you can do also, James," she went on, slowly. "The Bishop is ambitious, yes – and would be more than a bishop! He seeks a cardinal's hat. If you promised Scotland's voice, in the Curia at Rome, in his favour? Besought your Primate of St. Andrews for him . . .?"

"Ha! The Bishop is not the only Beaufort schemer, I perceive!"

"Do you think the less of me for it? I will do anything, James – or almost anything – to win you back to your Scotland. Not just that we may wed – but to undo a little of the grievous wrong that has been done to you, all these years. I will scheme for this, yes – even against Catherine!"

"Catherine! You? What can you do there, my Joanna? You, whom she hates – and because of me, I know."

"Because of you, yes. But . . ." The girl shook her head, and laughed a little. "Catherine de Valois is not a subject to discuss upon our knees, I vow!" She rose, and raised him up also. Keeping her hand in his she led him to the window. "I would not wound you in your manly pride, my dear – but Catherine is perhaps more catholic in her admirations . . . than some women! Highly as she thinks of you, she yet can admire others! In especial if she could see them as foes of her husband Henry! Part of her admiration for yourself, I think, was because of this – that she knew Henry did not love her. So she struck back, by favouring Henry's unfriends. And Henry used it again – as he would! Do I talk like some tavern wench, James?"

"Not so. I have thought something of this, myself."

"Then consider this. In the long weary months when you and Henry were in France, Catherine found another foe of Henry's to admire! A Welshman this time – of the princely family of that country, Sir Owen Tudor by name.

240

A strange, smiling cold-eyed man who turns my stomach. But not Queen Catherine's!"

"So! You scarce break my heart! But I know him not . . ."

"No. He came about the Court only when King Henry was away. For they hated each other. Tudor and his father fought with Glendower."

"You tell me this for some reason . . .?"

"If Owen Tudor was summoned to Court, the Queen's Court, it might be that Catherine would be less concerned at losing King James to Scotland!"

"Ah! So that is it! And would Catherine dare to do it? So soon? She is uncertain of herself, now."

"Not Catherine. My Uncle Thomas of Exeter. He is one of the two guardians of the baby King. And, being a duke, senior to the Earl of Warwick. He will in fact be the foremost of the Queen's Court. My uncle – and your friend! Surely this can be contrived?"

"I' faith – I see that Scotland is to have a notable Queen!"

"Queen . . .? Oh, James!" Suddenly the young woman faltered, and turned to gaze at him, biting her lip.

"Goodsakes, girl! Surely you have not failed to consider this? In all else? That you will be Queen in Scotland?"

"Not . . . not in this room, no. Today. It had not entered my mind – not as a reality. Oh, I have thought often of it, of course. After a fashion. It could not be otherwise. But not . . . not as fact, as something that rises before me as, as my fate!"

"And you mislike that fate so much, Joanna – now you see it?"

"I do not know! I do not know, James . . .!"

"You will be the fairest, truest queen that ever Scotland had, my dear."

She shook her head.

Seeing her still so strangely uncertain, she who never before had seemed so to him, but calm, serene, he went on urgently. "You, as queen-to-be, in Scotland, will greatly aid me. To win back there the sooner. See you, a king, even a prisoner king, may not wed without some prior dealings with his Council and people. By the Rude – do not mistake me! I would wed you if every man in Scotland said me nay! But some discussion, talk of it, there must be. A gesture only – but enough. So I have excuse. To send for envoys. From Scotland. To inform of my project of marriage. And these I can use to hasten the English permission for my return. Do you not see it? Henry said he had commanded that I be freed, allowed to return home. But Gloucester and the rest now temporise, talk of negotiations. And will do nothing. I will force their hands. Announce that I intend to marry you. Require commissioners to come from Scotland to discuss it. Discuss your style and titles. Your marriage-portion. In Scotland. Lands must be settled on you, as Queen. All this. And use these commissioners to push Gloucester and the English Council into the negotiations that they talk of."

"How . . . how long, James? Will it be? All this?"

"Who knows? I shall drive it at my hardest, you may be sure. Some months – it cannot be less, I fear. But, pray God – not more! Not years! Happily, as far as Scotland is concerned, this is a matter for the Church. And the Church is my friend. I can ignore Murdoch, who calls himself my Regent! I will write to the good Bishop Wardlaw, at St. Andrews. The Primate. He is old now – but still keen of mind, and my faithful friend. He was my tutor once. Henry Wardlaw will see to it. The envoys. Will choose them well. Murdoch cannot stop it. The new Scots Chancellor is a bishop also – Bishop Lauder of Glasgow. You see it?"

"I see it." Her voice was firm again. "And, God helping me, I shall not fail you, James. As helper. As wife. As . . . Queen!"

"Fail me . . .!"

They were in each other's arms again when a knock at the door revealed one of the palace secretaries, coughing discreetly.

"My lord Bishop requests your presence, my lady, in his library. And my lord James, if you please . . ."

Joanna had asked how long. And James had said months, perhaps, but not years. In the event he was only partly right. It was sixteen long months before wedding-bells, in fact, sounded across the Thames from Southwark, months of delay, frustration and obstruction, of sordid haggling and advantage-seeking, of piddling meannesses and sheer spite. Henry's stern and ruthless opposition was gone; lesser men now had their day.

Money, not policy, became the major preoccupation. Since Henry had, at the end, made it definite that the King of Scots was to be released – and for lack of any strong successor, Henry's shadow still dominated – the theory of release was accepted. The marriage, too, was well known to have been Henry's wish, so that this also was not seriously resisted. But conditions became the thing, terms, payments, claims, pickings, promises for the future.

At first, the word ransom was on every lip. But when James pointed out, in no uncertain fashion, that his capture, eighteen years before, had been contrived in time of truce, and therefore the terms of warfare and chivalry ruled out any question of ransom, a swift shift of ground was made. Expenses became the operative word. Housing, feeding, clothing, educating and equipping the King of Scots for eighteen years had been an enormous burden on the English economy, it seemed. Everywhere ledgers and account-books were looked up, assessments, computations and calculations made. Obviously the cost of guarding the visitor adequately had to be taken into account also. Forage, for instance, for the horses of keepers of royal castles and their staffs, must be refunded, in due percentage. The entertaining of Scots embassages visiting their king had cost money. Servants appointed to wait on James had been costly. Et cetera.

Never had the English genius for trade and merchantry been demonstrated to better effect. Detail was meticulous. The treasury pointed out, as example, that for twenty-four

days at Windsor, that notable May, the Scots monarch and
his people ate four hundred and sixteen loaves at a cost of sixteen shillings; milk and cream sevenpence; and for heating,
debited him with six hundred faggots at eighteenpence. This
sort of accounting, spread over eighteen years, was variously
computed to have cost England something between £50,000
and £100,000 – with only moderate interest. The Scots, to
get their monarch back, must in fairness produce it. Which
made talk of ransom sound distinctly silly.

John Lyon and Thomas Myrton, James's two clerical
secretary-chaplains, after the first outbursts of disbelief,
now proved their worth. They set to work to question, check,
verify and challenge. They suffered much obstruction and
reviling; but, with persistence and ingenuity they managed
to beat down the sum demanded to £40,000 – or £2,000 per
year, with interest. James himself refused to take any hand
in this undignified chaffering.

Or almost so, for, to Joanna's major humiliation, one of
the chiefest chafferers was Bishop Henry Beaufort, once
again Chancellor of England. And since the Bishop was
involved in the marriage agreement also, James could by
no means ignore him. Indeed, James had to bargain,
personally, on that count, over the matter of Scots support
for the Bishop's projected cardinalship, and it was difficult
to keep one set of bargainings distinct from another. The
Bishop himself made little attempt to do so – and a shrewd
bargainer he was.

As witness. When James pointed out that £40,000 was a
vast sum; that he had no penny of his own; that Scotland,
as far as money was concerned, was a poor country,
and that anyway the Scots Treasury was in the hands
of Duke Murdoch, who would be loth indeed to empty
it in order to import his own supplanter – listening to
this, the Bishop nodded sagely. So he well understood, he
admitted. But Holy Church was not poor, even in Scotland;
and the Church was, he believed, kindly disposed towards
its absent royal son. Undoubtedly the faithful would find
the wherewithal, in time. Especially if adequate and suitable

noble hostages for the payment were transferred to England meantime – to be maintained here, of course, at their own expense, until final payment was made.

James eyed the other long and hard – but appeared to cause the older man no embarrassment.

Moreover there was the matter of his niece, Lady Joanna's, dowry, the prelate went on. In the circumstances, with all the expenses of the proposed wedding having to be paid by the bride's family – which meant himself – a more modest dowry than was usual for so loftily-born a lady was surely indicated. The Lord James would not quibble about that, he was sure? In view of the general financial situation, it probably would be most convenient for him, as Chancellor, just to remit ten thousand marks of the £40,000 Scots indemnity, to serve as dowry – James could give him a receipt for the sum, on the celebration of the marriage. This seemed to be the simplest and most dignified arrangement; no actual money need pass between them.

James was all but speechless. He had never heard, nor conceived, of so startling a piece of legalised jobbery as was here outlined, and which amounted to nothing less than a private raid on the English Treasury for ten thousand marks – £6,700 – the realm paying the Beaufort dowry. That it was James's *own* realm that would gain the said dowry, and not himself or his wife-to-be, was but a side issue.

Joanna actually wept a few tears of shame when James told her of this situation, however certain it made the acceptance of their marriage.

Acceptance by Scotland was intimated rather differently. Although there were many comings and goings of couriers between James and his kingdom in the interim, Master Myrton practically wearing a discreet path to and from St. Andrews, it was not until early September 1423 that commissioners from the Scottish Privy Council came south, as far as Pontefract, to negotiate with their English counterparts the actual treaty for their king's release – Duke Murdoch's delaying tactics petering out. James himself travelled north to wait for them, in the company of the English commissioners – the same trio, as it happened, as at his previous abortive journey north, Bishop Langley of Durham, recently Chancellor, Henry Percy, Earl of Northumberland, and Ralph Neville, Earl of Westmorland, reinforced this time by churchmen and lawyers.

James was all but overcome with emotion when, at long last, the Scots contingent were ushered into his presence in the Great Hall of Pontefract Castle, led by the Scots Chancellor himself. Eyes clouded with held-back tears, James came forward from his guards, to raise them up as they sank on bended knees before him, to kiss his hand. Thomas Myrton had come south with them, and introduced them now.

"My lord Bishop William of Glasgow, Chancellor of Your Grace's realm . . ."

Blinking away the moisture, James peered, his eyes widening. Suddenly he was transported back over the years, back to a certain bright and breezy boyhood day on the Bass Rock in the Firth of Forth, when two stalwart smiling young men had climbed with him on the lofty gannet-thronged cliffs. One of them stood before him now.

"Willie! Willie Lauder!" he gasped, gripping the Chancellor's arm. He remembered how he had discovered, after the pair were gone, that one was in fact a priest. "Dear God – it is you!"

"Sire! Your Grace . . . remembers me, then!" The other's deep voice was notably unsteady.

James could not speak, for the moment. The Bishop turned, and ignoring the Earl of Dunbar and March who should have been next introduced, beckoned another closer.

"Your Grace will mind Rob also, maybe? My brother – now Sir Robert Lauder o' Edrington."

The second cliff-climber smiled, and grasped the royal hand to kiss it a second time, wordless.

James, it is to be feared, gave only superficial greeting to the others of the commissioners, so moved was he – to March, the Abbots of Cambuskenneth and Balmerino, the

246

Archdeacon of Glasgow, and three of Murdoch's men, Sir James Douglas of Balvenie, Sir Patrick Dunbar of Beil, and Master Patrick Houston, the Regent's own secretary.

"Your father? Old Sir Robert? My good friend. He is . . .?" James asked, when he could be alone with the Lauders later, after the formalities.

"Aye – he died five years agone, Sire. And Rob is now the Laird o' Bass," the Bishop said. "It is a long time – long. And you – Your Grace! A grown man, a fine, bonny, noble make o' a man! God be praised! For Scotland needs such, on my soul!"

"And *you* are Chancellor! Here's a wonder – and my joy! I never thought of it. I knew the Chancellor was a Bishop Lauder. But it never came to me that you it was."

"Myself it is – and for this purpose, Sire. To work for your return. It was, in the main, Henry Wardlaw's doing. All these years he has been working for today. Against the greatest in the land, who have been lining their purses at *your* expense, robbing the Treasury, stealing your royal lands, living in your halls, oppressing your folk! Most of the nobles of Your Grace's realm have betrayed you – for their own advantage. This Earl of March here amongst them. Albany first, then Murdoch, have bought them, with your Crown lands, offices, customs, sheriffdoms. But the Primate, Bishop Wardlaw – he has seen that the Church is leal, and that true men represent the Church in the Council. And, because we are prepared to work, and are lettered – and the lords are neither – we now control the Council, and I am Chancellor. When you return, the Church at least will welcome you with wide arms – and the Church is strong. For that, thank Wardlaw of St. Andrews, Sire – if any are to be thanked."

"I know it. Thank God for my friends. I will not forget you all."

"Aye – but Your Grace will not have to forget your enemies, either!" That was Sir Robert, speaking grimly. "You will have to deal with your enemies. And strongly. If you are to save your throne, save Scotland. The people

247

are leal, and the Church. But the nobles . . .! Never was there such a crew of shameless traitors, I swear, than Your Grace's Scots lords! When you come back, Sire, it must be with a strong hand and a drawn sword! No faltering grasp will hold your realm, Church or no Church!"

"I fear that is true," the Bishop agreed.

James looked at them both grimly. "Fear not that you have a gentle weakling for king, my friends," he said. "I have learned much, these last years. From notable schoolmasters!"

"The saints be praised for that, then! It is time, and past, that the Lion of Scotland roared loud and long! Before the jackals devour all. And you have jackals a-many – bearing the proudest names in the land! They have had eighteen years. Now must come the reckoning. And with a sword – not a pen!"

"Aye," the Bishop nodded, smiling a little at his vehement brother. "But, see you – there are uses for jackals. Other than as meat for leal warrior's swords! These English demand much money. And hostages for its payment. The money we have not got, I fear. But the hostages . . .! That, perhaps, is different!"

"You mean . . .?"

"I mean, Sire, that you have here opportunity to serve yourself and Scotland well. Let the English have the keeping of many of your enemies! A carefully chosen list of hostages could solve many problems! It would be my pleasure to make up such list for you!"

"And spare Scotland the haste and cost of redeeming them!"

James smiled. "I perceive that the Lauders of the Bass are practical men!" he said. "Between you, I am going to be shrewdly advised!"

"The advice, Sire, is one matter. The resolve and hardihood to follow it, another."

"You think I lack that resolution, Sir Robert?"

"Your Grace's life, as captive, may scarce have hardened you sufficiently to rule in Scotland. Forgive my presumption, Sire, in saying it."

"You forget, I think, who have been my tutors and gaolers – since I left Bishop Wardlaw. Henry Plantagenet – fourth and fifth! I suggest to you that, hitherto, no King of Scots has had so . . . so notable an education! Fear nothing, my old friends. It is Henry's pupil, rather than my poor father's son, that Scotland will gain for king. Tell you that to Henry Wardlaw when you return!"

Out of the silence that followed, Bishop William changed the subject. "Your Grace plans to marry?" he said. "There will be a queen to Scotland again?"

"That is so. A queen . . . and a joy!"

Swiftly they both eyed him.

"So that is the way of it, Sire!"

"That, and more, my lord Chancellor."

"Very well, so. And yet . . . so near to the English throne and rule?"

"In blood, yes. But in all else, a world away."

"Then your realm will be the richer, Sire."

"When does Your Grace marry?"

"So soon as I may. But, knowing my English hosts, not until the last penny has been wrung from me, the last advantage gained! You have come to a land of notable bargainers – as you will discover before this treaty is signed!"

"They want more than money? And hostages?"

"To be sure. They want a signed Border truce of seven years. No more Scots to be sent to France – and all Scots there to be withdrawn. This, I know, Murdoch and Buchan will never accept. But . . . they will bargain."

"So-o-o!"

"You have not been sent word of it?"

"No. This will cause delay, Sire. We have no authority so to treat."

"I feared it. I told you – these are notable bargainers! And delayers. It is their policy. The last advantage, as I said! Ah, well – I have waited eighteen years. Another few months will not be the death of me! But – of a mercy, my friends, make the delay short as you may. God knows I long to be away. And to wed the woman of my heart. Neither will they allow until this treaty is signed."

At the transparent pain and longing in the younger man's voice, the Bishop reached out to grasp his monarch's arm. "Rest assured, Sire – on our part, not a day will be lost. To bring you home. And your bride with you. I promise it . . ."

James and Joanna were not wed, neverthelesss, until fully five months later, in February 1424, with the Treaty of London signed, sealed and secure at last. The ceremony was performed with a strange mixture of pomp and perfunctoriness, in the church of St. Mary Overy at Southwark, Bishop Beaufort the Chancellor officiating, the young Earl of Somerset home from France to give away his sister – and showing no delight in the business – and the Dukes of Gloucester and Exeter, with the Earl of Warwick supporting the bridegroom. Queen Catherine did not attend. Joanna looked so unutterably lovely that even Chancellory and Treasury clerks, there to chronicle all expenses, were constrained to write of it.

At the banquet in Southwark Palace thereafter, James duly signed a receipt for ten thousand marks remission of indemnity, as dowry – a document which was to raise considerable trouble in later years for the Cardinal Beaufort, even though it was made out in the name of his brother Exeter, as looking better. For the first time, James heard himself addressed as Majesty by an Englishman; now that his niece was a queen, the Bishop could hardly forbear to accept her husband as a king.

That night the King and Queen of Scots perforce must spend under the roof of her uncle – since they had nowhere else to lie. But, when alone at last in Joanna's chamber, before losing themselves in the joy so long awaited, they gazed out of the window, hand in hand, it was northward they looked, northward where a new life awaited them.

All things must have an end, and a beginning.

PART FOUR

16

James Stewart reined up, on the crest of the little ridge beyond Cornhill, and waved an eloquent hand forward in a sweeping gesture, from left to right. The hand had to be eloquent, for the rest of him certainly was not. His throat was constricted and he had to fight back tears of emotion.

The ground sank quite sharply before them to a wide and silvery river. Beyond, an entire land was spread out, under the smile of the mid-day sun, a land of tilth and meadow and pasture, of green sweeping slopes and rolling ridges, low at first but ever rising until, a score of miles away but clear in that northern light, the tall blue hills of Lammermuir rimmed the far-flung prospect under the great skies. After the Northumberland moors it made a breath-catching sight.

Joanna looked from the man at her side to that fair panorama, and back again – and wisely said no word. But her eyes were warm and very kind.

He tried to get the word out, but could not – although behind them scores were pronouncing it easily enough, in varying tones of voice. Then abruptly he abandoned laggard speech for eager action, and grabbing Joanna's bridle, dug in spurs to send the two horses plunging downhill at headlong pace, towards the Coldstream ford of Tweed.

At the water's edge, with a crowd waiting on the other shore, he slowed their going only a little, to lean over towards his companion. Throwing an arm around her waist, with a single and notable exercise of muscular strength, he swept Joanna out of her saddle and over to the front of his own, even as she skirled in laughing protest and the waters of Tweed spouted up around them. Without pause, the King's horse plunged and splashed across the fifty yards or so of the ford's shallows.

At the Scots side, pulling up his rearing, panting beast before all the hastily scattering spectators, he jumped to the ground. Reaching up, he lifted Joanna down from the saddle. Then sinking to his knees on the sheep-cropped turf of the haugh, he put his face down and, lips to the earth, kissed the soil of his native land. After only a moment's hesitation, the young woman sank down beside him – but instead of kissing the ground, she lowered her head and murmured a little silent prayer of true thankfulness.

Even as they knelt there, and the excited cheers of the waiting throng died away in wonder, an old man in plain monkish habit stepped forward. Reaching out two trembling hands, and raising a surprisingly strong but mellow voice, he pronounced a moving benediction upon them both, and through them, upon the ancient kingdom which was mother to them all. Even as he spoke, and riders came surging across Tweed in the wake of the royal couple, the bells of the nearby Coldstream Cistercian nunnery pealed out in joyful greeting.

Rising, James looked at the old man – and then moved impetuously to enfold him in his arms. "My lord! My good and dear lord!" he cried.

Henry Wardlaw wagged his white head, stroking the younger man's arm – and however strong had been his voice a moment before, now he could only mumble the word welcome indistinctly, again and again.

"My dear – here is my old and most loved friend and father in God, Bishop of St. Andrews and Primate of this realm. Travelled this far to meet us."

"So long! So long!" Wardlaw got out. "But, glory be for what these eyes do now see! Lord now lettest Thou Thy servant depart in peace! My son! My son! And his bonny lass!"

Joanna took the frail hand in both her own. "And your daughter also, I pray, my lord."

254

"Daughter, aye. Your Grace gladdens these old eyes. And heart . . ."

The great company of welcome was presented amidst a storm of acclaim from the lesser folk. Eleven of the thirteen bishops of Scotland were present – Argyll being held by a member of the Albany family, and The Isles being too far distant. A host of abbots, priors and other clerics, knights and lairds, sheriffs, magistrates, provosts and townsfolk from the nearby burghs. In seemingly endless procession they came to kneel and kiss their monarch's hand, and thereafter that of their new queen – and all the while the bells rang out, not only the nunnery's musical peal but the more monotonous notes of Coldstream's two churches and that of Ladykirk down-river. Indeed, occasionally during quiet intervals in all this joyous din, a distant and sweetly melodious ringing could just be caught on the westerly April breeze. When James, in the midst of the presentations, remarked on it, Bishop Wardlaw nodded.

"Those are the great bells of Kelso Abbey, Sire. The river carries the sound. See yonder smokes on the hill-tops? Those balefires today tell of good tidings, not ill. Every abbey and priory and church in this your realm will be ringing your welcome, by now."

When at last all had paid their homage to their liege lord – and the English escort under Henry Percy of Northumberland were grown restive indeed – James turned.

"Master John Lyon and Master Thomas Myrton," he called. "Come you. These," he said, to the Primate, "have served me passing well. They are churchmen, and I cannot reward them with more than my gratitude and friendship. But you can, my lord – and I commend them to your good offices."

"They indeed deserve well of Holy Church, my son – and shall receive it, never fear."

"That is well. But there is another, whom I may thank differently. Of a house that has not always played my friend! To me, David Douglas." He looked over towards the wider circle of watchers. "And another. Who kissed my hand

255

amongst the rest — and perhaps feared that I had forgot him! Here to my side, as you were before, Walter Gifford!" James drew his sword. "On your knees, my friends."

He tapped each bowed shoulder with the flat of his blade. "David Douglas of Whittinghame, I dub thee knight," he said. "Walter Gifford of Yester, I dub thee knight. Arise, Sir David! Arise, Sir Walter! You bore long years of spurning and contumely at my side. Now, my first act as lord on this the soil of my kingdom acknowledges it."

Amidst the cheers Henry Percy pushed forward, quite the most splendid figure present. "My lord James," he said, "I have done my duty. I have carried you back to your realm, and gladly. I now return to my own place. But I have one last duty to perform. As Warden of this March and in the name of the high and mighty Prince Henry, King of England, it is required of me that I now receive from you, on your own soil, the confirmation of your royal oath that you swore at Durham. That the provisions of the treaty will be kept entire. The truce of seven years enforced on your people. No further Scots forces to go to France. And payment of ten thousand marks each year be made, until all thirty-four thousand pounds is paid in full — as you value your royal honour!"

At the low ominous growl which rose in hundreds of throats and swelled in volume into sheerest menace, James cleared the quick frown from his brow and raised his hand.

"I, James, swear before all here as on the Holy Gospels, that the treaty terms will be kept," he said curtly. "You have done your duty, my lord!"

"And a writing will follow? For my lord and Prince-Bishop?"

"A writing will follow. To Durham. Go in peace, my lord." James's voice quivered. Abruptly all the joy was wiped from the face of the day. James felt Joanna's hand slip into his, and press.

Henry Percy looked round at all the suddenly hostile faces, and then at the King, blinking a little. James, then, had a mind picture of the tall, thin boy in the Sea Tower of St. Andrews Castle, whom a smaller angry child had battered with his fists for dwelling so gloatingly on the grim details of the Duke of Rothesay's death. He managed to smile a little.

"I bid you God-speed, Harry," he said, more gently.

The other's perplexed features cleared. He bowed, and beckoning his English company to follow him, pulled his horse's head round and rode back into the ford.

"Harry Percy does not change, I see," Henry Wardlaw said quietly. "But . . . you do! Now, my son – the Prioress awaits you with refreshments at the nunnery . . ."

As the long cavalcade rode slowly westwards across the fair green champagne of the Merse, approximately parallel with the course of the great river, James was fully restored in his spirits. He rejoiced that he could show his bride that she had come to so handsome a land – since all in England deemed Scotland to be a place of wild mountains and savages. This terrain of meadows, cornlands and gentle ranges of sheep-pasture, dotted with the little stone towers of lairds, and grey churches, was rich as any to be seen in the south – and Joanna gladly acknowledged it. Only once or twice did James's glance cloud over, at a charred homestead or a smoke-blackened ruin.

It was when they came to an entire village so devastated, on a low grassy ridge so typical of the Merse, an ominous eyesore indeed in all that pleasing prospect, and still smelling of fire, that James halted.

"What place is this?" he demanded. "And why is it destroyed? Where are the folk? This is not long done. I have seen all too much of the like, in war-stricken France. But I had not thought to see it here in Scotland. Has this been English raiding?"

Bishop Wardlaw looked at Bishop Lauder, silent.

The Chancellor shook his head. "Raiding, I fear – yes. But not English I think, Sire." He turned in his saddle. "Where is Kelso? Have my lord Abbot to the King."

The master of Kelso Abbey – which was now only some four miles away, its bells still pealing, and sweetly, clear above some lesser, nearer chimes – was brought forward. A portly, fresh-complexioned man, richly attired and splendidly mounted, he was a mitred abbot, indeed with precedence over all others of his degree. He was asked what place this was, and why it was thus destroyed.

"This village was Toft of Eccles, Sire," he told them. "A dependency of the nunnery of St. Mary yonder, at Eccles – and so mine."

"And how came it to be destroyed, Sir Abbot?"

The stout man shrugged. "My lord of Drumlanrig . . . thought meet to do so, Sire. He would have his sister Prioress of this nunnery. Whose bells Your Grace hears."

"Drumlanrig? A Douglas! I know him. He came to me at Windsor. And again in France. Indeed, I signed his charter once, at Croydon. He is brother to the Lord of Cavers, Sheriff of Teviotdale, is he not?"

"The same, Sire."

"Then why . . . this?"

"He considers himself aggrieved, Sire. Because I do not evict the present Lady Prioress and instal his sister. Eccles is a rich nunnery, and he would have its revenues. So – he gives me warning!"

"By the Rude – you say so! And what have *you* done, my lord?"

"I have made protest to the Council, of course. But . . ." The other shrugged again, and looked at the Chancellor.

Lauder sighed. "That is true. But what could we do?" he asked. "They are Douglases. Powerful lords."

"And the Governor? Duke Murdoch?"

"The Duke, Sire is . . . otherwise occupied! Moreover, Drumlanrig is close friend to his son Walter. And this is only a small matter, I fear – compared with many. I told Your Grace, at Pontefract, that much awaited a strong hand, in Scotland."

James, set-face, gazed at the desolate blackened rows of cot-houses and barns, the broken walls and charred hay-ricks. Then his glance lifted to where, directly behind and perhaps a couple of miles off, a great castle crowned an upthrusting green hill, a strong place of towers and battlements, proud in the afternoon sun.

"What strength is that?" he demanded.

"That is the lord of Home's house. Sir Thomas's castle of Home. Warden of this East March."

"Home! Warden . . .? And he allowed this to happen? Under his very walls?"

"Sir Thomas is kin to the Douglases, Sire. He married a Douglas heiress. His son, Sir Alexander, is with the Earl of Douglas in France, even now."

James was looking at Joanna, but for once he scarcely saw her. "I see," he said quietly, almost softly. "I see." He paused. "Warden, you say. Warden of the East March. Then, my lords – should not the Warden of my March have been at Tweed to greet his sovereign this day? I mind not any Sir Thomas Home named."

There was silence.

"Nor indeed, did I hear the names of Sir William Douglas of Drumlanrig! Or the Sheriff of Teviotdale! No single great lord was of your company, my lord Bishop? All the lords spiritual – but where were the lords temporal?"

Again he got no reply.

James narrowed his eyes. "I think that I see a banner flying above Home Castle," he said. He turned. "David . . . Sir David Douglas. And you, Sir Robert Lauder. See yonder castle? Go there and convey my greetings to its baron, Sir Thomas Home. He will attend upon me here, forthwith. You understand? Bring him."

Breaths were indrawn all around.

"My lords and friends – and my lady wife. We shall rest here a little. It is a pleasant place – or was, once!" James dismounted, and went to lift Joanna down.

The two knights named eyed each other, and then spurred their horses into a gallop northwards.

Everywhere men were murmuring to each other, faces grave. James himself aided the aged Primate from his mount.

"You . . . you will have a care, my son!" the old man began, anxiously. "Home is powerful. He can field many – five hundred men."

"Aye – and all subjects of mine! As is Home, to be sure! Did I come to Scotland to be careful, my old friend? Or did I come to rule?"

"His Grace is right," Bishop Lauder said strongly. "All the land watches what is done this day. So be it."

"I know it, my friend. But Home is also close to Walter, as well as the Douglases. Between them they can do almost what they will in Scotland – to her sorrow! To antagonise them, the first day . . .!"

"A man must start as he intends to continue," James declared shortly. "This Walter? Twice he has been named. You mean my cousin Murdoch's eldest son, Walter Stewart? What of him?"

The two prelates exchanged glances. "The Lord Walter is a notably headstrong young man," Lauder said. "He grew up during Duke Murdoch's captivity in England, and sorely lacked a father's hand. He ran wild over the land – and still does. A law unto himself."

"His father can do naught with him," Wardlaw agreed. "With any of the three sons. But Walter is the worst. He slays and harries, rapes and burns, as he will. He defies his father at all turns . . ."

"He even snatched the Duke's favourite falcon from his father's wrist, hawking at Doune, before all," Lauder broke in. "And wrung its neck, laughing! He forcibly took and married the Lady Janet Erskine, heiress to the old Mar earldom, when his father had engaged to wed her to another. He is Keeper of Dumbarton Castle, and from there terrorises the land, and claims that he, not his father, governs Scotland. His friends, in consequence, have no fear of the Governor."

"It seems, my lord, that I did not return to Scotland before time!" James observed grimly. He turned. "And that

I have brought *you* to a sorrier kingdom than I knew, my dear!"

Joanna shook her head. "You will put it right, all right, in good time, my heart. I fear not."

"By the Holy Rude, I will!" he cried, passionately. He stabbed a finger, first towards the proud distant castle and then at a nearby clump of yellow broom where a few cattle-beasts grazed. "Let God but grant me life, and there shall not be a spot in my dominions where the key shall not keep the castle and the broom-bush the cow – though I lead the life of a dog in securing it!"

There was a notable silence at this outburst. Even Joanna was taken aback, so unlike James Stewart it was.

The King drew a hand over mouth and jaw, as though to smooth away the tension there expressed. He produced a smile of sorts, and led Joanna aside to the prattling burn which ran uncaring past the devastated hamlet.

If the royal party had some time to wait, they could not complain of lack of sensation when at length the King's couriers reappeared. Apparently these were successful in their errand, for they now rode under a great banner, with a third man between them, Behind came rank upon rank of others, armour and lance-tips gleaming in the sunlight, score after score.

Everywhere churchmen and commons gasped and involuntarily drew back at sight of that ominous armed host. The dread word mosstroopers sounded from a hundred lips.

"I feared it," the Primate muttered. "Here comes what truly rules in Scotland today. The Lord of Home seldom rides lonely!"

"The Lord of Home appears to be not a little uncertain of himself!" James said lightly. "Come – let us see if the mill-wheel there still will work."

The small group with the King were still examining the little wrecked mill by the burnside when the jingle and clatter, and not a little shouting, proclaimed the arrival of the contingent from Home Castle. James did not so much as pause to glance in its direction. He was poking away at the choked mill-blade with a charred stick. A pregnant hush spread over the entire company.

James's voice could be heard clearly, declaring that there were the carcases of dead sheep caught under the mill-wheel.

David Douglas came forward, on foot, doubtfully. "Sire," he said. "Here is Sir Thomas Home, the Lord Warden of this March."

"Ah, yes." The King glanced round. "I said bring him, did I not, Sir David?" He returned to poking with his stick.

Moistening his lips, the Douglas went back to the others.

There followed the sound of upraised, angry voices, and then the clank of armour, creak of harness and scuffle of hooves, many hooves.

James turned, at last, a hand under Joanna's arm, and looked up. He had to look up, for the line of horsemen had moved forward, still mounted, right up behind the group at the burnside, close, so close indeed as to be almost threatening. Only Douglas and Sir Robert Lauder were on foot.

In the centre of this line, under the green-and-white banner, a thick-set, elderly man, heavy-jowled and sparsely-bearded, sat on a black stallion that pawed the turf restlessly all too near the royal couple. He was carelessly dressed, with no attempt at tidiness – but a great jewel gleamed redly in the threadbare velvet of his plumed bonnet. He wore no armour. But around him and at his back the tight ranks of his body-guard, fierce, hard-riding, bearded Border mosstroopers to a man, sat bristling with arms and armour.

James looked him up and down, and then turned to Sir Robert, who stood, uncomfortably crowded and in danger of being stamped on by Home's horse. "Who is this man, Sir Robert?" he enquired.

The knight swallowed. "This is Sir Thomas, the Baron of Home, Warden of the East March, Sire. Whom you sent for."

"Is he so? Warden of my East March? I'd scarce have thought it, on my soul! I'll have to look to my officers,

262

I see! Have him down off that animal, Sir Robert. We would have word with him."

There was a choking sound from Home, and a snarling rumble from the ranks behind him.

"My lord Warden – you heard His Grace!" Lauder said tautly.

"God's eyes!" the man on the stallion got out thickly. "In the Merse, on Home land, none speaks so to Home – whatever his birth! I am Warden here . . ."

Still James did not look at him. "Sir Robert," he went on, with an appearance of patience. "Is there not here some mistake? This man cannot be my Warden – or he would have come to meet his liege lord at Tweed, on entering his territory. I fear he is an imposter, no subject of mine, even – since no subject sits his horse in front of his monarch dismounted! Or remains covered in his liege lord's presence. Have him down, Sir Robert, a God's sake! And uncovered. For I cannot speak with him so."

James turned away. He could feel Joanna's arm trembling. He patted her hand. "I am sorry, my dear," he said.

"Christ's blood!" Sir Thomas exploded. "If you are James Stewart, the Englishman, I'd mind you, sir, that there is not yet any crowned king in Scotland! I . . ."

"Englishman, did he say!" Like a whiplash that cracked out, as James swung round. "Did a man say Englishman? Of me – James!" Blazing-eyed, suddenly white-faced, quivering with a rage none had ever seen him in before, he dropped Joanna's arm and took a swift pace forward – and everywhere men, even Home himself, flinched back before the white heat of him. "For that word there shall be . . . a price!" The word was almost hissed out. "For that word a new Warden of my East March will be appointed forthwith. My lord Chancellor – you will find me a good and leal lord to ward my March. You hear? And I want the charters of the barony of Home, and all its pendicles, delivered to me. At your soonest. Yonder castle and lands deserve a lord who does not reek of . . . treason!"

263

There was something like a sigh went up from all who heard that dread word enunciated.

James repeated it. "Treason, aye! We will see, by the Rude, whether there is a king in Scotland!" He turned on Wardlaw now. "And more than treason. My lord Bishop of St. Andrews — you are Apostolic Protonotary, as well as Primate. Can you tell me any reason why this man, who allows Holy Church to be spoiled and ravaged beneath his very windows, and does nothing, should not suffer the penalty of excommunication? Aye — and all who do his bidding." The King's hot glance ranged over all the ranks of men-at-arms. "Excommunication! Cast off by Holy Church, to eternal damnation!"

It was Henry Wardlaw's turn to all but choke. His old lips trembled. He looked at the other prelates.

"Well, man! Tell me? You are the guardian of Holy Church, are you not? You have the power, from His Holiness, of excommunication? Have you forgot it?"

The other drew up his frail frame. "I have not forgot it, Sire. It shall be as you say. Here was sacrilege."

"As I say." James nodded grimly. "See you to it, my lords." He turned his back on them all, reaching out to take his wife's hand to lead her the few steps to the waterside again. And it was his arm in hers which quivered now.

There was something of a commotion behind them. Then a hoarse voice cried out. "Sire! My lord King! Hear me."

Taking his time, James paused, and then looked back. Sir Thomas Home had dismounted and come striding after him, in agitation. He snatched off his bonnet as he came.

James eyed him sternly, but said nothing.

The other paused, his heavy florid features working strangely. Then he sank down on his knees. "Your Grace's pardon . . . of a mercy!" he croaked. "Not treason! Not . . . the other. Not ex . . . excommunication! Of a mercy, Sire!"

The King stood stiff, unspeaking, a stocky, upright muscular figure, the lovely, pale-faced, great-eyed woman at his side.

Home reached out, in supplication. "I acknowledge my fault, Highness. It is so long. Since we have known a king. Near thirty years. I crave mercy. Give me your hand, Sire. I would . . . do my homage."

Still James waited, his glance lifting to run over the serried ranks of mounted mosstroopers behind – and not one glance met his own. Slowly, then, he extended his right hand towards the kneeling baron – and in it still was the charred stick, taken from a burned cot-house.

Gulping audibly, the older man dropped his cap and raised both hands to take between his two palms the monarch's hand, in the full traditional gesture of homage – and perforce must take the stick also, so that his bent grey head was within an inch of the burned wood, its smell in his nostrils.

Then James drew back. "Very well, my lord – on your feet," he said coldly. "Your homage, belated, is accepted. I require to know now why you did not protect this village – as Warden, if not out of love for Holy Church?"

Home rose, but kept his head lowered. "It was done . . . by ill men to cross. Douglas. A private quarrel, Sire – with Kelso Abbey. I deemed that the Governor . . . would not desire . . . my intervention."

"Speak truth, man! Drumlanrig is your friend. You are wed to a Douglas. Is there more to it than that?"

The other's lips moved, but no words came.

"So be it. My lord – your last act as Warden. You will ride now to Teviotdale. To Drumlanrig's house. You will bring him to me at Melrose, where I go to pass the night. Melrose Abbey. And his brother, of Cavers, the Sheriff also. You have men in plenty for the task, I see! I require of you these two, before nightfall. At Melrose. And shall then reconsider the matter of treason. And, who knows, my lord Bishop may do the same of excommunication! Go, you. This audience is ended."

Home hesitated, then bowed low, and turning, walked unsteadily back to his horse. He stood beside it for long moments, staring straight at its saddle. Then slowly, almost wearily, he hoisted himself up. He jerked his head to his standard-bearer, reined round the stallion and dug in spurs. With a great stir and clanking, the entire martial company pulled round and formed some sort of column behind their lord. They rode away from that broken hamlet, but in the opposite direction from their coming, south-westwards now, for Kelso where Teviot joins Tweed.

Queen Joanna moved to clutch at her husband, and buried her chestnut head against his breast. "Oh, Jamie, Jamie!" she cried into his doublet. "That was . . . beyond all! Praise God – I married a man! And a king! A king amongst men, indeed!"

"Hush, my heart," he murmured into her hair. "You married, I tell you, a very frightened man! I' faith, you did!" He dropped the charred stick, and held out the charcoal-blackened hand to the Primate. "Forgive me, my old friend, for speaking you so! But . . . it was necessary."

"It was necessary, aye." Henry Wardlaw acknowledged. "My sorrow that it should have been so. And that I needed minding of my duty. Forgive *me*, my son – forgive an old done man."

"Forgive us all – who could but stand and watch!" William Lauder said, his great voice ringing. "But, praises be to the Most Highest that there is a master again in Scotland. I asked much – but my cup overflows! God save the King, I say! God save King James!"

"He will require to, if I mistake not!" the monarch observed, quietly, as the cheers rang out. "Now, my friends – shall we ride for Melrose . . .?"

"Think you they will come?" Joanna asked, looking out from the Abbot's parlour towards the sunset which was making a gold and purple glory out of the shapely peaks of the Eildon Hills that rose so steeply above the magnificence of Melrose. "Think you that the Douglases will heed Sir Thomas Home? If *he* does not change his mind!"

"Who knows? I can but hope that the threats I laid on Home he will transmit to these others, and with like results.

Threats for the future and the hereafter, rather than for the present though they be!"

Joanna knit her brows. "This of excommunication . . .!"

"You blame me for using that?" he demanded quickly. "It is a dire weapon – but I have to use it. Since I have little else. I have the Church. And the good will of the common people, so I hope and believe. All the rest is against me – the lords, the nobility, the castles, the armed men. My threats of treason and the withdrawing of land charters are well enough – but they depend on force to make them effective – force which I have not got. As yet. But this other is different. Its force is the gnawing uncertainty in men's own minds. The fear of eternal damnation! This weapon the Church holds. It will not serve with all – but with many it must. The King's cause and Holy Church must be identified by all. I would be a fool not to seek such weapon."

She sighed. "It may be so. But I mislike it . . ."

"I mislike it myself. But what other can I do? My strength is only in the mind, in notions – not in reality."

"Your true strength lies in yourself, my dear. In James Stewart!" she said, reaching out to him.

They were alone in Abbot John Foggo's parlour, in the most lovely of all the four great Border abbeys which clustered in the vales of Tweed and Teviot – indeed the most lovely in all Scotland. James had made for Melrose deliberately, to pass the first night of his return to his native land in this most noble shrine – for here were interred the remains of two of Scotland's greatest and strongest monarchs, the heart of Robert the Bruce and the body of Alexander the Second. There had been only weaklings and boys on the throne ever since the Bruce had died, and his much-travelled heart had reached here via the Holy Land; now his great-great-grandson aspired that men should recognise that he intended to rule in the same tradition. Moreover, Scotland's other Queen Joanna, Alexander's wife, was buried here, at the door of the north transept. It was a strange chance that Melrose should also be a burying-place of the great House of Douglas.

They heard the beat and pound of many hooves, even above the sweet clamour of the Abbey bells, which had rung unceasing for many hours. Presently Sir David Douglas came to them.

"The lords of Home, Drumlanrig and Cavers await Your Grace," he said. "Shall I bring them here?"

"Not so. Have them to wait. Outside. In the forecourt. I shall see them . . . anon." As the other turned away, James asked, a little less assuredly. "Are they come well . . . furnished, David?"

"Aye, Sire. Another two hundred, I would say."

"So! Well – there is little difference whether they come with a score, ten-score or a hundred-score! I cannot fight them with swords and lances."

When Whittinghame was gone and James began to pace the parlour floor, back and forth, Joanna watched him.

"You keep them waiting, of design?"

"Yes. Or, say that it is myself I force to wait! For I am not the waiting sort." He shrugged. "Your English Plantagenet cousins taught me much of kings' ways – but I find it less than easy to follow them. I have been a captive too long! To use the high hand comes to me but awkwardly."

"Then do not follow the Plantagenets, James." She rose. "Be yourself. Always and only yourself. Let us go."

"You need not come, my dear. Not this time. You have had enough of painful scenes this day."

"My place is at your side. Where it may profit you. Here, who knows? A woman's presence may . . . restrain arrogant men." She took his arm.

The great courtyard between the monastic buildings and the tall, slenderly-beautiful rose-red church was filled with loud-voiced men and stamping horses; indeed they overflowed into much of the precincts, to the scandal of the monkish brethren – though even so there was room and to spare, for the Abbey's enclosing wall measured a mile around. At sight of the royal couple in the doorway, gradually the noise died away. Abbot Foggo sent a monk to stop the bells at last.

The three barons stood together in a cleared space. Home bowed deeply, the others less so – but bow they did.

"I thank you, my lord of Home." James raised his voice. "Sir William – we meet again. And this will be Sir Archibald, of Cavers. My Sheriff of Teviotdale. I rejoice that you have found it possible to come to meet and greet your liege, my lords!" He held out his hand.

The Douglas brothers hesitated. The big red-headed Drumlanrig looked at the more slender, dark Cavers. But they could not ignore the royal hand still extended towards them. They came forward, with some reluctance, to take and kiss that hand.

"Your Queen, my friends."

Joanna also extended her hand – and perforce they had to kiss it likewise.

It was stiffly done, but James affected not to notice. He spoke pleasantly. "We parted last at Corbeil, Sir William. You to the Earl of Buchan's army – I to Melun. There to see how a king might behave to those who crossed him! A sorry day for Scotland!"

"Aye, Sire. But we redeemed yon day. At Baugé!" Drumlanrig rasped.

"A great victory, yes. You were there?"

"With Stewart of Darnley I led the left array. Capturing, amongst others, this lady's brothers, I think!" That was said grimly.

"As well that the young men fell into such good hands, Sir William! After such gallant warfare, it must have cost your honour dear to make war on harmless and unarmed cotters, women and bairns, sir! At Eccles Tofts!" That was rapped out so suddenly as to take the big man by surprise.

The Douglas frowned, and cleared his throat. "That was . . . a private matter," he jerked.

"When subjects of mine are injured, and their homes destroyed, it is no private matter, sir! Not to me. This I'd remind you, is Scotland – not France!"

"Scotland aye. But *I'd* remind Your Grace – it's no' England either!"

James drew a quick breath, but with an effort controlled himself. He turned to the other brother. "Sir Archibald – you are my Sheriff of Teviotdale. I had expected to see you at Coldstream. When I crossed Tweed into my realm."

The dark man smiled thinly. "Alas, Sire – how was I to know? We are something remote, in Teviotdale. I received no message to attend."

"Nor did others. Yet hundreds gathered there, to receive me. From a deal farther than the Teviot sir!"

Cavers did not answer.

"Leaving that. Since you are Sheriff, it is your duty to uphold the law. How say you, Sir Archibald, of this burning and ravaging of Eccles Tofts? This private matter!"

"Eccles is not in Teviotdale, Sire. It does not concern me."

"I say it does. It concerns the peace of my realm. Therefore all honest men in my peace. Officers of mine in especial. How say you of the justice of this matter?"

"I say naught. Since it did not occur in my sheriffdom, I have not enquired into it."

"I see. Then, sir, I charge you to do so. Forthwith. If you would remain Sheriff of Teviotdale! Sir William's house of Drumlanrig Tower is in Hawick, in your sheriffdom. I want a full, fair and swift trial of the matter. Without fear nor favour towards any. All causes heard, full compensation ordered, and due punishment exacted. You understand, Sir Archibald?"

The other stared at him, then at his brother. He did not commit himself to speech.

"Sir William, therefore, is in your charge. Until the trial," James went on, evenly. "Naturally I hold you responsible for his appearance thereat. On pain of treason."

"God's death! This is beyond all bearing . . .!"

Drumlanrig's rough hoot of laughter interrupted his brother. "Dinna fret, Archie," he cried. "You'll no' need to bear it! I'll be gone for France any day now – and spare you the trouble."

"You will not go anywhere, sir," the King said. "Until you have tholed this assize. France least of all."

"I sail for France wi' the rest, Sire – so soon as ships may be assembled. All is in train."

James's fists clenched. "Ships assembled? All in train? What is this?" he demanded.

"The Lord Walter Stewart leads a great company to France, to the aid of his uncle, the Constable, my lord of Buchan. I act his lieutenant."

"By God, you do not! Walter Stewart again! What folly . . ."

"No folly. Buchan needs more men. We take them."

"But . . . the treaty! Signed at Durham. It declares that no further Scots forces shall go to France . . ."

"*I* didna sign that! Nor did Walter. He has spoken against siclike weak truckling to the English, all along!"

"But *I* signed it. Your king. As did the Chancellor of this realm, in the name of the Privy Council. And the Governor."

Drumlanrig's snort demonstrated eloquently what he thought of Chancellor, Council and Governor.

"My lord Chancellor! What is this? You know of this . . .?"

Bishop Lauder stepped forward, his brother Robert at his side. "Of the force for France – nothing, Sire. Some chuckle-headed ploy of the Lord Walter. He made loud talk at the signing. Against the provision to send no more men to France. And much other foolish talk. Belly-wind!"

"Belly-wind, you think!" Drumlanrig exclaimed. "That, from a priest! You'll see if it is wind and talk, my lord! I tell you, we but await the ships agathering."

"Talk or truth, it shall not be!" James declared strongly. "It controverts my honour, and the repute of this kingdom. Neither shall *you* go, sir, nor Walter Stewart, nor any other!"

"We shall see."

"You would disobey me? Defy your king!"

"My king, I'd remind Your Highness, isna yet crowned!"

"I am my father's son."

271

"And Walter is *his* father's son. And better, his grand-father's grandson!"

James's eyes narrowed. "What are you saying, Sir William?" he demanded quietly.

"This! Who has borne the rule and governance in Scotland these thirty years? Your line? Or his?"

"Dear God . . .!"

"Sire – here is outrage! Highest treason!" Sir Robert Lauder burst out. "Rebellion barefaced, no less! It bears out what was said. At the time of the signing. That Walter Stewart had engaged not only to continue to assist the Dauphin, but to prevent his subjects from maintaining the projected truce with England. *Subjects*, mark you! It is said he swore that he would continue the war, on coming to the kingdom or governorship of this realm."

"He . . . said . . . that!"

"So we were told, on our return to Scotland, Sire."

"Is this true? Did Walter Stewart say such words?" James swung on the Douglases.

"Some such, it may be." Drumlanrig shrugged. "You werena here, mind. And his father is a weak fool. Someone must rule in Scotland!"

"So-o-o! Someone *shall* rule in Scotland! And it shall not be Walter Stewart!" James raised his eyes to the great mass of armed Border horsemen, filling the enclosure, so patently behind the Douglases' frankness of speech. "My lord Chancellor – you will arrange the arrest of the Lord Walter, wherever he may be found. On my royal command. And you, Sir Robert, will conduct these lords from my presence. Sir Archibald Douglas to keep Sir William Douglas in ward until trial. He is on no account to leave my borders. See you to it."

The sequence of events thereafter was dramatic in its sudden exchange of action for words. Robert Lauder moved closer to Drumlanrig. Probably he had no intention of touching the other – but the big man appeared to assume it. Swinging round, he struck Lauder a violent blow on the

272

cheek and shoulder, sending him staggering. Then his hand dropped to the poniard-hilt at his waist.

Something like a great sigh arose from the watching throng.

James Stewart's action was as swift as the rest. "Hold!" he cried, his stocky frame tense as a coiled spring. A peremptory hand rose to point at Drumlanrig. "Here is shame! By all the powers of heaven – no man strikes another in the presence of the King of Scots! Sir Robert – that man's hand! Which struck you. Your sword, sir. Strike it off! Off, I say!"

The gasp of the entire company developed into part groan, part snarl.

James felt Joanna's hand tighten on his arm convulsively.

Even Sir Robert Lauder seemed utterly taken aback, uncertain. He gripped his sword, but did not draw it.

James's anger was a pulsing vehement thing that affected all by its sheer, fierce intensity. "Sir William Douglas – hold out your arm!" he commanded. "You have done the unforgivable, committed *lèse-majesté*! A soldier, you know it. No man strikes another in the presence of the king. It is your head, or your hand! If you choose the hand – thrust it out! Sir Robert – what ails you, man? You heard me?"

The screech of steel sounded thinly in the appalled silence, as Lauder drew his blade.

It was Joanna who broke that throbbing hush. "My lord! My lord King!" her voice rang out clearly, urgently. "Mercy, Sire! I pray you. Spare this thing, of your clemency. Spare Sir William!"

"Would *he* spare one of these?" James's hand sketched the circuit of the staring men-at-arms, Douglas and Home. "Would he spare a man who raised his hand in the face of his lord?"

"I know not, Sire. But *you* are not Douglas! You can be merciful. Oh, I know it well. See – I beg of you." Joanna slipped to the ground and knelt there at his feet, slender

273

hands upraised. "Spare this man, my lord – as you love me!"

Tight-lipped James looked down at her.

"Aye, Your Grace – have mercy," old Bishop Wardlaw entreated brokenly. "It has been so long. So long since this land had a king. Spare him, my son."

Curtly James nodded his head, once. He stooped to raise up the Queen. "Very well, my dear. So be it. This once." He raised his voice, so that it rang out vibrantly. "But take warning, all here. This is as far as my mercy goes. Drumlanrig's hand, his right hand, had better serve me well, henceforth! In this kingdom, only the king rules! Heed it well!"

No single voice answered him.

Drumlanrig stood like a man dazed. He had not made a move since the King's dire order. He had not raised his arm, admittedly – but neither had he lifted hunched shoulders, or moved his lips. Action had ever been the Douglas's province; stark action it seemed spoke to him louder than any words.

"Audience is over," James rapped out abruptly. Taking Joanna by the arm, he stalked back with her through the Abbot's doorway.

In the parlour again, the door shut, the young woman collapsed into the King's arms, frankly sobbing now. "Oh, Jamie," she gulped. "What have men done to you! What has this land done to you! Already. To make you . . . thus! I think . . . I think you should never . . . have left . . . England! I am frightened, James!"

He patted her head. "You have no need to be, my heart. I shall see that it is others who shall be frightened."

"Words, James – only words! You know it. I *am* frightened. And frightened . . . of you!"

"Of me? Never that, surely!"

"I am frightened of . . . of King James!" she repeated.

He smiled, but mirthlessly. "King James also was frightened. Back there. Frightened of those mosstroopers. Frightened that they would put their lord before their king. Unbidden. That they made no move, I think . . . I

274

think indeed I must have the people with me, the common people. Pray God I have! And I was even more frightened that . . . that – lest Drumlanrig's hand should indeed come off! There before my eyes! The saints be praised that you pleaded mercy, my dear, my white dove! But . . . I had to do it! You must see it? It was that – or I might as well have turned back for Tweed, there and then! This first day is all-important. Or, almost so . . .!"

"What do you mean?"

"I mean, tomorrow may be more so! Tomorrow, when we ride into Edinburgh. Into my capital . . ."

17

Second thoughts, and William Lauder's advice, delayed the approach to Edinburgh for another day. The Chancellor was strongly of the opinion that the news of the sort of king that Scotland had acquired ought to be given time to spread across the country – he believed to good effect. Consequently the next day's journey northwards through the rolling Lammermuir Hills stopped short at the Abbey of Newbattle near Dalkeith, seven miles from the capital, a daughter-house of Melrose.

The day following, again advance was delayed – for the sufficient reason that word was brought to the Abbey that a great company was approaching from the direction of the city, under a forest of banners. The reporter informed, with the catch in the voice which habitually accompanied mention of the name, that most of the banners seemed to blazon the Red Heart of Douglas.

The royal party advisedly waited. Dalkeith was the territory of the second greatest of the Douglas houses.

When the glittering and colourful host came riding down the Esk valley slope to the green water-meadows around Newbattle, however, Sir David Douglas was the first to point out that though indeed Red Heart banners predominated, the greatest and most prominent was not adorned with the crescent of cadency of Dalkeith, but was wholly plain, undifferenced. Which could identify only the chief of the name. And since Archie Tyneman, Earl of Douglas, was still in France, this must be his son and heir, Archibald, Earl of Wigtown.

The young man who halted his great array some distance

from the Abbey entrance, dismounted and came walking alone and bareheaded, was splendidly dressed and walked with a proud and lissome swing, a fresh-featured and fair-haired, stockily-built, broad-shouldered and muscular gallant. As he drew near, Joanna's eyes widened, and she turned to look at her husband and back to the approaching man.

"James – he is . . . he is . . .!" She exclaimed.

"Aye. He is," the King agreed, laconically.

James had never seen this Archibald Douglas – but he had heard much of him, in especial that he was a very different man from his silent and devious father, headstrong, forthright, bold, fond of women. He had the name of being a dashing cavalry leader in France, and with no fondness for the ways and policies of his parent.

Wigtown came striding forward, to fall on his knees before the King. He reached out both hands, palms together, in clearest gesture of homage. His eyes, upturned to those of James, were alive, vivid with laughter – and extraordinarily like those he looked into. Even in that moment, however, they flickered sidelong towards Joanna, in frankest appreciation of feminine beauty.

"Welcome, Nephew!" James said – and though that was short, there was a wealth of relief in the two words.

"Your Grace's most devoted servant, Sire – and Uncle!" the other cried, kissing the extended hand. He turned, still kneeling to do the same for the Queen – but with a smile she waved her hand to raise him up.

"My cheek surely!" she said. "Since it seems that I am your aunt, sir!" She was swift of perception, was Joanna Beaufort.

Wigtown rose to kiss her cheek with enthusiasm, having to hold her in the process, James looking on amused. None of the others looking on, amused or otherwise, could fail to note how alike these two men appeared, standing there together.

Archibald Douglas was indeed James Stewart's nephew, son of that Princess Margaret, eldest sister whom James had never known, who had been wed by Albany to Archie Tyneman when still a child. Only two or three years separated uncle and nephew, and they looked to have come out of the self-same mould – save for the colour of the hair and something of greater maturity and responsibility about the King.

"You are the most hopeful sight and sign that I have seen since I crossed Tweed, my lord," James said, trying to keep the thankfulness from sounding too evidently in his voice.

"Would that I had been there! At Coldstream. To greet Your Graces." Wigtown did not say why he had not been. "But now – I rejoice to see this day. Scotland has a man again to lead her! And beauty to adorn and delight her! Beauty – aye, and mercy, so I do hear!" And he bowed to Joanna.

"Tales are told, I see!" James commented. "Douglas ears are sharp!"

"Their swords are sharper, Sire! And at the service of a king who knows how swords should be used! And when *not* to use them!" That was significantly said. "I shall see that Drumlanrig's sword-hand strikes *for* you, in future!"

"I am content to leave it to you, Nephew."

"Good. Have I your royal leave to present my friends? Sir James of Dalkeith. Sir Henry of Lochleven. Sir William of Nithsdale. Sir James of Balvenie. And others of the name. All are here – and at your command . . ."

So, that late April afternoon, King James came to his capital under distinctly more favourable auguries – since in Scotland an escort of the principal Douglases was scarcely to be improved upon. On the last green ridge, of Gilmerton, they all paused, to look down towards the city, Joanna exclaiming her delight.

Strangely enough, it was also James's first glimpse of Edinburgh. His father had loved the west, the Castle of Dundonald in Ayrshire, and Rothesay on its quiet island in the Clyde. When he had to sojourn in the east, he seldom went farther than Stirling, from whose rock he could still see his western hills. He had never taken his second son to his capital.

278

Encircled by hills on three sides, and with the blue waters of the Firth of Forth to the north, Edinburgh rose like a grey leviathan out of the green coastal plain. James had never seen so strangely and nobly placed a city. A mile long and scarcely a quarter of that in width, it was built wholly on a thrusting narrow spine of ridge which lifted from the foot of the soaring bulk of Arthur's Seat up to the challenging bluff of the Castle Rock, like a mailed fist shaken in the face of the land. Because of the constriction of the site, its huddled buildings were forced to heave skywards within the tall walls, as in a jostling struggle for light and air, like plants sown over-close, tier upon tier thrusting upwards to a crazy skyline of pinnacles, steeples, towers and gables, wood and stone, some half a dozen and more storeys above the ground. Across the intervening plain, its church-bells sounded in jangling cacophony.

The Provost and magistrates met them at the fortified city gates, with the keys and a lengthy address in bad Latin – which James listened to with fair patience and a grave face. Within, the narrow streets were thronged with cheering folk, who shouted for their fine swack king and his bonny bride – even though they looked askance at the Douglas men-at-arms who beat an ungentle passage for the royal cavalcade. James might have wished for other harbingers than these, but recognising all too clearly the hard facts of the situation, smiled and bowed and waved cordially. Joanna, looking radiant, won all hearts.

"At least, it smells a deal less than London!" her husband shouted. He had to shout, so great was the din.

At the open space of the Grassmarket, directly below the frowning castle – open in the sense that the huddled buildings here drew back somewhat, though the space was packed with people – the busy Douglas outriders began to clear a way up a steep cobbled hill that rose towards the east end of the Castle Rock itself. James, glancing round for other openings, drew rein.

"Why do we climb up there?" he asked. "It leads but to the castle, does it not?"

"The Duke of Albany awaits you at the castle," Wigtown informed. "It is the foremost citadel of your realm . . ."

"Perhaps. But Murdoch shall come to me, not I to him! Moreover, I have had enough of castles and citadels to last me my life!"

"Sire – do not fear. No trap is set for you, I warrant. Duke Murdoch, I think, will be glad to yield up the government to Your Grace. It has brought him little joy! And . . . would any dare seek to shut you up in Edinburgh Castle, with Douglas at your side?"

James favoured him with a twisted smile. "I am much beholden! And reassured! Nevertheless, I shall stay away from castles, when I may. They mind me over-much of prisons! I prefer gentler lodgings." He was looking about him, over the heads of the crowd. "My lord Bishop – over there is a monkish house, is it not? A fair enough place . . .?"

"That is the monastery of the Greyfriars, Sire. They would be honoured, to be sure. But it is not large. For your train. Whereas the great Abbey of Holyrood lies scarce a mile off. Beyond the Canongate. Meet for your residence – if you will not have the castle."

"Holyrood then let it be. Send a messenger to inform the Abbot that I am coming, my lord Chancellor. And you, Nephew, send up to the pile on the rock, and tell my Cousin Murdoch to present himself to me at the Abbey."

So the procession, with difficulty, turned itself around and made its way down the long reaches of the South-Back Canongate, below the stern crags of Arthur's Seat, to the Abbey which crouched under the great green hill and formed the lowermost end of Edinburgh's extraordinary spinal site. It was a large and handsome establishment, if smaller than Kelso and less fine than Melrose.

"With my lord Abbot's permission, this will serve very well – until we ride for Perth," the King said.

"Perth, Sire . . .?"

"Yes, Perth. Scone is near to Perth, is it not? Scone, where the Kings of Scots are crowned. To Scone we go, just as soon as all can be ordered, and proclamations issued. For if there is one matter more than another which gives comfort to my enemies, it is that I have not yet been crowned. My coronation, therefore, is of the first necessity. See you to it, Willie Lauder. Commands for every earl, lord, noble and knight, as well as every prelate and cleric of note, to attend me at Scone without delay. To come prepared to bide some time, also. For after the coronation, I hold my first parliament. At Perth, it shall be. We have work to do!"

"So soon, Your Grace . . .?"

"Soon? Sooner, man! I have had eighteen years in English ward to think of what must be done. Time and to spare to consider my course, and my duty. Now is the time for deeds." He turned in the saddle. "And you, my lord Earl – action for you also. I gave command for Sir Robert Lauder, here, to go arrest me the Lord Walter Stewart, who it seems seeks my throne! He is Keeper of my Castle of Dumbarton, I learn. It may be something beyond Sir Robert's present power therefore. So go you, my lord of Wigtown, to take him, instead. So soon as may be, using what force you require. To be handed over to Sir Robert, who will ward him. Ward him in an excellent secure place I mind of. The Craig of Bass! The Lord Walter for the Craig of Bass, at the earliest, my friends. Now – let us see the Abbot of Holyrood . . ."

An hour or so later the Governor of the Realm, Murdoch Duke of Albany, presented himself at the Abbey. James, who had never liked or respected him, was much struck to see how changed he was. Always a pompous stiff man, at least he had had a tall and almost stately dignity at variance with his weak and shallow character as it was; now he appeared shrunken, hunched, unkempt, his manner veering between anxiety and feeble assertiveness, a tired, ageing man, sorry for himself and only too well aware of failure.

James had intended to deal in harsh and exemplary fashion with this usurping cousin, who had been ransomed and exchanged for Henry Percy ten years before, instead of himself; who had done nothing to secure the King's release since – the reverse indeed; who had ensconced himself in the rule of Scotland, even had his own Great Seal made, as though monarch; who had given away practically all the King's lands which his father Albany had not already given, as bribes to the nobility; who above all was his father's son. But, seeing him now, whining and declaiming by turns before him, James perceived that the man was not worth his long-cherished wrath. This was but a mouthing caricature of his sire, Albany, the terror of James's childhood, murderer of his brother. He now took from him the seals of office and other emblems of rule, and thereafter dismissed him almost like a lackey.

Joanna was glad. Vengeance on this Murdoch could only tarnish his honour, she said.

Right in the centre of Scotland, Scone lay distant from the town of Perth some three miles. There, by the silver Tay, in another ancient abbey, the kings of that country had been crowned for nearly seven hundred years, since Kenneth MacAlpine had united Picts and Scots and brought the famed Stone of Destiny to this the Pictish capital, while England was still centuries from becoming more than a collection of warring petty princedoms. To Scone Abbey, then, on 21st May 1424, King James and Queen Joanna came, from the Blackfriars Monastery at Perth, to be crowned – for contrary to usual custom, this was to be a double coronation.

James's fear that there might be only a very restricted answer to his command for attendance was in fact proved groundless. Whether on account of curiosity to witness a scene unseen in Scotland for thirty-four years, or because the word of King James's calibre and methods had not failed to penetrate to every corner of the land, there was a greater turn-out than for any coronation hitherto – despite the fact that not a few of the greatest men of the land were now, in turn, hostages for the King in England. Of the fourteen earls, ten were present, Buchan and Douglas being in France, and Moray and Crawford hostages. Hay the Constable and Scrimgeour the Standard-Bearer were there, though Keith the Marischal was hostage. Of the feudal lords, barons and great lairds there was a host such as never before had been seen together at one and the same time. Of the prelates, once again only Finlay, Bishop of Argyll, was missing.

James had commanded that all bring their ladies with them, something new for Scotland which it was his hope might have a gentling effect on proceedings. In consequence, he met for the first time three of his four sisters — Margaret, Countess of Douglas; Mary, formerly wife of Douglas, Earl of Angus, now wed to the Lord Graham; and Elizabeth, wife of Douglas of Dalkeith. The Princess Egidia, the fourth, had died. Also he saw once again his only remaining uncle, Walter Stewart, the same who had been Lord of Brechin and was now Earl of Atholl. None of these close relatives did he greet with much more than the most formal expressions of delight — since not one had lifted a hand to succour or comfort him in all his life. Perhaps he was prejudiced, but he did not particularly like what he saw of them now — though he perceived that Atholl, chuckling, couthy, wily, was a man to watch.

The impressive and lengthy ceremony went off satisfactorily and without hitch — even if it had a slightly sour start. It was the hereditary right of the Earl of Fife to commence the proceedings by conducting the monarch to his royal seat up near the high altar — and Duke Murdoch of Albany was still Earl of Fife. Indeed his eldest son Walter, now securely islanded on the Bass Rock under the care of Sir Robert Lauder, should have had the earldom; but Murdoch clung to it and its revenues — one of the reasons for their mutual antipathy. Murdoch therefore paced at his cousin's side to the throne in the crowded Abbey Church of Scone — and seldom can a man have looked less joyful in the occasion. His Duchess, Isabella, daughter and heiress of the old Earl of Lennox, another Stewart, did a like service for Joanna — and looked little the happier, a hard-faced ageing woman beside the lovely Queen.

Thereafter matters improved. The Abbot of Scone, gorgeously robed, performed the ceremony and service, as was his right, Murdoch placed the crown upon his former cousin's brow, and the Primate bestowed the anointing – to a great shout of the entire congregation – and Bishop Lauder of Glasgow, the Chancellor, preached the sermon. A notable sermon it was, too, emphasising all too clearly the state of the nation, the shame of its ruling classes, the dire apprenticeship of the King, the stern tasks now before the monarch, and the unwavering support of Holy Church. Seldom can a coronation sermon have cast down the gauntlet so plainly before an unruly and recalcitrant nobility. A lowering corporate frown settled over a large proportion of the assembly. King James had had a hand in the concocting of that homily – and none there doubted it.

The prolonged homage-rendering followed, conducted in strictest precedence by the Lord Lyon King of Arms, with Murdoch, as next heir to the throne, coming first to kneel and take the monarch's hand between his own palms. The proceeding took literal hours to complete – and it was a hungry and thirsty congregation that eventually spilled out into the May sunshine to partake of the vast provision Holy Church had produced for the occasion, in booths and on stalls and tables throughout the Abbey pleasance and orchards.

James, having given due warning and ample demonstration of his determination, was now concerned to show the other side of his nature. The rest of the day and night was to be given over to rejoicing. Temporarily at least he would wipe away those frowns from the multitude of noble brows.

In the afternoon therefore, the level haughlands between the Abbey and the Tay, cleared of their cattle, were the scene of pageantry, play-acting, music and singing, chivalric contests and manly sports, such as had never been staged in Scotland before. James organised it practically single-handed, since few others present had any experience in the matter. Moreover, he threw himself personally and wholeheartedly into almost every activity. He sang with the singers, accompanied others on the lute, ran foot-races and rode horse-races, challenged all comers at wrestling, waged sword-fights, fought in armoured tourney, practised archery and played at the ball. There were not a few who were shocked, outraged, at such behaviour on the part of a king, especially amongst the elder folk. His sisters, for instance, were black affronted. But most there were caught up in their liege lord's manifest enthusiasms, and entered into the spirit of the day, the young folk in the main notably so. And as James proved himself the champion in so much that went on, so the excitement grew.

Joanna co-operated loyally and happily – but even she, as the afternoon wore on, counselled caution, moderation. James would wear himself out, she claimed – do himself an injury. And some would be glad of it. She indicated the starched disapproval of much of the royal family.

"Heed not them, my heart," he told her, panting after a wrestling contest in which he had soundly beaten his nephew Wigtown. "Look to the young ones. Those I need to build up my kingdom. See young Angus, there – another nephew. Wigtown himself. Mar. Seton of Gordon. Young Graham. Are these frowning? These . . . these are learning to love me! And, God knows, I need men to love me! I do too much, yes. It is unseemly. Boastful. That I should win in so much. But – I do it of a purpose, Joanna. This is my opportunity – opportunity I have made. What happens here at Scone today, will resound throughout the realm. The Scots must have a king in deed as well as in name. For this they have lacked so long. And a king they can love, as well as fear. You understand, my dear? I overplay my part of a purpose."

"So long as the part you play is truly James Stewart, I am content," she said.

As a further demonstration of what kingship could mean, in an interval of the proceedings, James created no fewer than twenty-seven new knights. There had been no king's knightings almost in living memory – for such had not been Robert the Third's habit – and while knighthood could be conferred by others, the royal accolade was the more sought after. The young Earls of Wigtown, Angus and March were amongst those so honoured, as were the Constable, the Standard-Bearer and the Lord Lyon. Walter, the son of old Sir Walter Haliburton of Dirleton who had aided James to the Bass, was another. Though it went against the grain, he even knighted Lord Alexander Stewart, Duke Murdoch's youngest son, as a diplomatic gesture, spoiled and arrogant as he appeared to be; the other son, James, was none knew where.

That evening, there was a great banquet at the Blackfriars Monastery at Perth, and however unsuitable some might deem it, the monkish establishment rang with mirth, music and dancing all night. It was notably not the clerics who criticised, most of them contributing to the gaiety in varying degrees. Even the Primate, aged as he was, trod a measure with the Queen. He declared that there had been all too little cause for rejoicing in Scotland for long; far be it from the Church to cry halt this happy day.

In the course of the evening, after an interval of music and minstrelsy, James read aloud, as tribute to his new-crowned Queen, the first part of his own love-poem, *The King's Quhair*, to the wonder of all present.

The northern kingdom had learned a lot, in one day, about the character and abilities of her young monarch.

James allowed only another day or two for celebrations, and then insisted on convening his first parliament. All three estates, the lords, prelates and representatives of the burghs, were commanded to attend. The institution of parliament had fallen almost into desuetude. The Albanys, as Governors, had ruled without parliaments, almost without Privy Councils. The idea of corporate responsibility in rule had almost faded throughout the land. James had seen what a source of strength it was in England – and what a weakness its loss had produced in France. He found little enthusiasm for its revival in Scotland – but he was determined in the matter. His summons was reinforced dramatically by the announcement of a list of drastic penalties for such as should fail to attend, be they the highest in the land. When he learned that his uncle Atholl was in fact returning to his domains further north, he had him brought back, as a lesson to all others.

The parliament was held in the same refectory of the Blackfriars Monastery as had been the banquet and the dancing – the largest hall available in Perth. There were complaints that Perth was not the place to hold parliaments anyway – they had been most usually held at the royal castles of Stirling or Edinburgh – but James declared that he wanted to be as near the centre of his kingdom as possible. This raised eyebrows, for only if the Highlands were taken into account could Perth be considered central – and few Lowlanders were prepared to consider the Highlands as part of Scotland at all, but only a mountainous wilderness of barbarians; James, however, since that visit paid to him at Nottingham so long ago, by Red Hector Maclean of the Battles, and the holocaust of Harlaw thereafter, had thought much of his Highland subjects, guided in this by John Lyon who had been chaplain and secretary to the Lord of the Isles. Now, he was adamant.

The Chancellor, as of right, presided, but the King sat opposite, in the Abbot's chair as throne. The refectory was packed. There had not been so representative an assembly seen ever before, probably.

It began with flowery speeches from the spokesmen of the three constituent estates, all on the same theme, congratulating the monarch on his safe return to the bosom of his leal and loving people, of the lieges' joy and the realm's well-being. Old Atholl fell asleep and snored, while James himself fidgeted.

This over, the Chancellor banged with his gavel to still the chatter of relief, and in a businesslike voice, devoid of emotion, read the agenda.

"My lords spiritual and temporal, knights, barons, lairds, burghers and true men of this realm assembled," he began, "His Grace, our Sovereign Lord, requests, desires and

287

advises that this first parliament of his reign shall consider, enact and decree the following provisions, for the weal and peace of this kingdom. That private war between lords or others soever, be forbidden, under penalty of treason. That rebellion, disturbing of the King's peace, or refusal to aid the King in that peace, shall be deemed acts of treason, and the lands of all so acting shall be forfeit to the Crown. That no nobleman or other shall take the road, or otherwise ride abroad, with excessive retinue in arms – His Grace suggesting a score for an earl, a dozen for a lord or bishop, eight for a knight or abbot, and six for laird, prior or gentleman, as maximum. That all feudal holders of lands will produce their charters thereof before the King's Sheriffs, to justify possession . . ."

He got no further before the clamour broke out. Everywhere throughout the crowded hall nobles were on their feet shouting. For minutes on end the unseemly din continued, beat on his table with the gavel as William Lauder would. James watched, expressionless, as the proudest names in all Scotland shook fists, stamped and bellowed. At length, he made a sign to the Lord Lyon nearby, who ordered the three state trumpeters, from now on to be the King's constant attendants, to blow a fanfare. The sudden blare of neighing sound stilled all lesser noise. As it faded, James stood up slowly.

"Discussion there shall be, on every matter. Gross uproar there will *not* be, in my royal presence," he said sternly. "My lord Constable – you will escort from this place and into secure ward, any man soever who speaks other than with the respect due to the royal presence, or the dignity of this court of parliament. Proceed, my lord Chancellor." He sat down.

There was a faint rustle and muttering, and then Lauder's voice continued. "Furthermore, that the King's Sheriffs investigate and consider the present state of all former Crown lands and property alienated since the death of the late King Robert, of gracious memory . . ."

Something like a growl arose – but savage as it sounded,

it obviously came from only a small proportion of those present, however lofty their lineage.

The gavel slammed down. "That a tax of one shilling in each pound of land value shall be levied on all land-holders whatsoever, towards payment of the King's ransom." That produced an almost anguished wail – which petered off however as the Chancellor added loudly, ". . . in order that the present hostages held in England may be returned to their homes."

All who had sons, brothers and relatives amongst the hostages glared at those who had not.

"That there be suitable taxes imposed on all cattle and corn, that the Treasury of the realm be replenished. That all Customs duties, now given wrongously to certain men, be returned forthwith to the Treasury. That all gold and silver mines be declared the property only of the Crown. And that no gold be sent from these borders – in especial to the Papal curia at Rome."

It was the prelates' turn to blink, and the nobles to grin – for barratry, the petitioning of offices and livings in the Church direct to the Pope, for reward, was as rife in Scotland as elsewhere.

"That all burghs of this realm will gather and collect from burgesses, guilds, crafts and citizens, one-sixth proportion of the King's ransom, to the total of twenty thousand English nobles or ten thousand merks Scots, within the year."

There were actual guffaws now, from lords who had been so lately fuming, as well as chuckles from the churchmen. The burghs' representatives stared at the floor.

Lauder's voice went on steadily, inexorably, detailing export duties on cattle, horses and hides; foreign merchants to expend their gains in Scotland; a survey of national wealth; honest, national tax officials to be set up; fishery and game laws to be enforced, with close seasons; wapinschaws and archery training to be engaged in by all citizens between the ages of sixteen and sixty. Et cetera.

The first shoutings had wakened the Earl of Atholl.

He and others like him did not fall asleep again, throughout.

The discussions that followed were prolonged, hot, acrimonious. Frequently King James had to exert his authority to prevent proceedings degenerating into a brawl, and more than one flushed and proud noble was escorted out by the Lord Lyon and his minions. But the list of enactments had been drawn up with some subtlety, and their order of presentation given much thought. They were so worded, and so brought forward, that only certain sections of the assembly stood personally to lose by each, and the voting strength was cunningly split time after time. The private war ban, for instance, was only of major moment to the great lords – so that the prelates, burgesses and many knights and lairds voted for the resolution. Likewise the excessive retinue provision. Again, the investigation into the former Crown properties only would injure those who had received them from the Albanys; consequently nearly all others voted for this measure also. The barratry embargo on gold had all the secular voters, as well as prelates with a sense of shame, in its favour. And the burgh taxation gained no sympathy from lords, lairds or churchmen.

It took James and the Chancellor four stern and trying days, in that crowded refectory, nevertheless, to battle through this revolutionary programme – for it was nothing less than that. They did not get all that they wanted; measures were toned down, amended, ventilated with significant loopholes. But by and large the vast volume of unprecedented legislation was carried, something no Scots parliament had ever before been faced with. Men eyed their stocky, energetic monarch, sitting alert, watchful, throughout all the long sessions, passing constant messages to the Chancellor – watched and wondered. Here was something new in kings – a clerk ascended the throne! Only, of course, the prowess displayed on the sports-ground and lists at Scone gave warning that there was a deal more than clerkishness here – as did the much-discussed treatment of Home, Drumlanrig, Cavers and the Lord Walter Stewart.

It was said, moreover, that King James had distinguished himself in the French wars, albeit on the wrong side. It perhaps behoved wise men to walk warily.

The parliament of 1424 stood down, at last, somewhat dazed by what it had agreed to. But it was all words and paper as yet, of course – which was a comfort to many. To translate all this talk into deeds was quite another matter. The lords and their great retinues rode off homewards, every mile from Perth, every clank of armed men and thunder of hooves behind them, bringing them returning confidence. Indeed, the Earl of Lennox and Sir Robert Graham, Tutor of Strathearn, came to blows before they reached Auchterarder, on their way southwestwards – and the Abbey of Inchaffray had to treat some fifty wounded men in its hospice. So much for words, papers and King Jamie!

James was seeing off his uncle Atholl next morning, from the Blackfriars courtyard, when John Lyon, now Archdeacon of Teviotdale, brought him the news of the Lennox-Graham clash. As old Atholl hooted his mirth, his nephew stiffened with the effort of damping down his hot anger.

"By God's blood – this they shall pay for!" he cried, almost trembling. "This they *must* pay for. And at once. And all the realm must see it – or our labours are vain. They must be taken, both of them, and warded for trial."

"Hech, man Jamie – you canna do that!" his Uncle Walter declared, chuckling. "Maybe you can take Graham. But Lennox! He's an earl, man – and of our own house o' Stewart. And he's an old man – near as old as me! Forby, he's Murdoch's good-father. Take Lennox and you'll have the most o' our own name against you, lad!"

"The laws we have just made were made for Stewarts as well as other men, my lord. All shall learn it. John – fetch me my lord of Wigtown. Or . . . no. We must not put too much on him. We'll test another young man's loyalty – and another Douglas. Fetch me my lord of Angus. And the Constable. These two shall take Lennox and Graham."

"You'll no' send Douglases against Stewarts, Jamie!" Atholl cried, affronted. "It's no decent . . .!"

"I'll send anybody against law-breakers, Uncle – *anybody*! But Angus is also my nephew, and he has the men. He's young – but Hay, the Constable, will give him authority."

"And what then? What will you do with them?"

"They shall be held in strong castles. Awaiting trial. For some time. While others learn the lesson! And *I* decide what forfeit they will pay. This is the plain rebellion we debated. Our work spurned the first day! They shall pay, yes!"

"M'mmm. Forfeit." The Earl's sly old eyes considered his vehement nephew quickly. "I advise ye go canny with Lennox, lad. An earl's an earl. Say his age moves ye to mercy! Hee-hee!" he cackled. "But Graham, now – that's another matter. Graham is Tutor to young Malise Graham that's got Strathearn. Yon was Murdoch's doing. A right fell thing, to alienate a royal earldom, like Strathearn, and give it to a Graham. Here's opportunity, maybe, to undo a wrong. Aye, a wrong."

James looked at the other doubtfully. "Strathearn? I fear I do not know the matter fully . . .?"

"Then you ought to. It was aye one o' the Crown earldoms. My brother David, and your uncle, was the last true earl. He died, leaving only a daughter. She married Sir Patrick Graham of Kincardine – that was elder brother to this Robert Graham. Murdoch, the fool, granted him the earldom, in right o' his wife. A Stewart earldom! It should have come to me!"

"Or perhaps . . . to me!" James intervened significantly.

The old man huffed. "*My* brother's, it was. A younger son's patrimony. But . . . Murdoch bought Graham support with it. Graham died – Sir Patrick – and now this laddie, his son Malise, is Earl o' Strathearn. You saw him, at Scone. Little more than a bairn. And his Uncle Robert manages the earldom for him – Tutor o' Strathearn. And rides high, God rot him!"

"So?" Lyon had brought the young Earl of Angus now, with Sir William Hay, the High Constable. "Sir Robert

Graham lacks wisdom, I think!" James sounded grim. "The young Earl Malise will need another, and wiser, Tutor! To break my peace the day he leaves me, while playing usurper in a Crown earldom, is too much! My lords – I have work for you . . .!"

18

The Palace of Linlithgow rang with high revelry. Even down at the lochside, the sounds of music and laughter came floating on the still evening air, to mingle but strangely with the sleepy quacking of the mallards and the rustle of the reeds. The man and woman, strolling there hand in hand, listened and smiled.

"This old lake has not heard the like for long, I vow!" Joanna said. "You have brought not a few changes to Scotland, James."

"I brought *you* to Scotland, lass. Of that I am proudest."

"Foolish one! I meant that you had brought music and laughter."

"Have I not just said so!" His smile faded. "But . . . I misdoubt whether most of my realm thinks of me as a bringer of mirth and music! I have, I suppose, brought more of fear, harsh measures, imprisonment. I am spoken of as a hard man. With a mailed fist. God knows such is not the name I would have."

"No, James! That name you have only amongst the grasping and unruly nobles. The people of the land are doing as you hoped they would – learning to love their king. Everywhere we have gone, it has been the same – St. Andrews, Dundee, Edinburgh, Glasgow, Ayr, Galloway . . ."

It was true. In the months that had followed the parliament, James and Joanna had ridden the length and breadth of his kingdom – excepting only the remote Highlands – showing themselves to the populace, instituting new officers and sheriffs, personally righting wrongs, indicating to the nobility that the Crown was no longer some remote, heedless and ineffective name, but the ultimate power, all-seeing and long of arm.

"Aye. But it is an ill thing that before I can make myself loved, I must needs make myself feared by those on whose duty and support I should most rely. Was there ever such a crew of hungry, self-seeking rogues as our Scots lords! Ignorant, uncouth, arrogant . . .!"

She smiled. "You prefer the English ones, my liege lord?"

He paused in their strolling, chewing his lip. "Yours seemed less . . . brutish! Less subject to their own selfish passions . . ."

"Better mastered, perhaps. The Plantagenets have ever been great at mastery! With little concern for being loved. That is all." She shrugged. "That, and better schooled, it may be."

"Schooled, aye. There is the rub, I grant you. Unschooled and unlettered. Scarce a man of them who can do more than sign his name! How can I make use of such to rule a realm? When the only persuasion they know is of the sword! I am forced to use ever and always churchmen, since they at least have learning."

"You have made a start in this, my dear, with your university at St. Andrews. In time, this sturdy sapling will bear fruit . . ."

"But how many noblemen's sons do I find enrolled there? Tell me that," James demanded. "Would that I could force them to it. St. Andrews is well enough – but it is full of churchmen's bastards and the sons of burgesses and small lairds, eager to better themselves. But of lords' sons, never a one!"

"Patience, James. Time – give it time. Ten years old – that is all, is it not?" Joanna glanced down. "Perhaps one day *we* shall have a son to study at your St. Mary's College of St. Andrews!"

He put his arm around her. The Queen was pregnant and beginning to show it, a source of mingled joy, pride and dread to her husband. "Joanna," he exclaimed, "I forgot!

You will be tired? Weary. And I keep you walking here. A fever . . .? The night air is chill . . ."

"Hush you, foolish one! I am well. Strong. Think you no woman ever bore a child before? This suits me very well . . ."

Nevertheless, James bent their path up over the shelving pleasances of the park towards the handsome brown-stone building that shared the knoll with the fine Church of St. Michael – Scotland's only true palace, in the sense that it had been built as a royal residence and not a fortified strength. For that very reason perhaps it had been little used in the troubled past, no monarch deeming it sufficiently secure a dwelling. But if James would indeed make the key keep the castle and the broom-bush the cow, he must needs show a lead himself. So he avoided, as much as possible, the great castles and fortresses of his predecessors, and made his residence mainly in abbeys and the like, the Blackfriars Monastery in Perth in especial – but also here at Linlithgow, because Joanna had fallen in love with the place, set amongst rolling low green hills beside its pleasing loch. Now, it stood above them glowing like a beacon, every window lit up, banners flying from its every tower.

Pacing slowly, James reverted to the subject of St. Andrews and its new university college – for it was a matter close to his heart. "Henry Wardlaw is stubborn on this. It is the only issue on which we disagree. That, and his too great subservience to Rome. He would have it that the college is for priests and churchmen. I say it is for others also. The Bishop's professors and doctors would teach only clerics. This is folly. Learning is for all men, not only priests."

"The good Bishop grows old, Jamie. The university was of his own begetting, his child. You must have patience with him."

"I know it. His was the vision. A university for Scotland. But he could not make it alone. He required a royal charter and Papal authority. For these he required me, prisoner as I was. Many the letters John Lyon carried between us, on this. From the first I saw the worth of it, the blessing it could bring to Scotland. But always I saw it had not only to be for churchmen. The charter I signed those years ago, was not only for faculties of theology and divinity, but for the arts, the humanities. Now, the churchly faculties grow and flourish – but the others are mere shadows, names. I gave orders otherwise – but all the servants I can trust are churchmen! All the professors learned enough to teach are churchmen . . ."

They had climbed now to the palace on its green terrace. The stone walls seemed positively to pulse with sound and life – as well they might, for James's Court far out-taxed Linlithgow's accommodation. The royal couple strolled in through the gatehouse pend to the great inner courtyard. Two weary froth-spattered horses stood steaming there, held by one of the gate-porters.

"Visitors," James observed. "Who are these?" he asked of the porter.

The man shook his head. "I dinna ken, Sire. But in haste they came. Speiring for the Chancellor . . ."

The inner courtyard was packed, and weirdly lit in the soft September twilight by innumerable flaring pitch-pine torches. In the centre a space had been cleared, and from here surged the wild, barbaric music. A score of ragged fiddlers sawed and plucked and skipped there, clad in varied and tattered tartans. To the ranting strains many were dancing – but it was not the stately and formal dancing to which Joanna, and James also, for that matter, was used. It was a wild, jigging, capering dance, though with a fierce and vigorous grace of its own, in which legs and arms, indeed the whole body, was tossed about in a rhythmic abandon which yet somewhere contained a strange discipline. In the men, the effect was savage, challenging, disturbing; in the women, infinitely more so, with a frank and blood-pounding voluptuousness that could not fail to stir the manhood of every male present still not yet in his senility.

In front of James, unaware of the royal presence, a man in canonicals was staring, black-browed – none other than John

Crannoch, Bishop of Caithness. "Accursed Hielant hizzies!" he was muttering. "Shameless Erse jauds and harlots! And yon Kate Douglas as bad as any o' them!" But despite his strictures, the Bishop was licking his lips and tapping the flagstones with his toe.

Of the women dancers most were dressed, like the men, in stained and faded tartans – though these were all but shaken off their gleaming bodies by the vigour of their exertions; but two or three were otherwise, ladies in the flowing gowns of courtly fashion, skirts necessarily now hitched high. Most notable of these was a tall and strapping well-made wench, with corn-yellow hair and high complexion, who danced with a flair, expertise and flagrant lustiness which outdid all others, in wide-mouthed, laughing provocation. So wholehearted was she in her exercise that her gown was kilted well above her knees and her bodice had slipped from her fine shoulders, completely uncovering one of her jouncing and magnificent breasts, that glowed extraordinarily more white, save for the nipple, than her flushed features. Clearly she cared nothing for the fact, and bounded and cavorted with infectious enthusiasm.

"The Lady Catherine – excels herself!" Joanna murmured. "A young woman largely generous!"

"Aye," James acceded.

She looked sidelong at her husband. He had sounded somewhat abstracted. She perceived that, in common with most of the men present, he was by no means unmoved by the spectacle.

"You *still* find her to your taste?" she asked.

Preoccupied as he might be, James did not fail to recognise the slight emphasis on the word still. "Kate is, as you say, generous!" he answered. "And she has Highland blood in her."

They watched in silence for a while. Sheer exhaustion was bringing the dancing to a close.

"Highland dancing is not always thus," James went on, after a while. "Indeed, I think this unusual. These people perhaps feel more strongly than do Lowlanders. In all matters. They think us dull, heavy . . ."

Joanna was scarcely listening. "James," she said slowly. "I would not wish to constrain you, to limit you. In your . . . living. Now that I am pregnant and plain, in especial. It is not unusual for men to . . . amuse themselves with other women than their wives. Particularly kings! You must not think yourself . . . deprived."

He turned to her, smiling now. "Is this my Joanna I hear? My proud Beaufort? Say no more, my dear. You have filled my heart since ever I saw you that morning at Windsor. When you opened a new world for me. Think you that you shrink in that heart because you grow great in the belly with my child?"

"I know your heart is great, my lord. It might be that I would not grudge some small corner of it . . . to another."

"Liar!" he said softly, into her ear.

Gravely she accepted that. "Yes, liar," she admitted. "But . . . remember what I say. I do not fear for myself in your heart. But there are other parts. The Lady Catherine would be kind to you if she might, I think. As for me, I hope that I can be generous also."

"It pleases the King's Grace to make royal command," James intoned, taking her arm. "Such talk is unseemly in his ears, and shall not again be spoken. You hear, woman?"

"As it please Your Grace!"

"It does. As do you, my heart. I can look on Kate Douglas with a man's quick lust, I suppose – and give thanks to God for Joanna Beaufort."

"Which is what I said, in other words, is it not Sire?" Her laugh was silvery. "But – here comes Master Cameron."

A small keen-faced, neatly-dressed youngish cleric, modest, unsmiling, but somehow determined, came sidling through the noisy throng to them, to bow.

"I have sought Your Grace everywhere," he said, his voice harsh with the jerky roughness of Lothian. "I have news."

John Cameron was not yet thirty, and humbly born, bastard of a parish priest on the Douglas lands of Dalkeith.

But he had a nimble brain, marked ability and discretion, with an infinite capacity for work, qualities apt to bring their own reward in any age or society. In consequence he had risen with meteoric swiftness in the service of his feudal lord of Dalkeith, and become the Official of Lothian. Then the Earl of Wigtown had perceived his usefulness and made him his secretary and agent – necessary when the said illustrious heir of all Douglas could neither write nor read – and had him advanced to be Provost of the Douglas abbey of Lincluden. Now, with John Lyon keeping an eye on matters in the Borders, as Archdeacon of Teviotdale, and Thomas Myrton sent as Scots envoy to Rome, Cameron had been taken over as secretary to the King – an efficient machine for the carrying out of James's purposes and policies. He was looking very grave now, in that laughing, excited company.

"Couriers from France, Your Grace," he said. "There has been a great disaster. To the Scots forces. A great battle, at a place called Verneuil, south of Paris. The Duke of Bedford has triumphed, the French and Scots grievously defeated. My lord of Buchan is dead. As is the Earl of Douglas. His younger son, Sir James Douglas also. Sir Walter Lindsay. And many others. The Scots army in France is cut to pieces, Sire."

James stared at him, a chaos of emotions surging in his mind. "Cut . . . to pieces!" he almost whispered. "Buchan! Douglas!"

"Aye, Sire. A disaster."

"A disaster, yes." James was looking through the secretary, not at him. "Dead! All dead!" It was not wholly shock and desolation that sounded in his voice.

Joanna eyed him strangely, but said nothing.

"You will wish to question the couriers, Highness?" Cameron suggested.

"To be sure. You have informed my lord of Wigtown? Now, of course, my lord Earl of Douglas and Duke of Touraine!"

"I have informed none, Sire. I sought you only."

"I will go to my chamber. Bring me my lord. And the Chancellor. Tell no others, meantime . . ."

When Cameron had gone, James turned to the Queen. "Look at me, Joanna," he requested. "Am I a monster? An evil man? Lacking humanity? I hear of this defeat, this blow to our Scots army. The deaths of many men. Men I knew — indeed, men of my own blood and kin. Buchan was my cousin. Douglas my brother-in-law. Yet I feel nothing of hurt, of loss. Triumph, rather! For Archie Tyneman is gone, and Buchan is gone! The one, a man I could never trust, yet the greatest noble in my realm. The other, Murdoch's heir, an able fighter and one who might have served me ill indeed. Wigtown is now chief of the name of Douglas — and I think I have made him my friend. And Murdoch, I believe, I can handle — and the rest of his brood! This disaster, then — may not Scotland be the better for it? That is, if *I* am Scotland! Am I indeed Scotland, Joanna? Tell me, am I Scotland . . .?"

19

It seemed scarcely conceivable that a year could have passed since last James Stewart sat on that throne in the refectory of the Blackfriars at Perth, listening to William Lauder's deliberately impassive voice detailing the clauses, statutes and provisions, watching the faces of Scotland's unwilling legislators, wishing that he could be elsewhere. Yet there was ample to prove the passage of the twelvemonth, many steps taken on the hard road to a better governed kingdom, much wrong righted, many nobles' wings clipped, many lessons learned, by himself as well as others. Not least there was the bawling presence of a fine baby girl, through there with Joanna in the royal apartments of the monastery.

There had been many mistakes made too, in that year – James was the first to acknowledge it. Indeed, this second parliament was largely concerned with correcting those mistakes, rectifying statutes too hastily drawn up, modifying, clarifying, simplifying, tightening. He would have held this parliament anyway – for he was determined that the realm should come to look upon regular parliaments as normal and indeed essential, that the habit of corporate responsibility in government should grow and become established. But the faults, gaps and inequalities of the previous legislation, as well as the impracticability of enforcing much of it, had become all too apparent. If the new order was not to be brought into disrepute and neglect, amendment was urgently necessary.

But it was a wearisome business – and none more aware of the fact than the King himself who, whatever most of his lords might think, was a man of action and no hair-splitting clerk. This was the eighth day of the sitting – for amendment, rectification and elaboration are slower processes than are basic propositions. And there had been the statutes regarding the Lollard heresy to consider, required by the lords spiritual, with other measures to safeguard the position of Holy Church. The clerics were demanding their price for support of him.

The assembly was reviewing the first report on the alienated crown properties which Duke Murdoch and his father had sold, given away, or otherwise lost during their long years of misrule – and typically, Murdoch himself had slipped out of the hall when the Chancellor introduced the subject. Suddenly, a fiercely handsome, sardonic-featured, dark man in his early forties stood up, to interrupt. He looked at Bishop Lauder, not at the King.

"I am Sheriff of Moray, my lord Chancellor. I declare an interference with my rights and jurisdiction. One of my lairds, Farquhar of Cairnecht, was arrested, tried and hanged, without recourse to myself and within my sheriffdom. But a month past. I seek explanation and indemnity from this parliament."

Lauder was beginning to ask for further details, when the King intervened.

"Farquhar? At Elgin, was it not? This was my doing, my lord. I shall speak to it – for it is fresh in my mind. Over-fresh!" James's eyes met and held those of the handsome man across the floor.

Everywhere men who had been lounging or even dozing, sat up alert. This confrontation had been bound to come, sooner or later – the wonder was that it had not happened much earlier. These two Stewarts must come to terms, or be at each others' throats – the clash was inevitable. On how it would go depended much in Scotland.

For the Sheriff of Moray was, in fact, Alexander Stewart, Earl of Mar. At least, so he named himself – and none had hitherto contested his assumption of the title, least of all the Albanys. This Alexander was the eldest of the illegitimate brood of another late and unlamented uncle of the King, also

Alexander, previous Earl of Buchan, fourth son of Robert the Second, and known as the Wolf of Badenoch, a man of unbridled passions and utterly savage behaviour, who had been the despair of even that lax and heedless monarch. This son had at first seemed to follow in his father's footsteps, terrorising and ravaging at will in the family fashion. He had, at a surprisingly early age, captured Sir Malcolm Drummond, brother of the Queen and husband of the heiress Countess of Mar, richest woman in the land, killed him in prison, then laid siege to the Countess in her own great castle of Kildrummy, forcibly marrying her thereafter – old enough to be his mother – and thereupon assuming the earldom of Mar himself, disinheriting her children. All before he was out of his teens. But, as well as having such initiative, this active youth was a born military leader of men – so much so that at the bloody Battle of Harlaw in 1411, against his cousin the Lord of the Isles, he had assumed command of the Lowland side, and had emerged the victor. Since then Alexander had sought and found certain graces to superimpose on his basic character, developing gradually from Highland freebooter and sea pirate into a puissant knight and successful commander – the most successful in the land, indeed. Fortunately he had seemed to have no dynastic or governmental ambitions, presumably on account of his undeniably illegitimate origin. Hitherto he had kept his distance from the returned King.

"My lord of Mar," James said, civilly enough. "If I trespassed upon your shrieval rights, it may be that I had excuse. In making a progress through my kingdom, I passed through your sheriffdom of Moray. That you were not there present to receive me was my loss! But at Elgin a poor woman came to me, her King, seeking justice – was carried into my presence since she could by no means walk. This Farquhar of Cairnecht, it seemed, had stolen her two cows – all her living. When she accused him of the theft and said she would seek restitution before the Sheriff, he laughed her to scorn. Then she declared that she would not take the shoes off her feet until she had walked into the

King's presence, to tell me. Whereupon Farquhar laughed the more, and himself took off her shoes, to disprove her. But he did more, my lord. He caused two horse-shoes to be nailed to the woman's feet, in place of her own – and told her to walk to her King in them!"

Even that assembly, accustomed to aberrant behaviour, stirred a little.

"In your absence, therefore, my lord, I sent and took the man Farquhar, and questioned him. He did not deny the deed. I had him dressed in a white linen smock on which was painted representation of what he had done, back and front. I paraded him thus through the streets of Elgin, then had him dragged at a horse's tail to the gallows of that your town, and hanged! My lord of Mar, do you quarrel with my justice?"

The other smiled, then actually laughed aloud. "My lord King – far from it," he exclaimed. "Save in that you were over-gentle perhaps! I submit to your superior jurisdiction – but suggest that *I* might have improved upon the punishment!"

"You have, my lord, perhaps served a longer apprenticeship at such business!"

"Aye. My experience and, h'm, proficiency, are ever at Your Grace's service. In this – as in all other matters."

They eyed each other for long seconds, assessingly. Then James nodded briefly, and the other sat down. Everywhere men sighed either in relief or in disappointment. It looked as though the King had made another convert.

Inevitably further consideration of the alienated estates brought up the subject of the Crown's resumption of the earldom of Strathearn, a move which had provoked not a little criticism, partly on account of Earl Malise Graham's youth, and partly because his mother, being the only child of the late Prince David Stewart, the former earl, was his undoubted heiress. Chancellor Lauder was elaborating when again the King signed to him.

"This also I will deal with myself, since my name and repute is involved, my lords, and I moved personally in the matter," he announced. "Strathearn is a royal earldom, like Rothesay, Ross, Fife, Carrick, Atholl and the rest. It should never have passed out of the control of the Crown. That it did so was ill-advised. The heiress, my cousin Euphemia, should have been compensated in good measure – but the earldom itself resumed into the Crown. What should have been done by the Duke of Albany, I do now. But I also revive the old decayed earldom of Menteith, endow it with certain lands forfeited by the Earl of Lennox for his late shameful rebellious behaviour at Auchterarder, and make and appoint Malise Graham Earl of Menteith. If any in this parliament, my lord Chancellor, find objection, let them speak."

None protested – even those of the Clan Graham. Most accepted that this was fairly generous treatment for the dispossessed Malise – and perceived the poetic justice of making Lennox provide the wherewithal for the young man's support, since it was the Grahams Lennox had fought with at Auchterarder. Lennox was still shut up in Edinburgh Castle.

James went on, "I now propose to bestow, in liferent, the earldom of Strathearn upon my good and last remaining uncle, Walter Stewart, Earl of Atholl. The two earldoms being contiguous. To return to the Crown at his decease."

There was a hum of comment as men remarked that here was an astute move. Atholl was a cunning, untrustworthy and difficult man – but better to have with you than against you. So now the King bought his support – but bought it cheaply, for he was an old man and the liferent was unlikely to last long. In his seat Atholl smiled thinly.

"There is one other matter, my lords, not unrelated, which I would bring to your notice," James resumed slowly. "The Earl of Lennox was taken and warded and tried, and is now confined at my pleasure, for breaking my peace immediately on leaving the parliament of last year, indulging in feud-fight and tuilzie when we, and he, had just acted to make such unlawful. But, my lords, there was another to that fight – Sir Robert Graham, former Tutor of Strathearn. Where, I ask, is Sir Robert now?"

There was a deep silence in that crowded refectory, as men eyed each other, and then looked over to where sat the Earl of Dunbar and March. Robert Graham had escaped from ward at Dunbar Castle some months before.

"My lord of Dunbar and March!" James snapped suddenly, crisply. "Where is Sir Robert Graham?"

The Earl, the same sober individual who had come as part of the Scots embassage to Pontefract to treat for James's release after King Henry's death, rose to his feet uncertainly. "I know not, Sire," he admitted. "Beyond the Highland Line, somewhere, I have heard . . ."

"You have heard! God save us – you have heard, sir!" James thundered. "When I committed this man to your keeping, in your strong castle of Dunbar, I required more than hearing from you! I require Graham at your hands, my lord!"

"It was not my doing, Your Grace," the Earl protested. "I was not at Dunbar. I was at another house – of Ersildoune in Lauderdale. When he contrived escape . . ."

"Contrived! From one of the stoutest holds in this realm! The contrivance was not all Graham's, I warrant! He must have been aided from within. Does your captain of Dunbar Castle still sit therein, sir?"

"Aye. But he kens naught of it . . ."

"Then let him ken something else, my lord! The inside of a different castle. Edinburgh's! I want your captain warded in Edinburgh forthwith, sir – until you bring me Sir Robert the Graham."

"How can I do that, i' faith?" the Earl demanded. "The Highlands are wide and Graham strong . . ."

"And your purse deep, for the task. The deepest in my kingdom. Moreover kept well filled these many years by a pension from the Treasury of England! Buy me back Graham, sir!"

Breaths were indrawn at this disclosure – then uproar broke out. George Cospatrick, eleventh head of the almost princely house of Dunbar and March, descended from Malcolm Canmore and the ancient Celtic kings, owned

307

more lands than any other man had ever done in Scotland, her monarchs included, being also Earl of Moray, Lord of Annandale, Nithsdale, Morton, the Isle of Man and innumerable other baronies. Moreover he had inherited vast estates in England also. If Douglas was more powerful, it was in men, not in wealth. Because of his English possessions, he had long acted in ambivalent fashion, Scot one day, English the next. Indeed he had the strange record of having aided Douglas to defeat Hotspur Percy at Otterburn, and then aided Hotspur to defeat Douglas's son, The Tyneman, at Homildon Hill. That such a Croesus should be in receipt of an English state pension could be accepted as intolerable to every envious Scots noble – information James had received from Joanna's uncle, Chancellor Beaufort.

Listening to the noise, James was satisfied, for the moment. Without seeming to have engineered it deliberately, he had just taken major strides towards the breaking up of the mighty front of his haughty lords. He had reduced Strathearn, bought Atholl, won over Mar, and now set fists shaking against Dunbar and March – all in one afternoon's talking. It was enough, and he was weary of it all. He rose to his feet.

Immediately all must stand. James bowed formally to the Chancellor, and as the Lord Lyon's trumpeters sounded their fanfare to indicate another day's sitting over, he stalked out of the chamber.

But he was not to win back to Joanna's side just yet. Master John Cameron, his secretary, came hurrying after him down the long monastery corridor.

"Sire – your attention, pray. I deem it important," that quietly efficient cleric said. And since James had employed him because he *was* efficient, he paused in his pacing now. "A man seeks Your Grace's ear, urgently. A Graham. Graham of Mugdock. He has tidings, of moment."

"Can they not wait, man?"

"I think not, Sire. He would not tell me all – but enough! It is rebellion. Sir Robert Graham is in it – but more than he. This Mugdock has known of the matter – as have others,

308

no doubt. Because he is grateful to Your Grace for giving his chief, Earl Malise, this earldom of Menteith, he has decided to tell you. Belatedly. There may not be much time."

"Rebellion!" As James sighed the word, he drew himself up, straightening the wide shoulders hunched from hours of sitting. "I have been expecting this. Bring him to me. In the library . . ."

Mark Graham of Mugdock was a thin, desiccated, lame youngish man, anxious-eyed and obviously with a strong sense of inadequacy. The presence of the King had him stammering and gulping.

"Your Grace's pardon," he said. "Your Grace's pardon. If Your Grace will hear me? It is the Lord James. The Lord James Stewart. And the Bishop. Aye, and Sir Robert. Robert Graham. And others. Campbell's MacGregors. Highlandmen. Islesmen. They're all in it, Sire. To bring down Your Grace. In bloody revolt . . ."

"Take time, man," James told him. "Be not so hasty. You have learned of a revolt? A conspiracy against me? Led by the Lord James Stewart, Duke Murdoch's son? And a bishop. That will be Finlay, Bishop of Argyll, from Lismore? Who has never paid his duty to me. Murdoch's confessor — and brother, they say!"

"Aye, Sire — these. And many others. They have raised a host. From Argyll and the south isles. All Lennox has joined them. Much of the West. Many of my own name. Esteeming you the ruin of Strathearn, Your Grace. Sir Robert has worked on them . . ."

"And you, my friend, were one of these — until this afternoon!" James interjected grimly. "Else how did you know all this?"

The other shuffled his feet, and looked down. "I but *knew* of it, Sire. I was in grievous doubt. I am a leal man, Your Grace, and no rebel. I was against it. But others . . . my own kin . . ."

"Let it be. So long as you have chosen the right now. And if it is not too late! Where is this host assembling?"

"In the MacGregor country. About Glengyle and Loch Lomond. North of the Lennox. They are secure there, in the wild hills beyond the Flanders Moss, but near to the settled lands. And apt for mustering from North and West."

"To be sure. And do you know aught of their plans?"

"They say, to move into the Carse of Forth. Make speedy thrust for Stirling. To cut you off here, from the south, Sire. Stirling Castle will be yielded to them, and they will hold the Forth. The Duke Murdoch to be declared King in Your Grace's place . . ."

"Murdoch! King? I do not believe it!"

"Aye, Sire – but only in name. The Lord Walter Stewart to be released, and become Governor of the Realm. My lord of Lennox to be President of the Council. And Bishop Finlay to be Chancellor. Lennox to receive your Castle of Dumbarton and many royal lands. The Bishop also to be Primate . . ."

"So-o-o! It is all arranged!" James looked at John Cameron, alone with them in the Prior's library, but did not see him. "So far has it gone! And I? I am to die?"

The Graham bowed his head.

"Aye. Tell me – how many of yonder lords sitting in the parliament hall knew of this?"

Still the lame man looked down, unspeaking.

"Murdoch!" James barked abruptly. "Do you tell me that Murdoch himself knows naught of this?"

"I do not know, Sire. But . . . his castle of Doune is near to Glengyle and where the host assembles."

"Dear God! The House of Albany held my throne for eighteen years! Now, they would have it for all time! Curse them all for foresworn traitors! The young James did not devise this for himself, I vow. He is the youngest of the brood, and scatter-headed they tell me. Walter I hold. And Alexander is here in Perth, with his father." The King raised an open hand, and snapped it shut into a clenched fist, an eloquent gesture. "It is them, or me! This time, there must be an end." Drawing a long breath, he turned back to Graham. "The times?

310

Know you anything of when they move? How long I have?"

"I cannot tell, Sire. I would think they move so soon as they are full gathered. But soon, while Your Grace is still here at Perth. To cut you off from your southern realm. Any day . . ."

James interrupted him, rapping out commands. "Master Cameron — fetch me the Chancellor. And the Bishop of St. Andrews. Also my lords of Douglas and Angus. Do it quietly, discreetly. No alarm. To come to me forthwith. But singly. Aye — and bring also my lord of Mar! I have use, I think, for his peculiar talents! If he is for me. And if not, I would know it . . .!"

James paced the room while the secretary was gone, firing questions at the lame man, building up in his mind the full picture, reaching decisions.

"There is a more clever hand behind all this than Duke Murdoch's," he jerked, presently. "Or any of his sons'. Or old Lennox's, a year shut up in ward. Whose hand is it?" It was to himself that he spoke. "It is a stronger, surer, more cunning hand than Robert Graham's. I must discover it."

"Bishop Finlay of Argyll, Sire . . .?"

"I have not met him. But he is said to be a by-blow of old Albany's — therefore Duke Murdoch's half-brother. I cannot think him responsible. This is not Bishop's work. Bishops do not act thus. With armies, hosts and swords. Their minds are otherwise — plotting with pen and paper, intrigue and secret compact. No, somewhere a shrewder hand, used to the sword, plans my overthrow and death. And I cannot think that hand is far away!"

"Sir John Montgomery, Lord of Ardrossan, is very close to the Duke of Albany, Sire."

"Montgomery is but a jackal. I seek higher game than that!"

The new Earl of Douglas came in, followed quickly by young Angus. Before these potent lords, Graham of Mugdock all but cringed in a corner. Then Bishop Lauder arrived, supporting on his arm the aged Henry Wardlaw.

Cameron came back, to announce that he could not find the Earl of Mar but had sent pages seeking him.

In terse, unvarnished phrases James informed the new-comers of the situation. He ended by repeating his conviction that there was a master-hand behind it all, as yet undisclosed.

The others looked at each other.

"Dunbar!" Archibald Douglas suggested promptly. He was more or less at permanent feud with the Earl of Dunbar and March. His mother, James's sister the Princess Margaret, had been promised by King Robert to Dunbar, and then given instead by Albany to the Douglas.

"Mar!" said Angus, whose lands adjoined those of that potent character.

The clerics remained silent.

"We shall see," James said. "Meantime, I must act, and swiftly. I cannot move against these rebels in the west until I have gathered together a host. But I can seek to clip their wings, here in the east. Stirling must be secured. And if I cannot take the castle, at least Stirling Bridge must be taken, and held open."

"For that we need men, Sire," Douglas declared. "But none of us has men here in Perth – by your own command! I have but a score. Angus here the same. Before, I would have had hundreds!"

"And so would others! Others who must now be moved against. We must raise the men from nearby lords. The Constable's lands of Erroll. Murray of Tullibardine. Ruthven. Drummond, my own mother's people. Oliphant. Gray. No – Gray is not to be trusted. These are all here, at the parliament – but their lands are near. How leal they are, God knows – but I want every man that they can muster. To ride to Stirling. See you to it. The Constable, and Keith the Marischal, will aid you." James raised his chin and squared his shoulders a little further, an involuntary but telling gesture. "But first, my friends, I have another task for Hay, the Constable. He may require your aid. Go fetch him, Master Cameron. And the Marischal also. I want

312

the Duke Murdoch arrested forthwith. Also his son, the Lord Alexander. With all his household. And his friend, Montgomery of Ardrossan. This first."

"Arrest . . . the Duke of Albany!" Henry Wardlaw faltered.

"Yes."

"This . . . this could split the realm, Your Grace."

"The realm – *my* realm – is already split, it seems! We shall see whom the Scots follow – their King, or the House of Albany!"

"It should have been done ere this," William Lauder asserted. "There is no room in this kingdom for Your Grace and the Albanys both."

"I fear that is true. It must be done quickly and quietly. And be you thankful, Archie, that Murdoch also is restricted to but a score of men-at-arms! Once taken, he and the others must be carried secretly, by night, to a secure hold. Your castle of St. Andrews, my lord Bishop? They will be safe there, from rescue, meantime . . ."

The guard on the door opened it to admit the Earl of Mar. Standing on the threshold, that handsome man eyed the group around the King with a disparaging, fleeting smile.

"Do I smell plotting, Sire? Dark deeds? Heads close? Is this to be the end of poor Mar's freedom? I swear you all look sufficiently black of brow!"

"All leal men have cause to look so, my lord," the Chancellor reproved him. "Therefore, we hope, yourself!"

"You say so, Sir Bishop? Long faces are to be the sign of loyalty? God help His Grace, then!"

"Earl of Mar," James said bluntly. "How much do you love Duke Murdoch of Albany, my cousin?"

The other looked at the King from darkly saturnine eyes. "Would it be next to treason, Sire, if I declared to you that I can scarce bear to breathe the same air as he does? Even so, I love him better than I do his sons, Walter in especial – or they him!"

"Yet Murdoch made you Lieutenant of the North, my lord! And Sheriff of Moray."

"I already controlled the North, Sire – so he could do little else. And any other Sheriff of Moray would have found the office . . . difficult!"

"I see." James decided to take a chance. "I also am finding the Albany air difficult to breathe! Perhaps you will help me clear it, my lord?"

"With all the pleasure in the world!"

Succinctly the King told Mar of the situation – and, watching as he spoke, could not believe that the dark man had known anything of the plot.

At the end, the Earl barked a laugh. "Murdoch king! And Walter governor! I warrant Cousin Murdoch would not long warm the throne's seat! We'd have King Wattie – Christ God preserve us!"

"You prefer King James, then?"

"Sire – I swore fealty to you, did I not? At Scone. And told you in the hall this afternoon that I was at your service. I will go now and take Cousin Murdoch out of whatever hole he skulks in, and bring you his head on an ashet. Or whatever other part you would prefer!"

"Ha – not so fast, my friend. Let Murdoch keep his head yet awhile. His is not the head I fear. And it is the Constable's duty, I think, to take him. For you I have another task. You are not inexperienced in reducing castles, I believe!"

The other grinned. "There are castles and castles, Sire!"

"Aye. There is Kildrummy – and Stirling! How think you to fare at Stirling, sir?"

"Stirling . . .?" the Earl almost whispered. "Stirling Castle! Sir Robert Erskine!"

"Exactly. Sir Robert Erskine, the Keeper. Who, it seems, would prefer King Walter. His son-in-law!"

"I have a bone to pick with Robert Erskine."

Well James knew it. This Erskine was the true heir, through his mother, of the Mar earldom which the dark man so cavalierly had usurped. Mar would have married his bastard son to Erskine's only child and heiress, to regularise matters – and Murdoch had agreed, as the price of peace in the North. But the Lord Walter had defied his father, married the heiress himself, and was now claiming the earldom – with his father-in-law's support. James was fast learning that such knowledge was essential to rule in Scotland.

"Pick your bone, then, before Stirling is yielded over to my enemies," he said.

"It is as good as done, Sire!"

"Good! And you, my lord Chancellor – warn your brother at the Bass that there may be an attempt to release Walter Stewart. Though how any could hope to break the hold of the Bass, I know not. Ah – here is the Constable . . ."

20

At the next day's sitting of the parliament there were many notable absentees. But the King sat in his accustomed place throughout – and if he appeared a little abstracted at times, he by no means allowed it to hold up the business.

Murdoch Stewart was under arrest, and with his son Alexander, Montgomery, and his secretary Adam of Otterburn, was on his way to St. Andrews by secret route. Stirling Bridge was held in force, and James anxiously awaited news of the castle. Mar would take it by guile if he could, by battery if he must.

How much of all this had leaked out, the King did not yet know. Stirling was only thirty miles south-west of Perth, and the movement of armed men from local lairdships was bound to have attracted attention.

It was late afternoon before James was brought the message for which he waited. Mar was in control of Stirling Castle – by guile, presumably – and Sir Robert Erskine, its Keeper, had fled westwards.

When the subject under discussion was passed – a revolutionary idea of James's own, whereby advocates should be made available, free, to the poor to plead their causes before courts of justice – the King rather abruptly announced the prorogation of parliament until mid-May. This was something new for Scotland. With a rebellion on his hands, parliament could not continue to sit; yet it might be vitally necessary to have parliament available to carry through swift and extraordinary measures at short notice. Unfortunately, a new parliament could only be summoned on forty days' notice. To get round this, James introduced this English idea of prorogation, whereby it was the same parliament, its members only standing down for a limited interval. There were not a few grumbles and raised eyebrows amongst the delegates – but most were glad enough to get away home, for they had had nine days of it already. Scots parliaments in the past had not been apt to last longer than an afternoon.

That evening the Earl of Atholl came to the royal apartments. "I have heard tales, Jamie," he said, licking thin old lips. "Ooh, aye. This town's as loud wi' tales as a bees' byke! And I canna find yon other nephew of mine, Murdoch, anywhere! No that I greatly want him, mind – for he's a feckless body and I canna be doing wi' him."

"Then you will not weep over his departure, Uncle. Murdoch is gone a-journeying. Under escort."

"Ha! You say so?" The pale eyes, though washed-out, were very keen. "Journeying? Whither, lad – whither?"

"Shall we say – to another part of the kingdom."

"Aye." Atholl grinned yellow teeth. "So you dinna trust your auld uncle!"

"I trust you sufficient to give you the earldom of Strathearn, my lord."

"Uh-huh. To be sure. In liferent, though – only in liferent. And I'm near three-score-and-ten!" He cackled shrilly. "But I'm no' dead yet, Jamie! No' yet." He moved over to Joanna's side, and took her hand. "You've got a right bonny wife, lad. Aye. And how's the bairn, lassie? Fine and well? A pity it wasna a laddie, mind. Then Murdoch wouldna still be next heir to the throne."

James nodded grimly. "The thought had not failed to occur to me!"

"Aye. So Murdoch's gone travelling! Wi' Hay the Constable, they say? Young Alexander wi' him. Walter's locked up, and Jamie – the other Jamie – is raising the West."

"You are well informed, Uncle."

"Just the chatter o' the town, lad – nothing more. Och, you ken how talk goes on. They're a fine, swack, good-looking family – and all in line for the throne! Aye, good looks – and no' a particle o' wits between the lot o' them!"

James eyed the old man sharply. "That thought also came to me."

"Aye." Atholl was stroking Joanna's arm, little encouragement as she was giving him.

"I am convinced that there is a shrewder mind behind all this than has Murdoch or any of his sons. Everything points to it," James said. "I cannot think that it is the Bishop . . ."

"Finlay Stewart is a fat slug, who thinks wi' his belly!"

"Then, who?" It did not escape the younger man's notice that his Uncle Walter had known just who was meant by 'the Bishop'.

Atholl's hand was growing more venturesome – but when Joanna sought to pull away from him, he gripped her with fierce claw-like fingers.

"The ladies – bless their hearts! Aye, and their other parts, heh!" he chuckled. "Och, you do not want to under-rate the ladies, Jamie. Even such as ar'na just beauties, mind. There's some as has as good heads as men – and better. Eh, lassie?"

"What do you mean by that, sir?" James demanded.

"Just what I say. If Murdoch and his sons lack wits, that's no' to say his wife does! Yon Isabella o' Lennox could be a better man than her father! Or her husband! Or her sons. Hee-hee!"

"You think that she – the Duchess Isabella – could be behind all this? The revolt? Surely you are not serious?"

"You think no'? Aye, then – maybe I'm just an auld fool. Like her father Lennox, that you've shut up in Edinburgh Castle. Aulder but just as foolish as her husband, that you've sent . . . where? Or her good-brother Buchan that you starved o' reinforcements in France. Or Wattie that you've made a gull of, on the Bass! Or Alexander that you've laid by the heels, likewise. Hech, aye – Isabella is a dark and handsome woman, who could see hersel' wearing a crown! Fine she could! And she hates you, Jamie lad – she hates you!" His Uncle Walter crowed with such convulsive mirth that he all but choked himself, and could barely finish. "Moreover . . . 'tis said . . . said that she . . . finds amusement . . . wi' Sir Robert Graham!"

Stroking his chin, James eyed the old man askance.

Joanna took advantage of Atholl's paroxyms to break free and make for an inner door. "You will pardon me, my lord," she said. "My child – you understand . . ."

Later, when James was free to come to her, she clung to him, her normal serenity much disturbed.

"Have nothing to do with that old man," she cried. "He is horrible. Evil. Do not trust him . . ."

"I like him as little as you do, my dear," he told her, soothingly. "But I cannot ignore him. He is powerful, a man to be reckoned with – and with sharper wits, I think, than the rest of my curious family! What he says of the Duchess Isabella makes sense. It may be that I have overlooked danger there. Because she is a woman. I, of all men, should know how women are to be belittled at one's peril!"

"That old man is more to be feared than any woman in the land!" she asserted. "I feel it in my bones."

"Nevertheless, I think that I will call upon the Duchess Isabella, at Doune Castle. Perhaps you will come with me, my love? Since, it seems that she would wear your crown!"

"Or so says an evil old man. Who might not be averse to wearing a crown himself! Has it struck you, James, that if Murdoch and his sons were gone, your Uncle Walter would be next in line for *your* crown? It might be wise to remember it . . .!"

Doune Castle stood above a bend in the river, in the fair valley of the Teith, some score of miles south of Perth. Originally built by the old Earls of Menteith, Albany had acquired it by marrying the heiress, and had much added to it. In turn, Murdoch had greatly increased its size and strength, until now it was one of the largest private fortresses in the land, a towering mighty place in a sylvan setting, with its little town huddling nearby, just below the blue bastions of the Highland Line. James and Joanna came to it next

319

afternoon, with a fine company – but however fine, it was not a company which could take Doune Castle if the stronghold was indeed held against them. None knew it better than the King.

"A handsome place," he commented, looking down on it from the high ground to the north. "But too strong to be any subject's house in a realm which *I* rule!"

"At least the drawbridge is down and the portcullis raised," Willie Lauder said. "It seems that she does not seek to deny you entrance – since she will know well that you come."

The Duchess Isabella's welcome was otherwise less than evident, however. Armed men, silent, watchful, lined the approaches to the castle, the drawbridge itself, and made a bristling frieze along the lofty parapeted curtain-walls which enclosed the great courtyard and beetling keep. Moreover, as the royal party rode in under the gatehouse-arch, it was to find the courtyard itself packed with men-at-arms, drawn up line upon line. No single word of either challenge or greeting met the newcomers.

Nevertheless it was not the silent living who had most effect on James – and on Joanna – so much as the silent dead. Jutting out from the red stone of the keep's soaring walls were a number of timber booms. And from each dangled men, who swayed and twirled in the April breeze. James felt a rising nausea as he was abruptly transported back in years to France, to the gibbets outside the walls of Melun. In the hush, he heard Joanna, at his side, catch her breath.

Despite his repugnance, he urged his reluctant mare forward, underneath the nearest of those swinging bodies, peering up. By reaching, from the saddle, he could touch the feet and legs. He did so – and nodded grimly to himself. It was as he thought by the slack way the bodies hung; the victims were not cold, and rigor mortis had not yet set in.

He backed his mount to Joanna's side again, lips tight. He gripped her arm that trembled a little, for a moment. At his other side, Lauder spoke, low-voiced, almost in a whisper.

320

"A trap, think you? I do not like this, Sire."

"Nor I. But we are not intended to, I warrant!" James nodded upwards. "There is strange bait for a trap! A demonstration, rather, I would say – a warning, even. New-written!"

"Even so, we are grievously outnumbered. I'd be happier outside these walls."

"So the lady judges, I would think!"

"Your Grace – let us back," the young Earl of Angus, new returned from Stirling, urged. "Over the drawbridge. While there is time. We could be cut to pieces here. Then Murdoch, her husband, is king!"

"I am king, my lord," James returned, and raised his voice to declare it. "And I do not retire before the frown of any of my subjects!" He glanced back. "My Lord Lyon – your trumpeters, if you please."

The three royal trumpeters in their gorgeous heraldic tabards blew a fanfare, brassy loud in that enclosed space – and the ranks of narrow-eyed men seemed to sway a little at the assured authoritative blare of it. But none spoke or moved thereafter.

Haughtily James looked around. "Who is captain here?" he demanded. "I, the King, require your lady's presence – if she is here."

When still there was no response, Joanna touched her husband's wrist, and pointed upwards.

The wooden shuttering of a small iron-grilled window two storeys up was open, and the head and shoulders of a woman could be discerned, standing there, watching.

James raised his hand. "Greetings, Cousin Isabella," he called. "I come visiting. With the Queen. Have you no better fare to offer us – than these!" And he gestured towards the hanging men.

There was no response, not so much as a flicker of acknowledgement.

He moistened his lips. "Have you grown hard of hearing, Coz? Or do I speak less than clear?"

When still he received no reply, James knew that he must

321

act, and swiftly. He did not require to be told that the situation was indeed as full of menace as it had grown to seem. This time, threats as to treason would serve nothing – for a single well-aimed bolt or arrow would dispose of that. Himself slain, and it would be Murdoch, master of this house, who would declare what was treason and what was not. Or the woman who controlled Murdoch! James was suddenly afraid – for Joanna, whom he had led into this danger.

All balanced as on a knife's edge, he perceived. One false move and there would be slaughter – and a new king in Scotland. Yet move he must, for more of this and the storm would burst. Any climbing down, any diminution of his royal dignity and assurance, would be fatal. He must surprise. Yet without precipitating the very clash that he feared.

He raised his voice again, striving to make it sound easy, casual. "Bide you there, Cousin – while I bring you word of your lord, Duke Murdoch. No – do not come down. I command." He tossed the single word, "Wait!" to Joanna and his companions, and urged his mare forwards towards the door of the keep.

It was unthinkable that the King should dismount there, before them all, and uninvited climb the stairs to that upper window. But the King still on horseback was a different matter. Without hesitation, physical at anyrate, he rode his mount to the arched doorway and up the two steps thereat, waving aside the two astonished guards. He had to bend somewhat in the saddle to pass through.

It was a long time since he had done such a thing – at Nottingham Castle, and brought down the wrath of Lord Grey de Codnor on his head as a consequence. He was taking a distinct chance, both with his mare and with the stairway – but with good horseflesh, he believed that what counted was the rider's confidence, and he knew that in large castles such as this the winding turnpike was apt to be wide, at least as far as the first floor.

It was a tight squeeze in the narrow entrance lobby –

322

merely a stone passage in the ten-feet thickness of the walling – two more servitors cowering back into the little porter's lodge that opened off it. Then, with the great dark vaulted basement chamber yawning in front, where wide-eyed, open-mouthed domestics stared, the stairway rose on the right, corkscrew-fashion. Thankfully James saw that it was fully five feet wide and the twist consequently not too tight, that there was fair headroom, and that the steps were not deep, indeed smoothed and rounded by the passage of mailed feet. Bending low, he set his sidling, doubtful horse to the ascent.

After a stumbling start, the mare made a fairly good job of it, clattering and striking sparks but gaining height steadily without too much slipping. The noise James welcomed.

From the first landing opened a sort of loft within the arch of the basement vault – which was good, for it meant that the main hall of the castle would be a storey higher, and the stair would continue wide that far, in all probability. It did. As he passed the first-floor window, James caught a brief glimpse of the crowded courtyard below, every face upturned, motionless.

The twisting of the stair must have been awkward for the Barbary mare, and more than once James had his right leg rubbed painfully against the stone of the newel. But he reached the second floor still mounted – to find a distinctly disconcerted woman pressing back into the doorway of the Great Hall. Behind her two other women stood agape.

The King, still having to crouch somewhat in the saddle, threw his hand forward in what was partly salute, partly pointing indictment. "Well met, Isabella!" he said.

"What . . . means . . . this?" she got out.

"Play-acting, Cousin – nothing more," he confided. "Like yonder dangling corpses! Though something less . . . expensive a gesture! I counted near a dozen of them!"

The other did not take him up on that. Isabella Stewart was a woman who wore her years well. She must have been nearly fifty, but her dark good looks showed scarcely a silver hair, her alabaster skin scarcely a wrinkle. She was handsome in a slightly masculine fashion, strong-featured, big-boned, but though not slender her body was still taut and womanly. She had dark smouldering eyes with notably heavy eyelids.

James was glad to get down off his horse, in the circumstances, deliberately showing the animal at the window before he did so.

"Let us have done with play-acting," he said then, crisply. "You can dismiss your legions and come greet my wife."

She eyed him with no least hint of accord. "Why should I?" she demanded.

"Because, unlike some handsome women, you are not a fool!" he said, shrugging. "You have nothing to gain by further mummery – and a deal to lose!"

"I have done my losing. My husband, my sons, my father! At your hands."

"They are not all lost, surely? Yet!"

"They are in your hands."

"All my realm is in my hands, Cousin. Even yourself! Since I am king. But that need cause true men no moment's unease. Moreover – you still have one son who puts himself outside my peace, I am told? James, your youngest."

The Duchess did not answer.

James glanced towards the window. "You have a great host of men under arms, have you not? More than necessary, I think, for your . . . simple protection! And contrary to the decision of parliament. Could it be Cousin, that you assembled these to aid your son's insurrection?"

Still the other did not reply.

He shrugged, and turned to sooth the mare, which for some reason began to sidle and paw in the confined space.

"I would also be interested to hear, madam, what crimes those dozen men had committed? To cause them to hang there from your walls?" he went on, mildly enough.

"I have power of pit and gallows," she returned shortly. Apparently she was a woman of few words.

"Your husband has. Or had! But only within the law of

this realm. Hence I ask what crime these had committed. So many. And so recently!"

"They had refused their due service. To their lord."

"Ha! Rebellion! So you hanged them! Do you counsel that I do likewise, Cousin?"

She glared at him.

"You hold yourself justified, then, in hanging a dozen men because they countered their lord's command – as expressed by you? A matter of policy!"

Curtly she nodded.

"Very well. You cannot complain if *I* act on similar policy. I am your liege lord. That you cannot deny – or until your son's rebellion is successful! I command that you order these men below to disperse. Forthwith. Peaceably. Do so, madam – unless you can show me wherein I now differ from you?"

She threw up a proud head. "The difference is simple," she said. "I can *enforce* my commands! You cannot!"

"Think you so, Isabella!" he answered softly. There was nothing soft about his actions however. With a couple of long strides he was at her side and, as her eyes widened in alarm, an arm encircled her in an expert wrestler's vicelike grip, from the back. An almost immediate change of grip, and he had her arms pinioned behind her in a hold against which any struggling produced only excruciating pain – as the Duchess promptly discovered. The King's left hand whipped out the dirk from his belt, to flash steel before her eyes. Brief seconds were sufficient for the entire action.

"I have never . . . had occasion to use a lady so . . . before," he jerked, in her ear. "But then, ladies do not usually hang those . . . who disagree with them! And threaten their monarch!"

"Unhand me!" she panted. "Are you . . . are you a savage?"

"I was trained in the French wars!" he told her briefly. "Now – to the window, Cousin."

"No!"

"Yes, I say." He applied a little pressure.

She bit back a cry. "Brute . . beast!" she gasped.

"So would croak twelve men – with ropes round their necks!" He was propelling her over to the open window. "Now – command them to disperse."

"I . . . will . . . not."

"You will, Cousin – or taste sharper hurt than this! Cold steel!"

"You would not dare. Even you!"

"Woman – I am of the same blood as your sons, remember! Would they not dare? See down there, my wife. The warmth of my heart. Under the threat of your bowmen on your walls. Think you I'd flinch to plunge this knife between your shoulders to save my Joanna? God pity you – and receive your soul – if you so believe!" He pushed her roughly against the window-breast.

There, in the sight of all the staring, wondering throng below, Isabella Stewart still hesitated, biting her lip.

James pricked the needle-sharp point of his dirk into the fleshy part of her rounded shoulder. "Tell them!" he whispered fiercely in her ear, and twisted her arm even more tightly. "To their quarters. Without delay. Speak!"

He felt her swaying against him, and a great sob racked her fine body. He had a sudden panic that she might swoon, and ruin all – but she was made of sterner stuff than that. It was fury, frustration, which all but overcame her. She rallied.

"Go!" she called huskily. "Go, I say. All of you. To your quarters. Dougal – have them disperse."

Something like a sigh rose from the crowd beneath, and a ripple of movement, as of wind across a barley-field, emphasised the break in the tension of waiting.

"My lady!" a hoarse voice answered her. "Is it truth? Your wish . . .?"

Another prick of the dirk-point.

"It is . . . my command. Now – do you hear?"

The murmur below changed character and was lost in the shouting of commands and the stir of movement, as the ranks broke up. There was clearly a relaxation amongst the visitors also.

"That was wise," James said. But he did not slacken his grip on the woman's arm, nor sheath his dirk. "Now, we shall go down, for you to greet my wife, Cousin. As is seemly. You would not deny the Queen your courtesy?"

No answer to that was expected or received, as he marched the Duchess past the mare on the landing, and down the stairway.

At the entrance lobby, James shifted his grip so that when they came to the doorway his arm around the woman might only have been holding her companionably. Also the dirk blade was slipped up his own sleeve.

The battery of eyes that greeted them was urgent, questioning, but since he was the King, no-one spoke. Joanna's glance searched his own. She still sat her horse between the Chancellor and Angus, her lovely face set, pale.

"The Lady Isabella, to greet the Queen's Grace!" he announced.

Joanna took her cue, even though her voice shook a little. "I am glad to see the Duchess," she said. "I hope that I see you well, Cousin?"

Tight-lipped the other woman considered her.

"She is grief-stricken for my lord Duke's absence," James asserted. "A matter which we must set to rights." He was swiftly assessing the situation. There were still a fair number of the Albany men in the courtyard, even though they were no longer ranked and standing to arms. And up on the parapet-walk guards still paced. There was still danger. At the same time, his own mounted company remained a close-knit entity, capable of more immediate concerted action. He made up his mind.

"You come with us, Cousin," he said quietly. "Willingly or other, you come with us."

"No!" she grated.

"My royal command! And if your people seek to stay us, in any way, you Cousin are the first victim! That I promise you. Do not think I'd fail, because of your sex. I've seen women flayed of their skins, for lesser offence! One ill move, and you die!"

She closed those smouldering eyes for a moment, then re-opened them and gave a single short nod. Whatever else she was, the Duchess of Albany was a realist, obviously.

James looked up. "A horse," he demanded. "Quickly."

An esquire hurriedly reined forward, and dismounted. Barely was he out of the saddle before the King stepped over to grasp it with one hand. Only a man of great physical development and notable fitness could have achieved what he did then. Without loosing his hold on the woman, he put a foot into the stirrup and hoisted himself and his captive both, in a single complicated movement which landed him in the saddle and the Duchess before it – an exploit taxing of all his strength, for she was not lightly made. In the process he cut his forearm with his own dirk-point, but scarcely noticed it.

Almost before he was seated, his eyes were searching the castle battlements. Men were watching inevitably, and interestedly – but no hagbuts or bows were so far raised. His scrutiny went on to the gatehouse-tower, from which the portcullis could be lowered and the drawbridge raised, trapping them within. No hasty movement was evident there – though activity within could be masked.

"Mount behind another," he ordered, to the owner of the horse he now sat. "Leave my mare." He jerked a head towards the gatehouse-arch. "Come!" he said, and urged his double-burdened new steed forward over the cobblestones.

There was no great distance to cover, but the doing of it seemed to take an eternity. Every step might have provoked the feared reaction. James's arm, around the Duchess, was tense as an iron band.

No shot was fired, no arrow strung, no chain rattled, not even a voice was upraised, before their horses' hooves were clattering echoingly beneath the vaulted gateway pend. James sighed with relief as he saw that the drawbridge was still lowered, indeed with footmen pacing on it. It was all that he could do to keep himself from spurring onward across it in a gallop. His passenger said never a word. At his side, Joanna murmured an incoherent prayer of thankfulness.

Drumming hollowly on the timber of the bridge, the King's company trotted out from Doune Castle. To well beyond bow-shot or cannon-shot they went, without speech or pause or backwards glance. Then, on the rising ground across the green valley, James pulled up, and turned his head.

"Praise be!" he exclaimed, as he let out his breath. "Praise be that you were wise, madam – for I would not have liked to stain my blade with your blood! More than the drop on its tip!" He swung on Joanna. "My dear, my dear – I am sorry! To have run you into this. It was unforgivable. You might have died in that hold – for my folly!" He reached out his left hand to her. The dirk was still grasped therein.

Askance the Queen eyed its naked gleam, then looked from him to the Duchess. "What . . . did you . . . do?" she faltered.

"I did what I had never thought to do! But what had to be done," he said abruptly. "I mishandled a woman. Broke my knightly vows. God forgive me!" He managed a thin and rueful smile. "God *may* forgive me – who knows? But this woman, I think, never will!"

Isabella maintained her blank, uncompromising silence.

Big-eyed, Joanna considered them both. Then she extended a hand towards the other woman. "Cousin," she said uncertainly, "perhaps you would prefer to ride with me?"

Isabella turned away her head stiffly, coldly.

At the curt gesture, James's brow darkened. "Not so, my heart," he said harshly. "This woman has today slain a dozen of my subjects. Touch her not, for her hands are bloodstained. My lord of Angus – you will take the Duchess of Albany. Hold her secure. I suggest in your strong castle of Tantallon. Treat her fair – but be not over-kind. I shall require her at your hands. Here – see you to her."

As Angus edged his horse closer, Isabella Stewart turned and spat full in the King's face. Without a word, she reached out to the dumbfounded Douglas.

James wiped himself with his sleeve. "You will perceive my difficulty, Joanna . . ."

21

Queen Joanna gazed out from the lofty embattled brow of Stirling Castle into the scarlet and gold of the May sunset, her fair features glowing with the flush of it but her eyes strained, troubled, anxious. Down there amongst the lilac shadows of the great plain, the Carse of Forth, the beams of the sinking sun flashed and gleamed ruddily from a host of lancetips, spearheads, casques and breast-plates. The red of the sunset reflected blood-red more than gold on that approaching army, and Joanna sought to read no omen into it. A battle there had been – but nobody had brought her news of the result. Only that the army was returning, and slowly, painfully. Even a woman could perceive, and at distant range, that it came back in limping and battered style compared to the fine panoply of war in which it had set out three days before. King James had ridden gallantly at its head then; how did he ride now – if he rode at all?

For a man who wrote and sang of peaceful, lovely things, who delighted in beauty and the kindly arts of loving and living, James was a singularly unpeaceful man to be married to. He hated war, and least of all things was ambitious to be a warrior-king – such as he had seen all too much of in his days of captivity; but his nature was such that he must be in the forefront of all that went on, leading, displaying, enspiriting. He would be so in the battle that had been fought, undoubtedly . . .

But surely, had the King fallen, she would have heard? Somebody would have brought her word? Or would they not? He might be sore wounded . . .

She could see now that there were still banners streaming in the evening breeze over the host. Not so many, she thought, nor so regularly placed as when they set out. But still banners. Would they still fly if it had been defeat, disaster? They might. Even beaten men would not trail them in the mire!

It might not be *her* James's host, at all. It could be the other James Stewart, and his uncle the Bishop. The rebels. Triumphant. The victors coming to take Stirling. And . . . and if that were so, then she was no longer Queen of Scotland! For her Jamie would lie dead, at Dumbarton, since with him it would ever be do or die. Murdoch would be King. And the hateful Isabella, Queen . . .!

Then, in some clearer light amongst the shadows down there, probably the reflection of the sunset from water – for the first of the scattered array had now reached the edge of the Raploch, below the westmost castle crags – she saw the great banner of the Lion Rampant of Scotland, an ensign as red-gold as the sunset itself. Her heart lifted almost to choke her. She still could not distinguish the small figures who rode beneath – but surely none but the true James would ride into Stirling under his own flag. It must be he . . .

Waiting for no more, Joanna, panting already as she was, turned and ran, caring nothing that she was a queen. From the parapet, down the winding turnpike stair she ran, out across the inner courtyard, through the inner bailey, kilting her skirts high, across the great outer courtyard, where men-at-arms stared at the sight, and through the outer bailey to the towering gate-house. Past the guards at the drawbridge she ran, and on down the sloping forecourt area which was but part of the naked castle rock itself. Now she had a tail of runners behind her, men and women, young and old, children and barking dogs. When the Queen ran, others might well have occasion to run, also.

At the lower gatehouse, where the perimeter wall met the climbing grey houses of the town, Joanna halted, gasping – but even the pounding in her ears could not deafen her to the shouting in the streets below. Even as she clutched

331

the moulded stonework of the arched pend, beside the embarrassed sentries, the first outriders appeared out of the Broadgait, weary men on drooping horses. And close behind them, a pale Sir David Douglas of Whittinghame, bearing aloft the royal standard, torn almost in two by a lance-thrust. And beneath it, swaying in the great saddle of his steel-girt and caparisoned charger, the King of Scots.

"God be thanked for that sight!" a hoarse and pain-filled voice croaked, behind the Queen.

She did not turn, though she knew that it was the Chancellor, who must have hastened also, though he should not — for Willie Lauder was a sick man these days. All her attention was fixed on James, who in dented and mud-encrusted full armour, minus a helm, leaned slightly to one side as though holding himself carefully. Dried blood caked all the left side of his face. The tattered remains of his heraldic surcoat were also stained brown with blood.

At first, the King did not perceive who stood there within the pendmouth awaiting him — sure sign that he was less than himself. But when he did see her, the lines of weariness and pain in his features lifted abruptly, miraculously, in a fashion to turn over Joanna's heart, and his smile was warm and alive.

Though she ran forward to him, hands raised to prevent him from dismounting, she was too late. Stiffly and awkwardly he heaved himself out of the saddle, to stagger a little and actually steady himself momentarily against the horse's side. But one arm was out to encircle her as she came to him — and he was still smiling.

"Heart of my heart!" he declared thickly. "Here is joy! All joy!"

"Oh, my dear! My Jamie!" she cried. "Mary Mother of God be praised! That you are back." She clung to him, against his hard armour, and smelt the smell of sweat, man's and horse's, and of hot leather, and another smell which might have been blood, and her lips moved urgently against stiff unshaven cheek and gritty mouth. "I was so afraid, afraid . . .! I feared . . . that you . . . would not come."

332

"Foolish one! I told you that I would come again in a day or two, did I not? And here I am, well enough – and the better for your presence, my love."

"But you are hurt? Wounded? In pain? This blood . . .?"

"No, no. The merest graze, sweeting. Nothing." He mustered a mouth-twisted laugh. "Alas, no glory in *this* blood, lass! Shame, rather. I disgraced myself. Not for the first time! I fell off my horse, no less – was dismounted! And was soundly shaken, as I deserved. This foolish blood, from my brow, was my own spilling! Caused by my own helm dunting me as I fell. Such hero am I, James!"

"Your Grace – he does not tell you that he brought down three men in the doing of it! One the Lord James himself!" That was Douglas, with the standard.

"Tush – heed him not, Joanna. This one but seeks royal favours! And see you what he had done to my banner! Besides, the Lord James escaped me. He is still at large. Though wounded. And the Bishop likewise. A curse on it!"

"It was . . . it was a sore fight?"

"It was sufficiently bloody," he conceded briefly. "But the rebellion is crushed." Stiffly he stroked her hair.

"Thank God! But – you should not be standing here. And all these, behind you, waiting. I am sorry. Come . . ."

He started to walk, leading his horse, and when she protested that he must mount, shook his head. Better walking, he said – for he doubted whether he could indeed climb back into his saddle. He was more than a little stiff. Falling from a horse in full armour was apt to have that effect.

So the King signed such of his weary host as was entering the castle to move forward and past him, while he and Joanna walked slowly up the rise. He did not let his esquire take his charger, for he needed its support. The young woman would have taken his other arm, but clearly it pained him.

"I fell on that side," he explained. "Fortunate that it was not my sword arm. My shoulder is put out, I think. I was dragged down. Those Highlanders fought like wildcats. Unmounted, they sprang on us. Out of the very ground.

333

In their scores. We slew hundreds of them, but there were always more. Douglas and Angus were both unhorsed. And wounded. Dirks through the slits of their armour. Many of my people are dead – butchered on the ground. It was savage fighting. No knightly warfare. The like I have never seen. The clansmen care nothing for the rules of chivalry! They make the land fight with them – else, I believe, we should have been lost."

"The Earl of Mar, I think, is little better than a savage himself – for all his smiles!" Joanna said. It was not often that she sounded uncharitable.

"Perhaps. But it could be that you have your husband's life to thank him for, nevertheless! For he was a man where we were babes. And you must not call the Highlanders savages, my dear. Most men do, I grant you. But they are not that. They are different, that is all. They have their own honour. And are they not all my subjects?"

"Yet they would have slain you, their king!"

"They have been misled. Turned against me, by my enemies. I' faith, I will win them to my side, yet!"

"You say that the rebellion is crushed?"

"Aye. Meantime. But at a cost. Before we could reach them they had ravaged the Lennox, sacked and burned Dumbarton, taken the castle and slain Sir John Stewart of Dundonald, the bastard of my father's youth, and thirty-five of his men. The battle thereafter was a grievous slaughter, and we lost as many as they did. But, in the end, the field at least was mine. My cousin James and the Bishop are fled into the remote Highlands, their host broken and dispersed. We have many prisoners. Mar commands at Dumbarton now, unscathed."

"And you trust him?"

"So long as I am like to win, I can trust Mar! And God knows I need him, the best soldier in my realm!" James suddenly became aware of the man who was walking just a pace behind the Queen. "Ha – Willie, old friend! I did not see you. I have a damned stiff neck. It was a victory. Of a sort!"

"Aye, Sire — I have been listening. And giving thanks for your safe return," the Chancellor said. "My sorrow that I was not with you."

"It was no tuilzie for priests, Willie — even such a priest as you! Besides, it was for you to look to the Queen and the bairn. But now, I have another task for my lord Chancellor. I want the Duke Murdoch brought from ward at Caerlaverock. His son, the Lord Walter, from the Bass. The Lord Alexander from St. Andrews. And the Earl of Lennox from Edinburgh. All here to Stirling. To stand their trial."

"Trial . . .? You bring the Albanys to trial, Sire?"

"I do. Fair trial. Which is more than they have meted out to others! Trial before the highest court of all — parliament. I have enough evidence now, I swear, to close this long chapter. Parliament shall decide, once and for all, between the Albanys and the King!"

"I joy to hear it, Your Grace! It is not before time."

Joanna clutched her husband's arm the tighter, but said nothing.

Parliament, recalled, had never known a session like this. The Great Hall of Stirling Castle, the largest in the land, was packed. The King, on his throne, actually wore his crown, and held the sceptre in his hand, a thing unknown hitherto. And the Chancellor, who presided, though only a shadow of the man he had been, was clad in the most gorgeous robes of his bishopric, mitre on head, with the Great and Privy Seals of the kingdom on the table before him. The great officers of the realm, with the Sword of State, the Sceptre, the Ring and other insignia, were all in their places. The Primate sat on a throne almost more magnificent than the monarch's. The most potent authority in Church and State was here exemplified.

The prisoners were seated in a row at one side, directly opposite the King, and in no way detracted from the splendour of the occasion. Far from appearing cowed and apprehensive, all four looked assured, even arrogant, and were dressed in finery excelling any but the clerics'. The Albany family were all tall, handsome and of noble carriage, even Murdoch being a fine figure of a man. He sat stiffly, pensive now, a disapproving frown on his face — though that was habitual.

His eldest son was otherwise. The Lord Walter sat a little apart from the others, for he was being tried separately, his offences being deemed to be distinct. He was a blond giant, in royal blue velvet and cloth-of-gold, on which jewels glittered, his brilliant good looks marred only by a slackness of the mouth and chin. That he found occasion to smile in this business was strange — but smile he did, almost continuously, mockingly. Walter Stewart was like that.

His brother, the Lord Alexander, was different again, taking after his mother, a dark, sullen young man in black and silver, with features only redeemed from heaviness by his youth. He glowered around him now, haughtily. Next to him was a space, for the Lord James, although absent, was on trial also. Rumour had it that he had made good his escape to Ireland.

Lastly, the young men's grandfather, the Earl of Lennox, sat in thin-lipped snarling hate, like an ancient eagle, moulting and stooping but still dangerous. Chief of the senior non-royal Stewart house, he looked well capable of having the Duchess Isabella for daughter.

The Chancellor's voice was cracked and husky now, for the lengthy proceedings had been a great strain upon his ebbing strength. William Lauder was a man sick unto death, most evidently, a circumstance not without piquancy in this present trial.

". . . so stands the indictment, my lords. The Lord Walter Stewart stands before you accused of highest treason in that, as testified by many witnesses, and indeed not denied by himself, he declared that he would rule this realm; in that he took up arms against his sovereign lord the King; in that he insolently did make to treat personally with the Dauphin of France, as in the name of this realm, engaging to gather and send armies to France, against the policies and will not only of the King's Grace but of his own father, then Governor and Regent. All this, my lords, you have heard. And also the said Lord Walter's defence – which indeed it seems to me was no defence but rather an assertion of right to do as he did. This high court of parliament has heard all. It now falls to you, my lords, to pronounce your verdict, solemnly here before your liege lord King James, and before this assembly of the Estates of Scotland. I therefore ask you, seriatim – guilty or no? My lord Earl of Atholl?"

"Guilty, sir," the old man snapped, almost before his name was called, and sniffed loudly thereafter.

"My lord Earl of Cathness?"

"Guilty."

"My lord Earl of Douglas?"

Archibald Douglas, still bandaged from Dumbarton fight, nodded. "Guilty, my lord Chancellor."

"My lord Earl of Angus?"

Young Angus, who had had a Highland dirk thrust through his cheek, and for the present could not speak, raised a hand and gestured downwards, thumb extended.

"My lord Earl of Mar?"

Mar was as great a smiler as his kinsman Walter. Many in that great hall looked askance at him now. He had ridden in from the west only that morning, specially summoned for this occasion, leaving his tidying-up of the rebellion to lieutenants, with a strong force besieging the island of Inchmurrin in Loch Lomond where a sizeable body of the insurgents were still holding out. But despite these undoubted services to the realm's security, men drew back from him. The stories of his methods of dealing with the captive rebels were flooding Stirling, and proving indigestible even for stomachs seasoned to harsh courses. He was not the Wolf of Badenoch's son for nothing. Men dragged limb from limb by deliberately maddened horses was not the worst of his practices, it was asserted.

"Black-guilty, to be sure!" he declared now.

"My lord Earl of March?"

"Guilty."

"Sir William Hay, High Constable of the realm?"

"Guilty, my lord."

"Sir William Keith, the Marischal?"

"Guilty, my lord."

So the grim tally was taken. Although the trial was staged before the entire parliament, the jury itself consisted only of twenty-one of the greatest of the land. Not one hesitated in his verdict, or indicated other than guilty.

"Very well," Bishop Lauder commented. "You have made your decision, my lords – in full knowledge as to the penalty for high treason. Does any noble lord wish to advance good reason why the said penalty should not be imposed? If so, speak now."

Not a sound broke the vibrant silence of the hall.

"So be it. Then it is my painful duty, as Chancellor and Keeper of the Great Seal of this realm, to declare and pronounce your lordships' due sentence. Namely, that the said Walter Stewart of Albany shall be taken from this hall to that place under the castle of Stirling known as the Heading Hill, and there his head struck from his body. Forthwith, this day. And may God have mercy on his soul!"

A long tremulous sigh rose from the assembly, and died away, like a lost wind in a forest.

Walter Stewart's smile froze into a fixed and ghastly grin, as he sat there as though turned to stone, his expression fixed, graven for all time. It seemed that he had never credited that it could ever actually come to this. His handsome face, in those moments, was as of a dead man already.

Duke Murdoch uttered a strangled, choking noise, and extended a trembling hand towards his son, but did not speak.

William Lauder raised his head, to look across the floor to the throne on its raised dais. "This is the sentence of this parliament. I hereby order the officers to carry it out, without delay – unless the King's Grace declares his royal will to be otherwise?"

James Stewart was scarcely any less rigid, motionless, than was Walter. Face stern, as though carved in granite, he sat and stared directly ahead of him, unwinking.

Somewhere, from the crowded benches of the assembly, a single voice, out of almost a sob, quavered, "Mercy, Sire!" Like a stone dropping into a pool it sounded briefly, thinly, and was gone, leaving not so much as an echo in the hush.

Not a nerve of the King's features moved.

"Let justice take its course then," the Chancellor grated. "Officers – remove the prisoner. The trial of the other accused will be continued tomorrow. This session of parliament stands adjourned. God save the King!"

James abruptly stood up, turned on his heel, and stalked to the private door behind the throne, and out, without change of expression.

Walter Stewart died well, recovering something of his careless arrogance and mocking assurance, brushing aside the attentions of priest and confessor, and climbing the mound of the Heading Hill almost with a swagger. After a cool look round the great throng which watched below the castle-rock, but without special glance for the King, he knelt, and still smiling, laid his head on the block, carefully parting the long yellow hair behind his neck, that it did not blunt the sweep of the headman's axe.

Probably none saw the stark, wincing horror on King James's face as the blow fell – for all eyes were either trained on the block or momentarily closed. But swiftly, as the fair head rolled in the sand, and the fountains of vividly red blood spouted from between the jerking shoulders, the royal mask was resumed.

The King returned to the castle alone, his expression amply sufficient to deter anyone from approaching him. He did not go to the royal apartments but climbed in fact to the topmost tower of the keep, there endlessly to pace the narrow parapet-walk, round and round, back and forward, while the dove-grey evening settled on the land and the great barrier of the Highland hills first grew deep in shadow, then turned a solid inky black and finally faded into the background of the night.

But eventually he had to go down, to face Joanna.

She greeted him calmly, made no comment on his long perambulations, only urged that he eat. It was he who presently burst out at her.

"Why do you not say it? Out with it! What your eyes are saying loudly enough. Think you that I do not know your mind? I had to do it. Had to, I tell you! So long as he lived, my crown would have been in danger. And therefore myself. It was his life or mine. Would you have had me spare him, possibly to make you a widow and Margaret an orphan?"

"Have I said so, James?"

"Not with your lips. But in all else. Think you that *I* wished him to die? To have his blood on my hands? Though God knows he, like the rest of his family, has not flinched to take life, for his own profit or whim! But a king may not act just as he would. He must preserve at all costs the power and dignity of the throne, so far as in him lies – for the sake of his realm. I swore, at my coronation, to defend the throne and kingdom against all who would lay hands upon it. To the death, if need be – mine or theirs. To that end, the Sword of State was put into my hands. Today, I have had to use that sword – or the state has used the sword and I have not put out my hand to prevent it. Walter Stewart aimed at the throne – and said so."

"Yes, James."

"Yes James, you say!" Almost he shouted. "I tell you, it had to be! There was no choice. It is the Albanys or myself! This sword has been over-long a-forging. Since the day old Albany starved to death my brother in the castle of Falkland – to gain the throne. He sought my life also – and betrayed me to the English when he could not reach me himself. He did not gain the throne, but he broke my father's heart and gained the rule in Scotland. For all the long years of my captivity. He gained the release of Murdoch – but me he left to rot. But I did not rot! And when he died, Murdoch did not seek my release, but took the rule

340

himself. He did all he could to prevent my return. And now he fosters rebellion, and his sons act as though the throne was theirs of right . . ."

"All this I know, my dear. Do not fret yourself . . ."

"It is myself or the Albanys. How much more blood must be shed in Scotland before this issue is decided? Many men died at Dumbarton fight. Untold more will die, unless I pluck out this evil thorn from the body of my kingdom. Once and for all."

"James! Twice you have said it. That it is yourself or the Albanys!" Joanna was twisting her hands together. "Not just Walter Stewart, but the Albanys! You . . . you do not mean . . .?" Her words faded away.

He took a deep breath, staring at her, but did not answer.

"Oh, no! No! Not that, James – not that!" She ran to him, to clutch his arms. "Not . . . *all* of them!" Her voice sank to little more than a whisper.

"Murdoch is no less guilty than Walter. And a step closer to the throne. They are all in it. Lennox also. Think you that young James made this rebellion, of himself? We well know otherwise."

"Dear God – you must not! You cannot do it. A whole family . . ."

"What point in destroying one viper from a nest, woman?"

"I pray you, beseech you, James my dear – from my heart. Do not this thing. Imprison them. Send them away. Banish them the country . . ."

"And have others rise against me in their cause? Store up civil war for Scotland? No – no more of this, Joanna. If parliament tomorrow declares Murdoch and the rest guilty of treason, then they shall pay the due penalty. I shall not interfere."

Great-eyed she considered him. Wordless she shook her head. James broke away from her, and strode from their chamber.

That night, the King slept alone, for the first time in their married life, when they might have been together.

341

And on the morrow when parliament resumed to hear the evidence of the guilt of the remaining accused, of involvement in the planning of the recent revolt, of designs upon the crown, of usurpation and alienation of royal lands, of the persecution, imprisonment, deprivation and death of loyal subjects – hearing, the jury condemned again unanimously, and sentenced all accused, present and absent, to death, King James remained throughout, and during the customary question to the throne as to mercy thereafter, silent, seemingly impassive, withdrawn. Even with a letter before him from the Duchess Isabella, captive at Tantallon, he showed no hint of relenting or even of emotion. The die was cast.

Emotion James Stewart did display, however, as he watched the dire deed done which no other King of Scots had dared to do. Men saw his face ravaged as one after another the three Stewarts went to the block on the Heading Hill thereafter – Murdoch broken, feckless, stumbling; Alexander tensely white and staring, spasmodically protesting; old Lennox spilling hatred and venom to the last. Emotion of a different sort was displayed, too, before James turned his back on the bloody scene. He drew a paper from his doublet – the letter from Isabella Stewart – and thrust it at his secretary, Cameron, who stood nearby.

"Take this," he said harshly. "In it the Duchess of Albany accuses me of greed. Avarice. Of laying hands on her father, husband and sons only that I may have their great lands of the Lennox, Doune and Falkland. She declares me concerned only for their property. Take this, then, Master Cameron – and take that other property of hers, and return all to her!" He pointed, towards the reeking execution mound. "Those three heads – they are hers. Have them restored to the Duchess, at Tantallon."

"My . . . my lord King . . . !"

"Do as I say. *She* will understand me! For she has been the instigator of much of it, much of this evil. And should know that *I* know it. Besides, she may wish, who knows, to show them her own honour – for the bodies must be buried nameless and in secret, as are all executed for treason. She may have this, at least! See you to it. And the Lord Walter's head, also."

That evening, James Stewart did not pace the castle parapets. He rode out of Stirling town alone, on a fresh horse, westwards into the sunset, towards the wild marshy fastnesses of the Flanders Moss, where the darkling Highland hills marched down in secret phalanx, with word for none. Far behind, and unseen by him, two men rode quietly after – though soon they had to gallop indeed to keep the King in sight – John Lyon, Archdeacon of Teviotdale, and Sir David Douglas of Whittinghame. It was grey dawn before all three came slowly back to Stirling, weary, mud-stained, blessedly empty of feeling.

22

It was good to sit on the warm yellow sand and listen to the long recurrent sigh of the tide, as the curling rollers changed from deepest blue to translucent green and crashed in lace-white foam along the strand; idly to watch the baby Margaret, all plump and laughing mischief, toddle after her father at his pacing to and fro along the water's-edge, distracted every now and again to pick up a shell or piece of seaweed and to tumble as consistently as she toddled; and to eye James himself, strolling with less of that caged-lion stalking, looking more at peace with himself and the world than he had done for long. St. Andrews by the sea was undoubtedly good for them all. Joanna felt the stirrings of happiness for the first time for months.

They had been grim, grey months, for James, and therefore for Joanna – even though most of the rest of Scotland rejoiced at the downfall of the House of Albany and the removal of a menace which had hung over the land for so long. James, although a man of strong temper and deep emotions, was not one who could take ruthless and harsh action and then forget it, however justified the circumstances. Daily, nightly, he lived again through those executions, and went over and over in his mind the pros and cons of his decisions. He was hard on himself, and so on his wife.

But the sea winds of St. Andrews had applied a clean and healing balm, keen as they could be. Back in his boyhood haunts, even occupying the same modest but lofty Sea Tower room where he had heard of his brother's death – to the distress of Henry Wardlaw, who thought it unseemly accommodation for a King – James had in some measure come to terms with himself and his duty. The university, too, occupied his attention and enthusiasm – even though he clashed with his old tutor on this issue also. Indeed, he was curiously at odds with Wardlaw on another and vital matter likewise – but the clash of opinions by no means invalidated their friendship and mutual respect, so that it probably was no unfortunate circumstance, distracting the King's mind from unhealthy broodings. Joanna thanked God for Henry Wardlaw, for with him James could, and had to, argue by the hour, as with no other man. Plenty undoubtedly disagreed with the King, on occasion; none but the Bishop of St. Andrews would now frankly and honestly argue out their disagreements with him.

Only one other had been of the calibre and inclination to do that – Willie Lauder. And he was no more. Lauder had died in June, and now there was neither Chancellor nor Bishop of Glasgow in Scotland. His death was a serious personal blow to James, as well as a notable loss to the kingdom. And it high-lighted a major problem in James's ideas as to rule.

Nevertheless, Joanna knew a resurgence of happiness. Not once had she upbraided or further questioned her husband on the Albany executions – although often indeed he himself combatively brought up the subject. He had not done so now for many days. Moreover he was smiling again, chuckling and playing with little Margaret. She believed that the black days might be over.

James was spinning flat stones out over the water for the child when two men approached them from the castle which soared above the sandy beach, two men vastly different in background, outlook and age, who represented directly opposing traditions. Yet both were clerics, able, intelligent, and the loyallest supporters of the King. Joanna's heart sank just a little as she saw them come – Bishop Henry Wardlaw and Master John Cameron, Official of Lothian and the royal secretary. They walked side by side but a little way apart.

The Bishop stooped to talk to the little girl, who ran to him with a dried starfish. Cameron, after bowing somewhat stiffly to both King and Queen, remained standing silent.

"*You* may have come to gather shells on the seashore, my lord – but I warrant Master Cameron has not!" James greeted them. "How can I serve you?"

Cameron inclined his head towards the Bishop, but the old man seemed hesitant to begin.

"I have no secrets from my secretary," James pointed out.

Wardlaw shrugged. "Very well, Sire. I have just received a letter from His Holiness at Rome. It is as I thought. The Pope does not accept Your Grace's right to appoint an incumbent to the vacant see of Glasgow. He declares it a reserved see, to which he alone may appoint. He cannot therefore ratify your proposed appointment. Indeed he declares quashed the election of the Glasgow Chapter. I am sorry – but I foresaw this."

The King treated the other to a hard stare. "And *I* said that I did not accept that the Pope had any authority to appoint to office in my kingdom. The Chapter at Glasgow has lawfully elected, and I have appointed. Unless the Pope can deny confirmation on the grounds of open scandal or evil living – which in this case is not to be suggested – I cannot see that he may interfere."

"In most cases that is true, Sire. But Glasgow is a reserved see. As is this of St. Andrews. Reserved for Papal appointment."

"Who says so? Save His Holiness of Rome!"

"I fear that *I* do, my lord James. As Primate of the Church in Scotland. It has always been so. From time beyond memory . . ."

"From time beyond memory England has claimed that the see of St. Andrews is a pendicle of Durham, and therefore *you* are subject to the Archbishop of York! I do not think that you accept that!"

"Such has not the Papal authority, Sire."

"If it had, would you accept it, my lord?"

The old man hesitated. "His Holiness would never subject me to so unnatural a decision, Sire."

"Think you not? If it was to his advantage? I fear that I esteem the Holy See less highly than do you, my old friend. I abide by my appointment."

"But . . . but, Your Grace, how is this possible?" the other protested. "So long as the Pope withholds ratification and consecration, Master Cameron is no bishop, and the see empty. No episcopal appointment is valid if His Holiness does not concur."

James paced the sand for a few steps. "Then we must make it our business to see that he does concur, by one means or another. We rely on your great and wide experience, my lord. Eh, Master Cameron?"

The quiet man whose situation was being thus embarrassingly discussed, stood there on the beach expressionless, waiting. With perhaps the nimblest, most agile brain in Scotland, he gave no least impression of agility of mind or body. A still, reserved and withdrawn man he seemed, passive almost. The King had not been long in discovering him for what he was, however – able, tireless, reliable, patient. And humourless.

On Lauder's death, James had taken the extraordinary decision to make Cameron Chancellor in his stead. It had been no light choice, for it must inevitably offend the entire ruling caste of the land. Almost necessarily the Chancellor had to be a cleric, since only such had sufficient education to handle successfully the extensive paper-work of the realm's first minister. But since the higher ranks of the clergy were staffed almost exclusively with the scions of the nobility and gentry, there was no lack of suitably bred candidates for even this lofty office. To deliberately select a man of no breeding, illegitimate and of no great standing in the Church, was as good as a slap in the face for his betters. That it was all part of the King's policy to diminish the power of the nobles and use the regard of the common people to buttress the throne, was not something which could be readily explained to the complainers.

Since the Chancellor presided over parliament and meetings of the Council, it was essential that he should be at least of a rank no lower than those he sat over. A clerical Chancellor therefore had to be one of the lords spiritual – a bishop. William Lauder's own bishopric was the only one vacant. So James had persuaded the Chapter of Glasgow – whose Dean was his old envoy, Thomas Myrton – to elect Cameron. Henry Wardlaw, himself of ancient if not resounding lineage had opposed the entire appointment.

"No doubt, Sire," Cameron returned levelly, when the King brought him into the conversation. "I am a very babe on the ways of Popes. I am sure that my lord Bishop gives you excellent advice. It is not about such that I would trouble Your Grace."

"No?" A little put out by the man's careful neutrality, James frowned. "What is it, then?"

"It is the matter of the English ransom again. A messenger has arrived from the Border – from the Warden of the East March. Sir Robert Umfraville and the Lancaster King-of-Arms have come from England, seeking onward escort to Your Grace's presence. With complaints. The Warden wishes to know whether to send them on to you, Sire? Or to send them packing whence they came?"

"What ails them about the ransom, man? I have paid them all I can."

"They claim, Sire, that only nine thousand and five hundred marks has been paid, out of the thirty thousand still owing at the start of this year . . ."

"Nine thousand! What of the ten thousand paid over at Bruges, in gold, from our trade with the Low Countries? We have the Duke of Bedford's receipt for it – used to pay his forces in Brabant."

"They claim that was only payment of last year's arrears . . ."

"God-a-mercy – the hucksters! Preserve me from such a race of misers!" James glanced over at Joanna, suddenly recollecting that he spoke in the presence of an English wife. "There is no sense in letting these men come here to me, Master Cameron. I can give them no more money meantime. A pox on it – I have scraped the land for what they have already had! They know that. Scotland has but little of money . . ."

"They declare that since Your Grace has now gained the great lands of Doune and in Fife, formerly belonging to the Duke of Albany, they conceive you able to pay."

"I' faith, they say that! How dare they speak me as though I was some merchant they trade with! Here, tell them, we do not judge all by money, gold pieces! Little they know. Crown lands and castles I have won back – but little of money. Tell them so. The saints be praised, they cannot take from me what I have not got!"

The secretary coughed. "Unfortunately, Sire, they hold the hostages. They now say that they will not agree to the agreed exchange until at least most of the money is paid."

James did not require to be reminded of the potency of this threat. Much of his nobility was already restive over the pro-longed detention of members of their families in England. An exchange for a new crop of hostages had been all but negotiated. Any reversal now would cause serious unrest in Scotland. The King pursed his lips and made no comment.

"They also threaten a strengthening of the fortifications of Berwick and Roxburgh Castles, held meantime by them."

"That would be contrary to the terms of the truce."

Cameron shrugged slightly, in an almost French gesture.

"Damn them! What is to be done, then? What do you suggest? My lord Bishop – can Holy Church not find, even yet, some moneys hidden away? To satisfy this English greed for gold?"

Wardlaw spread his frail old hands. "The Church has already all but beggared herself."

"Scarce that, I think! The Church has been most generous, I agree – and I am grateful. Nevertheless, I swear that somewhere you could find a little more, in this pass. Not so far away, perhaps! Your Prior of St. Andrews here drips with jewels! He has more in his priory chest than all the royal Treasury, I swear. The richest in this land. Have a word with Master Prior, my friend."

"I only wield spiritual jurisdiction over the Prior, not temporal. He is an independent prelate. But . . . I will do what I can, Sire."

"And you, Master Cameron? Have you no suggestions?"

"Only this, Your Grace – that the answer to threats may be . . . threats."

"To be sure. If you have wherewith to threaten."

"There is always France, Sire. Scotland's most sure and age-old support when England presses sore."

"France is weak, helpless, rent – a frail support indeed to turn to. The Dauphin is hounded hither and thither." The Dauphin should have been King Charles the Seventh, for his imbecile father had died soon after James's return to Scotland; but in the broken state of his country, he had chosen never to have himself crowned.

"True – but there are stirrings of spirit again, in France." It was strange to hear this man speak so, in his flat, monotonous Lothian voice, a man for whom spirit might seem a wholly alien thing. "This young woman, the Maid of Orleans, is rousing them. There is talk of the Dauphin agreeing to be crowned. I believe there may be changes in France. And the English are not what they were. The Duke of Gloucester and the Cardinal Beaufort quarrel, at home." He bowed briefly to the Queen, at the mention of her uncle's name. "And Bedford is a sick man. Here could be opportunity for some small threat, Sire."

"But we are in no position to send armies to France, man! Nor to provoke English action on the Border. You know our weakness."

"Such was not in my mind. My suggestion is quite otherwise. I would point out that the Dauphin has a young son. And Your Grace a young daughter . . ."

"No!" Clear and vehement that denial rang out, as Joanna started up.

"A mercy, man – the bairn is not yet three years old!" James protested.

"Old enough, Sire, to be your threat! Babes unborn have served a like purpose, before this. Do not mistake me,

350

Madam. I much respect Your Grace's feelings and suggest nothing to upset them. No child-marriage or even betrothal. Only motions, feelers theretowards. I think there would be no lack of interest. In more than France."

"You mean, to threaten England with a royal alliance between the Scottish and French thrones?"

"To be sure. Naught need come of it, Sire. But so long as their young King Henry is claimed to be King of France, the English will seek to stop this at all costs. Word that you even consider such a match might well produce proposals that instead you promise your daughter to the child King Henry. It would not surprise me. Anyway, they would seek to halt the match-making. And there would be a halt to harrying Your Grace for money, while the matter was being thrashed out."

"M'mmm." James looked from the speaker to his wife, thoughtfully. "This deserves some thinking on. And talk with the Queen. What say you, my lord?"

Bishop Wardlaw stroked his chin. "There may be merits in the notion," he admitted guardedly, almost reluctantly.

"So long as it is understood that my daughter suffers nothing by your schemes," Joanna said quietly, firmly. It was seldom indeed that the Queen intervened openly in any discussion of state matters.

"Have no fear, my dear," James said, his hand on Margaret's curly head. "I value our child and her happiness more than any gold pieces. Is there anything more, Master Cameron?"

"Only that the tailor, Peter Brown, and Henry Knox of Knoxland, are both come from Edinburgh, at Your Grace's command."

"Ah, yes. See them well cherished. In especial the tailor. They shall have their set-to before we dine. Perhaps it may whet some appetites! Who knows . . .?"

The central courtyard of St. Andrews Castle, on its projecting cliff-top, made an excellent arena. It was packed that evening, save for the open square in the centre, the paparet-walk of the enclosing curtain-walls was thronged, and every window of the keep, Sea Tower and lesser flanking towers contained its watchers. James, a furred robe thrown loosely about his gleaming oil-smeared body, sat with Joanna, the Bishop and a few intimates on the gatehouse battlements with its own convenient stairway down to the quadrangle. The music of massed harpists rose meltingly into the evening air.

"If you would not be the cause of the sheerest heartbreak, cover yourself something better, my brave champion!" Joanna murmured to her husband. "Although it may not be her heart that is like to break, but something else! You must have mercy on the Lady Catherine. She is all eyes – and other parts. Near swooning for this great, glistening body of yours!"

James grinned, glancing across to where the young Lady Catherine Douglas – the same who had danced so voluptuously with the Highland gipsies at Linlithgow two years before – sat with her kinsman the Earl of Angus. "And you grudge her that small pleasure, my dear?" he asked, making no attempt to draw his robe closer.

"Not so. *My* heart bleeds for her! Indeed, I might almost concede her some small portion of you – since there is becoming enough and to spare, is there not?"

"Vixen!" He glanced down at himself, not without a trace of male complacency. Although he was still panting a little he had excuse, for he had just fought two wrestling bouts, and won both. Admittedly he was thickening just a little round the middle with the years, but there was no hint of fat about him anywhere, and his muscles remained hard and trim. "If we must discuss bellies . . .!"

"Who is to blame for mine, sirrah?" Joanna was pregnant again.

"I confess that there the fault may lie with me! At least, no spies tell me otherwise . . ."

"Hush! The Bishop will be hurt if you do not pay heed to his singers."

The harping had died away, and up on the topmost keep parapet-walk, where they could also be heard by the crowd of townsfolk who waited outside, the singing boys of the Cathedral choir were lifting up their sweet voices in chant and psalmody. The evening's entertainment was catholic in scope.

There was no question, however, as to what the majority there really waited for. It was the next item. The singers, it is to be feared, got but a divided attention.

The two protagonists were presently brought up into the royal presence, before the contest. They made an oddly assorted pair, in appearance as in manner. Henry Knox of Knoxland was elegant — or as elegant as a man can be in full armour — assured and slightly ruffled. Clearly he disapproved of the proceedings. His tailor, Peter Brown, was tubby, clumsy and self-conscious, a man consumed with anxiety and fright. In the presence of the King and Queen he was scarcely sentient. He wore armour of a sort also, but ill-fitting, unmatched pieces which only made him look the more ridiculous.

James sought to put the unhappy burgess more at ease. "This is a notable occasion, friend," he said heartily. "I hope that you are come prepared to give a good account of yourself?"

The other gulped, bobbed and achieved no coherent answer.

"Knoxland, you look very fine. Are you a veteran swordsman?"

"I have fought ere this, Sire. If that is your meaning."

"Aye. It may be that our friend here has not. Mind it, sir. Lest the bout is spoiled for us all by over-deft swordery. You understand?"

"I did not seek this encounter, Sire."

"I know it. But you did provoke it, I think? Now you must give satisfaction — I hope, to us all! As, I am sure, will this good citizen of Edinburgh."

Joanna smiled on them both.

The forthcoming and unequal duel had become the talk of the country. The Laird of Knoxland, dissatisfied with his tailor for some reason, had insulted him in public. Peter Brown had protested – and thereafter been slandered. In wrath he had challenged the laird to a duel – to be roundly scorned and abused by the gentleman, who of course was not prepared to soil his steel on a plebeian tradesman. He had however slapped the tailor's face and refused to pay his bill. Brown had sought the law's satisfaction, but with little avail – until by chance the matter had come to the King's ears. He had reversed the decision of others, that the tailor was an insolent upstart who deserved a flogging for daring to challenge a gentleman, and ordered that the duel should indeed be fought, moreover before himself and the Court. This royal fiat had, of course, caused grave offence. But almost equal desire to see the outcome. The common people, naturally, were delighted.

The contestants clattered down the stairway to the cleared arena, where they donned helmets, one gleaming and proudly plumed, the other over-large, rusty and plain. They took their swords and faced each other.

The King gave the signal to set to. A great cheer went up, largely derisive.

Peter Brown was no fool. He knew well that he was hopelessly outclassed in everything except possibly main strength. His only forlorn hope was to use that strength vigorously before the other's expertise had time to dominate the contest. Consequently, the moment the King's hand fell, he rushed in, smiting, eschewing all the feinting and posturing with which these affairs usually commenced. He wielded his sword windmill-fashion, and did achieve a measure of surprise in the first onslaught, Knox's fine armour ringing to a succession of blows. Almost certainly the laird had never before been attacked thus.

"Your man will not last long on such tactics, I fear," Henry Wardlaw commented. "On my soul, what does he think he's at?"

"Using what the good God gave him, I would say," James answered. "Only a modicum of wits perhaps – but good thews, strong lungs and a stout heart."

"He would have been wiser to stick to his needles and scissors, nevertheless," the Bishop observed. "Instead of vaunting himself to swordery."

James turned his gaze from the spectacle to consider his old friend. "My lord – is it not strange that so much that I know you taught me, yet that we should look differently on so many matters? I see this otherwise. *I* put the sword into this tailor's hand. By my edict, *all* able-bodied men in my realm must bear sword and be prepared to use it in my service. Parliament has enacted it. And if tailors, my lord, are fit to carry swords for their liege lord's defence, then I say they should be fit to use them in their own. Lords and lairds must learn it. Is that not just?"

"Your justice does you credit, my son – but more than that has to be considered. If the lairds must learn your justice, then the tailors must learn how to *use* their swords, as well as carry them! Look yonder."

Peter Brown, after driving the surprised Knox round the arena by the sheer whirling fury of his attack, had now in his rotatory flailing whirled himself right off his own feet, over-balanced by the unaccustomed and unwieldy armour. Great was the shout of mirth from the watchers. His opponent, who could have ended the business there and then by a single deliberate thrust, stood back, to lean on his sword, point to the ground. As the cheers continued, he bowed jerkily all round.

James frowned instead of laughing with the rest. "Aye, you are right, my lord – and the fault is mine," he said. "I shall have to see to it that the lieges are taught. How to use their swords. Having them is not enough. The wapinschaws, where all must show that they *have* the weapons, as enacted, will have to be changed so that all must there prove that they know how to handle them. Masters-at-arms must be appointed, in all sheriffdoms. Our tailor may at least take credit for making this clear!

Ha – look! He is up again, and still smiting. Possibly he has learned something."

Peter Brown had discontinued his windmilling, and had changed over to a mighty two-handed chopping and jabbing, which at least expended more of his energy approximately on the target area and less on the circumambient air. He was still on the attack.

"I said that he had a stout heart," the King went on. "Inside that armour, he must be sweating like a pig!"

"Yet this will serve him no better than the other."

The Bishop was right, of course. It was actually easier for a trained swordsman to elude the aimed blows and stabs than the aimless and unpredictable flailings. Knox parried almost every stroke with ease.

Soon he was playing with his attacker. Everybody knew it, including the latter.

But the tailor was not a man who gave up because he could not win. He laboured on, regardless of complete non-success, of flagging strength, of the derision and catcalls of the hostile crowd.

"That man may have the bearing of a bull, but he has the spirit of a lion!" Joanna declared warmly.

"There are unnumbered thousands like him in this Scotland," James nodded. "The ordinary stalwart folk – who cannot be beaten because they do not know the word for defeat! I need every one of them. Do you see, my lord Bishop? *There* is the spirit which will save Scotland – not all Knoxland's expert swordsmanship and haughty pride."

Certainly Knox's expertise and pride were being demonstrated in vivid fashion. Few could fail to recognise his intention now. He was, in fact, doing what had been his original intention – refusing to fight. He was wholly, scornfully, defensive, fending off the other's wild attacks with almost casual mockery, but refusing to demean himself by responding thereto, withholding his blade from any soiling by plebeian blood.

Brown was visibly failing, each stumbling blow an effort. Time and again he went down on one knee – and on each

356

occasion Knox refused to end matters, but most manifestly not out of any sympathy or generosity, choosing disdainfully to stand back. He was determined to let the other's own indomitable spirit defeat him.

James, well perceiving the inevitable and humiliating end to it all, stood up, and signed to his trumpeter nearby, who blew a single blast.

"It is enough," the King cried. "Have done. Honour is satisfied – for one man, at least! Since only one man has truly fought, I declare that man to be the winner. Peter Brown, of Edinburgh, tailor! Knox of Knoxland will leave this Court until it is my pleasure to recall him." He sat down.

In the hubbub that followed, the exit of the duellists and the arrival of a team of tumblers went all but unnoticed.

Joanna retired early from the dancing that night, pleading her condition. "You will not lack suitable and admiring company," she added, smiling towards the Lady Catherine Douglas.

"How does a man deal with such as Kate?"

"*You* to ask me that? I would have thought that any man would know how, with that one!"

"Aye, she is all woman. All the time she seems to demand a man's manhood. And yet – there is no harm to her, I swear. I would not name her wanton. Not truly. She is honest, at least – uses no wiles. She is just . . . Kate!"

"Just Kate, yes! And the King does not know how to deal with her?"

"That is so," he agreed, mildly.

"I would suggest that you tire her out. If you can! Perhaps you will tell me how you fared, when you come to bed, my lusty champion? Or perhaps you will not!"

When the Queen had gone, it did not take many minutes for the Lady Catherine to make her way to the King's side.

"Her Grace is wearied?" she asked concernedly. "The dance is not for her, in her state. But . . . she has the better part."

"You believe so, Kate? I would not have thought it."

"Ah, yes. Her Grace is the happiest of women. I would rejoice indeed had I your child within me."

Blinking a little at such frankness, James coughed. "You should get yourself married, Kate," he said. "I am surprised that you have not, indeed."

"Are you?" she asked, simply.

"H'rr'mm. It cannot be for lack of suitors. Men flock to you, like bees to a honey-pot. Marriage is an excellent state. I commend it to you."

"No doubt, Sire – to the one of your choice. Less excellent, perhaps, otherwise!"

"Let us dance," he suggested, abruptly.

Kate Douglas came to his arms with alacrity, and though the measure was a somewhat stately one where partners paced and dipped and circled each other at some little distance, she would have none of this and frankly pressed and rubbed her generous person against the King at every opportunity. At first he sought to keep her within a measure of discretion, to maintain at least some little dignity of his own; but quickly he perceived the hopelessness of this and elected to go along with her in spirit, but to inject a deliberately boisterous, almost comic tenor into the business, hoping to rob it of all significance in the eyes of the beholders. Other couples were not long in following the royal lead, and quickly the musicians perceived the mood and skilfully altered their rhythm and tempo to coincide. The dance became a romp.

So nearly all present laughed and cavorted and panted in a sort of abandoned jollity – but it is safe to say that none came near to rivalling Kate Douglas's sheer animal enjoyment of the occasion or lusty contribution and stimulation. James, however much on his guard, could by no means remain unaffected; no man who was indeed a man could have done so in the face of all that vivid, earthy, unabashed provocation. Her magnificent breasts leapt and bounced against him, her belly kneaded his loins, her thighs were hot against his own, her parted

358

lips yearned for his, her eyes devoured him. He could scarcely be other than roused.

Tire her out, Joanna had said. When that dance was over, James immediately ordered another, to the cried protests of many present – but not of Kate Douglas. This measure was as vigorous and prolonged as the last, and most couples had dropped out before the end of it. After that, a third, a Highland jig – and half-way through James and Kate were the only pair on the floor.

The young woman was flushed and breathless, the roots of her yellow hair darkening with sweat. But she showed no signs of exhaustion, and her eyes laughed up into those of the King. Although he was loth indeed to acknowledge it, he was probably breathing more heavily than she was.

It now became a contest, a battle, frank and apparent to all, as to who would last the longer. James was fit, and of great muscular strength, but the duties and cares of state allowed him considerably less time for bodily exercise than had the days of his captivity, and he was undoubtedly thicker, heavier than he had been. Moreover, he was now thirty-four, and a dozen years older than his partner.

The musicians were keeping up their ranting fiddling indefinitely now, and the dancers skipped and whirled, although admittedly their footwork was not what it had been. James was beginning to know some distress – but he had had that evening the notable example of one of his humbler subjects who, taxed to the physical limits, had refused to give in; he, the King, was not going to be outdone by any tailor! This duel might not be very kingly or dignified – but the challenge was there.

He did not know how Kate kept it up. She was no slight slip of a girl, but a big-built young woman with a deal of weight to carry on those twinkling feet. Her bosom alone, tossing and joggling like that, constrained and supported now by nothing of her clothing, must have been a major handicap. But though her face and throat were scarlet, her hands wet in his and her breathing chaotic, she still laughed up at him, kicking and flouncing as vehemently as ever.

With something like dismay the man was having to make acknowledgement to himself that he could not go on much longer, when, looking down into those eager blue eyes, he perceived that, despite the laughter on her lips, they were no longer smiling nor eager. Suddenly he realised that it was desperation he saw in the young woman's glance, a sort of agony that was the more real for being so resolutely unacknowledged. Kate Douglas was in direr straits than he was, but somehow kept going.

In that moment James knew a great pity, admiration and some affection for this strange creature. Somehow he mustered sufficient breath to gasp in her ear.

"You . . . have me . . . beat, Kate! Enough, I . . . pray you!"

He saw the relief flood into her eyes. As he slowed down at last she was clutching at him convulsively, but it was for support now, as she all but collapsed upon him. But he held her up, an arm round her, seeking to distract attention from the great racking sobs which shook her. He cried – though it was more of a croak.

"The Lady Kate . . . outdances me! Outdances . . . all!"

As the courtiers laughed and applauded, the King led the stumbling young woman to one of the Great Hall's stone window-seats. There he sat with her awhile thankful to be still, while an instrumentalist from Castile twanged and plucked staccato music for a dark-eyed, lissome gipsy girl who stamped and undulated and pivoted in provoking fashion without ever moving from the same spot. Catherine Douglas sat wordless, gasping.

At length, however, she stirred, and rose. "Air, for a mercy, Sire!" she exclaimed. "I must have air – else I choke!"

He nodded, and taking her arm, led her out on to the parapet-walk of one of the curtain-walls, where the cool evening breeze off the sea fanned them deliciously.

"You were kind, noble, back there, my lord James," she said presently, huskily, as they slowly paced. "You knew,

360

did you not, that I could go on no longer? And so you cried halt, to save me?"

"I was never more thankful so to do, Kate. You had danced me to that halt."

"Aye – but you could have gone on for a little longer. Whereas I could not. And you knew it. Only James Stewart would have done that. It was so like you."

"Tush, girl – do not make a hero out of me!" he said, almost roughly. "I am little different from other men. I am no monument of nobility, I assure you. If you but knew . . .! Only, I have seen so much of bound and hurt and captive things that I must seek to release them, when I can . . ."

"And you conceive me as bound? Captive?"

He jerked a short laugh. "Such would seem the height of folly, lass – for a more free and untrammelled woman than Kate Douglas would surely be hard to find, in this or any realm! Yet, somewhere, you are bound and tied, I think. You bind and tie yourself, perhaps. Inside of you. And so you more vehemently loose the bonds of your person . . ."

"I am no whore, James Stewart!" she said.

"No. No – I know that. It is a strange thing . . ."

"Nothing strange that *you* should perceive that I am bound and captive," she said levelly. "Since you have done the binding." She sat down on a watchman's bench in an open round of the parapet above the sheer cliff-face, and drew him down beside her. "My heart it is that is bound. Imprisoned here." She took his hand and laid it on her left breast, which still heaved deeply from her exertions. "You must know it."

He did not withdraw his hand. That would have been unkind, cutting. Besides, a more satisfactory place for a man's hand to lie would have been hard to find.

"I know, Kate, that you think well of me," he answered her slowly. "That is good. But as to binding your heart – that I think takes two to do. This heart I feel beats in love, yes – but not only for me. It is a warm and generous heart, Kate, in a warm and generous breast. I swear it will beat for any true and goodly man that you count as noble."

361

She shook her head, clasping his hand and thrusting it deeper. "Little you know me! I said that I was no whore, no strumpet, eager for any man! It is you I need and may not have!"

"And may not have, Kate!" he repeated softly.

"I know it — I know it. I may not have you as your Joanna has you. To my sorrow. But . . . I could be content with less, perhaps?"

He stared out over the grey plain of the sea to where it merged imperceptibly with the night. "I think not, Kate," he said. "You are one who requires all. And if not, nothing. You know it. I would not serve. Nor could I use Joanna so."

She was silent for a little. Then she drew a great breath, and he felt her trembling against him.

"I . . . I could make you want me!" she burst out.

"True. For I want you now!" he agreed. "This body. But is that all *you* would wish? Or require? I have taken women. In France. To . . . to appease the blood. Without a deal of satisfaction. For any of us." He was stroking the proud curves of her bosom with his forefinger. "Is that what you would have of me?"

She did not answer.

"I think not, my dear. So we understand each other, do we not? Our weaknesses and our strengths. And we are the closer therefore. *I* know that you would have my heart. And *you* know that you could have my body. Both know this is not enough. It is our secret. To cherish."

For a moment she laid her sweat-damp head on his shoulder, and the smell of her was strong, essential, potent, so that the man shook a little, and his fingers clutched. Then she rose, lifting out his hand as she did so, but gently.

"So be it. But . . . one day you may require Kate Douglas. In that day I shall be ready. Now, Sire, take me in — and go to your wife . . ."

PART FIVE

23

It was a far cry from Nottingham, where first James Stewart had crossed swords with an emissary of the Lord of the Isles. This was a very different place, a very different emissary – and James himself was no stripling youth but a mature and experienced man of thirty-five. It was even a different Lord of the Isles. Donald was dead, and his son, Alexander, reigning in his stead. Yet, although every circumstance was changed, the basic situation remained practically unaltered. A proud, haughty and independent princeling sent an equally stiff-necked envoy, not to convey duty and service to his monarch, however reluctantly, but to trade terms, treat, declare conditions, like an equal. From a subject to his monarch, it was not to be borne.

And yet, in some part of him, James could not but admire these proud Highland chiefs. Theirs was a pride distinct from that of the arrogant Lowland nobles, a pride of race and tradition rather than of personal power and position. They had an inborn dignity, however trying it could be, seldom found amongst the lords and lairds, despite outlandish costume and peculiar speech. James perhaps had something of a weakness for the Highlanders – indeed, he would not have been here otherwise; but it was not a weakness which must be allowed to weaken or injure his kingdom. The reverse was his objective. These people were his subjects, and had to be taught the fact in no uncertain terms, for their own sakes as well as that of Scotland.

"I fear, sir," he said quietly, "that I cannot accept your Alexander's observations and proposals as seemly from a subject to his king. My summons to the parliament

365

at Inverness *is* a summons, a royal command, which a subject, howsoever distinguished, must heed, and disobey at his peril – not an invitation to a parley! You must so inform my lord Earl of Ross."

The other barely inclined his head. "You refuse to meet Alexander, then?" he asked – and the King was struck anew by the extraordinary soft and melodious speech to issue from the mouths of these formidable characters.

"Not so," he answered. "I will gladly meet your Alexander – who is in cousinship to myself. In Inverness Castle. Prior to the parliament, if he so wishes. But not *instead* of his attending that parliament. Or to discuss conditions for his attendance. Like every other man summoned – yourself included, sir – he must attend on such summons without question."

"I shall convey your words to Alexander of the Isles. For myself, I acknowledge no such necessity."

"Here is plain and declared rebellion, Sire!" the Earl of Mar burst out. "Will you sit and listen to such treasonable talk? *I* deal otherwise with insolent savages."

"My lord of Mar – perhaps that is why we are faced with this trouble in the North! You are my Lieutenant of the North, yes – but while I am here, matters will be contrived my way." He turned back to the Highlander. "I would warn you, Clanranald, to consider well your position. And your words. I do not bear the Sword of State in vain! You *and* your Lord of the Isles will attend my parliament. As will all other chiefs and land-holders that I have summoned. In two days' time. There we shall talk of your complaints and troubles. Also of the complaints against you. With due heed and understanding. *You* understand?"

The big man eyed him levelly, unwinking, wordless. Alexander mac Godfrey mac Ranald mac Ruari of Moidart, Chief of Clanranald, was little less than a giant. Dressed in the fullest panoply of great-kilt, chain-mail, calfskin jerkin and winged helmet, he towered above the shaggy garron on which he had ridden up, seeming to make of it no more than a dog. Behind him his troop of running gillies, in short kilts, bare of leg and naked to the waist, wore each a shoulder-belted broadsword, and carried a naked dirk in each left hand. Before the royal array of mounted and armoured chivalry and fair ladies, they looked to belong to a different world.

James nodded curtly. "You may go," he said.

Clanranald stood his ground. After a moment or two he bowed and swept forward his hand in an onward gesture. "You may pass," he said, with the slightest emphasis on the you.

In almost anybody else it would have been sheerest insolence, but in this enormous and sternly dignified man it was just possible to esteem it otherwise. James drew a deep breath, while Mar rapped out a great oath and many of the other lords growled and exclaimed. Hands dropped to sword-hilts.

The Queen's silvery laughter rang out. "Our friend is gallant!" she cried. "He gives way to the ladies. Thank you, sir!" She waved graciously to Clanranald, and urged forward her horse.

James had no option but to follow – and on second thoughts was grateful to do so. With the royal example, all others must do likewise – and though many were the angry and malevolent glances thrown at the Highlandmen, nothing more dangerous developed as the King's host continued on its way to Inverness.

"As ever, my heart, you chose the better course," James conceded. "There could have been trouble there – notable trouble. When, God knows, we want no trouble!"

"Nevertheless, Sire," Mar intervened from behind them, "trouble you will have if you do not use a strong hand with these cattle. I *know*, who have been handling them all my days. That pirate would have been better on the end of a rope as example, than able to prate how he bested the King of Scots!"

"That pirate, as you name him, is one of the greatest chiefs in all the West! I have much against him, yes – but by rights he should be Lord of the Isles, not the other. Only because

John of the Isles married as his second wife one of my father's sisters, and my grandfather persuaded him to put *her* children before his elder brood by Amy MacRuari, is that man not Lord. But he is still a great chief, second in the Clan Donald Confederation. Had he died there today, representing the other Alexander, scarce a single chief would have come to my parliament. All the Highlands would have been aflame. It would have been war! Clanranald alone can field five thousand broadswords."

"He is an insolent rogue, nevertheless. And treacherous. A murderer. He will now go back to Alexander and declare you weak. All will hear of it. How will that serve your purpose?"

"So long as the chiefs come to my parliament, they will discover whether or no I am weak!" James returned grimly.

They were riding down the long, long slopes of the shelving heather moors into which the great mountains sink and dwindle towards the Great Glen of Scotland, the Braes of Drummossie. It was a fair scene that spread before them. To the right the blue levels of the sea, narrowing into the Moray Firth. In front, the moors giving way to rolling woodland and pasture till, six or seven miles away, the grey roofs of Inverness clustered round its castle. To the left, the long glistening sheet of Loch Ness stretched away south-by-west. And beyond, as behind, the mighty peaks of the endless mountains rose to all infinity.

It had taken the host four days to ride thus far, from Aberdeen, over the Mounth – for this was not an army, riding stripped for war. It was a vast and colourful cavalcade rather, an entire Court on horseback, officers of state, lords and their ladies, the Queen's women, prelates and clerks, musicians, cooks, servants. There were men-at-arms too, of course, by the hundred – but the great mass of troops had been left behind at Aberdeen, to come on two days later, on the King's orders.

James well knew what a risk he was taking, in thus leading a largely unprotected host, not to mention the Queen's household, deep into the wild Highlands – and he had been well enough warned against it, in all conscience. No monarch had ever done the like, or contemplated such a thing. Trouble was indigenous to this mountainous half of Scotland, and danger everywhere. But of late the troubles had been growing worse, in contrast to the rest of the country where James's strong rule was having its effect. Here, in the North and West, feud and bloodshed, pillage and sack, had reached appalling proportions, as the clans battled and harried.

James had decided that something must be done. Mar, as his Lieutenant of the North, had been successful in protecting the settled Lowlands from invasion and attacks, his sheer savage ruthlessness making a sort of devastated cordon around the Highland perimeter. But he had done nothing, attempted nothing, to rectify the internal chaos. His attitude indeed, like that of most Lowlanders, was – let the Highland barbarians bleed themselves to death, that they be the less trouble to better folk.

Not so King James. These were his people, and he accepted his responsibility towards them – even if they did not. Moreover he felt a certain guilt – not in himself but in his blood, his forebears; for undoubtedly much of the anarchy which prevailed north of the Highland Line was the fault of his grandfather Robert the Second. He, who had married his daughter to John of the Isles, had done so of a purpose – to divide and weaken. He had achieved his end, by spliting the mighty Clan Donald in two; but he had also removed the strong and unifying over-all control of the Lords of the Isles. The lordship still existed, but it was not what it had been. The lesser clans no longer feared its controlling hand. Divide and rule might be an excellent precept – but to divide without ruling thereafter was fatal. Anarchy was the inevitable consequence. James was determined to rule – in this portion of his kingdom, as in the rest.

But to rule in these vast and fearsome trackless wastes of mountain and torrent, of sea-loch and the myriad of islands, was not to be achieved by invasion with the largest army or even a large fleet. Every pass could be a death-trap, held by a few men. Every kyle of narrow sound likewise. The country, however beautiful, was a campaigner's nightmare, and the clansmen expert in making it fight for them. So James, ever against the sword as a persuader anyway, had chosen other methods. He proclaimed a parliament at Inverness, against all the counsel of his advisers, and summoned all the Highland chiefs to attend it. In state he progressed thereto, risking armed assault on the way.

That the risk was real was acknowledged by the fact that, before setting out on the expedition he had had all his principal vassals swear fealty and allegiance to Joanna, as distinct from himself. Just in case – since surely no Highlanders would slay the Queen. And they left the Princess Margaret, with the new baby Annabella, secure with Henry Wardlaw in St. Andrews Castle.

They rode into Inverness unchallenged. The streets were full of armed Highlanders – so evidently some of the chiefs had answered the summons. But experts on tartans and identifications declared that none of the really big clans were yet represented.

All the day following men were arriving, from the low country of Buchan and Banff and Moray, from the Black Isle, Cromarty and Easter Ross, from Sutherland and Caithness – Grants, Gordons, Inneses, Frasers, Chisholms, Rosses, Gunns, Munros. Some more of the lesser of the true clans came in also – Macphersons, Macbains, MacEwans, Mactaggarts and the like. But none of the really large names; most notably, none of the great Clan Donald Confederation, the Islesmen.

The Laird of Mackintosh arrived late that second evening, the first of the truly great chiefs – and James had to hold himself back from falling on the man's neck. The parliament was due to start in mid-forenoon the next day.

That night, until late, James Stewart paced the floor, despite all Joanna's entreaties that he came to bed. If the great chiefs ignored his summons and refused to attend, the parliament would be not so much a fiasco as a disaster, a proof to all that in the Highlands the King's word, his very presence, could be counted for nothing. And in that case, it was at least questionable whether any of them would win back to the Lowlands alive.

In the morning, the King scarcely touched his breakfast in his haste to be out pacing the battlements of Inverness Castle. The din from the town below was already alarming, with clan fights the order of the day and whisky flowing like water.

James continued his vigil on those battlements in a fever of impatience, concern, apprehension. Even Mar kept his distance so black was the royal brow.

Parliament was to open at ten o'clock. At nine, Inverness was strung to a tension that was all but unbearable.

Half-an-hour later, James was set-faced, snapping out curt orders as to amended procedure – for this was to have been a ceremonial state occasion, with crown, sceptre and all the regalia on show. It was the sound of music that halted him, the distant skirling of bagpipes thinly and intermittently heard above the nearby din. And that it could be so heard held its own significance. There must be a great many bagpipes. The sound came drifting from the north-west.

As the music grew in pitch and volume, all eyes were turned thitherwards. Even down in the town the noise and shouting lessened, as men heard and pondered.

Then suddenly the high shrilling martial music was louder, clearer, as over the green ridge of Tomnahurich came into sight, on a broad front, the first of the ranked pipers. Behind them, banner tips appeared on the skyline.

There were hundreds of pipers – how many was anybody's guess. And a score at least of banners beyond.

"A great company, a host," the Earl of Douglas said thickly, at James's shoulder. "Think you . . . think you they come peaceably, Sire? With that array? By God – I would that my Douglases were here!"

The King did not answer.

Presently beneath the banners there materialised a number of mounted men. And behind them rank upon rank of footmen. The entire host came on at a steady fast stride which was almost a trot, an extraordinary pace for blowing pipers to maintain.

Soon they could see that one great banner dominated the others, and bore the single uncomplicated design of a black galley, sails furled, on white. It required no interpreting even to the veriest Lowlander present; only one man would thus ride beneath the undifferenced Galley of Clan Donald – Alexander, Lord of the Isles and Earl of Ross.

James emitted a long sigh. "He comes, then! In . . . in his own fashion!"

"Aye – but does he come to your parliament, Sire? Or to show whose will prevails in the North?"

"We shall see."

"These other banners, Your Grace? They must represent many chiefs." The speaker was a stocky, open-faced young-ish man in only approximately clerical garb – George, the youngest of the Lauder brothers, now appointed Bishop of Argyll in place of the unseated rebel, Finlay Stewart. "It is a court he brings with him!"

"Perhaps. But at least they would not ride so if intent on battle, I think. Each would then have his own host. So he comes to talk. We shall see who talks loudest!" Sombrely James eyed the swiftly advancing throng, agleam with arms and ablaze with colour. "They come late to my parliament! The Council-General of this realm does not wait on late-comers. Parliament opens at the hour stated. Come!"

He turned about and strode for the stairway.

Since Bishop William Lauder's death and the Pope's refusal to consecrate John Cameron in his stead, there had been no Chancellor in Scotland, James refusing to appoint anyone else. He therefore presided over the parliaments in person, with Cameron at his elbow. On this occasion, the roll-call taken, he had introduced the first subject for discussion – that of compensation for Church and other lands in the North harried by raiders who could not be identified with any particular clan – and argument was well under way when, without warning, the hall door was thrown wide and a party of perhaps a score of men came stalking in, unannounced. Everywhere those within drew quick breaths, and held them. Everywhere, save on the throne.

The speaker of the moment, the Abbot of Kinloss, faltered and fell silent, as he stared at the newcomers.

These certainly were such as to catch the eye. Indeed never had most of those present seen anything to compare with this, in blazing colour, savage splendour, magnificent manhood and sheer proud flourish.

A pace in front of all the others strode a massive thickset man of apparently James's own age, who was in fact very tall but because of his taut bulk scarcely looked it. Bareheaded and simply dressed in a sort of long saffron tunic girded at the waist by a thick and heavy belt of solid gold, he wore neither weapon nor any mark of rank. Yet none could doubt by his carriage and demeanour, any more than by his foremost position, that this was Alexander himself, Lord of the Isles, Earl of Ross and high chief of Clan Donald. With a leonine head, plentiful hair prematurely grey, and vividly blue eyes, he bore himself like an actor in some high tragedy.

What Alexander lacked in spectacular adornment, armour and weapons, tartan, eagle's feathers and splendour of antique array, his companions more than made up. The dazzle of their strange barbaric jewellery hurt the eye in the streaming forenoon sunlight. No-one, least of all King James, required to be told that here were the great men of Scottish Gaeldom, the powerful chiefs *en masse*, whom he had summoned. Immediately behind Alexander was Clanranald.

"Your point is taken, my lord Abbot," James's voice sounded even, unhurried, only a few seconds after Kinloss had faltered to a halt. "These robbers were, you believe, Mackintoshes. Indeed two captured gave that as their names. Yet the Laird of Mackintosh denies that they were of his people. Declares that they must have been broken men, of various clans and none, and he can bear no responsibility for their actions. Nevertheless your granges of Hempriggs,

Struthers and Milton were sacked and burned, certain servants slain, and much cattle and plenishing carried off. You demand and deserve compensation. How thinks this parliament, then? Can we devise some expedient whereby the chiefs of any area, in company, shall be responsible for the maintenance of my peace within that area, not only on the part of their own clans but on that of all other men soever? Whereby they shall be bound to make good such damage – and in return obtain recompense from the realm's treasury? How say you, my lords?"

Apart from an initial glance towards the new arrivals, the King had not once looked in their direction. He had not altered his tone of voice, nor given the least acknowledgement of any interruption.

All men were not able or prepared to control themselves so. Everywhere eyes were on the chiefly group, attention held by the drama unfolding before them. Alexander and his company had come to a halt in the middle of the hall, and were looking around them at something of a loss – although their fierce dignity remained unimpaired.

George Lauder, the new Bishop of Argyll, came to the King's aid. "It is well thought on, Sire," he said loudly. "The jurisdiction of the chiefs is alike to that of the barons. Greater perhaps in certain powers but less in advantages that he may receive. I would move that they should be made the same, for the better governance of this realm. Moved that parliament votes accordingly."

"Do you move then, my lord Bishop, that all chiefs of clans, and chieftains of septs of clans, be made in effect barons of the kingdom?"

"I do, Your Grace. Provided always that the septs and clans are large enough so to warrant."

The Earl of Mar jumped up. He did not look away from the newcomers – indeed he glared at them. "I question the wisdom of such proposal, Sire," he cried. "The barons of your realm have certain privileges and position. Jealously guarded down the ages. These are not lightly

374

to be thrown away on . . . others. I move against." He sat down, grinning wickedly.

As a growl arose, James raised his hand — and his voice. "I hear two motions. How says the Laird of Mackintosh?"

That elderly chief dragged his gaze away from distinctly doubtful contemplation of the Islesmen, and rose uncertainly. "I . . . I do not know, at all," he declared. "I must think on this. It is a difficult matter. You must give me time, I say. Here are deep matters . . ."

"Very well, sir. Time you shall have. All of you," the King said. "To consider this proposal. We shall return to it at a later sitting of this parliament. Master Cameron — so note." James sat back in his throne, and at last allowed his eyes to rest on the group of Highlanders standing below him. He inclined his head. "This, if I am not mistaken, will be Alexander of the Isles, Earl of Ross? And . . . others. I bid you welcome to this parliament, Cousin — late as you are."

The other was slow to speak, and moments passed before he answered. His voice, when he did, was rich, deep. "I am Alexander, yes. And my life is not ruled by clocks, James Stewart! I came here to speak with you. Not to attend any meeting or assembly. As did these my friends." He turned, hand out towards those behind him, and with grave dignity announced the resounding catalogue of their names. "Alexander of Clanranald. Alexander of Glengarry. John of Isla. MacMath of Lochalsh. MacNeil of Barra. MacAlastair. Maclean of Duart. MacKinnon of Strathard. MacKenneth of Kintail. MacArthur. Angus Dubh Mackay. James Campbell of Lorne . . ."

The King listened attentively, bowing slightly as each name was enunciated. At the end of the recital, he spoke. "I welcome you all, my friends. It is good to see in the flesh such notable, indeed famous, names. We shall talk much, later. Meanwhile, the business of the realm's parliament must proceed. In session, it must be interrupted by none. I ask you to take your seats, my lords." James raised his voice, in a different and commanding tone. "Officers — bar the doors. We shall have no more comings and goings during this session. Or other. See to it. Parliament, the high court of the kingdom, sits. Master Secretary – what is the next business?"

The murmur from all sides was eloquent. In especial it rumbled in the throats of Alexander's chiefly party. They stared from the King to each other, and then, as of one accord, turned to face the door by which they had entered.

Armed guards had already moved in front of it, helmeted and breastplated men-at-arms, halberds in their hands.

For long seconds there was indecision. Some chiefs' hands fell to their sword-hilts. Some moved a pace or two towards the door. Some glances made a swift survey of the hall. There were whispers, grunts, muttered curses. No unified move eventuated.

That was not to be wondered at. The door could and would obviously be held against any undignified assault from within. The chiefs were outnumbered ten-to-one in that chamber and fully another hundred men-at-arms lined the walls. The Islesmen were trapped meantime.

James smiled faintly. "My lords and chiefs, the next measure much concerns yourselves. It refers to the right to levy tolls on shipping in certain narrow waters. Will you take your seats, that we may deal with this more happily? My lord Alexander, I would value your especial guidance and advice on this matter, since it is one in which you are much experienced. Come sit here at my side, where you may have my ear."

Alexander, after his usual due consideration, accepted the inevitable with a fair grace, stalking up to the throne-dais and taking the seat which John Cameron vacated for him. As he came, James murmured quickly in the secretary's ear. The other chiefs found no option but to drift to various vacant seats. Cameron slipped out by a small door behind the dais.

"Now, my lords, this issue of toll dues and exactions is an important matter for our sea-carried trade, all round our coast but in especial in the narrow waters of the West and the Isles where it is much practised. There are some who name it piracy — but I say that it need not always be that. Some dues are justified, where sheltered havens are offered, beacon-fires maintained to guide shipmasters by night, pilots provided for dangerous waters. On the other hand, there are those who but hold shipping to ransom, and seek to slay when they are challenged. I have specific complaint against MacNeil of Barra. By Dumbarton shipmasters. MacNeil is here. How say you MacNeil?"

With much huffing and puffing, the red-haired and bearded Hebridean chief rose to declare that the right to levy toll on passing shipping had been his and his ancestors' from time immemorial, that it was a matter for nobody else but himself and the shippers concerned, and that he certainly was not prepared to give it up at the behest of whomsoever.

James accepted this unparliamentary statement mildly enough, and turned to Alexander. "My lord, tell me. You have a great many galleys, lymphads and the like. Some hundreds, I understand. Do any of your ships have to pay toll when in waters around the Isle of Barra?"

The other raised pained brows. "MacNeil would never think to interfere with *my* galleys!" he said briefly, and without his due deliberation.

"Ah. Then MacNeil does not levy toll on all ships. Only, perhaps, on those insufficiently strong to resist him? It would seem, therefore, that either this means piracy, or else MacNeil is being defrauded of what is his by right by the armed strength of certain others. Notably you, my lord of the Isles."

Hoots of laughter from the Lowlanders and confusion amongst the Highlanders set the hall in an uproar, but James, raising his hand, declared that it was no laughing matter and that men's lives were at stake in this. He asked for reasoned and practical suggestions on the principles to be adopted by parliament.

A debate of sorts took place which, without the King's consistent and patient handling would have degenerated many times into farce, and worse, into free fights. Out of

377

it some pattern gradually emerged, and the clerks began to write.

Presently John Cameron returned, whispered at some length to the King, and remained standing nearby.

At length James declared that they had taken the matter as far as was possible at this stage, and that the clerks would draft a full measure to put before the next parliament. Then, sitting back in his chair, he spoke almost conversationally.

"A matter has been brought to my notice, my friends. It is something of no great consequence, indeed a formality. But I find myself duty bound, by act of previous parliament, to take some formal action upon it, I fear. It is reported to me that certain members of this parliament have brought with them to Inverness large numbers of men. It was most clearly laid down by the first parliament of my reign, the numbers of men any subject might have in his train – twenty for an earl, a dozen for a lord or bishop, eight for a knight or abbot, and so on. The numbers now brought, I am credibly informed, vastly exceed these – run into hundreds indeed. To ignore such breach of parliament's decision would be to undermine and make mock of all parliamentary discussion. I am left with no recourse, therefore, but to make some token enforcement of this law. The act says, my lords, that all who transgress in this matter shall be warded until the royal pleasure is known. In token whereof I must now declare that all those chiefs and others who have brought more than their due number of men to Inverness, are now in my ward and arrest. Throughout the term of this parliament. All are confined to this castle. Is that understood?" The King smiled. "Let it be also understood, however, my friends, that you will all be just as comfortable as if you were free men, all receive my best hospitality. It is a token only . . ."

The rest was drowned in uproar. It was as though pandemonium had hit that hall. Everywhere men were on their feet, shouting, waving their arms, pointing. It was safe to say that there was not a single chief present who had less than a hundred gillies in his tail.

James gave them time for the first fury to wear off. Then he banged on the president's table with the gavel – the first occasion he had had to use it. When that did not serve, he signed to the ever-present trumpeter, who blew a blast or two and soon had approximate silence.

"Here is shame!" James declared. "Be seated. All be seated, I say! This is the solemn parliament of the kingdom. I am the King of Scots. In it, and in my presence, no man stands and shouts. No voice is raised beyond the seemly. Would you trample the realm's dignity? And therefore your own? All shall be done seemly and in order." He paused. "I repeat. This warding is in token. And only for the duration of this parliament. I can do no other, without demeaning the supreme court of my realm. All are warded in this castle. But within it, all are free men. And my friends. Two days, three days, and you go where you will. But – hear this! The King's ward is true ward. Make no mistake. It is not to be mocked. Any man – I say *any* man, be he great or small – who breaks the King's ward, or seeks to do so, will pay the price. Any who seeks to leave this castle and town, lacking my leave, is guilty of treason. And the penalty for treason is death. This, on my word – the King's word. So you have it, my friends – and I do not break my word." In the throbbing hush he rose. "I declare this session adjourned. We shall resume later. Cousin Alexander – you and yours will honour me I hope, by eating at my table. Come."

The trumpets rang out in flourish.

Joanna looked down from her window on the rooftops of the town, which clustered within the bend of the river below the castle walls. It seemed to seethe and quiver, so full was it – full of men and full of tension. How many hundreds, thousands, of Highlanders packed Inverness that night no-one could tell. The King had ordered his own main host, come from Aberdeen, to the far side of the river, to minimise provocation. But this reduced the tension only by the merest fraction.

"This . . . this is as though we crouched below a great cliff," she said, almost panted. "A cliff which could topple, fall at any moment. Upon us. Crush us all. Do you believe, James — do you really believe that you can win? This struggle? Or even . . . survive?"

"I believe I can. And must."

"You hope it. But do you *believe* it?"

"Believe, yes. I shall ride out of Inverness King of all Scotland. Or . . .!"

"Or not at all!"

"Aye. Or not at all."

"Did . . . did you have to do this, James?" she asked presently, uncertainly.

"You must know that I did. The Highlands are half of my kingdom. Could I have long held one half while the other spurned me? I heired a *kingdom*, my dear — sorry state as it was in — not just so much territory to hold or to leave. By the grace of God, these are my subjects. No other man's. I must rule them — or yield to one who can!"

"Has any other Scots king sought to do this?"

"Not for long, no. But never has the kingdom been in such a state as I found it — lacking a king for eighteen years. And the failure of others does not absolve *me*. But . . . we have been over all this before."

She sighed. "Yes. Many times. And no doubt you are right, my dear. But now it is no longer what you will do, or ought to do. Now we are wholly in the hands of others. On what *they* do, all depends. They have overwhelming strength. And you have as good as challenged them to use it."

"It had to come to this, sooner or later, Joanna. My sorrow that you should be endangered by it. And yet, I brought you here, my eyes open. I came seeking a trial of strength, and brought my Queen with me, of set purpose. Did I wrong you?"

"No. Since I *am* the Queen. Not only your wife, but your consort. If the fate of the kingdom is to be decided,

380

my place is here. Do not blame yourself in that, my heart. I but asked, can you win?"

"And I say yes. See you there is overwhelming strength that could be used against me, yes. But perceive also the quandary these proud chiefs are in. These Highland hosts are the most personally led of all men – and all the leaders are held here within these walls. Their thousands down there are leaderless. They cannot know what their chiefs want of them. Moreover, they are all divided by feuds and dissensions. They are used to fighting each other, not a common enemy. Certainly not their king."

"That may be so. But do not tell me that none of these chiefs could win out of this castle, if so they chose!"

"True. But here again they are constrained. Pulled in sundry ways. These men are not united, however much they may seem so. My grandfather ensured that! Not all will be disloyal to me. Some will fear my threats. Some will be moved to acknowledge my authority. All have eaten my salt – which to Highlanders is a great matter. All this gives me encouragement."

"Yet you do not deny that men are strained taut as a harpstring? It but requires one false move and the string will snap."

"Aye – that is why I thank God that I have Mar and his like in this castle, under my eye – as much in ward as any of them. And that it is good and sober Sir Robert Lauder who commands my host out there across the river. He has his orders. He at least will not make that false move."

"Even so, I shall not sleep this night, I think."

"You must. And shall. For it is your beauty and grace, my dear – the Queen's grace – which sustains and solaces me. In this struggle. As in all else. It is vital to me. It must not be impaired, Joanna of my heart . . ."

In the morning, although the tension still was there – indeed with somewhere even a new urgency to it – no climax had yet eventuated. Alexander, breakfasting with the King, was silent – but then he was not a talkative man. James had to make all the conversation.

In the parliament hall thereafter, it did not take the King long to perceive that Clanranald was not present. He waited, during the discussion of close seasons for salmon fishings, for an hour. Then he quietly mentioned the matter to Cameron.

That calmly efficient individual conceded that he had noticed the absence of Clanranald. He pointed out also, however, that so far as he could gauge, five other chiefs were missing from the hall. He could not say who they were, save that one certainly was MacMath of Lochalsh, he of the limp.

James looked grave. "Search the castle, and inform me," he commented, even-voiced.

Presently Cameron was back, to report no sign of any of the six chiefs. But a rope of plaids tied together hung to the ground outside from one of the western flanking towers. According to Highland servants, the missing men were, besides Clanranald, Mackay of Strathnaver, MacKenzie of Kintail, MacArthur of Dunstaffnage, Campbell of Lorne and MacMath of Lochalsh.

The King sat very still for minutes on end. Then, as the Bishop of Moray sat down, he raised a hand, to interrupt the discussion.

"My lords," he said harshly, "I have grievous tidings. I learn that, in despite of my word and warning, six members of this parliament, held within my ward, have broken that ward and removed themselves from this castle. In fullest knowledge of my pledged penalty. These men, according to my information, are Alexander of Clanranald. Angus Dubh Mackay of Strathnaver. Kenneth Mor MacKenzie of Kintail. John MacArthur of Dunstaffnage. James Campbell of Lorne. And MacMath of Lochalsh. All, for whatsoever reason they have done this thing, are guilty of highest treason. Others, without a doubt, must have known of this act against my word and authority. But none informed their liege lord. I am gravely displeased. Has any man aught to say?"

The silence in the hall was absolute, uncanny.

"Very well. The King's word is not to be mocked, or the nation perishes. The penalty for treason is death, as was stated yesterday. Can any here offer good reason why these men, who have deliberately flouted my royal prerogative, should be spared the due penalty? Speak now. I heed the advice of parliament."

There were shufflings, coughings, stirrings, but not a voice was raised.

"So be it. I declare before all that it is the decision of the King in parliament, from which in this realm there can be no deviation or reducement, that the chiefs of Clanranald, Kintail, Strathnaver, Lorne, Dunstaffnage and Lochalsh are guilty. My officers will make all endeavours to bring them back to this castle forthwith, where they shall die, without delay or further trial." He turned. "Master Cameron – with all speed to Sir Robert Lauder, commanding my royal host. These men to be found and brought to me, cost what it may."

As Cameron bowed and withdrew, James resumed his normal tone of voice, though with an effort. "My regrets, my lords, for this interruption. We now proceed on the matter of the salmon. My lord Earl of Caithness, were you about to speak . . .?"

It is to be feared that the salmon got but divided attention thereafter. As did sundry other important measures.

It was evening before messengers came to announce that the fugitive chiefs had been captured, many miles to the north, apparently making for Mackay's country, where he could quickly raise men by the thousand. Sir Robert required instructions. To bring the prisoners and their captured followers through Inverness would probably provoke a riot and attack.

James gave orders that the chiefs' henchmen were to be kept meantime under strong guard in some hidden place well outside the town, but that the six leaders were to be smuggled into Inverness Castle at the quietest hour of the night, with all secrecy. In the morning they would deal with the matter.

In the morning, they did. An announcement was made that parliament would assemble at the usual hour, but in the courtyard of the castle. There the prisoners were brought forth, and the Justiciar of the North read out briefly the charges against them, the decision of the King in parliament, and the sentence. No appeal, plea or mitigation was valid, he declared. But if any of the guilty men wished to speak before the King, they would be heard.

Proud, disdainful, all six chiefs stared ahead of them, silent.

As men waited, into the pulsing quiet a clear voice spoke, a woman's voice, to turn all eyes to a window of the main keep. There stood Queen Joanna.

"Hear *me*, my sovereign lord King!" she called. "I ask you, pray you, to have mercy on these men. They have earned the sentence of death, no doubt. But it becomes a monarch to have mercy. Your Grace's fame will not suffer that in your strength you are clement. Spare their lives, Sire – if only for *my* sake."

James did not even look round. Long, intolerable seconds passed, as hundreds held their breath. Then he spoke, flatly, stiffly.

"No. It cannot be. Here is not my fame at stake, but the entire authority of the realm. To remit sentence now would be to discard all the dignity and authority of rule, governance and parliament. The Sword of State, which I have vowed before God at my coronation to wield in truth, would be but thrown away. Mercy is for those who transgress the law – not for those who deny it. I cannot grant Her Grace's request. Proceed, my lord Justiciar."

Joanna turned and ran from the window.

The Justiciar went on. "The due sentence for treason, for men of gentle blood, is beheading by the axe. We have knowledge howbeit that one of these men has forfeited that right to honourable death. James Campbell of Lorne was adjudged guilty, by the Court of Justiciary many years past, of the foul murder of John, Lord of the Isles, grandsire of the present lord. Also of the condemned Clanranald. He

384

never yielded himself to justice nor was ever captured. Here, hitherto, he has been protected by the privilege of parliament. Now, by his own treason, he has forfeited that privilege also. I therefore condemn James Campbell to the felon's death by hanging. The others will suffer beheading, on yonder block forthwith. God save the King's Grace."

And so it was done, there before them all – or such as had stomach for the business, which perforce had to include King James. All died like the haughty chiefs they were, without protest, display or any hint of emotion. Only young MacMath so much as opened his mouth to declare that he died a faithful son of Holy Church. His father-in-law, MacKenzie of Kintail, smiled thinly as he followed him to the block.

Later, with Campbell of Lorne hanging from a boom that projected from the keep's parapet, the King sought Joanna, with some hesitancy. But she was not reproachful.

"I feared that you must so decide, even before I asked," she told him, sadly. "It was almost bound to be so. But I had to try, James – I had to ask for mercy. Even as, I suppose, you had to refuse me. Do you understand?"

"I do, yes. Would God I could have granted it."

"They died . . . well?"

"Well, yes. With such men, that was assured."

"And you – and the kingdom – are advantaged?"

"I believe so. Already the others look at me with a new respect. Even Alexander. He rejoices to see the punishment of Campbell of Lorne, who murdered his grandfather – which he himself never dared to carry out. Strange that I must slay before men respect my authority. I believe that we shall have no more trouble. That having accepted so much, they will not rise against me now. The parliament will finish tomorrow, when I will free them all. They will have learned that I keep my word. In all things. And learned whose voice does speak loudest, even in their Highlands!"

"At a price!" she reminded.

"At a price, yes."

"And Alexander?"

"Alexander goes free also. But I hope to persuade him to come south with us. For a time. In my court. Make much of him there. He is my full cousin's son."

"You would tame the Lord of the Isles, James?"

"If that is the word. Teach him, at least, that he is better off as my friend than my foe."

"You will never change that man. Or break his pride."

"You think not? These Highlanders are a strange folk. It is all or nothing with them. They do not bend. They either resist – or break entirely. I have hopes of Alexander, son of Donald, son of John . . .!"

24

Nine months later it certainly seemed as though Joanna had been right, and James's hopes for Alexander of the Isles lay in fragments. The King was, in fact, heading for the Highland North again, the North-West this time, and not on any friendly visit. This time he did not progress in state, with courtiers and ladies; he rode hard and fast, at the head of a tight column of armed men, mainly Douglases – tight, bristling with arms, warlike, but pathetically small in numbers for the task in hand. However, he had sent orders for the Earl of Mar to join him with all the strength he could muster from the North-East, at Strathfillan, by the route through the central mass of the Highlands, by Tay and Dochart. Moreover, his messengers had gone ahead to raise Clan Cameron of Lochaber to his banner, whose chief had sworn his fealty at Inverness. Pray God his oath had meant something!

The situation was dire, sheerest folly and disappointment. Alexander had indeed been persuaded to come south with the King and Queen, from Inverness. He had been made much of at Court, loaded with honours. Then some drunken fool of a Lowland laird had undone all in a few grim seconds, had called the Lord of the Isles a Hieland stot, a barbarian with heather between his toes, a bog-trotting savage unfit for the company of decent men – this before a great company, though not in the King's presence. Alexander, unarmed, had snatched the laird's own sword and run him through the heart there and then – and thereupon stormed out of Stirling, on the road to the North-West without word to any. And now all the North was afire.

James, sick with fury and frustration when he heard, was forced to drastic action. All over the mouthings of a fool. Although it was possible that there was more than that to it. Rumour declared that the King's enemies, notably Sir Robert Graham, late Tutor of Strathearn, were behind this, in a campaign of hate. It was not impossible, for the offending laird, though not a Graham, had come from Menteith. But whatever the cause, the results were appalling. Alexander had hastily mobilised the whole resources of the Isles and his earldom of Ross, and at the head of an army estimated at between ten and twenty thousand, had marched south. The royal burgh of Inverness was now only a heap of smouldering ruins – although the castle still held out. From Inverness the Islesmen had turned south-west down the Great Glen of Scotland, burning and slaying through the settled lands, searing a wide blackened swathe through the country, with the declared intention of not pausing till Stirling town itself, and in the process killing or driving out every King's man in the Highlands.

There was no great deal to stop him.

James's hard-riding company thundered up Loch Lomondside. At its head, at Crianlarich, they found Mar's advance-party awaiting them, with word that the Earl and eight hundred men were on their way, with more to follow in a couple of days. Scarcely cheered by this news, the King led his inadequate force onwards, northwards, by the vast emptiness of the Moor of Rannoch and the savage grandeur of Glen Coe, to the sea. At Kinlochleven, Mar caught up with them.

Even in his present state of mind, James could not but be much affected thereafter by this his first sight of the Sea of the Hebrides. He had heard of its fairness, its mountain-girt vistas, the myriad of islands. But nothing had prepared him for the colour, the translucence of light, the haunting beauty of it all. Gazing out at the glowing skerry-strewn, isle-dotted sublimity, he all but forgot the bloodshed and the animus which brought him to it, in wonder.

But not for long. Tidings reached him that Alexander was, in fact, camped with all his host in the low ground at the foot of Loch Lochy, a bare dozen miles to the north. The man who brought the news was a Cameron, whose country this was. He also informed that his chief, Donald Dhu Cameron of Strone, with his whole strength, was with Alexander. He had raised his clan, according to the royal command, but to have faced the Islesmen alone would have meant annihilation. He had joined them meantime, therefore, but was ready to change sides at the right moment.

On hearing this, Mar flew into a fury of rage and suspicion. It was just as he had always declared, he said — these people were not to be trusted further than a rope would swing them. It was just a trap, the device of treacherous rogues and cowards. The Camerons would wait to see which side looked like winning before committing themselves.

James demurred. Donald Dhu had pledged his word at Inverness. To a Highland chief that meant much. In the circumstances, his strategy was sound. It would have served no advantage for the Camerons to be cut to pieces before the royal force arrived — and if Alexander came on them assembled, they must either join him or fight him. He must trust Donald Dhu, he thought.

The courier, looking daggers at Mar, added a further detail. Alexander had summoned the Clan Chattan to his colours, from Badenoch. They were on their way down the Great Glen now, under their Captain, the Laird of Mackintosh. That was why Alexander was waiting, camped in the Haughs of Lochy. But the Clans Chattan and Cameron were linked — and Mackintosh did not love Alexander of the Isles. He was prepared to change sides likewise, given the signal.

"So! The Laird of Mackintosh also. How many men has he? And your chief?"

"Donald Dhu has two thousand here. Mackintosh three."

"Five thousand in all. To add to my thousand of chivalry. And Alexander? How large is his host?"

"Fifteen thousand."

"Six against fifteen! But with surprise to aid us, armour and horse. It may serve. How think you, my lord of Mar?"

The Earl snorted. "I think that if Your Grace relies on these cattle, none of us will see another morning's light! I say that you can forget your five thousand, Sire. Reckon but on your chivalry, and the surprise. As did I at Harlaw!"

"I reckon rather on my judgement of men, my lord. We shall see who is right."

Although James Stewart spurned Mar's advice on strategy, he was not so foolish as to do so on tactics. Mar was undoubtedly the ablest tactician in the land. Given the situation which the King envisaged, he was not slow to size it up to best advantage. Divesting himself of all responsibility for the results, he prepared a plan of action which could hold the seeds of success.

James asked no more of him.

Using the Cameron as a guide, they left the coastal levels and climbed sharply up into the steep but low hills which flanked them on the east. Behind the first ridge, they turned north again, and made their laborious way along the high ground, by peat-hag and corrie, cliff and shoulder. Mile after weary upheaved mile they went, leading, almost dragging their horses most of the time, sweating in their armour and mail, until they came to the deep dark glen of Nevis. Here, safely hidden, they waited, resting, confronted by the mighty bulk of the mountain ahead, while the Cameron and one or two agile young men went on, on foot, to try to discover the progress of the advancing Clan Chattan.

They came back, having climbed most of the way up the ben, to inform that a large company, almost certainly Mackintosh's people, were in sight from up there, coming down Loch Lochy side. Alexander's host was still camped where it had been, in the level haugh half-way between Lochs Lochy and Linnhe. A question from Mar elicited that the oncoming Clan Chattan would still be more than four miles from the Islesmen.

There was no time to lose if they were to attempt their plan. The entire column of some thirteen hundred men set off down the trough of Glen Nevis.

Their plan involved keeping themselves completely hidden until the last moment, and this demanded much trying doubling and traversing of the lower western flanks of Ben Nevis. But eventually James had his woefully scanty host approximately where he wanted it, and, he believed, unobserved. They were ranged behind the last green ridge, called Torr Sonnachain, east of the Haughs of Lochy, and the noise of Alexander's great army came up to them on the evening air from little more than half-a-mile away.

With Mar and some of the leaders, the King moved up to the crest of the ridge, on foot, to peer over. All the wide haughland below seemed to stir and seethe with activity, to overflow with it. But it was not the urgent activity of a host preparing for battle; it was the easy and domestic bustle of vast numbers of men preparing their evening meal, with cooking-fires by the hundred sending up their blue columns into the still air. There appeared to be fully as many cattle as men spread over that green plain – the booty of innumerable ravished straths and glens. Here was an army, however potent and fierce, glutted with easy conquest, made careless by lack of opposition, overconfident in the sheer superiority of its own numbers, power and fame.

"There it is, my friends," James said. "Better by far than it might have been. With God's help, our own resolve, and the good faith of the Camerons and Mackintoshes, we put all to the test."

"But be ready to forget your resolve, and ride for your lives, if God or the Hielantmen fail us!" Mar added, with his sour laughter.

Back behind the ridge, James marshalled his force. Two companies of one-hundred-and-fifty each he detached, one for the left flank and one for the right. He put the Earl of Angus in charge of that to the left, with the Cameron envoy. The right-hand group were commanded by Sir David Douglas of Whittinghame. With him lay the greatest responsibility of the day. It should have been Mar's task – but James would not trust that man with the necessary tactful liaison with the Clan Chattan.

These two contingents rode off north and south, their instructions definite and clear. Then, stringing out his remaining thousand horsemen in an extended line, only two deep, James moved the entire half-mile-long front forward and up until it was halted just below the grassy crest of the ridge, to wait.

While they waited, the King sent orders up and down the line that every man who could find something of cloth about him – cloak, shirt or saddle-blanket – was to tie it to the head of his lance, to look from the distance like a banner. Every true banner and pennon was hoisted around the great Royal Standard, in the centre.

It seemed a long wait, with the sunset beginning to stain the western sky and great purple shadows to well out from every hollow and fold of the mountains. But at last David Douglas's signal showed, a single black smoke column rising from a small hill-top a mile to the north, burning heather which was to touch off a greater conflagration. Clan Chattan was there, and at least nominally prepared to co-operate in the King's plan.

James raised his hand. "My lords," he cried, "now for either the most easy or the most sore battle of your lives! No single move other than to my order." And he signed to his trumpeters.

High and clear the bugling challenge pealed out, to echo and re-echo from a thousand mountainsides. And slowly, deliberately, the long, long double line of horsemen moved forward to top the summit of the ridge – and there to halt, five hundred banners seeming to fly in support of the great Rampant Lion of Scotland.

The effect on the armed camp below was instantaneous and notable. At first, all save cattle seemed galvanised into immobility. Then, as realisation flooded in, the entire haugh began to swarm like an ant-hill disturbed, and everywhere the deep baying of chiefs' warhorns sounded their urgent summons.

Other sounds now added to the din. From the north came a long sustained roaring as, headed by the seven-score Douglas horse, the Clan Chattan, the Tribe of the Cat – Mackintoshes, Macphersons, Shaws, Farquharsons, Cattanachs and the like – surged round the last flank of hill at the loch-foot, pipes skirling, broadswords flashing. No doubt the Islesmen knew that they were approaching – but as summoned allies not as attackers at a desperate moment.

At the other side of the haugh, Angus's men, led by the Cameron, burst out from the screen of alder and birch scrub where they had been hiding, and galloped towards the camp, yelling. The Cameron slogan was somewhat involved – *Chlanna nan con thigibh a so's gheibh sibh feoil!* meaning "Sons of the hounds, here and eat flesh!" This naturally was quite beyond the Border horsemen. But they could all shout "A Cameron! A Cameron!" at the pitch of their lungs, which was sufficiently clear.

Within the camp, at this sign, Donald Dhu's clansmen raised their true slogan in savage chant. They did not actually attack the Islesmen around them, but surged in a body towards the Cameron-shouting Douglases – a sufficiently disconcerting move.

Up on the ridge of Torr Sonnachain the long beflagged line of chivalry, armour and weapons gleaming blood-red in the level rays of the setting sun, stood silent, motionless, menacing.

Confusion reigned amongst the Islesmen. In the circum-stances, only magnificent generalship and strict discipline could have saved the situation. Alexander's host had neither the one nor the other. In a sea-fight, with galleys, nothing could have outfought them. In an onset, they would have been irresistible. But scattered, taken unawares around their camp-fires, uncertain where the main attack came, unsure who was friend and who foe – and above all, presuming, as they were meant to do, that the great half-mile line of waiting horsemen poised above them was but the bannered front of a much mightier royal army – they fell a prey to chaos and panic. Clanranald might have preserved the situation – for he had been a steely, cool-headed leader; but Clanranald was dead, and Alexander had none other like him.

James signed to the trumpeters again, and once more the stirring, martial blaring rang out, this time prolonged in vehement command, on and on.

It was the last straw for the Islesmen. From confusion and runnings to and fro they progressed to outright flight, in the only way left open to them, westwards, leaving all their gear behind. Smitten by the panic, the captured cattle stampeded with them, much adding to the chaos. As yet not a blow had been struck.

"Now!" Mar exclaimed. "Before they can rally. Smite them! Ride them down!"

"Aye – but not all of us. Lest they see how pitifully few we are," James ordered. "Take your half, my lord. One rank only. Leaving most of the banners. And, Mar – be careful that you smite the right Highlandmen!"

So the rout became a pursuit, where running men scattered far and wide. There was, however, comparatively little slaying – for in their own bogs and heather Highland gillies are not easy to ride down.

Presently, with the light swiftly fading and the wide valley filling with lilac gloom, James turned to his fretting companions.

"I thank you, my friends," he said. "The day is won, I think. By your patient standing here. And faith. In God – and in the words of sundry Highlandmen! Let us go down . . ."

There was no rally of the Islesmen. Not that night, at anyrate. And by morning Lochaber held neither hint nor hair of them. Alexander may not have been roundly defeated, but he had been most resoundingly outmanoeuvred and brought low. Worst of all, for so proud a chief, he had been utterly humiliated. He would not quickly live down that evening's debacle.

After a couple of days, leaving Caithness, Atholl's son in command at Lochaber, and ordering all and sundry to capture Alexander and bring him to justice, James returned to the south, well satisfied.

It was Palm Sunday of 1429, so that James had been five years returned to his kingdom, five energetic, eventful and fruitful years. This Easter-tide therefore was to be a special period of celebration, not only for those years, for peace at home and abroad, but for the successful outcome of his battle with the Holy See; for the Pope had at last relented, being for the moment short of allies, and James had his way, so that Scotland had a Chancellor again – John Cameron, Bishop of Glasgow.

All the pride and circumstance of the realm was assembled in the church of Holyrood Abbey, at Edinburgh, that Sunday, in consequence. James and his Queen occupied golden thrones up before the high altar, with their two daughters nearby, the service being conducted by the Primate, Henry Wardlaw, very frail now, assisted by the Chancellor and the Abbot of Holyrood.

It was upon this solemnly splendid scene, with the choir chanting sweet harmony, that an unseemly disturbance drew all eyes towards the church door – which was abruptly burst open and a gigantic and extraordinary figure staggered in, the guards there hurled aside before a great windmilling sword. Everywhere men gasped and women screamed.

The intruder presented an awesome sight, almost as comic as fearsome. Long hair wild, beard unkempt, the man, bare-legged and bare-footed, was clad in nothing but a shirt, and carried only the huge two-handed sword. The fact that the features were noble, dignified, though contorted now with a extremity of emotion, but added to the absurdity of the spectacle. The man was Alexander MacDonald, Lord of the Isles and Earl of Ross.

Up the central aisle this apparition ran, stumbling. Behind trailed hesitant guards, at a loss as to how to cope with the

King's cousin running amok, and preoccupied with the crazy flailings of that mighty sword.

James, frowning, drew a hand over his mouth. Joanna rose from her seat and stepped swiftly to her husband's side, to grasp his hand. Then, remembering the young princesses, beckoned them behind her.

All over the church men started forward to the King's aid – but none was armed with anything more potent than a jewelled dirk, for swords were not worn at divine service. The choir faltered into a silence hardly noticeable in all the shouting. Bishop Wardlaw raised trembling forbidding hands at the high altar, and Chancellor Cameron came pacing down with a crucifix held high, in protest.

But the Lord of the Isles ignored and avoided all. Lurching, he reached the chancel, and tripping up its steps plunged onwards, thrusting Cameron aside with a sweep of a bare arm.

James was on his feet now, pushing Joanna out of harm's way. The two little girls stared wide-eyed.

Alexander, despite his apparent crazed state, performed a complicated manoeuvre. Pulling himself up before the King, he tossed his sword in the air, to catch it expertly by the point – a feat in itself, for the great two-handed brand must have been enormously heavy. Then he flung himself down on his knees, and leaning forward, one hand on the floor, held out the weapon in the other, hilt-first to James.

"Mercy, my lord King!" he panted. "Mercy! I, Alexander, submit myself to Your Grace. I confess my fault and crave your royal mercy. Hear me, Sire, and be clement."

A sigh of relief arose from the congregation.

James did not echo that relief. He stared down in perplexity at the long-legged, beshirted suppliant, scarcely able to believe what he saw and heard. He looked at Joanna, and then back to Alexander.

"Up, man!" he jerked, distastefully. "Grovel not so."

But the other was not to be put off in his self-abasement. "Your Grace," he cried, "Hear me and forgive. Of your excellence, have compassion. Into your hands I place my

396

person and all my lordship, all the Highland West and the Isles of the Sea. In token, take this my sword. To use as you will!"

James did not fail to perceive the method behind this madness. These Highlanders, whatever else they were, were actors all. This prostration, however headlong, was that rather than wholehearted – of the head not of the heart. Here was a beaten rebel, a hunted fugitive, seeking to salvage from the wreck what he might. By the offer of his sword, as by abject confession of error, he was subtly changing his status from that of rightless outlaw to honourably defeated opponent. Moreover, by the very extravagance of his surrender, he was making it very difficult for the monarch to repulse him – especially here before God's altar and in the sight of so great a company. Here was another aspect of Highland character for him to take into account.

He schooled his voice to its sternest. "Alexander of the Isles," he commanded, "rise to your feet. You are a condemned traitor, twice pardoned, a man of blood and slayer of the innocent. Your tarnished sword I will not so much as touch! The sword that made a reeking ruin of my royal burgh of Inverness! Officer – take it from him, and destroy it. Up, Islesman – on your feet, I say. I mislike a cur that cringes!"

Alexander, presenting the sword to the uncomfortable officer of the guard with a flourish, rose to play another part – that of the noble savage. Dignified now, sorrowful, he bowed his head. "Our rude island ways do not school us in the ways of courts, Sire. My offence, no doubt, is great – but none the greater, I say, that I am not bred as you are. I place myself in your royal hands." For a man of few words, he was using them to good effect.

"*You* do not place, man! I *take*!" James declared harshly. "We are not treating, you and I! By the law of this realm you are a felon thrice over. You have well earned a felon's death. No talk or mummery will make it otherwise."

The other spread his open hands. "I did not come to Your Grace for justice – but for mercy," he said simply.

James drew a great breath, and looked at Joanna again, something like appeal in his eyes.

Almost imperceptibly she nodded. "Again, my lord King – I crave your indulgence," she said. "The Lord Alexander admits his grievous fault. He yields himself to the law. He does not deny the law, as did those others. He craves your mercy, who administers that law. I add my cry to his, Sire. Ward him as you will – but grant him his life. Here, in God's house. On this holy day."

James inclined his head. "As Your Grace desires. It shall be so. The sentence of death passed by parliament on the traitor Alexander MacDonald I hereby remit. His lordship of the Isles is forfeit, his earldom of Ross confiscate to the Crown. My lord of Angus – you will take him into your custody. Secure him surely in your castle of Tantallon. This realm will require him at your hands. My lord Bishop – pray proceed."

As Angus came forward to take his charge, Alexander's eyes met those of James for a long and eloquent moment. A world of meaning, recognition, even understanding, passed between them in that glance. After all, they were cousins.

As the richly formal service continued, no doubt James Stewart's was not the only attention that wandered. Yet there was thanksgiving deep within him, for all that. Whatever the way of it, the Highland half of his kingdom was his now, as he had made the Lowland half. At last. Five years. It now remained to deal with England . . .

He turned to consider his lovely English wife. She smiled to him, gently, warmly, and touched his hand. He had been right when he told her that he could tame the Lord of the Isles. After a fashion . . .

25

Henry Beaufort had changed but little. A Cardinal now, and still Chancellor of England, he was if anything more pompous, more insincere – but still the shrewd, crafty and unscrupulous bargainer, the merchant of statecraft. Beside him, Henry Percy, Earl of Northumberland, seemed but a bladder of lard, pompous too but ineffective, and the Lord Scrope, English Warden of the Middle March, but a wooden soldier.

The Cardinal was put out, indignant, that he had had to come all this way, to this barbarous place of Coldingham – but he did not show it. He had proposed the meeting for Durham – which was surely far enough north from London for any reasonable man, more than half-way to Scotland. But King James, in his arrogance, had refused to set so much as a foot in England. Worse, he had even rejected a meeting on the Border itself, on the claim that this was unsuitable save between monarchs. So there had been nothing for it but to travel the dozen miles farther north of Tweed into Berwickshire, to this Priory of Coldingham, named by the King of Scots, distressful as it was.

That the Cardinal had forced himself so to agree was not without its significance for James Stewart. There had been many proposals of meetings, from English sources, prior to this, and none had come to anything because of James's insistence on the venue being in Scotland; presumably England now wanted something from him very much indeed.

James was, for him, very silent – the effect on him of

Beaufort's smooth wordiness. It was Joanna who contributed most of the replies to her uncle's verbosity.

Undoubtedly the Cardinal had been surprised to find his niece awaiting him at Coldingham – and more than that, displeased to have her present at their discussions in the Prior's study, where women were quite out-of-place. But James had brought his wife for good reason – as was frequently the case.

"My brother Somerset is now done with the French wars?" she asked. "Home, at court? With his wife?"

"Yes, yes," her uncle answered testily. "One folly forsaken for another! He is an ill-advised young man. Too proud-blown by far. On my soul, I think I liked him better in France!"

"Which is no place for headstrong young English lords today, I hear, my lord Cardinal!" James put in drily.

"M'mmm. The campaign, Your Highness, is at a stage of . . . attrition. We shall soon have the French on the run once more, however."

"To be sure. But running which way, my friend? This Maid of Orleans would seem to have changed the direction of the French running most notably!"

"Faugh! Superstition! Idle talk! She has spurred Charles de Valois on to further resistance – that is all. It will take more than witchcraft and a peasant wench to make a man out of Charles."

"Perhaps. But if she unites the French people, that may serve to make up for the feebleness of the King of France."

"The King of France, I would remind Your Highness, is Henry Plantagenet, sixth of his name!" Beaufort said stiffly.

"Ah, yes. To be sure. All save the French know that!"

Joanna intervened. "So you call it witchcraft, Uncle Henry? This Maid's belief in her divine mission?"

"What else? The ignorant dreamings of a country trollop! None with any wits or judgement would call it other."

400

"That is so," Northumberland agreed heavily. "A sorceress and deceiver."

"Yet, if I mistake not, she it is who has brought you all to Coldingham this day, my lords!" James commented.

There was an outraged huffing and puffing, but nobody was in a position flatly to contradict the King of Scots.

"Our visit is for the mutual benefit of our realms," the Cardinal declared hurriedly. "To bring Your Highness the love and regard of our liege lord King Henry, and to convey His Majesty's congratulations on the gift of a son and heir."

"For which we are gratified, and greatly thank you, and our Cousin of England." Three months earlier Joanna had given birth to twin sons, Alexander and James. The former was a sickly child, and soon died, but James throve. The King nodded. "But I think so resounding an embassage did not come all the way to Coldingham merely to convey greetings? Is not the fact that Scotland is in ancient alliance with the Kingdom of France something to the point?"

The Cardinal looked at his plump finger-tips. "Perhaps so. We would consult Your Highness on a most privy matter." He glanced at his niece. "Namely, the marriage of our sovereign lord King Henry."

"Ha!" said James.

"His Majesty is now almost ten years of age. It is time that this important matter was considered. The Privy Council – and of course Queen Catherine – feels that the elder Princess of Scotland might make a suitable consort for our young monarch. In view of her mother's nearness to our royal house. And . . . and other circumstances."

"Aye. So there we have it! You come seeking a Scots princess."

"We come to consider the matter. And the elder princess, of course."

James looked from the three Englishmen to his wife, and back. "My lords – I have always believed that you in England were notably well informed. You must know therefore that the Princess Margaret, our elder daughter,

401

is promised already to the Dauphin of France, Charles's son."

Scrope spoke. "That we would wish undone," he said bluntly.

Beaufort cleared his throat, and frowned. "A matter for . . . adjustment, perhaps," he suggested.

"I do not see how that is possible. Margaret has been promised to the Dauphin for almost three years now."

"Promised – but not fully betrothed, I think, Highness?"

"My daughter is but six years of age," Joanna put in quietly.

"To be sure. That is my point," the Cardinal agreed quickly. "The princess is still too young for a full betrothal. Therefore matters may still be amended, bettered."

"Bettered for whom, my lords?"

"For all. For both realms. For the child herself. Better surely that she should be wed to the King of England and France than to a beggar-prince lacking a throne!"

"Beggar princes sometimes regain their thrones!" James said evenly. "*I* did, you may recollect. And France seems more like to throw off your English invasion than ever before."

"Not so," Henry Percy put in. "This is but a pause. A lull, see you. Before we drive them, once and for all, into the Middle Sea."

"Well said," Scrope commended.

"And you would seek to bring this about by breaking the Auld Alliance between Scots and French? By this projected marriage weakening France and tying my hands? My lords, do you take me for a fool?"

"Never think it, my lord James!" Beaufort exclaimed. "Rather we think you to be wise. Wise enough to perceive where lies your true advantage."

"How shall I, or Scotland, be advantaged by being tied to England?"

"England has much to offer."

"I have tasted of England's offerings. Over many years!"

"There is much new that we could give."

402

"Much that I would wish to have?"

"The Border truce renewed."

"With France resisting you, that is more important for you than for me."

"We are the stronger," Scrope declared. "The truce will be of more value to the weaker."

"Try us, my lord, and see how weak are the Scots!"

"Such talk is profitless," Beaufort said. "If we were allied, the fortresses of Berwick and Roxburgh could be yours."

"Berwick and Roxburgh are mine now. They will ever be Scots. Shamefully held against me, in time of truce, by usurpers. Would you have me trade my daughter for them?"

"No, no, Highness. I but rehearse some advantages to you of alliance with England. I can think of others. A remission in the payment of the ransom moneys . . ."

"Dear God!" James all but choked. "Ransom! For piracy done near thirty years ago, you would still exact payment! What are you, by the Rude? Jews? Usurers?"

The Cardinal looked pained. "Your Highness is pleased to jest. But it is scarce jesting matter, I think. Your release was agreed on for a sum those years ago – a sum which as yet has by no means been fully paid. Sum and interest. This matter we would consider anew."

"You are generous, my lord Cardinal! How much will you offer for this betrothal of our daughter?"

"It is a token of esteem."

"You say so? Then, we have another daughter. The Princess Annabella. But three years younger than Margaret . . ."

"James!" Joanna cried.

"Ah, no, Highness – that would not serve." Her uncle reacted almost as quickly. "Not another. It must be the elder. The King of England could not wed a second daughter. It is not to be considered."

"I thought as much, my lords. It is not that you want a Scottish queen – only that you would deny one to the French! I have the measure of your esteem, I think!" James rose – and they must all rise. "Sufficient of talk for this day."

"But . . . but there is much yet to be said, Highness!" Beaufort protested. "What is decided . . .?"

"Decided that I do not break my word, my lords. To France, or other. The Princess Margaret remains promised to the Dauphin – that is decided."

"And the truce? What of that? We . . . we could offer a permanent peace . . ."

"Permanent . . .?" James stared. "This . . . this, my lords, is something different!"

"No doubt, Highness. But it is for consideration."

"Aye. As you say – for consideration! Long consideration. But not today. The truce I will renew for five years further. On condition that the English garrisons are withdrawn from Berwick and Roxburgh."

"But . . . my lord James . . .!"

"But nothing, sir. Details you may discuss with my Chancellor, the Bishop of Glasgow. This audience is at an end."

The King had never intervened so little in one of his parliaments. Patiently he listened hour after hour as the wordy battle raged, seldom contributing so much as a word. From an early stage he had had little doubt as to the consensus of opinion, and was gratified that it coincided with his own. But those who took the contrary view were eloquent, vehement, and included some of the most illustrious of the land.

In a way, this session was the crowning achievement of James's reign. From the very start he had set out to make something new in Scotland, a responsible legislature representative of all that was substantial in his realm, a parliament which could and would consider, discuss in detail, and come to decisions on the major problems confronting the country – a thing hitherto unknown in a land where the king, or more often those who controlled the king, decided all. He had made mistakes in it all, of course, gone too fast, taken unwise short-cuts, had to accept appearances for the reality; but achieved great advances nevertheless. Today, at Perth, they were seeing something of the substance of his vision – a crowded national debating chamber at work, thrashing out a momentous line of high policy which must affect Scotland's future and security for long years to come. And it was no mere façade, the King's party triumphing; not only were the burghs and lesser lairds well represented and speaking up, but there were Highland chiefs sitting with Lowland barons as of right, and giving their views without coaxing. Indeed the last speaker had been none other than Alexander of the Isles, released from ward and restored to his Lordship – though not to the earldom of Ross. Alexander had spoken in favour of the English peace – which was perhaps not to be wondered at, for the Isles had more often in the past been more friendly with England than with the Scottish Crown.

The peace party was led by James's Uncle Walter, the Earl of Atholl, and many of the King's closest associates were supporting him, including the Earls of Douglas, Moray, Crawford, and Sutherland. Also, not a few of the bishops – for Henry Wardlaw, the Primate, though now too frail to make the journey from St. Andrews to Perth, had made it known that he was persuaded to the English permanent peace proposal.

The opposition, or French party, had throughout the discussion been headed, strangely, by the lesser prelates, the abbots, priors and deans, with James's own confessor, John Foggo, Abbot of Melrose, their chief spokesman. Without doubt they had the great majority of the parliament with them, in their contention that a permanent peace treaty was but an English ruse to tie the Scots hands while France was battered into subjection – whereupon England would turn upon her ancient and now isolated enemy, peace treaty or none, and rend her. This was James's own belief, but he had not said so, desiring a free and full exchange of views.

George Lauder, Bishop of Argyll, had risen to refute certain statements of Alexander of the Isles. ". . . he says that the succouring of France is costly folly. I say that it is less costly than having to fight on our own soil for the protection of our lives and freedom. In all their history the English have been aggressors. To our cost we know it. Think you that they have of a sudden changed? This proposed treaty would give them the free hand in France, which they have long wished for – no fears of attack at their backs. Our Auld Alliance with France is born out of mutual need, to contain England – not great love for each other! The need is no less great today – as we shall find out to our dire hurt if France goes down. Then it will be our turn. His Grace has renewed the truce for five years. It is enough, I say. This of permanent peace is but a trap. I counsel you – put it from you!"

A man jumped to his feet before the Bishop had sat down, hand raised to catch the Chancellor's eye. Cameron looked swiftly, enquiringly, at the King.

It was Sir Robert Graham, late Tutor of Strathearn and James's chiefest hater. In the same amnesty which had released Alexander from Tantallon, he had been pardoned of the sentence of outlawry and made free to come and go as he would, as part of the King's policy for a fresh start now that he had both Highlands and Lowlands reduced to obedience. Many had declared it a mistake, folly, but James saw it otherwise. The former outlaws had even been called to attend parliament; now they possessed all the privileges of immunity which such calling gave them.

The King nodded.

"Sir Robert Graham of Dundaff will speak," Cameron declared, as though with distinct reluctance.

"My lord Chancellor," Graham cried, "I say that you have been listening to lies! Lies! Told by churchmen in the pay of the French. They would have us spill our blood in France. For why? That they might seize our lands when we are gone! The Church, ever greedy for land and power . . ."

The uproar drowned his passionate voice. Everywhere men rose to their feet, shouting. Few indeed exclaimed in Graham's favour. Even those of the English faction deplored this sort of behaviour and recognised that nothing would be gained by attacking the Church.

The Chancellor banged and banged with his gavel.

"Silence!" he ordered. "Silence, I say! In the name of the King's Grace – silence. Here is shame . . ."

When he had gained a measure of quiet, he addressed the Graham. "Sir Robert – if you would speak further, you will watch your words! Such abuse and calumnies are unworthy of this parliament. You will utter no more of the like, or I will silence you . . ."

"Is this the vaunted freedom of speech that we were promised?" the other demanded. "Is this the parliament where a man may speak his mind without fear? Speak as King and Chancellor would have you, or you will be silenced . . .!"

Cameron banged again. "For the last time, sir," he said, "you will speak to the subject of debate, and civilly, or sit down."

"You will not muzzle Robert Graham! You, nor any man. Least of all, traitors to this realm of Scotland!"

"That is sufficient," the Chancellor decided. "We shall have no more of this. You will sit down, sir, or I will call upon the High Constable to have you removed from this assembly."

"My lord Chancellor," the King intervened at last. "Sir Robert has said too much – and yet not enough, I think. To silence him now. He spoke of traitors to this realm. Before this parliament he may not make such allegations without substantiation. I pray you, let him speak – so long as he makes good his charge."

"As Your Grace wills. You hear, sir? Of the King's clemency, you may speak further. You have spoken of traitors. I say it comes but strangely from the lips of a former outlaw and rebel! But now you must say more. Name your traitors – or stand for ever shamed."

The Chancellor's words seemed to wholly infuriate the irascible Graham. His voice rose to a shout. "You, John Cameron! Yourself, I name. Traitor! Lick-spittle! Sold to the French! You and your master, both!"

The normally imperturbable Bishop Cameron went white of face. He rose from his chair, fists clenched, while the hubbub mounted in the Blackfriars hall. He tried to shout, but his voice was no match for that of the almost insensate Graham.

Arm outstretched, finger jabbing accusingly, the man pointed – and not at the Chancellor but at the King. "There!" he yelled. "There is the greatest traitor of all! James Stewart. Man of blood! Dispossessor of the innocent! Seller of his own realm . . .!" The accuser choked with his own emotion.

This time, with the terrible words out, the pandemonium died away to an appalled hush. Although the King sat still in his throne, apparently unmoved, consternation gripped the entire assembly.

The Earl of Angus found his voice first. "This man is mad!" he cried. "Crazy-mad! Constable – seize him!"

Sir William Hay, the High Constable, was already striding forward, minions at his heels.

At the sight of him, Graham also added action to words. Whether or no he expected accomplices in the parliament to join him is not to be known. His seat was at the end of a row, and the Constable had to move down some distance behind. Graham leapt forward and down, across the well of the chamber, and up on to the dais whereon was the King's gilded throne. He shouted as he ran.

"To me, true men! To me! Here sits a tyrant! He misgoverns. Misgoverns our land. Tramples on our liberties. Ruins our noblest families. He must be put down! To me, all true men!"

He reached the throne. James sat motionless yet, even if he had stiffened somewhat in his chair. The Chancellor left his table to come forward, hand out. Shocked, the great assembly stared.

Graham, his not unhandsome features working strongly, pointed in the King's tight-lipped face, all but screaming. The monarch's immobility seemed to send him over the very verge of folly. He did the unpardonable thing – he laid hands on the royal person. Reaching out he grabbed the King's shoulder. In his frenzy he half-swung James round in his

408

seat, and in the same movement lurched round, himself, to face the gathering.

"I arrest the traitor! The tyrant! In the name of freedom!" he shouted. "Here he is! James Stewart. Is it not as I say?"

Although everywhere men were on their feet, this extraordinary and dramatic gesture and demand for the moment froze all movement, all speech. For seconds on end the panting breath of the speaker was the only sound in that parliament. James did not struggle or open his mouth, but gazed straight ahead of him.

The Graham, feverishly scanning the rows of horrified faces perceived that no single man, whatever may have been said in private beforehand, was going to support him, in word or deed. In that instant of truth and reality, he seemed to collapse physically, to slump, shrink in on himself, all the vehemence and command to drain out of him. The hand that clutched the King's shoulder dropped limply to his side.

As though released from some dire spell, the Constable and his guards rushed forward belatedly to grapple with the offender.

James spoke, at last. "Constable – escort Sir Robert Graham from this chamber," he said, keeping his voice steady with an enormous effort. "He is not well, I think."

The gasp which swept the gathering was astonished, incredulous. Then the clamour arose.

"Hang him!"

"Death to the dastard!"

"To the gallows with him!"

"Slay him, Hay – slay him!"

James rose to his feet, hand up. "You heard my command, Sir William? Escort Sir Robert hence, I said."

"Yes, Sire. To be sure. And then?"

"Escort him from this town. Let him go where he will." Hay's men had Graham held fast, unresistant.

"But . . . but . . . not to hang him, Sire? He has earned the rope if ever man did! He struck Your Grace!"

"Touched, not struck. That is *lèse majesté*, yes

– but, as I say, he is not well. I promised immunity, the privilege of parliament, to all who attend. Let such immunity cover this day's folly. Escort him hence, I say." James turned. "My lord Chancellor – pray continue with the session."

As Graham was led out, no amount of beating with the Chancellor's gavel would still the uproar in the assembly. Men exclaimed, discussed and argued. Clearly there would be no more constructive and worth-while debate that day.

James bowed to the inevitable. "My lord," he called to Cameron, "I suggest that you take the vote. On the English peace proposal. It has been sufficiently discussed. Then adjourn the session."

The Chancellor was glad enough so to do. The vote showed an overwhelming majority against the treaty of permanent peace with England, and in favour of maintaining the alliance with France. Atholl trumpeted disgust, but the die was cast.

James went in search of Joanna.

26

The two couriers arrived at Stirling within an hour or two of each other – and set town, castle and court in a stir indeed. The first came only from the East March of the Border, sent by the Warden thereof. He reported that a large English force under Sir Robert Ogle had crossed Tweed, near Wark, and was at large in the Merse, burning, harrying and slaying. The Warden was doing what he could, but he had insufficient men to confront the invaders successfully. Help was required urgently.

The second messenger came from farther afield, but he had been awaited. He was from France, via the Clyde and Dumbarton, and he brought notable tidings. The Princess Margaret had duly reached France, and had been triumphantly received; but not without prior incident. Her squadron had been attacked at sea by an English fleet of great size, especially sent to intercept her, and only the timely appearance on the scene of a Flemish merchant flotilla bearing the season's wine harvest from La Rochelle – which the English had mistaken for French warships – had saved the bridal company from a sea-battle. Even so, discovering their mistake, the attackers had pursued Margaret's squadron almost into La Rochelle port itself. She had nearly suffered her father's fate of thirty years before.

There was still a year of the five-year truce to run.

Few had ever seen James Stewart so angry as these tidings made him. He was greatly fond of his children, in especial his firstborn, Margaret, who had grown into a winsome and sweet-natured girl of nearly eleven, showing every promise of being almost as beautiful as her mother. The parting with Margaret had been one of the sorest occasions of his life, and he had put it off and off, despite King Charles's representations, until the latter had at length sent three special ships to bring his heir's bride and her suite to France. So at last she had sailed from Scotland, under the care of the Earl of Orkney, son of the man who had taken a like journey with her father all those years before, accompanied by a brilliant escort of prelates, lords and knights, waited on by no fewer than 144 youthful squires of good family. That the English should have planned to attack this company, attempted his daughter's capture and endangered her life, left King James all but speechless with rage.

It was a rage which had to be translated into action, swift and drastic action. Angus, chief of the Lothian and most reachable Douglases, was ordered south, with five thousand men, to reinforce the Warden. And the King sent out heralds and couriers up and down the land, sounding the call to arms. It was not yet war; James had not lost his head. But at least he would show that treachery and truce-breaking could have painful results.

In three days there was good news to cheer on the recruiting. Angus had come up with the English raiding force, glutted with their spoils, at Piperden, and completely routed them, with major slaughter and a great number of captives including Sir Robert Ogle himself. The few survivors had fled back across the Border.

That threat was eliminated, that lesson taught. So far so good.

It took two weeks more to prepare for the second lesson, geography and mileage being what they were. But at the end of that period, towards the close of July, the Burgh-muir outside Edinburgh was a vast armed camp, thronged with the levies of great lords, Lowland lairds and Highland chiefs, to the number of almost thirty thousand. More were on their way, from farther afield, but James decided that he had sufficient to make a start. On a fine late July morning of 1436 he put himself at the head of his great army, waved farewell to Joanna and his children, and set off southwards.

412

They perforce made a slow progress, for the army was burdened with much heavy cannon, siege-engines and impedimenta. They went by Dalkeith and Oxenford, to cross the Tyne, and up and up by Fala and Soutra, into the green Lammermuirs, choosing the slowest gradients for the sake of the lumbering oxen-drawn artillery. Through the sheep-strewn passes they wound, down into Lauderdale, to mid-Tweeddale, to follow that broad and silver stream south-eastwards, by Dryburgh and Mertoun, to Kelso Abbey and the little town which had grown up around its walls. Near here was the junction of Tweed and Teviot, and in the very apex of that junction, in an immensely strong position guarded by the broad rivers on all sides save one, rose the great fortress of Roxburgh and its dependent burgh.

Roxburgh had long been one of the headaches and heart-aches of Scotland. Yielded to the English nearly a hundred years before, by the traitor Edward Baliol, it had ever since remained in their hands. This was partly on account of its own strength, partly in that it was so near the Border as to be aided and reinforced readily from England; partly because the proximity of its burgh, which climbed around its steep skirts, meant that any wholesale bombardment must inevitably result in great loss of life amongst the people thereof – and though this was of no matter to the English assailants, to fellow Scots it was a major concern.

James set up his quarters at Kelso Abbey, and divided up his great army. Almost half he sent, under Angus, down Tweed to Berwick, the other Scots stronghold held by the English. Berwick was to be invested but not actually besieged, as yet – there being a grave shortage of heavy cannon and siege-machinery. When Roxburgh was reduced, then the artillery would be transferred. Angus was to see that no help reached that walled town from England, and that the Governor of Berwick sent no aid to Roxburgh. Another detachment of ten thousand or so James sent to line the banks of Tweed itself, mile after mile with smaller parties to hold the Cheviot passes. He did not wish to be disturbed.

And so began the great and difficult siege of Roxburgh, none underestimating the task. First a summons to surrender was sent – and rejected. Then, from the opposite river-banks, just out of cannon-shot from the castle, the King's trumpeters and heralds ordered all his people of the burgh of Roxburgh to leave their houses in the said burgh and make their way to Kelso, by command of their liege lord James. There they would receive full compensation for all goods, gear and livestock left behind in the town. Before the Provost could reply to this, the English keeper broadcast the counter announcement that any townsfolk seen leaving the burgh would be fired upon by cannon, and a proportion of the remainder taken as hostages and executed, men, women and children.

The Provost held his tongue.

None of this had been unexpected, of course. James methodically set about the protracted business of siege-warfare which he had had to learn so thoroughly in France.

That night, royal emissaries swam Tweed and Teviot secretly, to coax townspeople to cross the rivers under cover of darkness, by boat, raft or swimming – and some few complied. Unfortunately there is but little real darkness of a Scots summer night, and time was notably short. Next morning, the muzzles of the castle cannon were depressed to their fullest extent, to blast at portions of the town which clung so trustingly beneath its walls.

The night following there were no more escapers.

Since the castle itself was out of effective cannon-shot of the far river banks, and the walls were so strong and high as to be impervious to assault unless they could first be breached, there were only three possibilities for the attackers – a straightforward assault along the narrow isthmus of land between the rivers, ditched, moated and defended in depth as it was, and a most evident death-trap; a sit-down siege to starve out the defenders – which might take months; and efforts to mine the walls by infiltrating parties at night. James sought to make use of all three methods.

The head-on approach along the isthmus quickly proved too costly. This was the very thing that the fortress had been designed to withstand. Such a system of outworks, redoubts, flanking-towers, obstacles and hazards, all with concentrated cannon cover, barred this land approach, that there was just no way to force flesh and blood across. If James could have bombarded the town immediately beyond, he might have been able to isolate these outer defences, and so counter them piecemeal; but he could not contemplate this. There was nothing for it but to try gradual night operations here also. And the nights were so woefully short.

So the pattern of the siege took shape. By day, tourneys, contests of arms, sports and entertainments – anything to keep idle soldiery, and their masters, interested and out of mischief; by darkness, parties of sappers and miners slipping out, burdened with picks and crowbars and gunpowder, with their guards, rafting across the river, creeping along the isthmus, burrowing beneath stout walls. Explosions by night, murderous encounters in dark narrow streets, blazing beacon-fires on castle walls, screams, savagery and sudden death.

Gradually the isthmus was conquered, towers blown up, redoubts levelled, ditches and moats filled in, cannon captured or made useless. Much the defenders were able to make good again the next day - but not all. A road was being cleared. Gaps were beginning to appear in the main castle walls also, and though these were quickly barricaded up, they represented the weakness necessary for a final all-out assault to succeed.

It was on the fifteenth day of the siege that a hard-riding party galloped into Kelso from the north – and no-one was more surprised than the King to discover that its leader was his own Joanna. She quickly made it clear that she had not come on any light or casual errand. James, superintending a wrestling match, left it to lead her into his pavilion in the Abbey precincts.

"My dear, my dear," she cried, "I bring you ill news! George Lauder has had word of it, and brought it to me. I came to you myself, for this is no matter to entrust to others, not knowing whom we *may* trust. And Bishop Lauder can serve you better elsewhere. There is a plot to overthrow you, while you linger here. To seize the throne in your absence, bring an English army in from the west and a fleet of ships into the Clyde, and so to bring you down."

"Dear God! Here surely is nonsense, lass! The imaginings of some disordered mind? Never has the throne been so secure as now. Never have I been so strong, so sure of the regard of my people. Never so many men assembled to my banner . . ."

"Can you trust them all? Who knows how many are in the plot?"

"But this is folly, Joanna. Who could unseat me of my throne? Without taking my life. And that of young James . . .?"

"One man could. Your Uncle Walter. My lord of Atholl."

"Atholl? No, no – not Uncle Walter. He does not love me, I think – but not this!"

"After Jamie he is next male heir to the throne."

"He would not murder me, and my son, to gain it!"

"He may not require to. The plot, as George Lauder heard it, is to pronounce you as in wrongful possession of the crown. To claim that you are of bastard blood. You yourself not illegitimate, but your father. Your grandfather, King Robert the Second, was married twice. First to Elizabeth Mure of Rowallan, by whom he had your father and the Duke of Albany. Then Euphemia, daughter of the Earl of Ross, by whom David of Strathearn and Walter himself. The plot is now to declare that the first was no marriage. That Elizabeth Mure was within the prohibited degree of relationship, cousin to the King in some degree . . ."

"That is an old tale! It was discovered, after they were wed, that they were in fourth degree cousinship. But

416

that was a minor matter. And anyway it was put right by Papal dispensation."

"Perhaps. But is sufficient for the purposes of this plot, it seems. The claim is that your father should never have been king, nor you after him. David of Strathearn, elder son of the second marriage, should have had the throne – and since he is dead, without son, Walter of Atholl is the rightful monarch!"

"Saints of God – whoever heard the like! Is my uncle in his dotage, then? To have thought of this? At his age? And after all these years . . ."

"Lauder doubts if he it is who thought of it. He believes another mind to have conceived it – Robert Graham's!"

"Ha! A sick mind indeed! Sick with hatred."

"No doubt. But a nimble mind, too. Trained to the law, remember. More dangerous than Atholl's."

"Atholl may not be behind the plot, then? Only Graham?"

"Lauder could not be sure. But there *are* important and powerful men behind it, he said. Of the English faction, of which Atholl is the leader. Moray. Crawford. Erskine. Some churchmen also, he believes."

"And you say that an English force comes to aid these?"

"Yes. A large army. From Cumberland and the Solway. By the West March. To slip behind you here. Reach mid-Scotland at Dumbarton. There to be joined by an English fleet in the Clyde. Lennox to yield Dumbarton Castle to them. Stirling also. So they will cut the land in half. You will be pinned in this corner. Then other English forces to strike over Tweed . . ."

"Aye – that is well devised, at least! However foolish the rest. It means that I cannot linger here. Devil take it – it means that I must raise this siege! Hurry back. Like any whipped cur! With my tail between my legs! God damn and burn them! What is it, in the Scots, that they are so wed to treachery? It is our stain and curse – to betray each other in the face of the common foe! Of what sort of people am I monarch?"

She reached out both hands to him. "I am sorry, James – so sorry. When all looked better, fairer. I had hoped that we might be winning out of trouble, at last." She sighed. "But . . . never fear, my love. You will overcome this, as you have done all else."

"Aye, that I will! I have not come so far to be beat now. How weary are you, my heart? Of riding? Give me but two hours, to settle matters here. And we ride for Edinburgh this night. Pray God we are in time . . ."

So the siege of Roxburgh was ignominiously raised, and that of Berwick scarcely begun. The Earl of Angus was left to guard the line of the East and Middle March, with ten thousand men, while the Earl of Douglas was sent west up Teviotdale with the great mass of the Scots army, to hold the passes of Liddesdale, Eskdale, Annandale and Nithsdale. James himself with a tight body of some five hundred knights and men-at-arms, rode hotfoot due north, his wife at his side.

Joanna had brought her message just in time. The Keepers of Dumbarton and Stirling Castles were relieved of their positions by their royal master himself, without explanation. A scratch force was hurriedly assembled at the latter town, in a central position to be despatched where most needed. An English fleet, sailing towards the mouth of the Clyde, found itself attacked out of the setting sun by a great swarm of the long, low galleys of the Isles, twenty-, forty- and sixty-oared vessels, the most vicious and manoeuvrable craft to sail the seas – and wisely took advantage of an easterly breeze to turn tail and make for Irish waters. The English spy-network ever efficient, got word of the changed situation promptly down to Cumberland, and the army mustering there at the Solway drew back discreetly towards Lancaster. Walter Stewart, Earl of Atholl, innocent or guilty, decided to open the hunting season early, and disappeared northwards into his own trackless Atholl mountains in keen pursuit of the deer.

Once again the situation was saved. But at a cost – the cost of James Stewart's faith, confidence and belief in his destiny. A heavy price to pay. Something indefinable went out of the King of Scots. Most men did not perceive it; but Joanna knew, and grieved for it.

27

At Queen Margaret's Ferry, the boatmen awaiting the royal party were seeking to drive off the old Highlandwoman who insisted on haunting the vicinity of the landing-stage, despite the chill, driving rain. She shook her bony fist at them, screeching at them in her outlandish Gaelic. But she had the English also, for when King James and Queen Joanna, with their train, appeared from the direction of Edinburgh, muffled against the December weather, she ran towards them, shouting.

"Go back, lord King!" she cried, a wild, ragged scarecrow of a figure. "Do not cross Forth this day, at all. Heed me, lord. Do not go."

"Tush, woman!" James had to rein up, or he would have ridden her down. "What's to do? Out of my way."

"Woe and sorrow are to do, lord! Pain and desolation! Heed me. Cross not Forth, I say."

"For why? The sea is calm. The crossing short. What ails you, woman?"

"Sire," the ferry skipper intervened. "She has been troubling us this hour. Not to sail. It is that she fears we shall sink, I believe. Och, she's crazy, just."

"No, no," the old woman exclaimed. She flapped her hands at the seaman. "It is truth. You are fools, fools! And if you take the lord over this sea – murderers! I tell you!"

"Come now, mother – here to be sure is foolish talk," James said. "These are honest shipmen. The vessel is sound. The passage short, and I have crossed it a hundred times. There is naught to fear."

The woman looked at the Queen. "Lady – will not *you* hear? I have seen it. Seen this thing. The King, in his shroud! You must not let him go, whatever."

Troubled, Joanna turned to her husband. "James – should you not heed her . . .?"

"Heed what? Would you have the King of Scots to turn back from crossing this scant mile of water because an old wife says so?" He shrugged beneath his wet travelling-cloak. He was an impatient man, these days. "Woman – what is it that you fear? What of hurt? Is it that you think the ship to sink?"

"I do not know, lord – I do not know! Only . . . that you must not go."

"Save us – if you cannot say better than that, here's an end to it!" James waved on his fretting party towards the ship.

As they boarded and cast off, the old woman continued to wail and clamour after them.

All the way across to North Queensferry, Joanna clutched her husband's hand tightly staring at the slate-grey, white-veined water.

Safely at the far side, James mustered a smile for her, and she bit her lip, relieved, and yet vexed with herself. There was a certain amount of laughter from their companions – and any laughter was perhaps welcome in the King's present temper, as well as to lighten the cold and unpleasant journey to Perth.

James was an angry, frustrated and humiliated man. His pride had suffered three resounding blows – the English displays of contempt, this latest Scots treachery, and his consequent inglorious retiral from before Roxburgh. Joanna had never known him so moody and brooding. It was at her suggestion that they now made the awkward journey to Perth, in inclement winter weather, to pass Christmastide at the Blackfriars Monastery. He had held a parliament at Edinburgh, after the recent abortive revolt, to take all necessary dispositions; now she wanted him to get away from it all for a space. James was usually at his happiest at Perth, where there was no castle, fortress or other reminder of things warlike. She planned that this Yuletide should make up for much, a peaceful, if possible joyous, interlude, for refreshment and restoration.

And now, this foreboding note.

Despite prophecies of woe, they reached Perth suffering nothing worse than the discomfort of the elements. Quickly Joanna took charge thereafter, organising the court, and indeed the Prior and monkish brethren, for a prolonged season of Christmas and New Year activities. It was something like a conspiracy to distract, arouse and involve the King. Few failed to co-operate – and none did so more warmly and essentially than the Lady Catherine Douglas.

James responded sufficiently to start a new poem, the first for many a day.

It was one dark and windy night, after an evening of song and tale and card-playing, that Sir David Douglas came back from an errand to the Chancellory Office at Edinburgh, and in handing over to the King a letter from Bishop Cameron there, announced that the same old Highlandwoman who had accosted them at South Queensferry was down at the monastery gatehouse, demanding to see the King and prophesying disaster again.

"Sainted Mother of God!" Sir Robert Stewart exclaimed. "Is that old hag come again? I have sent her away a dozen times. I' faith I'll have her whipped out of the town . . . !"

"No, no, Rob – you will not!" James said. "She means no harm. Believes that she serves me in this. Use her not harshly, if it is out of love for me that she besieges us."

"She wearies the guards with her importuning, Sire. Even the good friars are out of patience with her."

"Yet you did not tell me, Rob? This is the first I have heard of her since the ferry."

"I conceived it my duty to protect Your Grace from such."

Sir Robert Stewart was the new Chamberlain, a handsome and stalwart young man and James's cousin once removed.

He was in fact Atholl's grandson, the only son of the Master of Atholl, who had died in England as one of the hostages. James had given him this appointment, as master of his household, partly to compensate for this misfortune and partly because, though the young man was Atholl's heir, he was known to be at odds with his grandfather, and gained little substance from that tight-fisted old man.

"I told her to go away," David Douglas went on. "Not to trouble Your Grace. But she insisted that as a Highland clanswoman she was entitled to speak with you, as Ard Righ, her high chief."

"It is their custom, yes. They all think to be in cousinship with their chiefs, and so have the right to approach them personally." James yawned. "But it is too late tonight, Davie. Tell her I shall see her in the morning. Now – let us have the parting-cup, before I fall asleep at this table!"

This was normally the signal for the ladies to retire; but Joanna had already gone to the royal bedchamber, with her ladies-in-waiting.

The great silver loving-cup passed round, the company bowed themselves out of the royal presence – all save Walter Straiton, the night's duty page, Sir David Douglas, gentleman of the bedchamber, and Sir Robert Stewart, Chamberlain. The monastery was, as usual, overcrowded, and most of the courtiers had to find their lodging outside.

The King rose, and stretched luxuriously. "A good night to you, then, my friends," he said.

"Shall I assist Your Grace to undress?" Douglas asked.

"No, no – I have not drunk so much as all that, Davie! You will be tired from your long riding."

"I shall see to the guard and the doors, Sire," the Chamberlain assured.

James strolled through into the next chamber. All the rooms intercommunicated. This was his dressing-room. Here he took off his clothing, and slipped on a furred bed-robe. Then he knocked on the inner door beyond.

The King always insisted on this knocking – even though it was to gain admittance to his own bedchamber. He had his own especial knock. There was a laughing chorus of invitation from within. He pushed the door open and entered.

It was a pleasing scene that met him. The large arras-hung room with the sheep and deerskin rugs on the dark bees-waxed floor-boards, was mellow with the glow of candles and the flickerings of a richly aromatic birch-log fire. The great four-poster bed dominated all, but there were presses, garderobes and chests to hold the Queen's dresses, with other furnishings. In a chair, near the fire, Joanna sat, wearing a silken robe which left her fine shoulders bare, having her hair brushed by Catherine Douglas. Another young woman, Elizabeth Douglas, daughter of Douglas of Lochleven, busied herself with putting away the Queen's clothes.

Greeting them more genially than of late, James went over to stand, with his back to the fire, legs straddled, to watch. This had almost been ritual with him, of a night, for he greatly loved to watch Joanna's hair being brushed and combed. It was long and thick and lustrous, reaching well below her waist, a rippling cascade which demanded a deal of brushing and attention. He was not averse, either, to note at the same time the play of light and shadow on Kate Douglas's strong rounded arm and rich, overflowing bosom. Often, during the brushing, the Queen hummed or sang gently to the rhythm of it, her ladies joining in. It seemed a long time since James had done so also, but tonight he added his deep note to the simple repetitive melody.

Joanna smiled to him, quietly, happily.

Presently she interrupted her crooning momentarily, to speak. "Jamie," she murmured, "of a pity, lower the skirts of your robe! Behind. Against the fire. You quite distract Kate here. My hair is suffering for it!"

James grinned. "Kate makes her own distractions! You all do. Is a man entitled to no self-defence?"

Giggles from over at the garderobe where young Elizabeth Douglas folded clothing.

Catherine Douglas spoke with mock solemnity. "Shall I bring another candle closer, Madam? His Grace's royal figure is such as to block the firelight somewhat!"

424

"Baggage! *You* to speak! You grow fair mountainous, Kate! In a fashion no *man* may rival! You need a suckling bairn at you. Or a pair!"

"As Your Grace wishes!"

"Come now," the Queen observed, but easily, equably. It was long since her lord had jested thus. "Whose bedroom is this, pray? *I* shall say when my husband grows too fat."

"Fat! Shrive me – here's treasonable talk!" James glanced down at his sturdy wide-spread legs complacently – and if anything hitched his robe slightly higher at the back, to warm his buttocks. He had thickened of late undeniably, but at forty he was still a tough, stocky, muscular figure without hint of flabbiness. "I will still out-wrestle any man in this kingdom, in the ring," he declared. "Or, i' faith, any woman on a bed!"

"I think you . . . exaggerate, my heart," Joanna murmured.

"Such claims stand void until proved, Sire!" Catherine Douglas said, demurely. "And Her Grace, though the most beautiful, lacks the weight of some!"

"Enough!" the Queen commanded, holding up her hand. "Before my hair is clean tugged out of my head! Elizabeth yonder is too young for such talk – and I fast growing too old, I think! Have the warming-pan out of the bed, girl . . ."

The Queen's voice faltered away, before a noise from outside.

They all stared towards the door, suddenly alert, tense. The noise was angry shouting and the unmistakable ominous clanking of steel-clad men.

The sound was not one which anyone in James's position, however valiant, could listen to with equanimity. It came from beyond the door by which he had entered. Still at some little distance. In a few swift strides the King was over at the nearest window, to open the wooden shutters and peer down through the wet darkness. He stiffened. Only one or two torches flared down in the monastery courtyard – but they were sufficient to show that the place was full of men. And not monks, nor courtiers. These men, silent as they stood, were kilted and wearing Highland bonnets. The torches gleamed on the naked steel of drawn broadswords and dirks.

James closed the shutters, and turned back to face the anxious listening women. "Treachery!" he jerked. "Armed Highlanders below. By the hundred."

Even as he spoke a high-pitched urgent cry rang out from no great distance away. "Sire! Sire! Flee! Begone! Treason, I say – treason! A-a-a-ahh!" The voice rose to a choking scream, to die away in a bubbling horror.

As the women gasped, James exclaimed. "Dear God! That was Davie Douglas!"

Joanna ran, to throw herself into her husband's arms. "Oh, Jamie! Jamie!" she cried. "Flee? How may you flee . . .?"

Well might she ask. This bedchamber was at the end of a row of intercommunicating rooms. It had only the one door. And the windows were iron-barred, and anyway opened only above the crowded courtyard.

James remembered something. The drainage vault. This was a monastery, and the religious were nice about certain matters. The like was not to be found in any castle, but under the floors of this principal range of bedchambers ran a slanting stone drainage-passage, for the emptying of slops and privies. It was no longer used, but some years before he had discovered the trap-door into it, in the flooring beside the fireplace – for always the royal visitors used this same suite of rooms. No doubt there was a similar trap in the floors of the other bedchambers.

He strode to the fireside, and kicked aside the sheepskin-rugs there. Yes, the square of cut edges was just evident beneath the polish of the beeswaxed floorboards. He dropped to his knees, to prise open the trap.

"See," he said, "this drain. This passage. It leads out into the back quarters. It will be clear, there. They will not think of the back. If I can get out. I will rouse the town. Bring help. If I can get down . . ."

426

He had the trap-door open now, and was peering in. "A candle," he demanded.

"Oh, quickly! Quickly!" Joanna panted. "They are coming. I hear them."

There was the sound of scuffling and fighting, near at hand, grunts and groans and curses.

"Go bar the door," James said, as he took the candle from Kate Douglas. The light showed that there was a sizeable drop to the floor of the drain – fully nine feet. An unpleasant musky smell came up on the dank, cold air.

James wasted no time. He lowered himself with fair agility into the hole, hung for a moment by his hands, and then dropped the foot or so, his bare feet jarring on the stone flags.

"Are you all right?" Joanna demanded, gazing down. "How is it? Can you stand . . .?"

"Yes, yes. It is well enough. See you – you should come also, Joanna. Better together . . ."

"No, no! They will not hurt me, a woman. It is you they want. The King. Go, James – go! I shall close this trap-door. Stand on it. The skins . . ."

"Hand me that candle down . . ."

But the onset of events denied him the candle's light. There was a scream, and the crash of a falling body just beyond the bedroom door, and hoarse shouting. The Queen, instead of reaching for the candle, turned towards the door, commanding Kate Douglas to bar it.

That young woman had already gone to do this. Now she glanced back, unhappily. "The bar is gone!" she wailed. "Mary-Mother – it is gone!"

Four great iron open staples, shaped like squared hooks, two in the door's timbers, one on either side let into the stonework of the wall, served as sockets for a stout timber bar to be inserted to barricade the door from within. This bar normally hung by a chain at the door-post. Tonight bar and chain were missing.

Even as Kate stared, the door shook. Men's savage voices were immediately beyond. Quick as thought the young woman hurled herself backwards against the door-post, and flung out her bare rounded arm. Into the sockets she thrust it, a flesh and blood bar linking one door-post hook and the two on the door itself, the second of which she could just grasp in her hand.

"Quick!" she cried, and gestured downwards to the Queen with her other hand.

As the wrench came at the door, and was held, with a gasp of pain, Joanna lowered the trap-door on the King. She hastened to fling the rugs over it.

Furious shouts came from outside, with demands to open. The door rocked again, and Kate bit back a scream.

The Queen had the skins in position. She stood on them, hand to her throat.

This time men hurled themselves bodily against the door, with all their strength. The snap of breaking bone was clear to hear, and with a high whinny of agony Kate Douglas lurched in a half-swoon, her grasp on the second staple yielding as she slumped forward and down. This sagging at the knees dragged down her shoulder, and the now limp arm slid out of the first staple. The door was flung wide and six armoured men rushed into the bedroom, dripping swords in their hands. In doing so they had to step or stumble over the bloodstained twisted body of young Walter Straiton, the page, who lay just beyond the threshold. One kicked Kate Douglas aside as they entered.

Of the six men, three were known to the Queen. One was Sir Robert Graham himself. One was Sir John Hall, formerly of the Duke of Albany's household, and the third was Robert Stewart, the Chamberlain. Of the others, one young man bore a striking resemblance to Graham, and was presumably his son.

The panting intruders glared about them, at the three women, at each other. One of them rushed forward, to peer under the four-poster bed. Others hurried to open garderobes and presses, tossing out clothing in search for their quarry.

"Where is he? Where is the King?" Sir Robert Graham demanded presently, with their search unavailing. "Where does he hide?"

No-one answered him.

Fiercely he turned on the Queen. "Madam – do not think you can save the tyrant by your silence. We shall find him. He must be here. Better for you, I say, that we find him quickly."

"Would you threaten *me*, sirrah? The Queen?" Joanna spoke with difficulty, even though she drew herself up proudly, hitching her robe more closely about her.

"I will do more than threaten, 'fore God! Think you we are here for civilities, woman? Where is he? Where does he lurk?"

"He is gone. From here. Gone, I tell you. And . . . and even if he were not, think you I would tell you? Treacherous dastard! Traitor!"

"I am no traitor! I threw off all allegiance to the tyrant, the usurper, months since. Said that I would bring him to justice. Now I do so. Where has he gone? He shall not escape me, by the Lord God!"

"You name the Lord God, miscreant! I wonder that He does not strike you down . . ."

"Leave her," Sir Robert Stewart interrupted. He had been opening the shutters and looking out. "If she will not talk, others may." Dirk in hand he swung on young Elizabeth Douglas. "You, girl! Where is the King? Speak, if you value your life." He held the dagger-point to her white throat.

Wide-eyed, breast-heaving, she shook her head, biting at her lips.

He shook her violently. "Answer, fool! Think you we cannot make you speak? God's blood – you shall see!"

"Take your hands from that girl!" Joanna exclaimed. She was starting forward, towards them, when she remembered that she must not move. "Are you brute-beasts, as well as traitors? His Grace is gone, I tell you. He left this bedchamber. You are too late."

"He cannot be gone. There is no way out, save by this door. It has been watched . . ."

"Aye — watched, by you, His Grace's trusted Chamberlain!" Joanna felt that she had to keep talking now, to give James time. "You, of the blood-royal. Whom he raised up and favoured. Of all men, to wrong and betray your prince! No doubt you it was who removed the bar from this door . . .?"

"Wrong him!" the young man shouted, flushing. "*I* wrong him? Is it not he who wrongs me? My father dying as hostage for him in your England. He that usurps the crown that should be mine! *Will* be mine! *I* should be the King, I say — and will be. My grandsire will not live long. He is old, and will die. Till then, I shall be Governor. Then King! *I* am not of bastard stock . . .!"

"You act as though you were, I swear! A base-born coward!"

Furiously Stewart stepped over, and struck the Queen across the face.

With a moaning cry, Catherine Douglas, who had been leaning against the arras of the wall, clutching her broken arm, and deathly white, flung herself to her mistress's aid, clawing with her sound hand. She knocked Stewart bodily aside, and turned to place herself in front of Joanna, gasping but eyes blazing, like a tigress at bay.

Elizabeth Douglas also ran to join herself to them, sobbing.

Beside himself, the Chamberlain rushed at them, dagger raised. It was the youngest man there, who so resembled Graham, who dashed to knock up Stewart's arm.

"Fool!" he cried. "Are you mad? What serves it to hurt the Queen? It is the King we want. This is folly."

"Aye," his father agreed. "We but waste time. James is not here — that is clear. Wherever he has gone."

"That we may get out of these women," Stewart jerked, glaring at young Graham.

"And waste longer — while all the time the tyrant betters his escape. He must be in the house still. We have it

430

surrounded. There is no way out. We shall discover him. Wherever he hides . . ."

"He must have slipped out. Before we came," one of the others declared.

"Whittinghame did not know it, then," Stewart declared. "He shouted warning – before we quieted him. Shouted Sire, Sire! He believed him here. As did the page . . ."

"Then they were wrong – as were you, sir. That at least is evident. Come – this is profitless. We shall find him, if we have to tear this monastery stone from stone!"

"Leave the women . . .?"

"The house is ours. They can do nothing."

The men hurried out, as they had come, ransacking the next chamber, the King's dressing-room, as they went. Catherine ran to slam the door behind them, and to lean against it, her body racked with pain and emotion.

"Thank God! Thank God!" Joanna exclaimed. "Mary-Mother – the savages! The animals! And Rob Stewart!" She ran to Catherine. "Kate! Kate, my dear! Your arm? My brave, gallant Kate! What have they done to you? It is sore hurt, is it not . . .?"

"It is naught. T'will mend," the other jerked. "His Grace? How fares he? In that hole?"

"Pray God he has won clear. Outside. He said it opened to the back. A drain. But . . . they said that they have all surrounded. If that be so . . ."

"His Grace is strong. Valiant. They will be stretched thin. They will not hold him. In the dark . . ."

"Listen! That noise? Shouting. That is from the town. It must mean that the town is roused. They have discovered what is to do. Praise be! Douglas and Angus will come. Save us."

"Madam – I hear a sound. Below." Elizabeth was still standing on the trap-door. She pointed towards her feet. "Listen!"

They stared at each other, troubled.

Joanna hurried to the fireside, and bent to listen. "I hear nothing."

"It was a tapping . . ."

"Sainted Saviour! Perhaps . . .? Perhaps . . .?" The Queen turned. "Watch the door, Kate. Elizabeth – help me with this trap."

They pushed aside the rugs, and raised the trap.

Down there, the King stood, staring up, blinking against even the mellow glow of fire and candles.

"Shrive me – it's black as the pit down here," he said. "They are gone? I heard them go . . ."

"Yes, yes. They have gone. To search the house. But – Jamie I had hoped you far from here! Won clear. They may be back . . ."

"It would not serve. The devil's own luck! That tennis-court. You remember? Only three days ago I ordered yonder hole to be walled up. The balls kept running into it. That was it. I realise it now. The opening for this drain. I could not get out. It is all stoned-off. Sealed."

"Oh, my dear! What now, then?"

"They have searched here. They will not come back for some time. If I can be clothed. Some armour. A sword in my hand. By God – they shall not need to search for me! *I* shall search for them!"

"No, no, James! Do not say that. Stay where you are safe."

"In this stinking, black pit! Like a rat? I am King of Scots – have you forgot? Here – help me out."

But though, by kneeling on the floor and reaching down, the Queen and Elizabeth could grasp the King's hands, they could by no means hoist him up. He was no light weight, and though his arms were very strong, there was nothing for him to grasp save the women's wrists, nothing to climb against.

After considerable fruitless heaving, James desisted. "This is of no avail," he panted. "Elizabeth – get a sheet from the bed. Twist it into a rope. Anchor an end to something of weight. That I may pull myself up by it. Quickly!"

While the girl did as she was bid, James demanded details of Joanna. "It was Graham, was it not?" he asked.

432

"Graham, yes. And his son, I think. But also, Robert Stewart of Atholl."

"Robbie? Rob Stewart? No! Not Robbie!"

"Yes. He struck me. And Elizabeth. Raised his dagger at us. Said he would be King . . ."

"He . . . struck . . . you! Struck the Queen? Dear God — for that he shall die! I swear it!"

"So long as *you* do not die. It is nothing, James I am not hurt. But Kate is. Kate's arm is broke, I think. She barred the door with it . . ."

"Christ-Lord! They broke Kate's arm? I' faith — get me out of this hole . . .!"

Elizabeth brought the sheet, twisting it, and lowered the end to the King.

"Now — turn it around something. Both hold on to the end. Say when you have it fast."

From deep in his hole, of course, James could not see what they were doing above. In fact, Elizabeth Douglas had little idea what was required of her. She wrapped a length of the sheeting around her middle, handing the loose end to the Queen.

"Now!" she called, bracing herself.

The inevitable happened. As James threw his whole weight on the sheet, hoisting himself up, the girl was jerked off her feet. Joanna clutched at her, but the combined drag was much too great for her to hold. Elizabeth was wrenched to the edge of the hole, and over. Down she fell, bodily, on top of the King. Together they crashed to the foot of the drain. The Queen only just saved herself from following them.

That fall of Elizabeth Douglas might be said to have determined the course of history. Or, not so much the fall as the scream she emitted as she fell, a loud and piercing scream of fright.

Sir Robert Graham had left one of his party, Thomas Chambers, at the door of the far room, the large apartment where the evening had been spent. He heard the scream and came running. Catherine tried to hold the door again, but

433

was now in no state to do so. She was hurled aside, as Chambers crashed into the bedchamber. Joanna, when she heard his running footsteps, sought to lower the trap-door. She was not quite in time. It dropped with something of a bang, just as the man entered. He could not fail to note it.

"Ha!" he cried. Striding forward, he pushed Joanna roughly aside from the stance she had taken up on top of the door. "So that's it! This is where you have him!" He pulled up the trap, throwing it wide. "Save us all – a bonny, cosy scene!" He pushed the Queen away, as she came at him desperately. "See you what goes on down yonder, Madam! Your lord has one o' your wenches down there! Ooh, aye!"

James, knocked flat on the floor by the girl's weight, had smashed his head on the stone, and was half-dazed. Elizabeth lay sprawled over him, winded and sobbing.

The intruder raised his voice. "Here! To me! To me!" he yelled. "I have him. The King!"

Furiously Joanna cast about for something to use as a weapon. She saw the poker for the fire. Grabbing it up, she flung herself at the man.

He fended her off, cursing – but when Kate Douglas came also, one hand clawing, he backed away. Turning, he ran for the door, and out, shouting.

Frantic with anxiety, the Queen called down to James, telling him that he must get out, somehow. At once. To throw up the sheet. They must try it again.

The King seemed not himself, partly stunned, strangely inactive.

Joanna, despairing, hurried for the other sheet from the bed. Realising what had been wrong before, she searched around for something to tie it to, or loop it around. She saw nothing sufficiently heavy save the bed itself – and it was much too far away. Could she and Kate move it closer?

She called the other over – but it was too late. Shouts from the adjoining rooms told their own tale.

Thomas Chambers came stamping back, with three other men, including the Hall brothers. These wasted no time. While one drove the Queen and Kate Douglas, at sword-point, into a corner, Sir John Hall tossed his sword to one of the others, and drawing his dirk, jumped down into the hole on top of the King.

James had recovered sufficiently to cope with the almost hysterical Elizabeth. He had just enough warning to be on his feet to meet the attack from above. Although Hall all but knocked him over, he had glimpsed the glint of the dagger in the candlelight, and he grasped the man's wrist in a vicelike grip. For the rest, it was not difficult for an expert wrestler although he was hampered by his dizzy head and the cramped nature of the passage. He threw the knight over his shoulder, and brought him down hard on the masonry. He knelt over him, reaching for the dirk.

He had not quite got hand on it when the brother descended upon him, all but flattening him on top of the other. This man also had discarded sword, for close-range fighting, in favour of the knife. In a stabbing fury he inflicted a couple of wounds on the royal chest and shoulder. Then the King had him pinned down half-over his brother, and again he strove to grasp the vital weapon.

It was not to be. Thomas Chambers now dropped down upon them – and James could spare only half his attention for him, for the two Halls below him, although injured and shaken and much in each other's way, were still in the fight, and with cold steel in their hands.

A chaotic and crazy struggle ensued in that dark and odoriferous hole, as unkingly a battle as was ever fought. James had only one advantage – that whoever he struck at was an enemy; for Elizabeth Douglas had dragged herself aside a little way down the passage. Against such advantage, he was practically naked, pitted against steel-plated foes, unarmed, and already wounded in a number of places, his hands lacerated by the knives he had tried to grasp. But he was a fighter, by character as by training – and he was fighting for his life.

If the odds had remained even thus, it is possible that James Stewart might have won the day, bloody but the victor – for he had forced Chambers to drop his dirk, and was scrabbling for it whilst fending off the others' blindly flailing arms. Had he managed to get the knife, all might have been otherwise – for his strength was far from run out, and his wrath steeling into cold, killing fury. But now Sir Robert Graham himself appeared on that grim scene, not throwing himself in wildly but easing down with care, and then reaching up for his sword, handed to him by an accomplice above.

The King freed one arm, to grasp the newcomer round the ankles, and wrench – causing the short, jabbing sword-thrust to rip down his thigh instead of plunging into his belly, as aimed. Despite the searing pain, he reached up to grab the sword-arm wrist, but his hands were so wet and slippery with his own blood that his grip did not hold. A stab in the shoulder from one of the squirming men below him spun him round, groaning.

Calmly, deliberately, Graham withdrew his blade, based his feet firmly, and awaiting his opportunity as the struggling pile of men below him heaved and lashed, drove the sword deep into his monarch's chest.

A convulsion caused him to miss the heart by an inch or so. His steel plunged through a lung. A bright red flow came surging up, to smother James's cry of mortal agony.

That fight – and James Stewart's much longer fight – was over. Though he sought still to struggle, with the life-blood pouring out of him, there was no strength now behind his efforts, and from above and below the red steel plunged and plunged. When, if ever, James desisted, and his thrashings became merely the uncontrolled twitchings of a dying man, is not to be known. But he sought to form words, at least, thick with spouting blood as they were, words hard to interpret.

"Mercy, is it? Mercy!" Graham shouted, the cold savagery now given way to more typical excited ranting. "You – who showed no mercy to others! To your own kin. There is no mercy for you – now, or in hell!"

James managed to shake his head. Again he sought to gasp a single bubbling word.

"Confessor, you say? You want a confessor? By the Mass, tyrant – you shall have no confessor. Save this steel! Here is the confessor meet for you!" And he drove downwards.

This time his aim was true. The sword plunged straight into the heart.

In a great shuddering convulsion, the bleeding body arched high, on shoulders and heels, and then sank inert. It lay still.

So died, like a rat trapped in its hole by terriers, James, King of Scots, the first of his name, the most far-seeing and gifted monarch that ancient land of heroes and traitors had known or was ever to know.

The Lion was wholly loosed, at last.

Historical Note

Although the King's assassins, alarmed by the growing uproar outside, made good their escape from the Blackfriars Monastery, they were pursued and all the principals captured. Thereafter, their punishment and execution was carried out with a harshness, almost barbarism, which however merited was little credit to the enlightened government and corporate responsibility which James had striven so hard to raise up. Graham, after unmentionable tortures, and his son beheaded before his eyes, died bravely, the fanatic to the end; Robert Stewart's head was fixed to the gates of Perth; his grandfather, Atholl, was executed, and an iron crown clamped to the decapitated head.

It was centuries before the parliamentary institution, the most ambitious and profound of James's projects, reached anything like the level it did during his reign; indeed it might be said that it never did reach to the promise thus foreshown.

In due course, Queen Joanna, whose romance was surely an epic amongst royal matches, married again – since it was almost inconceivable for a Queen-Mother with a young family to remain unwed and a prey to all the warring factions which would seek to gain possession of the infant king, and so power in the land. But she tried to choose shrewdly, marrying three years later another James Stewart, the Black Knight of Lorne, of the royal blood but safely illegitimate, so that there could be no intriguing for the throne. She brought up her son James to be something of the man his father would have had him be. It is another of the tragic ironies of history that the promising James the Second

439

should have been killed, while still in his late twenties by the bursting of a cannon when engaged in besieging the English in the self-same Castle of Roxburgh which his father had had ignominiously to abandon twenty-five years before.